BLEEDING
KANSAS

G. P. Putnam's Sons   *New York*

BLEEDING
KANSAS

Sara Paretsky

G. P. PUTNAM'S SONS

Publishers Since 1838

Published by the Penguin Group
Penguin Group (USA) Inc., 375 Hudson Street, New York, New York 10014, USA • Penguin Group
(Canada), 90 Eglinton Avenue East, Suite 700, Toronto, Ontario M4P 2Y3, Canada (a division of Pearson
Penguin Canada Inc.) • Penguin Books Ltd, 80 Strand, London WC2R 0RL, England • Penguin
Ireland, 25 St Stephen's Green, Dublin 2, Ireland (a division of Penguin Books Ltd) • Penguin Group
(Australia), 250 Camberwell Road, Camberwell, Victoria 3124, Australia (a division of Pearson
Australia Group Pty Ltd) • Penguin Books India Pvt Ltd, 11 Community Centre, Panchsheel Park,
New Delhi–110 017, India • Penguin Group (NZ), 67 Apollo Drive, Rosedale, North Shore 0632,
New Zealand (a division of Pearson New Zealand Ltd) • Penguin Books (South Africa) (Pty) Ltd,
24 Sturdee Avenue, Rosebank, Johannesburg 2196, South Africa

Penguin Books Ltd, Registered Offices:
80 Strand, London WC2R 0RL, England

Library of Congress Cataloging-in-Publication Data

Paretsky, Sara.
    Bleeding Kansas / Sara Paretsky.
        p.   cm.
    ISBN 978-0-399-15405-8
    1. Rural families—Kansas—Fiction.   2. Iraq War, 2003– —Influence—Fiction.
3. Iraq War, 2003– —Protest movements—Fiction.   4. Fundamentalists—Kansas—Fiction.
5. Conservatism—Kansas—Fiction.   6. Social conflict—Kansas—Fiction.   I. Title.
    PS3566.A647B56   2008   2007035962
    813'.54—dc22

Printed in the United States of America
10   9   8   7   6   5   4   3   2   1

BOOK DESIGN BY MEIGHAN CAVANAUGH

This is a work of fiction. Names, characters, places, and incidents either are the product of the author's
imagination or are used fictitiously, and any resemblance to actual persons, living or dead, businesses, companies, events, or locales is entirely coincidental.

While the author has made every effort to provide accurate telephone numbers and Internet addresses at the
time of publication, neither the publisher nor the author assumes any responsibility for errors, or for
changes that occur after publication. Further, the publisher does not have any control over and does not
assume any responsibility for author or third-party websites or their content.

For Nicholas, Jonathan, Daniel, and Jeremy
Fellow refugees from our own patch of bleeding Kansas

The promised peace has not yet come to Kansas. With many fears, and many sufferings before them in the cold months coming, they will look forward to a day of deliverance, when the new reign of peace and righteous laws takes the place of oppression and tyranny.

—Mrs. Sara Robinson, *Kansas,* 1856

THANKS

I attended a two-room country school but know nothing about farming. Without the help of the Pendleton family—John and Karen, their children, Margaret, Will, and Liz, and John's parents, Al and Loretta—I could not have begun to write this book let alone finished it. Needless to say, the errors, which are doubtless legion, are all my own. Further, there is no resemblance whatsoever between any real Kansans, whether friends of my youth or the amazingly energetic Pendletons, and any of the people in this novel. All the characters here, especially Nasya, are creations of my own hectic imagination.

Thanks to Karen Pendleton, I am a proud honorary member of the Meadowlark chapter of Kansas 4-H; the many skills Lara Grellier learns in 4-H in this novel are a real sample of what Kansas kids actually do learn.

I spent an informative afternoon at the Newhouse Dairy near Topeka. I am grateful to a very overworked Will Newhouse for taking time out of a day that starts at four each morning, for the first milking, to talk to me. As he warned me, that was scarcely a beginning of understanding dairy farming, so I apologize for the numerous liberties I have taken with cows in this book.

Professor Allan Lines, at Ohio State University, provided much useful information on farm economics.

Sue Novak, at the Kansas State Historical Society, was generous with her time and resources as I began my research into Kansas pioneer history. Sheryl Williams, curator of Special Collections at the University of Kansas, was most helpful in directing me to sources on the early history of settlement in Kansas.

My brother Jonathan helped in many ways, from talking over the book as it developed, introducing me to Douglas County DA Angie Wilson, who generously provided information and advice on Kansas law and Douglas County courts, to helping create the Hebrew-speaking heifer.

I have taken a number of liberties with the Douglas County government, including times of bond hearings, and the behavior of the sheriff's department, which I modeled more on Cook County, where I live, than on the real behavior of Douglas County deputies. In addition, for my own story needs I moved the county fair from August to July, which would never happen in reality. I have also added about a mile to the landscape between Lawrence and Eudora to accommodate the Schapens, Grelliers, Fremantles, Ropeses, and Burtons so that I need not displace the Pendletons, Wickmans, and other actual farmers in the valley.

If you are ever in Douglas County, look up the Pendleton Country Market. My old two-room school, Kaw Valley District 95, where I played baseball with more zest than skill, is now a high-end prep school not too far from Highway 10. It now boasts many rooms.

With the exception of Z's Espresso Bar, every place and person mentioned in this book is fictional.

BACKGROUND

I grew up in eastern Kansas in the valley of two rivers, the Wakarusa and the Kaw. On maps, you'll see the Kansas River, but we call it the Kaw, as the Indians who first settled there did, and that is the name I use in this book.

I've been away from Kansas for forty years, but it still is in my bones. The landscapes of childhood are so familiar that it is hard to write about them. I see Chicago more clearly now than I do the prairies, where my brothers and I hiked and worked and played. It took eight years of thinking about the people and places I knew before I could write this novel.

In the 1850s, the ferocious struggle over slavery in Kansas earned the territory the nickname "Bleeding Kansas." The wars fought on that soil were among the bloodiest in our nation's history, as pro- and anti-slavery forces battled over whether the territory would join the Union as slave or free. John Brown's name is well known, but at least a thousand anti-slavery emigrants were murdered in cold blood by "border ruffians," as they were called, who poured into Kansas Territory from the neighboring slave state, Missouri, with the tacit consent of territorial governor Wilson Shannon, himself a slave owner. In 1861, Kansas came into the Union as a free state, but Lawrence suffered a bloody massacre in 1863 in which hundreds were murdered by raiders led by the Missouri slave supporter William Quantrill, who took advantage of most of the able-bodied men being away fighting for the Union.

I grew up on that history, on knowing I shared a heritage of resistance against injustice. Harriet Beecher Stowe's brother, Henry Ward Beecher, sent "Beecher's Bibles" into Kansas Territory: trunks full of rifles for anti-slavery forces covered with Bibles so they could get past the slavers who controlled access to Kansas. I grew up proud of the role of pioneer women, who sewed bullets into their crinolines to smuggle them past the slaver guards.

A century after Kansas came into the Union as a free state, it was painful to acknowledge that Lawrence was a segregated town. In the 1960s and '70s, in a reprise of Bleeding Kansas, the town of Lawrence and the University of Kansas became the site of some of the bloodiest campus battles in the nation—over segregation, over women's rights, the Vietnam War, American Indian rights, African-American rights. Some of the town reacted in alarm, convinced that Communists had taken over the town, the university, and the county. The Republican revolution began then. People who thought African-Americans and women were out of line demanding their rights began taking over government at the grass-roots level to ensure that old-fashioned values would prevail.

This novel is set in the present, against the backdrop of that history. It is set on the farms of the Kaw Valley, where I grew up. In 1958, my parents bought a farmhouse east of town to escape the poisonous segregation of the era, which affected African-Americans the most but, to a lesser degree, Jews as well. The house we lived in had been owned by the Gilmore family, who at one time farmed ten thousand acres in the Kaw Valley. My family lived in that house for forty years, but locals still call it the Gilmore house, never the Paretsky house, and in this novel the Fremantle house is treated in the same way. Like the Fremantle house, "our" house had a Tiffany chandelier in the dining room, a silver-backed water fountain in the upper hall, and many beautiful fireplaces.

CONTENTS

Part Three MIRACLE

Part Four HALLOWEEN

Part Five   **CODA**

Part One

PROTEST

One

THE CORN IS GREEN

HEAT DEVILS SHIMMERED over the cornfield. It was late July, the midday sun so hot that it raised blisters on Lara's arms. It turned the leaves into green mirrors that reflected back a blinding light. Lara shut her eyes against the glare and held out her hands, trying to reach the edge of the cornfield by feel, but she tripped on the rough ground and fell, grazing her knees on the hard soil. She'd had plenty worse falls, but this one so humiliated her that she started to cry.

"Don't be such a baby," she whispered fiercely.

She sat up to inspect the damage. Her dress had a long streak of dirt up the front, and her knees were bleeding. She'd made the dress as part of a summer 4-H project for the county fair. It was pink lawn, with a placket up the left side edged in rose scalloping, and she'd won first prize for it. She got up, her knees stinging when she straightened them, and hobbled the last few yards into the cornfield.

The corn was so tall that walking into the field was like walking into a forest. After a few dozen steps, she couldn't see the house or any of the outbuildings. The rows looked the same in all directions, neat hills about two feet apart. If she turned around in circles a few times, she wouldn't know what direction she'd come from. She'd be fifty yards from home but would be so lost she could die in here. Probably she'd die of thirst within a day, it was so hot. Blitz and Curly would find her bones in October, picked clean by prairie hawks, when they came to harvest the corn.

She lay down between the rows and stared at the sky through the weaving of leaves and tassels. The corn was as tall as young trees, but it didn't provide much shade: the leaves were too thin to make a bower overhead the way bur oak would. She scooted close to the stalks so that leaves covered her face and blocked out the worst of the punishing sun. It was a close, windless day, but when she lay completely motionless she could hear a rustling in the leaves, a sort of whooshing, as if they created their own little wind within the field.

Grasshoppers whirred around her. A few birds sang through the rows, pecking at the corn. The ears were just taking shape, the kernels at blister stage. The smell was sweet, not like the icky, fake-flavored corn syrup you got with your pancakes at the diner, but a clean, light sweetness, before anyone took the corn and started manufacturing things from it.

She lay so still that a meadowlark perched on the stalk right above her. It cocked a bright eye at her, as if wanting her opinion on the world.

"They'll make the corn dirty," Lara told it. "Here in the field, it's clean. But then they'll take it to their stupid factories and turn it into gasoline or plastic or some other nasty thing."

The bird chirped in agreement and turned to peck at one of the ears of corn, trying to get through the thick husk. When Lara reached up an arm to strip the husk back, to help out, the bird took off in fright.

In the distance, she heard her father calling her name. She squinched her eyes shut again, as if that would shut out sound and sight both, but in a few minutes she heard the louder crackling of his arms brushing back leaves.

"Lulu! Lulu!" and then louder, closer, more exasperated, "Lara! Lara Grellier! I know you're in here. Blitz saw you go into the field. Come on, we have to get going."

With her eyes shut, she felt his shadow overhead, heard his sudden intake of surprised breath. "Lulu, what are you doing down there? Did you faint? Are you okay?" And he was bending over her, smelling of shaving cream—so strange, Dad shaving in the middle of the day.

It didn't occur to her to lie, to say yes, the sun got to her, she fainted, she was too ill and weak to go. She sat up and stared at him, imagining how she must look covered with dirt and blood.

"I just fell, Dad. I'm okay, but I wrecked my dress. I can't go like this, I wrecked my dress." She burst into tears again, as if the loss of a stupid dress mattered. What was wrong with her, to cry over her dress at a time like this? But she sobbed louder and clung to her father.

He stroked her hair. "Yeah, baby, you look like you decided today was mud-pie day. It's okay, the dress'll clean up fine, you'll see. You run in the house and wash up and put on something else."

He pulled her to her feet. "No wonder you fell, wearing those crazy flip-flops in the field. I keep telling you to put on shoes. You could step on a nail, get tetanus or ringworm. Aphids could lay eggs under your skin."

It was a familiar litany, and it eased the worst of her sobs. When they got to the house, he hesitated a moment before letting go of her arm. "See if your mom needs any help getting dressed, okay, Lulu? And don't forget your trumpet."

LATER, WHEN SHE'D been away from Kansas for years and finally came home again to run the farm, with children of her own who couldn't tell the difference between a stalk of corn and a sheaf of wheat, the colors were what Lara remembered from that day. Most of the other details she'd forgotten, or they'd merged in her mind with all the other shocks and horrors that made up one long year of grief.

What her aunt Mimi and uncle Doug said when she shoved past them in the kitchen or Curly's sour remark to Blitz, just loud enough for her to hear, "Are we supposed to drop everything and clap, now that Lulu's turned into a drama queen?" let alone Blitz's rumbling warning to Curly to get off Lara's back, "She's been through too much for a kid her age," none of that stayed with her.

All she remembered was the heat, green leaves against blue sky, the red-brown blood on her pink dress. Oh, yes, and her mother, sitting on the edge of her bed in a bra and panty hose, staring blankly at the pictures of Chip and Lara on the wall in front of her.

The sight terrified Lara. Her mother was the active presence on the farm. Jim was cautious, uneasy with change, but Susan was a gambler, an experimenter. After he took physics, Chip labeled her a perpetual motion machine, "p-double-m" in teenspeak, because she never sat still, not even in church or at the dinner table—there was always someone who needed a helping hand up the aisle or "Just one more shake of salt will make this dish perfect."

That hot July day, Lara shook Susan until her mother finally blinked at her. "You're hurting me, Lara. I'm not a pump. You can't draw water out of me by yanking my arm up and down."

But she got up, and let Lara choose an outfit for her, a gold linen dress that Lara loved for the way her mother's auburn hair looked against the fabric. Susan sat while Lara pulled up the zipper and tied a dark scarf around her throat, Susan smoothing Lara's own brown curls away from her daughter's face with a wind-roughened hand. She seemed so very nearly like herself, even on this day of all days, that some of the tightness went out of Lara's chest. Nothing would ever be right again, but it wouldn't be so horribly wrong if her mother started moving.

IF THE DETAILS of the year blurred into a long memory of grief for Lara, her father thought of them as a string of tornadoes roaring down on him. Jim saw himself as small, bewildered, holding out his hands in a futile effort to push back the funnels of wind.

For a long time, he played that most useless of all games: if only. If only I had paid more attention to Chip, seen how unhappy he was. If only I hadn't argued so much with Susan about the bonfires or the war. If only I'd told John Fremantle no one could live in his parents' old home because it was too run-down.

For some reason, that last one gnawed at him most, maybe because it was the one thing he thought he could have controlled: letting Gina Haring come to live in the valley. Not that it had been his decision, but he and Susan had been keeping an eye on the Fremantle house ever since Liz Fremantle died. Her three children had come back for her funeral, had looked at the old house and agreed with Susan that it would take a lot of work to restore it to the splendor of its early days, and had fled again, to New York and London and Singapore.

And then right before Thanksgiving last fall, John Fremantle called out of the blue to say he was renting the house to Gina Haring. Gina was his wife's niece. She'd been through a difficult divorce and needed a cheap place to live while she figured out how to pull her life back together. And all Jim thought was, one less burden. Not, what will a stranger do to the subtle balance of relationships in the valley? Well, no one does think about that, do they?

Two

LOOKING TO THE PAST

THE NEWS THAT the Fremantle children were renting out their parents' house had whipped around the Kaw Valley that previous fall. Before Jim and Susan decided whether Blitz, who worked for Jim and was a first-class mechanic, should try to fiddle with the Fremantles' old octopus furnace, let alone the best way to get keys to Gina Haring, all their neighbors knew she was coming. In fact, two days after he heard from John Fremantle, Jim ran into Myra Schapen at Fresh Prairie Cheeses. Jim had stopped in to buy a slab of cheddar; Myra was delivering the raw organic milk Annie Wieser used in making her artisanal cheeses.

"What's this I hear about the Fremantles?" Myra demanded when she saw Jim.

She was eighty-something, and her false teeth fit badly so she clacked like a loose combine shoe when she talked.

"I don't know, Myra, what do you hear?" Jim said.

"John Fremantle's letting some hippie take over the house. Or, worse, a sodomite."

"Then you've heard way more than me," Jim said. "I only know that his wife's niece is moving in next week. She's had some hard times, and he's renting the place to her."

"Hard times? Her husband divorced her because he found her in bed—"

"Myra!" Jim interrupted. "You weren't there anymore than I was, so neither of us knows what went on in the lady's life. My only business is to make sure the house is fit for her to move into and try to make her feel welcome in a strange place. She's been living in New York City—the country's going to seem like a foreign land to her, most likely."

"Make her feel welcome!" Myra's jaws worked around her teeth. "In *your* place, I would have thought about my neighbors and spoke up. We don't need our children exposed to people like her. I'm not surprised you don't worry about your own pair, the way you let them roam around doing whatever they like, but I care about my grandchildren's immortal souls."

"I expect Junior can look after himself," Annie Wieser said briskly. Junior, who played football at Lawrence High, had been an enthusiastic bully since he started first grade.

"'Every sound tree bears good fruit.'" Myra half smiled, taking Annie's comment as a compliment. "But Robbie, that's another story altogether. Takes after Kathy, and I can't whip it out of him."

When she stumped out of the barn, Annie made a face at Jim. "Poor Kathy. I'm not surprised she ran off, although I've never understood how she could leave those two boys with Arnie and Myra. Of course, she tried to take them that day she left, but when Arnie stopped her she just seemed to let them go. Or maybe the gentleman in the case didn't want a great lout like Junior on his hands. But why not take Robbie?"

Jim only grunted. It made him uncomfortable to be drawn into conversations about his neighbors, the endless speculations on who did what and why. Arnie had shot at Kathy when she drove out to tell him she was leaving and that she wanted her sons; she'd stopped at the Grelliers' farm afterward, trembling and crying, until she was calm enough to drive off. That was the last anyone around Lawrence had ever seen of her—as far as Jim knew, anyway.

"How does Myra get her news?" He fumed at supper that night. "I haven't told a soul about John Fremantle renting out the house."

"No more have I," Susan said. She was peeling an orange, trying to cut off the rind in a single piece without touching the fruit with her fingers. She'd been practicing all fall. Tonight, she held up a perfect spiral in triumph.

"Way to go, Mom." Chip grinned, and gave Susan a high five.

"Myra's installed a mike in every house in the valley," Lara said. "Then she listens in on our conversations and posts the juiciest parts on the Schapen website."

"She knows when you've been sleeping," Chip sang off-key. "She knows when you're awake, and who you wake up with."

Susan laughed, but Jim shook his head gloomily. "I hope she doesn't want to make trouble for the young lady. When I asked Myra why she said Gina Haring was a sodomite, she clacked her teeth and said it was common knowledge."

"I didn't think women could be sodomites," Chip objected.

"Why not?" Lara asked.

"Because—"

Jim cut off his son. "More than I want to hear on the subject, especially at mealtime."

"Myra has that cousin in St. Jo who grew up with John Fremantle's wife," Susan said. "That's probably who told her about Gina Haring. And then Myra might have embellished Ms. Haring's story so she could get angry about it. Myra has to be angry about something all the time, you know. If she was ever happy, she'd probably fall apart."

Myra's rages had been part of Jim's life since he and his brother, Doug, came to live on the farm. They'd always spent a few weeks with Gram and Grandpa in the summer, but they'd never been part of county farm life until their parents died and Gram and Grandpa took them in. The brothers—Jim, nine; Doug, eleven—had been startled by how much the other children knew about them when they started at Kaw Valley Eagle School in the fall. Two town boys suddenly transplanted from schools with more students in each classroom than made up all eight grades at Kaw Valley, they were furious at the way the other kids discussed their parents.

It seemed to Jim that their classmates knew more about his dad's childhood than he did himself, repeating stories they heard from their own parents, who'd grown up with his father. Arnie Schapen, who was Doug's age, liked to needle the Grellier boys by insisting that their dad had been drunk at the wheel when a Santa Fe freight train crashed into his car. Arnie also taunted the brothers for being sissies.

"You don't know a baseball from an ear of corn," Arnie yelled when Jim overthrew first base and the ball landed in the cornfield behind the school. Jim had never liked fighting, but Doug jumped into the ring—really, into the cornfield—with zest, punching away his grief and anger over their parents on Arnie Schapen's nose and shoulders.

That was the first of dozens of encounters between the two. Once, when Doug broke Arnie's front tooth, Myra marched over to the Grellier farm, waving a dental bill under Gram's nose. "You better pay that bill, Helen Grellier. Seventy-eight dollars your hoodlum grandson cost me."

Gram made a shooing gesture. "You want to pay my doctor bill for Doug's broken nose, Myra? That was a whole lot more than seventy-eight dollars, but I'd be ashamed to ask someone else to take responsibility for my boy's behavior. You go on home and hoe some peas. That'll take your mind off this nonsense."

Jim's grandparents were just a little older than Myra, who had married late. Arnie, Myra's only child, was born when she was past forty. Gram said that before Arnie was born, Myra had five or six miscarriages. Gram thought that's what had soured Myra on life, all those losses combined with the hard-line religion she practiced. Schapens and Grelliers used to be Methodists together, but when Myra married Bob Schapen, she took her husband, and later her son, to Full Salvation Bible Church.

Jim, under his own wife's influence, had also left the Methodists, in his case for the Riverside United Church of Christ. Susan had insisted they join because it was the church Jim's many times great-grandmother helped found. Gram shook her head, exasperated by Susan and what Gram thought of as her fads; she and Grandpa stayed with the Methodists.

The three families, Schapens, Fremantles, and Grelliers, had first met in 1855, when they came to Lawrence as anti-slavery pioneers. They had staked neighboring claims near Lawrence for safety.

More than once, the first Robert Schapen had come to Jim's ever-so-great-grandmother's rescue: her husband was an idealist, a French disciple of Emerson and Alcott, who often forgot his farm and family when he was in the grip of a transcendent idea.

The Fremantles brought money and status west with them. Horace was a judge, Una one of the Salem Peabodys, and they built what looked like a mansion to the rest of the valley. After their first house was burned by Quantrill's raiders in 1863, Horace built an even grander place when the Civil War ended. Marble fireplaces with Venetian tiles set into the sides, a grand staircase leading down to a formal parlor, a veranda that enclosed three sides of the house, these had all been extraordinary in pioneer Kansas.

When Jim was a boy, it was still a wonderful place, but after Mr. Fremantle died old Mrs. Fremantle stopped trying to keep on top of repairs or modernizing things that badly needed it, like digging a deeper well to get below the rusty water that was rotting out her pipes. Jim tried to pitch in when he could, but he didn't have the skill or the money to repair the roof or the flashing around the chimney. By the time Liz Fremantle died, the mold along the chimney walls and cat urine in the floorboards had turned the place squalid.

Every time Jim or Susan went over to check on the roof after a microburst or tornado swept through the valley, they e-mailed John Fremantle with a catalog of decay. Jim got Blitz and Curly to help him seal up the basement so that cats couldn't get into the house, and Susan, one hair-raising afternoon, climbed up to replace the flashing around the three chimneys. They couldn't afford to take on other repairs themselves.

Despite its decay, Susan loved the house. She'd fallen in love with the history of the three families and their fight against slavery before she'd fallen in love with Jim. Abigail Grellier, who Jim only thought of as the grim-faced woman in the photograph on the front-room wall, was a living person to Susan.

The first time Susan visited the Grellier farm with Jim, back when they'd been students together at Kansas State, she'd asked a thousand questions about its history that Jim couldn't answer. He and Doug never thought about things like Quantrill's raiders, or the way the anti-slavery women circumvented the slavers' posts along the Kaw River. Grandpa was entertained by Susan's enthusiasm. He showed her however many great-grandmother Abigail's diaries and letters in the tin trunk in the attic.

Susan had stayed up half the night poring over the faded ink, reading bits out loud to Jim. "You mean you've never even read these? But, Jim, this is the trunk she brought with her from Boston. She had to keep her food in it the first year on the farm because it was the only thing the mice couldn't eat through. I can't believe it, can't believe I'm sitting on the same trunk! And that piano down in your gram's parlor, that's the piano Abigail carried out here."

Jim tried to explain to her that his family's history meant something different to him, something he found hard to put into words. It was a sense of having a place in the world, a place ordained for him. Susan, whose father, unable to hold on to a job, had moved every two or three years, responded with a kind of wistful eagerness that Jim found touching.

She'd finally let him pull her down next to him, finally let him turn out the light, make love, but she'd been too excited to sleep much. Jim had grinned idiotically all through breakfast the next day while Susan catechized his grandparents about Abigail. How many of her children had survived? How had she decided who inherited the farm? Could Jim's grandmother run the farm herself the way Abigail did when her husband was away?

Grandpa couldn't resist Susan's flushed face and bright eyes, but Gram found her questions naive or pointless. This was a farm, not a museum. Even after Jim and Susan were married and Susan proved she could carry her weight at harvesttime, Gram often treated her as if she were a child who had to be indulged or restrained.

When Lara was little, Susan used to take her over to visit the Fremantles. Mrs. Fremantle would give Lara sour lemonade and chocolate chip cookies while Susan wandered through the house, tracking the descriptions in Abigail's journals against the floor plans.

Now and then, Liz Fremantle let Susan lead a tour through the house for the Douglas County Historical Society or a Riverside Church study group. Susan showed visitors the outsize flour bins where Una Fremantle had hidden Robert Schapen and Etienne Grellier during one of the slaver raids and the basement room where Judge Fremantle stored guns for the anti-slavery militia in Lawrence.

Susan mourned the fact that the Grelliers' old two-room shanty (rebuilt after Quantrill's raid in 1863) had been replaced by a proper house in the 1860s. That house had been demolished in turn in the 1920s, replaced by the comfortable two-story, brick-and-frame place where the family still lived. Susan wanted to feel herself in Abigail Grellier's two-room lean-to, with the slats so wide apart the mice and snakes came in and out at will.

Susan wished she could explore the Schapen place, to see what remained of their original buildings, but if she'd suggested that to Myra or Arnie they would have assumed she only wanted to snoop and sneer. It seemed to be a point of honor for Myra to live in almost-punitive austerity. She still bent over the low zinc sink installed in the 1920s when her father-in-law brought plumbing into the house. The steep stairs to the second floor weren't carpeted, and only the cheapest rugs—rag in her father-in-law's day, discount bath mats for Myra—lay at the front and back doors.

Susan told her daughter that Myra lived like that to increase her grievance with the Universe. "Everything in the world works against the Schapens. Myra to this day blames your grandpa for the death of their dairy herd in the thirties. She'd only just come there as Bob Schapen's bride when the drought took hold. She thought the Grelliers should have sacrificed half their beef herd and shared out their hay with the Schapens."

No matter what happened, whether it was a hailstorm or a county tax levy, the Schapens felt that they'd been cheated—sometimes by the thieving Fremantles, sometimes the lying Grelliers, sometimes the government, or the Indians or the Jews. But someone was always trying to drive them out of the valley, take what they'd fought for.

Over the decades, the Schapens turned more and more inward, away from the rest of the farms around them. By the time Chip and Lara came along, everyone was so used to thinking of the Schapens as surly that the Grellier children didn't even try to be friendly to Junior, who was Chip's age, or Robbie, who was in Lara's grade at school.

It was different for Susan, at least when she first married Jim. She actually tried to visit the Schapens, inspired by a friendship between the original homesteading Schapens and Grelliers that she'd read about in Abigail's diaries. Jim's grandmother warned Susan that Myra and her son, Myra's husband having died some years before, struck by lightning as he rode a load of hay in from the fields, "liked to keep to themselves," but Susan laughed, and said the Grelliers owed them some kind of hospitality gift to make up for all that Arnie Schapen's ancestor had done for Abigail.

"I'm a new face here—maybe they'll take to me," she said to Jim's grandmother. Young wife, triumphant in her youth and sexuality, sure they made her invincible.

She baked an apple pie, using Baldwins from the Grellier trees—the offspring of wild trees Abigail had found on the land—and Abigail's recipe for crust, which meant buying lard, since, to Susan's disappointment, the Grelliers didn't butcher their own livestock. One raw November morning, she drove down the narrow gravel lane that connected the Schapens to the rest of the world.

Myra Schapen came to the door. "Oh. You're Grellier's wife. What do you want?"

Susan was taken aback. She managed to hold out the pie pan and stammer that she wanted to meet Arnie and Arnie's wife, Kathy, that this was a neighborly visit.

"We don't need charity in this house," Myra snapped. "Especially not Grellier charity. You tell Jim Grellier and that grandmother of his that I wasn't born yesterday, I know what they're up to sending you over here."

"What are you talking about?" Susan said, her voice high and squeaky, as it always became with stress or excitement. "They didn't want me to come at all."

"Maybe you're lying, maybe you're telling the truth. Either way, we don't need any Grellier pies." And Myra shut the door on Susan.

Susan flushed a painful red. She ran back to the car, slipping on the gravel in the yard so that she ended up dropping the pie. She didn't notice Arnie come out of the barn and take a tentative half step toward helping her back to her feet. She clambered into her car and drove home, blinking away tears, sliding in through the unused front door of the house so she could change out of her dirty jeans before Gram saw her and said, "I told you so."

Over at the Schapens', Myra recounted her triumph to Arnie and Kathy. Kathy, who worked at a bank in Lawrence to help pay the farm bills, said she thought it was time they got over all this grudge holding. "It was brave of her to come here, Mother Schapen."

"Brazen, you mean," Myra clacked. "I know you dated Jim Grellier when you were in high school, but you married my son, and I expect you to remember it. And remember that you're a saved Christian and they're no better than pagans. No, they're worse than pagans, because they have the chance to hear God's saving Word and they turn their backs on it."

In Myra's eyes, people who worshipped at Riverside United couldn't have been closer to hell if they'd been Catholics.

June 22, 1855
Kansas Territory

My new home! what is there in it to raise my spirits? We are settled in a fine piece of land about five miles east of Lawrence, but M. Grellier was unable to find lumber for a house, so we dwelt for four weeks in a tent, where I also was delivered of my son, whom I have christened Nathaniel Etienne, in memory of my dear father and my babe's own father. How I have need of my father's spirit and guidance in this land.

As I lay ill, not knowing if I should live to suckle my little one, Mrs. Schapen, who has arrived to keep house for her son Robert, came to visit. She is one "whose mercy never fails," for she saw the straits in which I was reduced, and her son, a fine young man of some two and twenty summers, appeared the very next day with a party of other young men, and within two days had a prairie home built for us. In truth, it is a rude shelter, and I try not to sigh too loud for the comforts of my mother's home, the carpets, the glass windows: here, we put in sheets of unbleached muslin to keep the fleas and mosquitoes as far removed as is possible. And the unfinished floor allows the prairie mice to dance merrily around me as I nurse my little Nathaniel. But we are able to assemble a bed and raise it above the ground. We have a roof that keeps out the prairie showers, and with these good neighbors I would be unworthy of the love of God if I had a disposition like a perpetual dripping on a rainy day.

The Fremantles, whom we also met on our journey westward, are settled near us as well. We are three little sailboats on the Kansas prairie, the Fremantles, the Schapens, and us. When you ride the California road west from Kansas City, and then turn a half mile to the north, you come first to the Fremantles, where Mr. Fremantle, who was a Judge in Boston, is building a fine house, two stories, and a stable to house three horses and a team of oxen. Then you arrive at our rude shanty, and a quarter mile farther on Robert Schapen and his mother, who live as simply as we do.

July 17

The Missourians pour into Kansas territory every day, seeking to harm us, and a woman alone with an infant is not an invitation to their mercy but to their rapacity. Last week, I heard horses' hooves upon the road while I was washing Baby's skimpy clothes and saw a cloud of dust as a band of eight or nine of these ruffians rode toward Lawrence along the great California Road. I gathered little Nathaniel and lay beneath the bed, pressing his face against my breast so that he should not whimper. I heard the men say, "No one here, shall we burn the place?" and another reply, "No, for we may want to move into such a nice home by and by," and then off they rode again.

August 22

Mrs. Fremantle came to call when Mr. Schapen was helping me hang a front door on our shanty home. She herself, of course, lives in great comfort in the mansion Mr. Fremantle is building for her. I try to suppress the sin of envy, for we are not to be concerned with "what we should eat and how we should dress," but I confess in my secret self that I would dearly love a wooden floor rather than an earthen one. So why would she grudge me a real door to replace one of hopsack that lets in every piece of dirt and vermin to attack my poor wee mite of a baby?

"Mr. Schapen, you must be well ahead of the rest of us with your plowing," said she with a broad smile, "if you have time to help Mrs. Grellier with her housekeeping."

"Mr. Grellier is so busy with his school that the rest of us are pitching in," my kind neighbor said. "A school benefits the whole community, and I've never seen anyone so fired up with ideas for the improvement of mankind as Mr. Grellier, even if I can't always understand him."

My husband's French accent becomes heavy when he is excited, as he often is these days, both by our political woes and by his own ideas for the improvement of mankind. When we are alone we speak French together, but of course few people here can converse in that tongue. Mr. Grellier's mind is so lofty that he seldom remembers the trivia of daily existence.

I will not pine for the fleshpots of Boston, like the apostate children of Israel in the desert. I will not indulge in regrets, remembering my dear mother questioning me, "You are so prone to impetuosity, my dear Abigail. Perhaps we should not have named you so, your spirit is too often highly exalted, and then, as if in reaction your spirit goes into mourning (meaning in Hebrew my name signifies 'father of exaltation'). I hope, my beloved daughter, that you do not find yourself in a period of mourning for this impetuous marriage." And I, dear Mother, thinking I knew better than you, and knowing that Mr. Grellier is a good man, a disciple of Fourier and of our own beloved Bronson Alcott, thought not of the hardships the women in Mr. Alcott's community have endured.

Oh, let there be no repining, nor any attention to Mrs. Fremantle and her insinuations! I will boil water for the laundry and the dishes in a tin pan that I have to carry some two hundred paces, from where we were able to find a well of potable water, and bear my yoke like a Christian, for I am here not for my own comfort but "to ease every burden and to let the oppressed go free." And in my own darkest moments I know that my life is free and easy in comparison to the bondswoman.

Three

THE PASSIONS OF SUSAN

THE WEEK BEFORE Gina Haring moved in, Uncle Doug and Aunt Mimi came down from Chicago for Thanksgiving. Doug was a litigator, Mimi a financial consultant, and their one child was around seven. The brothers didn't see each other often—it was hard for Jim and Susan to get away from the farm, and Mimi, frankly, hated country life. Chip and Lara had spent a month with them in Chicago the previous summer, but Mimi and Doug hadn't been to the farm for almost three years.

Thanksgiving morning, Chip took off early to spend the day with his girlfriend. Neither Susan nor Jim was crazy about Janice Everleigh: "Surely he can do better than that," they'd worry, after she spent a day on the farm with Chip, wearing heavy eye makeup even while going out on the combine in the hot sun with him, giggling, flirting, but never talking. Jim, looking at Janice's large breasts bobbing up and down under her tank top, gritted his teeth and talked to Chip about safe sex, keeping his opinions of the girl to himself. Don't make her into a martyr in his eyes, Susan had cautioned.

Susan didn't like Chip abandoning his family for the Everleighs, not on a major holiday, and not while his aunt and uncle were visiting, but Jim put a finger over her lips when she tried to argue Chip out of it. "I don't think your folks liked you spending all those Christmases with Gram and Grandpa before we got married, Suze."

"That was different! My parents' house was so—so *dreary*. Here, it always felt like Christmas, and I try to make it feel like Thanksgiving, too. But you're right, I mustn't be a possessive mother. Let Chip spread his wings."

Chip bent her backward in a sweeping bow and kissed her. "Don't worry, Mom, your little bird will come home in time for Grellier apple pie."

"Her little turkey bird, is more like it," Lara yelled at him as he went out to his car.

While the turkey cooked, Lara and Susan showed Mimi and Nate the X-Farm. This was Susan's latest passion, but Lara was, if anything, more enthusiastic about it than her mother. Doug and Jim watched them from the kitchen window

"Susan doesn't wear out, does she?" Doug said. "First the bread oven, then the co-op market, now an experimental farm. What'd Lulu say they were going to grow? Confection sunflowers?"

"We figure we can't compete with the big producers if Susan tries for an oil-use crop, but everyone wants to eat healthy nowadays. Organic seeds should be a hit in the health-food stores."

Jim spoke tersely, not wanting his brother to see he was worried about Susan and the X-Farm. Doug and Susan had never really hit it off, going back to those Christmases and summer vacations when she'd visited the farm. Doug would tease her about her interest in local history, but there was always a bite to his teasing that made Susan flare up.

When Jim told Gram and Grandpa he was thinking of asking Susan to marry him, Doug had exclaimed, "You sure you want someone that intense on a working farm, Jim?"

"Mind your own business," Jim snapped back. "You never wanted to work this farm, you're running off to law school to turn into one of the leeches who suck the life out of the land, and now you don't want to admit the country bumpkin can attract a woman as amazing as Susan."

"All I'm saying, Jim, listen, she's beautiful, she's fascinating, but she carries on about those old diaries as if Abigail and our farm were a movie. Can she be happy living real farm life, not a made-for-TV romance?"

Jim had tried to knock him down, which led nowhere, because even though Doug was in law school he was still stronger than Jim.

Jim thought about that conversation from time to time, when Susan's enthusiasms swept away everything in her path. The ill-fated co-op market had been the most disastrous venture, because it had been the biggest, but there'd been other smaller actions along the way.

Many farmers in the valley had a small market on their property where they sold fresh produce in the summer. Many also went into Lawrence twice a week to set up a stand at the town's farmers' market. One year, Susan decided that a co-op market would be the salvation of the area's small farmers. Everyone would bring their produce to one central location, the families would staff it to cut down on overhead, and they'd eliminate the brokers who took all the farmers' money and gave nothing back.

Susan brought a missionary zeal to the idea, talking it up at the extension office, visiting neighbors with pages of cost projections, produce suggestions, and profit possibilities. When Susan had a head of steam, she could persuade most people to do most things.

Although the Schapens and Greynards said they weren't giving up their private markets so a Communist like Susan Grellier could make money off them, Liz Fremantle agreed to it. The Fremantles, even when they were old, widowed, the last of their line to farm, carried a lot of weight in the valley; nine more farms followed suit.

Jim remembered how excited Lulu was the day the Kaw Valley Market opened. She kept waking him, demanding to know if it was time to get dressed. She insisted on skipping school to help Susan open the doors. Once it got going, the market garnered interest all over the three-state area. Susan gave interviews on Nebraska and Missouri public radio as well as the Lawrence television station. Her picture was on the cover of the *Kansas Farm Bureau Journal* and in the *Douglas County Herald*. Lulu brought all the articles into school, and Mrs. Lubbock put them on the bulletin board.

For eighteen months, Susan rose at four and drove round all the participating farms, collecting whatever they had for sale at the moment—flowers, pumpkins, lettuce, dried gourds, goat cheese, even emu steaks. Every Sunday afternoon, she'd tot up the week's sales and scrupulously divide the proceeds among the participants.

The market was a success of sorts, in that people did drive out from Lawrence and Eudora to shop, but the store never made enough money to hire a manager. The burden fell on Susan to keep the market open and staffed; the other families taking part didn't treat working there as a serious commitment. During the co-op's last six months, Susan slept less and less, and she had a feverish flush all the time.

One morning, Susan slept through the alarm, slept through Jim getting up to make coffee. She was still asleep when he came back at noon for lunch.

Susan finally got up in the middle of the afternoon, her face stained with tears. "I can't do the store anymore, Jim. I'm not strong enough, or good enough, or—I don't know what enough—to inspire the rest of the families to help me out, and I can't keep it going on my own."

"Then let's make a plan for closing it down. Give people notice."

"They don't give me notice when they don't show up for their shifts and I have to drop what I'm doing on our own place to fill in!"

"Baby, I know you're right, but you can't just turn your back on it. That's a recipe for courting ill will. It was a hard enough job getting people to sign up. Now they'll call you a quitter, and it's not good to get people riled up, even if they're in the wrong. You can't farm out here if you're on bad terms with your neighbors—our farms are too small. We have to cooperate to survive."

"Then tell your old friends to cooperate with *me* for a change. I'm tired of it being a one-way street. I've been neglecting Chip and Lara to help out the neighbors. Chip's playing in a big game over in Shawnee tomorrow—I'm driving over to watch. If people get upset enough to start pulling their weight, then maybe I'll get involved again."

The next morning, Jim sent Curly out to collect the produce, even though he'd been planning on using Curly in the oat field that day, and Curly kept the store open for a few hours.

Curly—Tom Curlingford—worked in the winters for a cousin who had a construction business in town; he was a font of news about everyone across northeastern Kansas. Jim knew Curly would tell the whole world some exaggerated version of Susan's behavior, but he didn't know what else to do—he couldn't take the time to run the store himself, and he couldn't spare Blitz, who was more like his right arm and best friend than a farmhand.

Sure enough, although some people, like Annie Wieser, spoke up for Susan, and others, like Peter Ropes, who farmed south of Grelliers' and had always been a mentor to Jim, refused to discuss Susan at all, most people had a field day at her expense.

Lulu was heartbroken. She loved that market. She'd gotten into fights at Kaw Valley Eagle with Robbie Schapen and Chris Greynard over whether the market was a Communist idea. Two days after Susan turned her back on the project, Jim got a call from Mrs. Lubbock at Kaw Valley Eagle to say Lulu hadn't come in. Jim found his daughter down at the market, trying to shift hundred-pound bags of produce, crying with rage and helplessness. She was ten years old, tall for her age, but Jim picked her up and carried her to the truck, and spent the day with her, away from the farm, from school, treating her to a hot-fudge sundae and a movie in town.

The building still stood at the crossroads on Fifteenth Street, the paint on its sign peeling, the Jayhawk strutting across the board faded to a pale blue. Junior Schapen and Eddie Burton had shot out all the windows, and the inside smelled of mold and rat droppings.

The market had come after Susan's passion for starting a bakery. The stone oven, where she could make five hundred loaves a day, still stood behind the greenhouses. Occasionally, she'd fire it up and make bread for a church fund-raiser or to raise money for uniforms for Chip's baseball team. Susan had built the oven herself, over Gram's objections, and made it work, too. She'd even signed up a half-dozen grocers in the county to carry her homemade bread, but, as with the market, the effort had never turned into a paying proposition. Susan had dropped it with only a week's notice to her customers.

Along the way, she took up lesser projects, learning how to make flashing for the chimneys, setting up a loom in the front room so she could weave cloth the way Abigail Grellier had done, re-creating the Freedmen's school Etienne Grellier started in 1863 and coaxing the Lawrence schools into sending their classes to see it one spring.

Her latest enthusiasm was for organic farming. "We can all do our part to make our carbon footprint smaller," she announced. "Farms are terrible energy users, and if we could farm organically our profit margins would be so much better."

Jim had argued about it with her for over a year, wary now of Susan's enthusiasms. His wife could accomplish anything, and he loved her for it, but she didn't have staying power and that was a problem when you had such a cost-sensitive business as a farm. Besides, the climate in eastern Kansas wasn't great for organic farming. The plains, unsheltered by mountains, were swept by winds as cold as northern Canada's in the winter and burned by heat as warm as northern Mexico's in the summer. Crops were too vulnerable to drought and pests in such weather extremes. You had to be able to fall back on some chemical interventions.

In the end, Jim agreed to let Susan experiment with fifteen acres across the tracks south of the house. The Fremantle children had sold off their parents' farmland after Liz Fremantle died, keeping just ten acres around the house. The X-Farm was part of the land that Jim had bought. It was a triangular plot, with a point sticking into Peter Ropes's field at the south; the hypotenuse of the triangle ran along the western boundary of the land the Fremantle children had kept with the house.

Susan had stayed with the X-Farm for three years, a record in a way, although Lara, who'd been cautious at first—Susan's withdrawal from the co-op market still festering—had done a great deal of the day-to-day work. They'd get their organic certification this coming summer if everything went well.

Jim wasn't going to tell his brother any of that history. To be fair, Doug had never criticized Susan again, once she and Jim were married, but he always tightened in his sister-in-law's company. Even her small projects, like learning how to peel an orange in a single beautiful spiral, rubbed him the wrong way. Jim wasn't going to say he worried whether Susan could stick with the X-Farm long enough to show a profit on her crop.

Four

FIRE BOMB

THE SATURDAY AFTER THANKSGIVING, while Chip drove Janice, Lara, and little Nate into Kansas City to watch the tree lights turn on in the Plaza, the four adults went over to scrub down the Fremantle house.

When Jim unlocked the door to the kitchen, Mimi wrinkled her nose at the odor. Despite Jim's embargo, the cats' urine and spraying lingered, so that the house smelled faintly like the lion enclosure at the zoo.

Doug said, "Someone's been doing dope in here, little bro. Who uses this place?"

Jim sniffed deeply. Sure enough, mixed in with mold and cat was the sweet smell of marijuana. Faint but unmistakable.

"Maybe Junior Schapen's been breaking in," Susan suggested.

"Arnie's kid?" Doug asked.

"Arnie's three-hundred-pound gorilla, is more like it," Jim grunted. "He's way more aggressive than Arnie was at that age. Myra seems to like it, seems to egg him on, all in the name of Jesus, of course."

The brothers scouted the ground floor, but couldn't see any signs of broken windows or forced locks.

"Chip?" Doug suggested.

"Certainly not!" Susan flushed. "That would mean Etienne had stolen the keys behind our backs, which he'd never do. Besides, Etienne wouldn't be so—so idiotic. He's an athlete, baseball is his life. He wouldn't do something that jeopardized his playing. Anyway, where would he get it?"

Mimi laughed. "Susan! Athletes use drugs all the time—it's all over the news every day."

"Why do you call him 'Etienne'?" Doug demanded, distracted from the main argument.

"It's his name."

"He hates it. You should know that by now."

"He'll grow into it," Susan said serenely. "It's a name with a noble heritage in your family, Doug."

"No Grellier has been named that for a hundred fifty years. Chip—"

"Etienne," Susan corrected him.

"*Chip* complained to me about it when he visited Chicago last summer."

While his wife and brother bickered, Jim walked through the house to see if he could find a stash of weed. Junior Schapen wasn't smart enough to break into a house without leaving a trail of broken glass. But Chip was, and several times in the past year Jim had wondered about his son's behavior. Chip had started having mood swings and outbursts of anger at odds with his usual disposition. When he'd asked Chip, point-blank, if he was doing drugs, his son had laughed at him, then left to go to the Storm Door with his baseball buddies.

Chip and Curly were pretty tight; Curly might buy dope for Chip. Or maybe at school—when Jim had gone to high school, you could get a nickel bag openly on the premises. He thought the school had tightened up its drug monitoring, but maybe not. He'd have to talk again to Chip, which he didn't relish.

He went back to the kitchen, where Doug and Susan were still arguing, and dragged them off to start scrubbing. "Doug and I'll do the walls and ceiling if you gals will take on the floors."

There were five big rooms on the ground floor, and then the front hallway, which itself was bigger than the Grelliers' family room. By the time the women had worked their way into the hall, they were black with soot. Susan had a tangle of spiderwebs in her auburn curls.

"This smell is never going away." Mimi sat back on her heels in exhaustion.

The front hall had taken the worst of the cat invasion: the two women had scrubbed urine stains, scooped feces. It was up to Susan to dispose of mouse and snake remains; Mimi had blanched at the sight of the mummified carcasses. She looked at the grand staircase, with its carved newel-posts and balustrade. It all needed to be cleaned, as did the carved double front doors; the etched-glass panels were black with dirt and webs.

"They'll have to strip all these floorboards and refinish them, unless they decide it's too much trouble and tear the house down completely," Mimi said, tossing her scrub brush aside and getting to her feet.

"Don't say that to Susan," Doug called from the front parlor. "She'll never forgive you for even suggesting it."

"It's true, I do love this house," Susan said. "I guess it seems silly to someone who doesn't know or care about the history, but I like to think about a time when people were so committed to doing the right thing that they'd even risk their lives for it."

She climbed a ladder and began wiping off the red globes bracketing the tops of each of the four doorways that opened into the hall. Mimi, perched on the bottom landing of the staircase, asked if they were some kind of emergency light.

"They're fire extinguishers. Una Fremantle was terrified of fire after Quantrill burned down their first house. That little bead sticking out of the bottom holds sulfuric acid. The globe on top has baking soda in it. If a fire got hot enough, the glass would break. Baking soda would fall on the acid, so the room would fill with carbon dioxide and choke off the fire. At least, that was the theory. I don't know that these globes would create enough CO_2 to do any good."

"We could burn some of these floorboards." Doug came into the hallway. "That would get rid of the stench and test the bulb doohickeys at the same time."

Mimi, seeing her sister-in-law redden, got to her feet. "I vote for lunch. Nothing like hard work to make leftover turkey sound good."

After lunch, they went up to the second floor, using the back stairs off the kitchen, with its narrow risers enclosed inside narrow walls. A big patch of plaster had fallen from one wall, exposing the laths.

Doug shook his head, and said he couldn't believe any of the Fremantles cared enough to put money into saving the place. Susan disagreed, saying it should be on the National Register of Historic Places. So Doug began baiting her, with the sarcasm that made him effective in court.

Privately, Jim agreed with his brother, but he didn't want to raise Susan's agitation level any higher by weighing in on the discussion. "Come on, you two," he called from the top of the stairs. "Enough quarreling over something neither of you has the power to control. Let's see if we can make this bathroom and bedroom bearable for the lady."

The other three joined him, but their morning stint had drained their energy—especially Doug and Mimi's, who weren't used to such hard physical work. However, even Susan felt daunted by the second story. Liz Fremantle had stopped housecleaning some years before her death, and the six bedrooms were filled with old newspapers, a train layout, laundered clothes that had never been put away, as well as boxes her children had sent home for safekeeping while they moved around the world.

Susan clucked her tongue anxiously over the patch of blue-black mold around the master-bedroom fireplace. She pulled out a tape measure, and announced that the mold had spread three more inches since she'd last looked in August.

The four of them did their best to clean the main bedroom, with its fireplace, marble washbasin, and heavy cherry furniture, but gave up on the rest of the second floor.

"If this Gina Haring cares about clean, she'll take care of it. If she doesn't, she won't notice," Doug pronounced.

"No one could help noticing all this," Mimi said. "I hope the Fremantles aren't charging her much. Really, they should pay anyone who's willing to stay here."

They packed up their cleaning gear and stowed it in the truck. Before they started home, Jim walked the perimeter, making sure the basement was sealed. He saw that the two-by-four was still bolted across the outside entrance to the old coal cellar but didn't bother to check the bolts. Mimi and Doug came over to him.

"Susan just remembered that all the dishes are dirty. She's washing enough to set out and look hospitable, or something," Doug said.

"What's that house out there that's fallen over?" Mimi asked.

Beyond the barn, visible in fall through the bare trees, stood the remnants of a small single-story house.

"It used to be a bunkhouse," Jim said. "Back when the Fremantles farmed ten thousand acres, they had four, maybe six, hands who lived there."

"And they just let it fall over?" Mimi said. "It's so—so dreary, like the House of Usher, or Miss Haversham."

"It burned down," Jim said, "the first year Doug and I were living with Gram and Grandpa."

"Mrs. Fremantle took it into her head to rent it to some hippies," Doug explained. "You know, back in the wide-open sixties Lawrence was quite the counterculture heaven, and there were a lot of communes dotted around the county, kids trying to harvest the local weed."

"Local weed?" Mimi wrinkled her forehead.

"During the Second World War, when the Philippines were blockaded, the government tried to get farmers all over the Midwest to grow marijuana for hemp, because we got all our rope hemp from the islands," Doug said. "It made poor-grade rope, and poor-grade dope, but if you were a lazy hippie you could get enough of a crop to make enough cash to buy the real thing. So Liz Fremantle, who liked to thumb her nose at local convention, she rented out the bunkhouse to some hippies. It really riled Myra Schapen. And then one night the bunkhouse burned down."

Jim had only hazy memories of that fall. He was nine, and his parents were newly dead. Arnie Schapen used to talk about the hippies all the time at school. He was Doug's age, two years older than Jim, and he was always bringing tales into school about what the hippies were doing. He said they had orgies, which Jim thought, in the confused way of children, meant the same thing as ogres, and he started watching for one-eyed giants coming out of the bunkhouse.

One of the girls in the commune mooned Arnie's mom when she went over to complain to the Fremantles about the hippies. Jim had been in the kitchen with Gram when Myra Schapen stopped off on her way home, shaking from head to foot in her fury.

"We survived Quantrill," Gram said to Mrs. Schapen. "Don't you think we can survive a bunch of confused college kids?"

That only got Mrs. Schapen mad at Gram. "Be your age. These people are Communists. Maybe they're too naive, or too duped or indoctrinated over at the university, to recognize what these so-called hippies are up to, but they're taking over our town. Now they're trying to take over our farms, and Liz Fremantle thinks she's hip or cool, or whatever their lingo is, because she's helping them do it. There's been a fire-bombing every day over in town for the last nine months, in case you hadn't noticed, but you don't care if a bunch of Commies blow us all up in our beds."

Gram said she had better things to worry about than a few college dropouts. "And how do you even know what they're up to, Myra? I live closer to them than you do, and I've never seen one-tenth the stuff you're reporting."

That had sent Mrs. Schapen away in a huff. Gram laughed about it with Grandpa over dinner. The fire had taken care of the problem for all of them. The Schapens said the bombs the kids were making blew up on them, but the sheriff figured they burned candles and incense when they were stoned and the place went up. He said there wasn't any evidence to show they'd ever made bombs, or even owned a gun, although that didn't stop Arnie's folks from spreading the story.

Jim remembered the fire. It was October, and he thought the Fremantles were making a bonfire for Halloween. He'd grabbed Doug, and they'd raced across the tracks and along the road to see if there would be marshmallows and cider. The two of them stopped when they saw the bunkhouse. It looked like some kind of fancy Fourth of July display, a house shape pulsing with fire.

Then Grandpa came running, along with the Ropeses and the Wiesers, who lived east of the Fremantles, even the Burtons from their ramshackle place over near Highway 10, to keep the blaze from spreading. Jim and Doug had formed part of a bucket brigade.

The kids from the bunkhouse, sobered up by disaster, pitched in, too, the girls working as hard as the boys. Only the Schapens hadn't helped. Doug said later he saw Arnie standing with his folks in the background, watching all of them work but not lifting a finger. When it was all over and Liz Fremantle really did hand out hot chocolate, the Schapens took off.

It was then that one of the girls started screaming that someone was missing. When the Fremantles and Grandpa got it all sorted out, they discovered that one of the boys had died in the fire.

"Did you ever know the name of the kid who died that night?" Jim asked Doug.

"Nope. Just that the girl blamed the Schapens for setting the fire, and Myra said they'd done it themselves. The girl was sure the Schapens were Minutemen or something," Doug said. "No one ever proved it one way or another, but I think Mrs. Fremantle let the kids stay in the big house for a month or so while they sorted themselves out. Gram said Mrs. Fremantle always felt it was her fault the boy had died. She said she should have made sure they had a fire extinguisher out there, but I don't see how she could have known they'd blow themselves up."

"So there was a bomb?" Mimi asked.

"Oh, no, I don't know. Not a bomb, but they were doing drugs and burning candles all night long, and a fire was almost inevitable. Jim, get your wife before she decides to reupholster the furniture—I'm freezing my ass off out here."

Five

FAMILY THANKSGIVING

IT WAS STARTING to snow as they drove home, big, wet flakes that melted on the windshield. By the time Chip drove into the yard with his sister and cousin, the snowfall was heavy enough to coat the fields, but not bad enough to make Doug and Mimi think they wouldn't be able to get to the airport in the morning.

Mimi started a load of clothes while Lara helped Susan set out leftovers in the kitchen. Doug put a bottle of wine on the table. He and Mimi almost always drank with supper. Since Jim and Susan didn't care much for alcohol, drinking rarely and only on festive occasions, Doug always brought four or five bottles with him. Tonight, after asking the blessing, Susan gave a self-conscious laugh and let Doug fill a glass for her. The wine flushed her and softened her. She even flirted a little with Doug.

Jim, watching her eager smile, the light glinting on her pale freckles, thought how much more vital she was than her small, elegant sister-in-law. Mimi worked out every day, but Susan worked, and it made her more vivid, at least to Jim. I scored so much better than you did, he thought in silent competition with his brother. You went for looks, but I won on personality.

Nate was full of everything he'd seen and done with his big cousins today—the lights, the zoo—all the things he saw regularly in Chicago seemed magical because he'd done them with Chip and Lara. Chip had even bought him an early Christmas present, his very first big-league baseball glove. "Me and Chip, we're going to be in the outfield. For the Cubs."

"Royals, doofus." Chip grinned, and cuffed Nate lightly on the ear.

"How'd the cleanup go?" Lara asked.

Mimi detailed the day's woes, but Doug interrupted to ask about the marijuana. "Who'd be in there doing dope?"

Mimi looked worriedly at Nate. He was arm wrestling Chip, who faked a strenuous effort and then let Nate knock his arm over half the time.

"Maybe Junior Schapen," Lara suggested. "He and Eddie, they go all over on Junior's bike. They could ride across the fields to the house and no one would see them."

"Peter Ropes would if they came in from behind," Susan pointed out.

Mimi wanted to know who Eddie was.

"Eddie Burton," Chip said over Nate's head. "He's kind of a retard."

"Etienne! You know better than to use that language."

"We know, Mom, we know," Lara put in hastily. "He's a sad case. Maybe he got lead poisoning as a baby, from sucking on all those rusted-out cars in their yard, or maybe something else that stopped him being able to learn even the whole alphabet, but you have to admit he's gotten pretty creepy now he's older. Even when we were still in school at Kaw Valley Eagle, he was doing stuff like starting fires in the trash cans."

"Yeah, but Junior sicced him on that," Chip interrupted her.

"Maybe," Lara said, "but did Junior make him come into the girls' bathroom and crawl under the stall to look up Kimberly's skirt?"

"Eddie Burton?" Doug echoed. "What's he doing with Junior Schapen? I saw Hank Drysdale when I went into town yesterday, and he was full of some rigmarole about Clem Burton assaulting Arnie, or something. He was surprised that I didn't know, until I reminded him that my brother was the original trio of hear-no-evil monkeys rolled into one."

"Burtons have a hard enough time of it without me spreading their problems all over the U.S.," Jim said through thin lips. "You know good and well that you can't farm in the valley—"

"—if you're on bad terms with your neighbors," his children and brother finished in a chorus.

"Which makes no sense," Doug added, "because the Schapens go out of their way to be on bad terms with everyone."

Hank Drysdale was the county sheriff. When he and Doug were in law school together, Hank used to come out to the farm for picnics or to pick sweet corn; he got to know a number of the area farmers, who'd mostly supported him when he ran for sheriff—except for the Schapens and Greynards. Arnie, already working as a deputy, was convinced Hank Drysdale was a liberal, if not an outright Communist.

"Drysdale wondered why you and Susan never drop in on him when you're in town," Doug added.

"I figure Hank's a busy man, running that department. And he was always more your friend than mine," Jim said.

"You should cultivate him," Doug said. "It never hurts to have the top lawman on your side. If I hadn't run into him, I wouldn't have known what was going on around this place. He told me Myra Schapen put up some nasty comment about one of the Burton girls on her home website, and Clem went over, threatening to blow Arnie to kingdom come."

"Yeah, that was pretty dumb," Chip put in. "But only a Burton would be dumb enough to go over to Arnie face-to-face like that, with him being a deputy sheriff and aching to put the whole valley behind bars."

"Of course, Myra could drive stronger men than Clem Burton round the bend." Doug laughed. "What was it she said? Hank couldn't remember, or wouldn't tell me."

Ignoring warning signs from their parents, Lara and Chip explained, "She keeps this 'News and Notes' column on the Schapen website. Mostly, she brags about how many people Junior massacres at football every week. But then Cindy Burton had an abortion, and Myra wrote, 'We believe all life is sacred, so it grieves us when an innocent child is slaughtered. If a family can't feed their children, they should learn the virtues of self-control.'"

"How did she even know?" Mimi demanded.

"That's the point, Aunt Mimi," Chip said. "Eddie Burton, he's Cindy's brother, he probably told Junior, and Junior told Myra. He knows Myra worships him, and every now and then he throws her a bone."

"Listen to you two." Susan was distressed. "A, you don't know for sure that Cindy had an abortion, and, B, if she did, you can't know that Eddie told Junior."

"Oh, Mom! It was all over the county," Chip said, "except for you and Dad refusing to admit it was going on. And, you know, Curly says the reason the Burtons made Cindy get an abortion at all is because Eddie was the father."

"Etienne!" Susan's face was flushed. "I won't have that kind of talk in here."

"I suppose it might have been Junior Schapen," Chip conceded.

"Yes," his sister agreed. "You know, lots of times I see Junior trying to hide that old Honda of his in between the used cars in the Burtons' front yard."

"Yeah," Chip said. "And of course Eddie will do anything for Junior, even—"

Jim reached across the table and cuffed Chip on the shoulder.

"Oh, all right," Chip grumbled. "But you can't blame Clem for being pissed off that Schapen made Burton's business everyone's business. And then when Clem got fined a thousand dollars just for threatening Arnie, he went and shot holes in the Schapens' milk barn in the middle of the night."

"Enough!" Jim slapped the table. "I won't have such mean-spirited talk in here, especially not during a family holiday. You want to laugh at me for hearing and speaking no evil, be my guest. I'd rather be a naive fool than spread so much poison around."

His children and even his brother fell silent. Mimi murmured something about laundry and packing, and got up from the table. Susan, after giving her husband a look, went to help her. While Lara started on the dishes and Doug took Nate into the family room to play Foosball, Jim steeled himself to talk to Chip about the marijuana they'd smelled in the Fremantle house that morning. It wasn't the best time—his outburst had left everyone on edge—but he wanted to get the conversation over with as fast as possible.

"Why do you keep harping on me about dope?" Chip glared at his father. "Do you think I'm some kind of addict?"

"I want to know you're not breaking into Fremantles' and smoking," Jim said doggedly. "And if you are using marijuana, I'd like to know where you're getting it."

"Why?" his son demanded. "Do you want some?"

Jim's own temper rose. "What kind of crack was that? If Curly is supplying you with drugs—"

"Curly is not supplying me with drugs, okay?" Chip stared at his father with hard, hot eyes. "And I won't lie to you: I sometimes smoke with the guys on the team, but I don't do it often. And I don't do it when I'm alone."

He turned on his heel and ran up the stairs, slamming the door to his room. Chip was supposed to be helping Lara with the dishes, but Jim didn't feel like confronting his son for a second time in five minutes so he went into the kitchen to help her himself. She saw how upset he was; she gave him a lighthearted rundown of their day in Kansas City, trying to coax him into a better mood.

Jim kissed her forehead. "Baby, I'm a crab cake tonight. You go on up to your homework—I'm better off doing the dishes myself."

When he'd finished, Jim went into the family room and challenged his brother to a Foosball match. Nate jumped up and down with excitement, cheering on his dad, who beat Jim by two points. Nate demanded a turn with Jim, who let his nephew win. The little boy's glee slowly brought Jim back to his more usual level spirits.

Lara, bored with her history book and drawn by the laughter, came back downstairs. She challenged Jim and Doug to a team game, she and Nate against the brothers. Jim was surprised all over again by how competitive his brother was: even though it was his own son he was playing, he put everything he had into the game, even snapping at Jim for letting Nate kick a ball past his defenders.

"We won, we won!" Nate squealed. "We beated them."

He and Lulu exchanged high fives, and then Lara scooped him up under her arm. "Come on, shrimp. Even Brian Urlacher has to go to bed sometimes."

"I am not a shrimp. I'm a giant. Put me down!"

Later, in bed, Jim told Susan about his abortive conversation with

Chip. "The way he reacted makes me think he *is* smoking over there at Fremantles'. You don't think you could talk to him, do you, Suze?"

"If Etienne swore he wasn't using drugs often, I think we have to believe him," Susan said.

"He didn't. That's the point. He won't lie to me directly. But he did a good job of dancing away from my questions."

"After Tuesday, when this Gina Haring moves in, it won't be a problem anymore." Susan turned out the light. "It'll be good to have the house to ourselves again—I'd forgotten how crowded this place feels with seven people in it."

"So seeing Nate running around doesn't make you wish we had another little person here?" Jim said, only half teasing. He liked all children, especially his own, despite his recent brushup with Chip. It was going to be hard when his son went off to college next fall.

"Oh, Jim, I'm forty-five now. I can't go through another pregnancy." To soften her response, she put her arms around him and pulled him close to her in the bed.

Six

DRUG BUST

Sunday night, Lara and Chip slipped out of the house, muffling their laughter against their parka sleeves. They'd told their parents they were going to stay up late to watch a movie. If their father was surprised that they'd agreed so easily on what to see, he didn't say anything.

They sat in the family room, watching *March of the Penguins,* for half an hour after the lights went out on the second floor. When they were sure all was silent in their parents' room, they slipped out of the house through the garage, leaving the television on as a decoy. Chip didn't turn on the flashlight until they'd reached the gravel road on the far side of the train tracks.

Yesterday's snowfall was starting to melt. Wheat stubble poked through the snow in the Ropes field like stubble in an old man's beard. The dead stem grasses along the drainage ditches waved ghostly arms in the wind.

Chip switched off his flashlight, and said, in a deep, soft voice, "They're in there, you know, waiting to jump out at you."

"They are not," Lara said, louder than she intended, because, in the dark, the towering grasses looked menacing. "Don't be an idiot. I'm not stupid Janice Everleigh, who's going to cling to you and screech, 'Oh, Chippie, protect me, you're so big and brave.'"

Chip picked up a handful of soft snow from the road and tried to stick it down Lara's back. She struggled with him and slipped in one of the deep ruts in the road. He grabbed her and pulled her to her feet.

"You okay, Lulu? Don't go spraining anything—I don't want to have to explain it to Dad."

"Well, don't push me, turkey."

They continued, arm in arm, skirting the holes, until they reached the Fremantle place. This was the part that Lara dreaded: going into the basement in the dark through the old coal chute. Dad had nailed all the basement windows shut, and seen to it that all the downstairs doors and windows were locked, when he was struggling to keep the cats out of the house. He'd even boarded over the coal chute and bolted it shut, but Chip had slipped the bolts free.

He and Lara had been using the Fremantle house as their private clubhouse for the past two years. Chip did go there to smoke dope with Curly or occasionally with a friend from the baseball team. Lara kept her diary tucked behind the overmantel in the master-bedroom fireplace where it had slipped away from the wall.

Lara loved the feeling of privacy, of owning the place, that she got when she went to the mansion. She could poke around in the rooms that hadn't been used since old Mrs. Fremantle's children left Kansas forty years ago. She'd found Mrs. Fremantle's wedding dress in the back of one closet and preened in front of the watery mirrors in it.

When Mrs. Fremantle died, her kids had taken most of the valuable furniture. They'd left a rolltop desk and a cherrywood table that dated to the Revolution, as well as a rickety piano that Susan thought could be valuable. All the windows had brocade drapes that now hung in shreds from the cats scratching them.

Lara would sit in a window seat in the master bedroom, writing by candlelight, pretending she was Abigail Grellier listening for Border Ruffians, while Chip and Curly horsed around in the back parlor.

Lara's favorite thing in the house was a Tiffany chandelier in the dining room. It was made of stained glass, like a church window, only its six sides showed people doing things with grapes—planting or picking them or making wine out of them. A big piece had broken off, the piece that would have shown the tub with people stomping grapes to make wine.

Before Prohibition, Mom said, every county in Kansas had at least one winery, and the chandelier commemorated the one the Fremantles used to own. You could see where they had grown their grapes, out behind the old hay barn at the back of the property. Mom said it would cost thousands of dollars to get the piece made to match the rest of the glass. Lara tried to make the broken panel in her art class at school, but she couldn't get the colors to turn out right.

Before she started the X-Farm, Mom had toyed with the idea of creating a vineyard and a winery herself: Château Grellier. Lara loved the idea of it, mostly because of the chandelier. She even designed a wine label in her art class, with a tub of grapes set in the middle of a wheat field. In the end, though, after going over the numbers, Susan had to agree with Jim that the payback horizon for wine was too far.

When she was little, Lara had loved her mother's stories about the early days in Kansas. Susan would copy pages from Abigail's diary into her own commonplace book, because the diaries were so fragile she didn't want to destroy the paper by handling them too often. Then she would read bits to Lara, and tell her the history, the battle raging over slavery in the Kansas Territory, what the women did, how the Delaware Indians, who used to live north of the Kaw River, helped the anti-slavery settlers. Susan would write notes to herself on the edges of her commonplace book, almost as if she were communicating with Abigail.

Susan also put her own family's stories into her commonplace book, the clippings about the co-op market that ran in the *Douglas County Herald,* or the time Chip's home run won the Northeast Kansas Little League tournament. "A hundred years from now, your granddaughter will want to know how we were living, how we faced up to the challenges, just like we want to know about what Abigail did," Susan explained to Lara.

Lara couldn't imagine that anyone would find her life as interesting as a pioneer's. How could playing basketball or working on the X-Farm compare to Abigail's hacking off the head of a snake that slithered through the great gaps in the floorboards or lying on top of her baby to keep him from crying while Border Ruffians ransacked the house? But when she was ten, Lara dutifully started a diary. Sitting next to her mother at the dining-room table, she would write about her day at Kaw Valley Eagle or how she rescued the meadowlark fledglings she'd found in the cornfield.

When she turned thirteen, the previous year, she also turned secretive. The privacy of the deserted Fremantle house became like a cloak of invisibility she could wrap around herself. Lara left her diary behind the mantel, where her mother wouldn't be able to find it, and she would sit in the east-facing master bedroom, where there wasn't a danger that Dad would see her flickering candle from the wheat field when she wrote in it. For the same reason, Chip and Curly hung out in the back parlor, the one used for receiving special visitors back in pioneer times.

Tonight, she and Chip wanted to retrieve the private things they'd left here. Chip was especially worried about his stash of dope, but Lara didn't want to lose her diary.

When they got to the coal chute, Chip undid the cover and slid down first. He waited at the bottom for Lara, who dallied: she was terrified, and didn't want him to know. For all the money they'd put into building a fancy house, the original Fremantles had left the basement unfinished. It had a dirt floor, where snakes and wolf spiders roamed. Lara didn't mind them so much in the daylight, but she didn't want to land on one in the dark.

"Come on, Lulu," Chip yelled up at her. "We want to make it snappy."

She shut her eyes, took a breath, and slid down the chute. He caught her at the bottom.

"Point the light on the ground. I don't want to step on a spider. And don't fool around with me, I don't like it," she added as he crawled his fingers up her scalp.

They ran up the steep stairs to the kitchen. The house smelled like bleach, from yesterday's cleanup, but the acrid stench of cat spray underlay the bleach, making Lara sick to her stomach. Chip pushed through the swinging door into the dining room while Lara headed for the staircase to the second floor.

Her foot was on the first step when the kitchen door opened. She couldn't hold back a scream.

"Hello, Lulu."

"Dad! What are you doing—"

"What am I doing here? More to the point, what are you two doing here?"

"It was a dare," Lara said quickly. "Chip dared me that I was too chicken—"

"Lara, don't lie to me. If you don't want to tell me the truth, just keep quiet."

Lara flushed and dug her nails into her palms so she wouldn't cry. Chip said he was sorry, they had left a few things here.

"So you have been breaking in here!" Jim said. "I tried talking to you about this Friday, and you were too cowardly to tell me the truth. How do you think that makes me feel? I was asked to keep an eye on this place, and not only did you take advantage of my responsibility here, you lied to me."

When neither of his children spoke, Jim said, "And what 'things' did you leave here? Dope? Don't tell me you've been letting Lulu smoke."

"No, of course not. Me and Curly, we come over here sometimes."

"After what you said Friday night? When I—"

"I told you Curly wasn't buying drugs for me. That's the truth."

Jim breathed hard through his nose, then he turned to look at Lara. "And what were you coming here to get?"

Chip said, "She just tagged along for the adventure. She was going to watch from the upstairs window to see if you were coming, but you beat us to it."

Jim's hard eyes stayed on his daughter for a second. Lara didn't know why Chip had lied for her, but she was too upset to say anything. Jim made Chip get his stash, which he'd stored inside a beat-up piano in the house's front parlor. When Chip and Curly got high, they'd play the piano. They thought it was excruciatingly funny to play songs where you could only get half the notes to come out.

"This is real," Jim announced, smelling it. "I thought maybe you were harvesting the local weed. Where did you buy this?"

"From a guy in town, okay, Dad? Now you have it, does it matter?"

"Of course it matters, because even if I throw this out you'll just get more. Is that the life you think I want for you, breaking into other people's houses, getting stoned there?"

"What are you going to do? Tell Arnie Schapen to search me every time I drive past his place?" Chip spoke with a kind of fake jocularity that always got his father's goat.

Jim and Chip both knew Arnie would think he was in hog heaven if he caught one of the Grelliers breaking any law, but Jim was too angry to think clearly, so he said, "If that's what it takes to keep you from doing dope or breaking into empty houses, maybe it's not such a bad idea."

At that, Chip lost his own temper. He flung open the back door and took off down the Fremantle drive toward the road.

Jim knew he'd overreacted, but he was still angry with both children. He glared at his daughter. "Were you in on this? Were you joining those drug parties?"

She shook her head. "I smoked some once, but I didn't like it. Anyway, Chip didn't want me to, he only let me because I begged him. I wanted to see what it was like. And we never hurt this house, so don't act like we're robbers or something."

"Not robbers, housebreakers, and too ignorant to cover your tracks. Come on. It's past midnight, and you have school in the morning, so let's get home."

Once they were outside, Jim closed the coal chute. He found a screwdriver in the pickup and rebolted the two-by-four to the cellar cover. When they were heading back home, Jim emptied the bag of marijuana out the window. Tijuana gold mixing with wild Kansas hemp—maybe they'd breed a wonderful hybrid that would bring a new generation of hippies to the area.

The truck passed Chip, trudging down the road. Jim was seldom angry, and never for long. The sight of his son walking through the snow in his sneakers made him feel ashamed. He swung down from the cab and apologized to Chip for losing his temper, but he couldn't apologize for throwing out the dope or caring about his kids breaking into the house. Chip climbed into the truck, but he stayed angry with Jim for a number of days.

Later, Jim wondered if his anger that night had been a catalyst for disaster. If I had kept my temper, if I had seen it from Chip's point of view, he would think over and uselessly over.

Seven

BEING NEIGHBORLY

SUSAN AND LARA'S BREATH made white puffs in the cold air, barely visible against the gray sky and peeling paint of the porch. Lara stomped her feet, which were freezing in her running shoes, but Susan stood still, not wanting to jar the pie she was carrying.

"Maybe we should just go in and leave the pie on the table," Lara suggested. "She must know we're here but doesn't want to answer the door."

"Not the first time we come over," Susan said firmly. "She won't know who we are or why we left a pie."

It was two weeks before Christmas. Neither Susan nor Lara had met Gina Haring yet. The day Gina moved in, Susan had a church board meeting, so Jim had shown Gina the house and explained the workings of the old octopus furnace, with its eight outsize arms pushing hot air into the house.

Lara knew Gina's car, a battered turquoise Escort, from all the trips she'd made past their house on her way to Lawrence. The Escort stood in the circular drive, alongside a newer car, one of the Honda hybrids. They didn't recognize the hybrid model—no one who lived out here would own a car too small to take the punishment of country roads—but it had Douglas County plates, and a bumper sticker that proclaimed WITCHES HEAL.

Susan had waited until eleven to drive over, not wanting to seem like a busybody. Lara came with her, hoping her mother and Gina Haring would get into some deep conversation so she could slip upstairs to retrieve her diary.

The morning after she and Chip had broken into the house, her father had bolted two large planks across the coal-cellar doors. Lara didn't know how she'd get in again uninvited unless Gina drove off and left the doors unlocked, and she couldn't sneak through the fields a million times a day to see if that had happened.

Susan was finally agreeing with Lara's suggestion to leave the pie with a note for Gina when Gina opened the kitchen door. Lara couldn't keep back a little gasp of admiration. Gina had on jeans, but they'd been ironed, and the big sweater she wore was made from yarn so soft Lara wanted to reach over to pet it. Not even her aunt Mimi wore such expensive-looking clothes. Gina also looked older than Lara had expected, her face thin, with well-defined bones, her dark hair combed severely behind her ears. Although it was Saturday morning, she even had on makeup, and tiny gold earrings.

Susan rushed through the business of introductions: My name is— You met my husband—my daughter— If there's anything you need— Here's a pie.

After a moment's hesitation, Gina invited them into the kitchen. No one else was there, which made Lara wonder if the hybrid was hers along with the Ford. Gina didn't smile or say anything, just stood holding the pie as if it were a foreign object she'd never seen before. Lara flushed, wondering what she and Susan could have done to make her so unfriendly.

"I re-created the recipe as best I could from my husband's great-great-grandmother's papers," Susan was saying. "Of course, she didn't list ingredients in detail, or proportions, but I did as much research into pioneer baking as I could. Since you're going to be living here, I thought you'd be interested in a pie that comes out of the history of this area. The apples are from the trees behind this house, and they still have branches going back to the 1850s. I think it's pretty authentic."

"It also tastes good," Lara ventured, seeing that Gina was looking even more forbidding.

That made Gina laugh. Her front teeth were crooked, which seemed somehow glamorous to Lara, the little flaw that made the rest of her look perfect.

She finally murmured something that might have been a thank-you, adding, "I'm not much interested in pioneer history."

"Oh, but once you start learning about it, you'll change your mind." Susan ignored Gina's chilly tone. "This little triangle, where we and Fremantles and Schapens live, was at the center of some of America's most violent battles in the 1850s. Not this house, but the people who lived here—this house wasn't built until 1871, but the Fremantles, and my husband's family, even—"

"Mom!" Lara interrupted, embarrassed because Gina was looking stern. "She doesn't care about all that stuff, she just said!"

Gina said, "It's always engaging to hear from someone who is enthusiastic about a subject."

The words showed interest, but her tone was cold, smooth, like ice cream. Embarrassed though she'd been by her mother, Lara couldn't bear for anyone else to make fun of her. She said abruptly, "It's freezing in here. You know, if you don't turn the furnace on, the pipes will burst. Do you want me to light the pilot?"

"Lara!" Susan was embarrassed in her turn. "She doesn't need you telling her how to run the house."

"Maybe I do," Gina said. "I've never lived in a palace before. The furnace is on, but I can't afford to heat a palace. I put space heaters in the rooms I use. The rest of the place stays a nice fifty-five degrees, perfect for the spiders and the mice."

Lara looked at her, baffled. It was impossible to tell what Gina meant, because, despite the sarcastic words, she sounded enthusiastic, as if she wanted to make the house attractive to vermin. Lara decided it was safer not to say anything else. Besides, she couldn't believe Gina didn't have any money: not only did her clothes look as though they cost a fortune, she had a big cappuccino machine on the counter; one not even that fancy was for sale at Z's Espresso Bar, and it cost twelve hundred dollars.

Gina glanced at Lara's troubled face and smiled, a genuine-looking smile, and said with genuine-sounding warmth, "I'm sorry, I'm a little distracted this morning. I know your house, because your father pointed it out to me when he drove out with me last weekend to open up this place. Who lives behind me? Do they own all those cows?"

"The cows belong to the Schapens," Lara said. "You can't see their house from here. Really, you can't see it from anywhere, not even our hayloft, because their farm is built so far back from the road. The Ropeses live behind you."

Lara pointed at the gray clapboard house across the field, where her best friend Kimberly had grown up. Kimberly and her parents lived in town now, but Kimberly's grandfather still farmed the land. She and Lara had gone to Kaw Valley Eagle together, before Kimberly's dad gave up on farming and took a job in the maintenance department at the university. Now Lara and Kimberly were in ninth grade together in town. They played basketball on the junior varsity team.

"Your husband told me you were an expert on the house," Gina said to Susan, still in the same warmer-sounding voice.

It was all the encouragement Susan needed. She launched into the story of Abigail's journey west, how the Fremantles and Schapens had helped her when Etienne Grellier was too busy thinking great Transcendentalist thoughts to work the fields, how Abigail's oldest son married Una Fremantle's daughter and that's how the Grelliers ended up with all the papers about the house.

Lara watched Gina's face. She was blinking under the avalanche of Susan's information, but she continued to listen. Her face didn't have that blank look people get when they are really thinking about lunch or their date to the game instead of what you are talking about.

Susan showed Gina the flour bin where Una Fremantle had hidden her husband during Quantrill's raid, a waist-high receptacle that pulled out of the wall at an angle. When Lara was a child, she used to beg Mrs. Fremantle to let her climb into it, so she could pretend to be hiding out from Quantrill.

"Quantrill burned down my husband's family's shanty and the Fremantles' first house—this is the one Judge Fremantle built after the Civil War. The Fremantle kitchen survived Quantrill, fortunately, or the judge would have been murdered. Una Fremantle was always obsessed with fire after that. Have you seen the study? Once, Jim and I took a trip to Boston so I could see where the Grelliers and the Fremantles had started their pilgrimage, and I got to tour the house that Horace Fremantle grew up in. This room here is an almost exact replica of his father's office. I fixed it up so you can work in here, if you want."

Susan ushered a dazed Gina across the small foyer at the bottom of the back stairs, through a bathroom next to it, and into Horace Fremantle's study beyond. Lara knew all about Horace and his effort to look important in his father's eyes. She knew how much the marble in the fireplaces cost and where it came from, and how when the wagon hauling it from Kansas City sank in the Wakarusa River the first Mr. Fremantle and the first Mr. Schapen rescued the marble and the oxen. She waited until her mother was in full flight in the study, then ran up the back stairs. The boards didn't creak if you moved fast and light.

The stairs ended next to Lara's second-favorite thing in the house, a drinking fountain built into the hall wall. It hadn't worked for years, but it was beautiful. The back was a silver shell, and the fountain part was more of the same marble as the fireplace. Lara could hear her mother at the bottom of the main staircase, her voice high and squeaky, as it always was when she was excited.

Lara tiptoed to the south end of the hall. The bedroom in the southeast corner had a closet that connected with the main bedroom. It had been cold in the kitchen, but it was freezing up here. Lara felt a sneeze coming on, tried to hold it in, succeeded only in exploding in the middle of the connecting closet.

"Gina? Is that you? I thought I heard more voices downstairs."

Lara froze at the entrance to the main bedroom. A woman wrapped in a heavy dressing gown was sitting up in bed, drinking coffee and reading a newspaper.

She dropped the paper and flung aside her reading glasses when she saw Lara. "Did they send you on a reconnaissance mission? Do you want a full report on my name and who I am?"

Lara flushed. "I'm sorry: I didn't know anyone was up here."

"Then why did you come up? Didn't you know Gina was living here? In town, we don't wander uninvited through people's houses."

"I'm sorry," Lara repeated helplessly. "Honest, if I'd known you were here I would have stayed downstairs."

"You didn't see my car standing out in the yard all night and wonder if someone had a breakdown and needed a jump? That was the previous *visitor's* excuse."

She gave "visitor" a sarcastic emphasis, meaning Lara was just one more nosy intruder. "Gina!" she added, leaning forward in the bed to shout. "I've caught a live one. Do you want to come get her?"

Lara turned a deeper red. Already embarrassed, she found she couldn't move her legs, much as she wanted to back up and disappear. She heard her mother and Gina's steps on the hall stairs; an instant later, they were in the bedroom.

"Lara!" Susan cried. "What are you doing up here?"

Lara looked around wildly and saw the blue-black patch of mold around the fireplace. "I came up to see about the mold. It's gotten worse, you know, and they could get a bad lung infection from breathing that stuff."

"She's right," Susan said to Gina, "it isn't healthy to breathe in those funguses. But, Lara, you're almost fifteen, you know better than to think you can still parade through here without permission. I'm sure if you'd told Gina—"

"Doesn't anyone out here mind their own business?" the woman in the bed demanded.

"Of course," Susan said stiffly. "I'm sorry my daughter broke in on you, but it was with the best intentions. I'm Susan Grellier. My husband and I were the caretakers until Gina moved in. I didn't realize it would take Lara so long to adjust to being a visitor instead of someone with the right to be in the house. We'll leave now. But you have our phone number, or Gina has it, if something goes wrong, or you're lonely—"

"How can we be lonely when everyone in the county waltzes in before noon?" the woman said.

"Autumn, I think they're different. Susan's a neighbor. She baked a pie in the best tradition of the Old West. She's a historian—at least, she's an amateur historian—and she knows a lot about the house. She came over to tell me about it."

Once again, Lara couldn't decipher what Gina was saying. She sounded as she had when they first came in, as though her meaning didn't lie in her words but in her inflection. The woman in the bed seemed to understand her because the angry lines had smoothed out of her face, making her look younger.

"Autumn Minsky runs Between Two Worlds in Lawrence," Gina said. "We met when I went in for—supplies last week."

"As the sheriff was at pains to find out early this morning," Autumn snapped, but then suddenly laughed. "You should have seen his face when I gave him one of my business cards—he acted as though it would turn him into a toad. Which I wish it had, once he told me he'd been keeping an eye on my store!"

Lara knew Between Two Worlds. It was a New Age store where you could buy incense or books on pagan religion, but they also sold jewelry, little gold suns on gold chains that cost hundreds of dollars, earrings in the shape of crescent moons with turquoise or lapis set in them. Some of the things weren't so expensive, though. Her friend Melanie Derwint had four piercings in her ears and wore silver moon-shaped studs she'd bought at Between Two Worlds.

"The sheriff?" Susan asked. "Has Hank Drysdale been out here?"

Gina shrugged. "I didn't catch his name. He stopped by at eight in the morning because he saw Autumn's car in the yard. He claimed to be worried about my safety."

"He wasn't as bad as the other one." Autumn shuddered. "At least it's possible the man was a sheriff, although he didn't have a uniform or a marked car."

"What was he driving?" Lara asked at the same time her mother asked, "What other one?"

"Some horrible-looking lout straight out of *Cold Comfort Farm* had climbed up the big tree outside the bathroom window and was peering in when I got up to pee around six this morning," Autumn said.

Lara was startled to hear a grown-up woman use that word boldly in the middle of conversation: I have to pee, she rehearsed in her mind. Would Kimberly and Melanie go, "Ooh, gross," or would they think she was totally cool?

"What happened?" Susan asked.

"I opened the window and shouted at him. He grinned as though he'd just done the cleverest thing on the planet and kept hanging on the branch while I kept shouting, until I suppose his hands froze and he more or less fell out of the tree. And then got up and ran away."

Lara said, "Was he about twenty, maybe? With dark curls and red cheeks?"

"He had on a stocking cap, and anybody outdoors on a December morning would have red cheeks," Autumn said impatiently. "Is he your boyfriend? Did you two dare each other to spy on us?"

"No!" Lara cried. "I don't have a boyfriend, and it wouldn't be him if I did, if it's who I think it might be."

"Calm down, Autumn." Gina walked to the bed and put a hand on her friend's shoulder. "Who do you think it was, Laura?"

"Lara," Susan corrected automatically, while Lara said, "Mom, don't you guess it was Eddie? It's the kind of thing he does."

"Who's Eddie?" Autumn demanded. "Remember, we don't have a playbill."

Lara blushed again. "Eddie Burton."

"Lara," Susan said warningly, meaning don't say something you can't back up with facts.

Lara knew her mother didn't like to hear about perverse acts. Susan wanted to believe that people had pure and ardent spirits, that no one, from her beloved abolitionists to the most tiresome of her neighbors, ever abused their children or raped a heifer or did any of the other grotesque things that went on day in and day out somewhere in Kansas, even right here in Douglas County, if you could believe Curly and Chip.

"Mom, if he's climbing their trees and staring in the window at them, they have a right to know who he is—or, at least," Lara corrected herself conscientiously, "who I think it could be. And they should let Sheriff Drysdale know, because otherwise Arnie Schapen will just use it as an excuse to lock up Eddie, or come in here and snoop around."

She turned to Autumn and Gina. "The Burtons live down the road to the south—Schapens are to the west. You can't see Burtons' from here because it's off behind the Ropeses' house, but if you drive up the county road toward Highway 10 and see a run-down place with about a hundred cars up on blocks in the yard, that's Burtons'. And Arnie— Mr. Schapen, I mean—he's a deputy sheriff, so it could have been him who came out this morning to check on your car, but the Burtons are, like—"

She caught her mother's headshake before she brought out the word *retarded* and changed it to, "They don't always, well, catch on as fast as most people. Especially Eddie. He was at Kaw Valley Eagle when I was, even though he's a whole lot older, and his whole lesson, every morning, was saying the alphabet, which he never could remember past the letter *f,* and then he'd get a nosebleed and have to—"

"But does he climb trees and spy on people?" Gina interrupted.

"Oh! That's the first I ever heard of him doing that, but he used to crawl under the bathroom doors to look up our skirts, me and Kimberly's, and now he likes to set fires—"

"Lara," Susan cut her off. "You have to get into town for basketball practice."

She turned to Gina. "If you wouldn't mind bringing the pie pan back when you're done—I used one of our real ones. They make better pies than the throwaway pans. And, please, people out here are friendly. Don't get the wrong impression just because of one little incident."

"Yes, indeed," Gina said. "They might burn down your house if you're an abolitionist, but perhaps since it was winter they just wanted to be helpful, heat the place up for you. So they climb the tree outside your bathroom to make sure you haven't frozen during the night. That sounds very friendly indeed."

Lara giggled, but her mother shepherded her from the room. As they walked down the back stairs to the kitchen, Lara heard Autumn Minsky say, "Honestly, Gina, when I told you Lawrence was a center for the arts in the Midwest I wasn't expecting people to reenact *In Cold Blood* for you. Maybe you should rethink staying here. It smells and it's cold—"

"And it's cheap," Gina said. "My uncle isn't charging me anything but utilities and taxes to stay here. Nowhere in New York could I find a place that cheap, let alone a gothic horror like this. Maybe I'll write a novel about it while I'm out here, *Cold Comfort Farm* meets *In Cold Blood*—I'll call it something like *Cold-Blooded Farm.*"

Eight

UNDERGROUND WARS

ON THE WAY to Lara's basketball practice, mother and daughter talked over their morning with Gina Haring.

"She can't really be poor, the way she says she is, can she?" Lara said. "Did you see her cappuccino machine? Or her clothes! Did you notice that sweater? It must have cost a hundred dollars, easy."

"Easi*ly*," Susan corrected automatically. "I can't imagine what it cost—your aunt Mimi sometimes spends a thousand dollars on an outfit, but even her clothes aren't that fine. I think Gina's husband was very wealthy—she probably has the wardrobe she bought while she was married."

"And then he divorced her because she was sleeping with women, and he didn't give her any alimony or anything."

"Lara! How can you say such a thing? We don't know anything about her marriage or why it ended."

"Melanie Derwint told me. She goes to Full Salvation Bible with the Schapens, and she says Myra told Mrs. Derwint."

"And if Myra Schapen says something, it must be the gospel?" Susan demanded. "Until Gina chooses to confide in us, we won't make any assumptions about her private life. All Mr. Fremantle told your dad was that she'd gone through a difficult divorce, and we don't have any right to ask her questions or guess what that means."

"Oh, all right," Lara agreed sullenly, all the while planning to talk over what she'd seen with Kimberly Ropes at basketball practice.

Her mother's mind wandered into a different place. "Did you hear what Gina was saying to Autumn as we were going down the stairs? That she would try to write a novel about the house? It would be wonderful to have that kind of creative gift."

Susan's voice trailed away, trying to imagine the special light that must flood the mind of someone with a poem or a novel coming to life inside them. Different from having a baby, which anyone could do. An artistic vision would sustain you in hard times, the way Abigail Grellier's vision had sustained her. Susan would have to share some of those old diaries with Gina.

"She talked in such a funny way," Lara said. "I don't think she's serious about writing a novel—she just likes to say things. Why would she do that, say things like 'living in a palace,' when you know she was probably thinking it was the worst dump she ever saw."

"Artistic irony," Susan murmured, bathing Gina's rudeness in an inspirational glow. "If she really has a vision, she may not realize how she sounds to other people."

"And the woman from Between Two Worlds," Lara went on. "Did you see that bumper sticker? 'Witches Heal.' Is she a witch? Do you think Gina might be one, too? She said she went into the shop for 'supplies.' I should have gone into some of the other rooms to see if she has a witch's altar set up. Maybe she can conjure the spirits of the dead—she could set up a séance for you with Great-Great-Grandmother Abigail!"

"Lara, no. I've seen Autumn Minsky at the farmers' market in town. I'm sure she doesn't believe in anything so superstitious."

"But, Mom, Ms. Haring said she'd gone into the store for 'supplies.' What could that mean, unless it was for some kind of witch ceremony?"

Susan cast around in her mind. "Incense," she decided. "To cover up the smell of cat."

"Even though we didn't smell any when we walked in? That was lame, Mom!"

"No one burns incense in the morning," Susan said firmly. "Not even confirmed witches."

They had pulled up in front of the high school. Lara grinned and said, "Good try. Me and Kimberly will be at the library at one, okay?"

"Kimberly and *I*," Susan corrected, but Lara was already halfway up the walk.

When Susan and Lara reported on the visit to Jim that night at supper, he looked narrowly at his daughter. "Your mother is wound up about the mold and the Fremantle house, but it's hard to believe you are, Lulu. I'd like to know what's in that bedroom you care about so much."

"Nothing, Dad," Lara said earnestly. "Mom was telling Gina all the stuff I've heard a million times, about the fire extinguishers and the marble in the fireplace and everything. I just wanted to—"

Her voice trailed off. She couldn't think of any reason that made sense for why she had gone up to the main bedroom. No matter what she said, it was snooping, exactly as Autumn Minsky from Between Two Worlds had said. Lara was as bad as Eddie Burton, or almost. The thought made her squirm, but also suggested a diversion.

"Dad, those women, they said Eddie Burton had climbed that old evergreen on the south side of the house and was peeping in at the bathroom window."

"Lara!" Susan exclaimed. "We don't know it was Eddie."

"But, Mom, who else could it have been?" Lara was aggrieved.

"Maybe Myra Schapen," Chip suggested. "Getting ready to add a little paragraph to 'News and Notes.'"

It was the first night Chip had joined them for supper since his blowup with Jim over the marijuana at Fremantles'. The rest of the family was so relieved to see him that they laughed loudly, especially Lara, who was happy to have the spotlight turn away from her.

"Yes, Myra has a periscope into every house around here; it's the only way I can figure how she knows everybody's private lives." Jim said. "She and Gram had some real fights about it when your uncle Doug and I were boys."

"Maybe Arnie was her spy when you were boys together," Lara said, "and now she has Junior and Robbie doing it for her. It could have been Junior up that tree, because the lady from the witch store, she said whoever it was grinned like he was the cleverest guy on the planet, and whenever Junior gets away with something slimy he does grin like that."

"Junior would break the tree," Chip objected. "Maybe it was Robbie."

"Oh, yeah, like Robbie would do *anything* for Junior. You know Junior bullied Robbie even more'n me when we were at Kaw Valley."

"So he bullied Robbie into spying for him," Chip said.

"You see," Susan exclaimed, "you two just started a new rumor. Two new ones. In five minutes, you've gone from claiming it was Eddie Burton up the tree to saying maybe it was Junior Schapen, or even his brother. Do you understand now how wrong it is to put out your opinion and claim it was fact?"

"And please remember that you two aren't to call Arnie and his mother by their first names. They don't like it, and we don't need to go out of our way to stir them up," Jim added.

"I bet Lulu's right, though," Chip said, "that it was Eddie Burton peeping in through the bathroom window."

"But why?" Susan demanded.

"Because he's a creep," Chip said. "Also, because he's been Junior's gofer since we were eight. People have been wild to know what Autumn Minsky is doing with Gina Haring ever since her car first showed up last week, so it figures that Myra—Nanny Schapen—would want to be the first to know. Curly will find out all about it and tell me."

"Chip, don't. I don't like the way Curly spreads news all over the place—he's like a wind blowing stalk rot to every farm in the valley. Don't encourage him to blow up Ms. Haring's troubles bigger than they already are. Leave Ms. Haring alone."

"Oh, Dad! Anyway, we don't need Curly to tell us what Autumn Minsky is doing out at Fremantles'—everyone knows."

"They do?" Susan said sweetly. "And exactly what is that, Etienne? And exactly how do they know it?"

Chip reddened and didn't answer, but Lara said, "You mean, because she was in Ms. Haring's bed, Chip? But I thought you said women can't be sodo—"

"Lara, you're displaying your ignorance, not how cool you are, so put a lid on it."

Lara subsided into a glower. She found relief in kicking Chip under the table for raising the subject to begin with. Chip kicked back and hit her chair leg.

"I'm worried about the Burtons, anyway," Susan said to change the subject. "Ardis is coming into the food pantry once a month now, they told me at the church board meeting. That fine Clem got for going over to Arnie's with his shotgun is really taking a toll on them."

"Mom," Chip chided mockingly, "that's gossip, you know."

Susan bit her lip. "You're right. It's just—I feel for Ardis, with five children all living at home, plus Clem's great hulking father, who has to have his diapers changed every few hours. How are they ever going to pay off that fine on what she makes clerking at By-Smart?"

"They could if Clem would get off his butt and work his land, or even find a job himself," Jim said shortly.

Lara stopped foot fighting her brother to say, "The lady from Between Two Worlds said someone from the sheriff's office came around checking on her car, you know, that red hybrid. Maybe that was Mr. Schapen."

Jim made a face. "I guess I could give Hank Drysdale a call, just ask him if he sent someone out there. I don't want Gina Haring being bothered, not when she's taken that house off our shoulders. Which reminds me, Lulu, whatever you were doing there this morning, don't. Even if you left your own stash of dope in the master-bedroom fireplace."

"Dad! That's unfair. I told you last week I don't do drugs, and I'm not a liar."

"I don't like to think of you spying on the neighbors. Whatever you were doing in Gina Haring's room, I don't want you snooping around like Myra Schapen. You've got enough going on in your own life not to add the neighbors' activities to your list."

"I wasn't snooping, Dad, at least not like that. Besides, it's so unfair to compare me to Myra Schapen. I don't go around threatening people with hellfire and damnation, or put stories about them on the Web!" Lara's eyes were swimming with hurt tears.

"But, sugar, gossiping is as bad as putting it on the Web," Jim said.

"I know you don't like gossip, Dad, but the Schapens are such jerks, and Eddie Burton *is* creepy. If I can't talk about them, it will all fester inside me."

"And give you a terrible complex?" he suggested. "And a farmer's daughter can't afford a fancy psychiatrist to sort out her problems so it's my duty to let you gossip so you don't build up weird complexes?"

Lara laughed reluctantly, unwilling to give up completely on her grievance. "Something like that, Dad. Of course, maybe Mom and I will make the X-Farm into such a huge success that we can all afford therapy."

He pulled her over and ruffled her hair. "I'm spending my share on a fancy trip. When you and your mom are organic-sunflower millionaires, talking to your shrinks about how hard it is to have all that money, I'm going to be hanging out in Argentina all winter with the bobolinks."

FROM ABIGAIL COMFORT GRELLIER'S JOURNAL

July 23, 1855

The sum of money my dear mother gave to me on our parting is fast depleted by the exorbitant price the Missouri ruffians charge for the basic needs of living. With a sack of wheat $6, we make a baking of bread do for a week. I must store it in my tin trunk to keep the greedy mice from it! We have apples a plenty, for there were trees on the land that M. Grellier staked out, and they are a great gift and mercy to us.

I used some of my precious hoard to buy a cow, and "Mrs. Blossom," as I christened her, has some days been my dearest friend, for M. Grellier is very busy in the town with the militia that will try to protect us from the ruffians. She stands near me while I tend my vegetable garden, dug for me with great kindness by Mr. Schapen, who has a team of oxen. One acre of this prairie sod is now under cultivation! And my radishes, peas, and corn are all rising well.

Nine

THE MILKMAN

"Yeah, Soapweed, it all sucks."

Robbie Schapen leaned his head against the Guernsey-Jersey's flank. The urge to curl up around her warm body and go back to sleep was so strong that he sat upright again. She hated—all the cows hated—automated milking. No matter how careful you were, the rubber tubes and vacuum pump moved milk through them too fast for comfort. If he fell asleep, she'd bellow in agony when her udders were stripped. That would be cruel to her, and would also bring his dad—or, worse yet, his grandmother—to see what new blunder he'd made.

He scooted over to Scurf-pea and attached the teat cups, moved on to Bittersweet, Daphne, and then Connie. Five cows on a side—his side—move them out, bring in the next five. A race of sorts that he won about once every three months.

Junior could outmilk both Arnie and Dale, but that was because he didn't worry about hurting the cows. The ones he milked always had the highest rate of mastitis on the farm, so Robbie thought it was fucking unfair—*Sorry, Jesus, but it really is*—for Dad to hold Junior up to him as an example. A cow with mastitis has to be on antibiotics, and you can't use her milk—you take it from her, but you have to throw it out until she's well again. So the faster Junior milked, the more money they lost. But try telling Dad that.

Today, fortunately, Dale Bracken was on the other side of the drainage pit. He was a tired, quiet man who worked for Arnie, coming out to help with the early milking and doing odd jobs, like spraying the lagoon, which collected wastewater runoff from the grazing pastures and milking shed.

Robbie turned on the pump, watched the milk flow through the Lucite tubes, checked the udders, turned off the switch, and removed the hoses. "Okay, girls, out you go." He slapped Cornflower's flank. She was the lead cow in this lot, and once she moved out the other four would follow. As soon as Soapweed, last in this group, was in motion, Robbie trotted back to the yard and brought in his next five.

Naming the cows was his job. It was actually a punishment, something his grandmother thought up because he'd broken his leg, or maybe because he'd been crying when the broker showed up to buy the cows after his mother disappeared. Robbie couldn't remember very clearly: he'd only been nine at the time.

First, Nanny had told him Mom was dead. But Junior, who was eleven back then, said, "She's not dead. She ran off with some guy she met at the bank." So then Nanny said Mom was a harlot who couldn't take family responsibilities, and that was the main story she repeated so often it was like a routine part of daily conversation: "Hello, Nanny, how are you?" "Your mother was a harlot."

She usually repeated it when Robbie did something to annoy her. With his olive skin and skinny frame, Robbie looked like his mother. Blond, broad Junior, he was a true Schapen. Nanny was also very fond of saying that.

Robbie didn't remember his mother clearly. After she left, Dad, or maybe Nanny, had thrown out all her pictures. Robbie rescued three from the garbage when his grandmother was in the field and Junior and Dad were in the barn. He kept them taped under one of his bureau drawers where Nanny wouldn't find them. She was always snooping through his things, looking for clues about whether he was queer, because Robbie liked to play the guitar and hated sports.

Junior was a defensive end. He was hoping for a football scholarship from Tonganoxie Bible College for next year, which meant he couldn't flunk any more of his courses this year. He was flunking biology this fall, but the college didn't care about that, because in Lawrence you had to study evolution to pass biology and Junior told the people at Tonganoxie he'd been flunked because he was the only student to take a stand against forcing students to disregard the sacred Word of God. Really, Junior had failed because he never did any work for the class. He hardly did any work for any classes, but most teachers passed him because he was on the football team. Only Mr. Biesterman, the biology teacher, and Ms. Carmody, in English, refused to give a free ride to the football players.

Of course if Tonganoxie found out what Junior and Eddie Burton had been up to, good-bye college, good-bye football. Robbie sometimes thought about telling, especially when Nanny was raving about Junior like he was one of the elect sitting at God's right hand. The fact that he didn't wasn't out of loyalty—he and Junior had always sacrificed each other on the altar of Nanny's anger—or even that he was afraid of Junior. He was a little afraid of him, of course, his brother being so big and so prone to use his fists. You'd be an idiot not to be somewhat afraid of him. But Robbie's reasons for not telling were more complicated than just fear of Junior. For one thing, he only suspected, he didn't know for sure. More than that, Robbie was afraid if he put his suspicions into words he'd make them real.

Robbie used to have to go to all Junior's games, but last year he started playing guitar for the Salvation Through the Blood of Jesus Full Bible Church's youth programs. The teen group met on Thursday nights, when a lot of Junior's games were scheduled.

Nanny snarled about his lack of family commitment, but Robbie took her hands and said in a wistful voice, "Nanny, I have to put my commitment to Jesus first, because didn't He tell us that 'he who loveth father and mother more than me is not worthy of me'?"

Nanny had scowled at him and snapped something about Satan and Scripture, but Robbie only smiled a kind, patient smile, one that he had practiced in front of the mirror for a long time: you cannot be punished if you are soulful and solemn. "Pastor Nabo says our metal band is an important Christian service, because we get kids to come to Jesus through music."

Nanny thought music was a waste of time. If she'd been the last person on the tractor, you could count on the radio being tuned to Rush

Limbaugh and William Bennett. If Robbie was the last one using it, he left it tuned at top volume to a heavy-metal station. The sound always jolted Nanny when she turned on the engine—a small pleasure, the price of which was a lecture on Mick Jagger and the dangers of hell waiting for people who jumped and danced on stage and were sodomites when they left it. No matter what Pastor Nabo said, Nanny wouldn't believe that rock or metal weren't the devil's playthings.

Nanny essentially worshipped Junior's football playing. Come to think of it, she was an idolater, with a golden football instead of a golden calf on her altar. She still talked about Dad's stats from when he'd been in high school thirty years ago, and for the last four years all she'd talked about had been Junior's, how he'd made more tackles than Dad in a game against Shawnee Mission or fewer in the homecoming game against Wyandotte. Robbie tried to imagine what she would do if he said, "Nanny, you and Dad have turned Junior and his football team into a statue of Baal."

"I'm not brave enough for that, Jesus," he whispered against the cow's side. Anyway, maybe Jesus didn't want him thinking up ways to torment Myra. "Why should I do your work for you," Robbie said out loud. "She'll die one of these days, and you can torment her yourself."

Dale, working across the pit from him, looked over. "You say something, Robbie?"

Robbie blushed, hoping the machines were too loud for Dale to have made out his words. "Just practicing my lyrics."

And then he did start practicing the new song he'd written last night for him and Chris Greynard to sing at youth group next week:

Who moves the mountain?
King Jesus!
Who moves our hearts?
King Jesus!
Hearts and mountains
Big and small,
They're nothing to the King,
He can move them all!

In His Spirit
We can move them, too
Hearts, minds, mountains,
We move them all
With the power of your love
Your precious, precious love,
King Jesus!

He started to sing more loudly, then remembered where he was: in the milking shed. Not that the cows, or even Dale, would tell on him, but Nanny sometimes came out unexpectedly in the middle of milking to inspect him.

She never worked with the cows, not because she was eighty-seven and couldn't handle the workload, but because the herd had been her daughter-in-law's idea. The Schapens used to raise cows back in the early 1900s. They even had their own dairy, Open Prairie, back then, but during the Dust Bowl Robbie's great-grandfather had to butcher or sell the herd—they couldn't cultivate their own grazing land during that long drought, and they couldn't afford to buy fodder for the herd.

Nanny blamed the Grelliers. Back in the Depression, they raised beef cattle, which they grazed on their acres down by the Wakarusa River. Nanny thought the Grelliers should have sacrificed half their herd and shared their grazing land and fodder with Arnie's grandfather. Just imagine if the Grelliers had suggested the same thing to them! Nanny thought Susan was a Communist who was bound for hell just for running that co-op market. If she'd said kill half your cows for us, Nanny probably would have burned down the Grellier house.

According to Junior, his and Robbie's mom thought she could start Open Prairie up again when the organic craze first got going twenty years ago. She'd bought a mixed herd of Guernseys, Jerseys, and Brown Swiss, starting with fifteen cows. She looked after them herself, before and after her day job at the bank. On her own, while Dad and Nanny scoffed, Mom had dug and lined the lagoon. And she had gone around the county to all the independent grocers, finding buyers for her milk.

His mother's job at the bank in Lawrence had been essential for the family to make ends meet. Like most small-farm families, someone had to work outside the farm if they were going to keep the land—that's why Dad had become a sheriff's deputy after Mom left. When she started the herd, though, she had had high hopes for her cows. She'd thought they might let her quit the bank job and stay home with Robbie instead of leaving him in Nanny's care.

When he was little, Robbie loved going out in the early morning with his mother to do the milking or make rounds with her to the local grocery stores. He could hardly believe it now, leaning against Gilly's side, trying to keep his eyes open. He'd stayed up too late last night, working on the new song, which he had to do almost silently so as not to bring his father or grandmother in on him. He and Junior took turns doing the early shift with Dale. He didn't know what would happen when Junior left next fall— Robbie would probably have to get up every morning to do the milking.

Mom and Robbie had named the cows. That was their secret together, Robbie's and hers, because Dad and Nanny thought naming cows was a sissy thing. He hadn't been supposed to let Dad know the cows all had names, although now that he was older he realized it wasn't that big a secret: Mom used to write the names on the backs of their ear tags. Each tag showed the breed, the date of birth, the registration number, and, on the back, the name she and Robbie had given it. They tried always to give new calves names that started with the same letter as the mother.

It was how he learned his alphabet, Mom squatting to look at him, her face smiling. "Okay, Robbie, Sunflower starts with S. Now we need another S-word for her baby daughter."

"Superman," he shrieked, jumping up and down.

"It's an S-word, all right, but is it a good name for a girl?"

And then he thought of Sugarplum, because it had been near Christmas, and she'd read him about visions of sugarplums, not that he knew what a sugarplum was.

Nanny had this bitchy attitude toward the cows because when Mom took off Dad planned to sell the herd. He'd turned against the cows, probably because Mom loved them, and he caused mastitis in a lot of the herd by his rough handling of the milking machine—information Robbie got from outsiders, at 4-H or the farmers' market.

"You're the one who made us keep those cows, Robbie," he could hear his grandmother saying. "You're the one who can name them."

It didn't make sense, but there never had been anyone Robbie could discuss it with to try to make sense of it. Nanny made it sound dire, as if naming the cows was like mucking out the milking shed, so that the pleasure he'd had with his mother in thinking up names had disappeared.

He reckoned in six years he had named over a hundred cows. He was running out of ideas and was starting to reuse names from cows who had died, starting to hate the whole routine. Only the unspoken knowledge that his grandmother would feel triumphant if he stopped naming the animals kept him going to lists of wildflowers and colors, even turning to foreign languages, to come up with new ideas.

He slapped the last of his cows on the side and urged her out the shed door. Dale had finished already and was bringing in the water hoses to swab out the pit below the milking stands. Robbie disconnected his milk lines and took them out to the washroom with his milking jars and teat cups.

It was still dark, but it was almost always dark for the morning milking. They started at five, finished around six-thirty, and this time of year the eastern sky was barely turning gray even when they finished.

He hurried to the washroom and dumped the equipment into the sink at the corner. Dale would disinfect it and set it out ready for the evening milking.

The light was on in the kitchen. Nanny would have breakfast ready. He mustn't dawdle, but he still took a chance and ran over to the new enclosure, where Soapweed's new calf stood in a lonely state. She was bawling, longing for company, for her mother, for food. She was only four weeks old.

Robbie hated that part of dairy farming. It was cruel to take babies from their mothers. The other calves didn't fare much better than Soapweed's calf, being pinned next to little sheds outside the main barn. Working cows couldn't be sharing their milk with their own offspring. It all had to go to the farm. At least the other new calves were outdoors. They all could see the sun and each other.

Soapweed had cried for forty-eight hours straight when Serise was taken from her. And poor Serise, she was in this god-awful—*sorry, Jesus, but it is*—pen, no sunlight for her, no friends. Robbie undid the lock and went in to pet her.

"King Jesus, He moves the mountains," he crooned, rubbing her nubby red head.

The cow nuzzled him and tried to suck his fingers. He smelled of milk. He had it on his clothes. She wanted to nurse so badly it hurt him.

"Your bucket of ultrapure is coming soon, girl, don't you worry. And when you're rich and famous, don't forget who looked after you, either, you hear?"

"Hey, Robbie!"

Robbie jumped, but it was just Dale, who added, "You know Arnie don't like you in here. And I seed your Nanny looking out the kitchen window for you. Maybe you'd better go on inside."

Ten

THE RED HEIFER

"WHAT TOOK YOU SO LONG?" Myra asked. "I saw Dale cleaning out the jars before you showed your head."

"Yes, Nanny," Robbie said. It was easier to agree with her than to offer excuses.

"Those Jews are coming from Kansas City this afternoon to look at the calf," Arnie announced. "Make sure you're not playing that music of yours while they're here. We need them to give us a favorable answer, and that guitar churning up the air isn't going to put them in a good frame of mind any more than it does me. And don't wipe your mouth on the back of your hand. What do you think that piece of paper is next to you? A copy of the Ten Commandments?"

Junior snickered. Robbie gulped down his eggs and raced upstairs to shower. He couldn't stand to go to school with milk on him. It had happened earlier this year, when he started in ninth grade, in town, and the memory of the girls mooing in the hall as he passed still made his ears burn. Lara Grellier had been in the group. He suspected it was she who told the others. They were city girls, who wouldn't know how fresh milk smelled, just that Robbie smelled funny.

He stood under the shower until the hot water ran out, then rubbed a clear space on the mirror to inspect his upper lip. Junior had only started shaving last year, when he turned seventeen, but Robbie was hoping that dark-haired musicians grew mustaches faster than blond football players.

"I won't wait all day for you, Romeo!" Junior bellowed, rattling the bathroom doorknob.

Robbie sprayed himself with the bottle of aftershave he'd started keeping in his backpack after Junior filled a previous one with ammonia. He pulled on his black BECOMING THE ARCHETYPE T-shirt. They were his favorite Christian metal group, the one he modeled his own sound on. He'd stenciled JESUS ROCKS on the back. Nanny hated the message, hated the shirt, and she'd ruined his first one in the laundry by deliberately pouring bleach on it. It was another thing he kept in his school backpack, folded flat inside his social studies notebook.

Robbie ran back down the stairs, his backpack draped over his shoulder. More than once, Junior had gone to school without him and he'd had to hitch a ride. Robbie had been lucky one time back in September, getting to the crossroads just as Chip and Lara Grellier were pulling out of their yard. Chip was going to drive on around him, but Robbie jumped in front of the car, waving his arms frantically, and explained that Junior had left him behind.

He'd scrunched into the back of Chip's Nissan, his knees around his ears, his nose almost resting in Lara Grellier's soft brown curls. Her hair smelled like fresh grass, and he could see the line where her tan ended beneath her tank top. He felt himself contract with longing. Was this love? And could he be in love with Lara Grellier, who had broken his front tooth in a fight when they were in sixth grade, whose family always went out of their way to hurt the Schapens? Besides which, she went to a church where they believed in evolution instead of the Bible, so according to Myra, Arnie, and Pastor Nabo she was bound for hell. Maybe it was his—Robbie's—job to save her.

When they got to school and she jumped out, he'd been imagining her breasts under his hands as his passion guided her to Jesus. Her mocking "End of the trail, milkboy" made him blush, as if she had seen his thoughts.

The next several times that Junior left without him, Robbie had sprinted to the crossroads, hoping to get there ahead of the Grelliers, but each time they had already left for town and he'd been forced to walk the long mile to the main road before getting a lift.

After that he'd tried harder to be ready ahead of Junior, since Myra thought it was good discipline for Robbie when Junior left without him. "This is what it will feel like when Jesus comes again in glory, to be left behind with the sinners. So you learn to be ready, ready for school, ready for the Lord."

When it was his turn for early-morning milking, he imagined his workload next fall if Junior went on to college. The one good thing was, he'd get to take the pickup to school himself, no more of this hassling by Nanny and his brother. Chip would be gone, too, probably, taking his little sports car off to college, so maybe Lara would ride with him, Robbie Schapen.

"Lulu" was what her family always called her. Back when they were in grade school at Kaw Valley Eagle, he used to tease her: Lulu makes doo-doo, Lulu the boo-boo. Now he blushed with shame. No wonder she called him milkboy.

"Lulu," he murmured into the foggy mirror.

Junior rattled the knob again. "Last call."

Today, as he bolted out the door, Nanny shouted, "You change that shirt when you get home from school, young man. I want those Jews to see you looking like a Christian, in a real shirt. You hear me?"

"But this is a Christian band, Nanny," Robbie called, jumping into the truck, which Junior was starting to put in gear.

"Says you."

Junior sprayed gravel as he spun out of the yard.

"Says me, says Pastor Nabo, and says anyone who isn't too ignorant to listen to music."

"Yeah, when the roll is called up yonder Nanny will be miles ahead of *Becoming the Anti-Christ* in the line. So listen to her, knucklehead."

"*Archetype,* not anti-Christ, you ignorant ape. Anyway, why is Nanny so bent out of shape about some Jews coming to the farm?" Robbie complained. "Lawrence is full of Jews. We know lots of them from school and the market. Why do we have to put on good clothes and let a bunch of strange men fool around with Soapweed's calf?"

"If you'd get your head out of your ass and listen to something besides your own useless guitar, you'd know that this could be the end of the world starting right here on our farm. We could be so rich we'd never have to milk another cow again."

"If the world comes to an end, we won't have to, anyway, we won't need money. Besides, we're not supposed to lay up treasure on earth."

"I'd love to have me a little car like Frenchie Grellier drives," Junior grumbled. "It'd be great to rub those golden Grellier noses in our shit for a change."

The remark reminded Robbie again of sitting squashed behind Lara, the smell of her hair, the softness of her skin at the nape of her neck. If Junior had a little sports car, he and Eddie Burton would ride around in it, terrorizing the county. Not that they didn't already, on Junior's bike.

"Chip bought the car with the money he made working last year's harvest. Do you know that Mr. Grellier *pays* him for his time in the field at harvest? Can you imagine Dad paying us to do the milking?"

"If Soapweed's calf is this special heifer the Jews need, we'll be able to hire two men to do the milking for us," Junior gloated.

All that day at school, Robbie thought of Soapweed's calf, alone in her special pen behind the barns, crying for company. Then he thought of buying his own sports car, of Lara Grellier sitting next to him. They'd be parked out back of Clinton Lake, with the top down. He'd be playing a song to her, a love song. Her lips parted, eyes glowing at him, her blouse unbuttoned so he could see her breasts. He drew a picture of them in his Spanish notebook, small, firm, the nipples little raspberries.

When the bell rang, he saw her in the hall, laughing with Melanie Derwint and Kimberly Ropes. The trio passed him as if he weren't there, so they didn't notice the blush that turned his dark skin to mahogany.

When he and Junior got home a little after three, Pastor Nabo was already there, pacing restlessly around the front room, the room they opened up only when company came. Myra had lit the oil heater, so that the room was warm but smelled greasy.

Robbie went upstairs to change into the blue-striped shirt Nanny had ironed. The sleeves were already too short, but she wouldn't buy him another shirt until next year. Arnie would never pay him for his work on the farm; he and Myra thought the Fifth Commandment was the cornerstone of Christian faith. More than not committing adultery or murder, you must honor your father and grandmother.

Robbie studied his reflection in the bathroom mirror. If he rolled up his sleeves, the shirt wouldn't make him look so much like a chimp, his too-long arms swinging at his sides.

He went to the landing and peered over the banister. Junior was sucking up to Pastor Nabo, calling him sir and laughing heartily at something the pastor had said. "Yes, sir, Pastor, I suck dick," Robbie muttered. He pulled a grimy notepad from his back pocket and sat on the top step.

> *Love your neighbor*
> *As you love yourself.*
> *Jesus taught us this.*
> *Jesus taught us this.*

> *I love my neighbor.*
> *Her hair is like bronze,*
> *Soft bronze,*
> *Living bronze,*
> *It moves in the breeze,*
> *Shines in the sun.*

> *I love my neighbor.*
> *Her breasts are like—*

Like what? Like little ice-cream sundaes with cherries on top? He'd never seen any girl's breasts, just snuck looks in a magazine when he was out on his own in a place where no one could possibly tell on him. Lara's breasts weren't like that, not those huge, gross mounds of flesh in the photographs. Hers were small and white. When she wore a tank top to school, he could see the soft shape through the fabric, so small his hand would completely cover them.

I love my neighbor, but she doesn't know I exist, and if she does think about me she imagines I'm the same kind of jerk as my brother. He put the notepad back into his pocket and went downstairs before his grand-mother sent Junior up to find him.

"Ah, Robbie," Pastor Nabo said when he came into the front room. "I understand the mother has been your special charge."

"Yes, sir," Robbie said, pulling his mind away from Lara to Soapweed and her calf. "She's a Guernsey-Jersey mix, and we bred her with a bull we've used before, a Jersey-Canadienne up in Wisconsin."

"And this is the first time you've had a solid red calf?"

"Yes, sir," Robbie said. "Sometimes they'll be born all one color and the markings will come in later, though. And Serise, well, this calf, she's only four weeks old, so it may be too early to tell if she'll stay solid."

"Yes, yes." Pastor Nabo rubbed his hands together in the oily room. "I think we all understand it's too early to be certain that the Lord is send-ing His messenger to us here in the valley of the humble Wakarusa and Kaw rivers, but we can pray, we can pray for spiritual guidance, for the strength to be worthy of His grace if He is showering it on us."

"Roll down your shirtsleeves, Robbie," Myra snapped, before bowing her head along with Arnie, Junior, and the pastor.

Pastor Nabo was only a minute or two into his exhortation when they heard the Jews' van pull up in the yard. He gave a hurried amen, and rushed out with Arnie and Junior to greet them, Nanny stumping along in her black Hush Puppies.

Robbie hung back, unexpectedly nervous. When the party returned to the parlor, Robbie bit back an exclamation. The three men were noth-ing like Mr. Lewin, who taught chemistry at the high school, or Julie Sugarman's dad, who owned one of the shoe stores on Massachusetts Street. They looked like a picture out of his history book, with their long, dusty coats, their beards, and the corkscrew curls that stuck raffishly out underneath their black hats. They were dressed identically, which made it hard to tell them apart. Two were heavy, with round cheeks puffing out from their graying beards. The third was short and slender, with a square jaw that made him look like Abraham Lincoln.

"So let's go look at this miracle heifer," the short man said. "You mustn't get your hopes up, you know. If she's only four weeks old, well, a lot can happen in the next thirty-five months."

"We know that," Pastor Nabo assured him. "And we aren't calling her a miracle. But it did seem like, well, something special, that she just *happened*. I've read about these efforts to breed a perfect heifer, and I've always thought God would provide one when the time was right, that it was *sinful*, almost, to try to breed against His will, if you follow me."

"Sinful?" the tallest of the trio said. "I wouldn't say sinful. If we are to rebuild the Holy Temple, we have to prove we are willing to labor for it. The work is large and the day is short. We must do as much as we can."

"Nonetheless, if we're to believe the Seventy Weeks prophesied in the Book of Daniel, the end of days is near," Pastor Nabo said, "and the Lord will show us by giving us a sign that He is ready for the final battle between Chri—between the forces of Light and the forces of Dark."

The tallest man said something in a foreign language. Was it Hebrew? Robbie wondered. Was this how Jesus had talked, in that funny language they'd used in the movie about His Passion?

Arnie, with Junior and the pastor in tow, led the trio to the special enclosure they'd built for Soapweed's calf. Robbie followed. When Myra tried to come along, too, the Jews said sternly that no women must come near the calf.

"Has she been handling the animal?" the short man asked.

"Nanny doesn't have anything to do with the dairy farm," Junior said. "But what difference does it make?"

"What difference, young man? Because a woman in the enclosure could pollute the heifer even before she's reached maturity." It was one of the two heavy men who spoke. "I hope we haven't wasted our time in coming here."

"No, no," Arnie said. "No women have been near the calf. My mother is the only woman on the place, and she never works with the cows."

The party moved on to the enclosure where Soapweed's calf stood in lonely splendor. Arnie had set up an array of work lights so that the Jews could inspect the heifer. The three men stopped inside the enclosure; the tallest gasped in amazement. The calf was a dark orangey red, from the bridge of her nose to the end of her scrawny tail, a red heifer without discernible flaw.

The perfect heifer was bawling; she was hungry and lonely. Robbie wanted to put his arms around her and let her suck on his fingers, but now he felt nervous about what you could and couldn't do around the calf.

The three men had brought rubber mats with them, which they knelt on to inspect the calf. They looked at her hooves, lifted her tail, studied her belly. They dipped rags in some kind of glycerin mix and scrubbed her sides to see if the Schapens had dyed her.

"Right now, she looks as though she has potential," the short man finally said. "We'll come back once a month to check on her. In the meantime, no women in the enclosure, no leaning on the animal or any other act that makes her work."

"Leaning on her makes her work?" Robbie asked, wondering if he should confess that he sometimes hugged her—well, every day, really—because she was so lonely.

"She has to exert force to prop you up. That is work," the short man said as if it were elementary physics and Robbie was too stupid to follow.

"Keep her clean, as you are doing. Make sure no sharp objects are in the compound—a cut on her flesh would be disastrous. And don't let her become a spectacle for sightseers," the tallest man added. "I know the temptation is great with an animal that potentially may be this special, but that is work for the animal, having to put up with the eyes of strangers. And a crowd is hard to control; someone might start touching her—a woman in her impure time might touch her."

Her impure time—when she had her period—everyone knew that. Robbie was so tired of these men and the way they were bossing him and his dad and even Nanny around, he almost blurted it out. Arnie was beaming with pride, and nodding as solemnly as if God Himself were talking to him. *Sorry, Jesus,* Robbie whispered to himself, *but you know what I mean.* It embarrassed him to see Arnie, the toughest man in the county, kowtow to these creepy-looking men in their round hats and long coats.

Arnie and Pastor Nabo walked with the Jews back to their van. They conferred again in their guttural, secret language, then told Arnie he needed to build the calf's pen above a rock base, preferably obsidian, since that was the rock where the Holy Temple had been built. If she came in contact with the earth, she would be in contact with death. And Arnie nodded and agreed, although even Nanny muttered about the cost and where would they find obsidian around here?

The three men lived in Kansas City, with a group of Jews who all wanted to rebuild the Temple in Jerusalem. Pastor Nabo had heard about them from another Salvation Bible Church, in Kansas City. Before they left, they assured Arnie they'd be back about the same time next month.

Pastor Nabo beamed and rubbed his hands. "I think we can tell the elders, Brother Schapen. Of course, it wouldn't do for television cameras to show up. They'd startle our heifer, maybe make her injure herself. But it wouldn't hurt for the church elders to know what may be in the wind."

Arnie nodded slowly, thinking it over. "As long as they operate in complete secrecy."

He turned to Robbie. "Well, well, who would have thought it'd be you who'd bring us fame and glory. Don't you go calling that calf one of your flower names. She's a holy animal; she's destined for glory. If we keep her free of any impurities, they'll use her in their Temple sacrifices and that will pave the way for Jesus to come again in glory."

He stopped smiling and looked stern. "You boys have to promise me you are not going to talk about this outside the family. If people like Jim Grellier or his crackpot wife get hold of this information, no telling what they'll do to try to make us look bad. You hear me?"

Both his sons mumbled "Yessir." Junior added, "These Jews don't even have a Temple, right? And they want her when she's three? Don't tell me they're going to rebuild Solomon's Temple with all his cedars of Lebanon and cubits of this and that by the time this calf is three!"

"No, no," Pastor Nabo said. "But they have the instruments prepared for her ritual slaughter, and they only need her ashes—"

"Slaughter?" Robbie cried. "You mean they want to *kill* her?"

"Of course they want to kill her," Arnie snapped. "Did you think they wanted to breed her so they could pour her milk over the doors of the Temple? Haven't you read your Bible, Robert? Don't you know the Jews were always commanded to make burnt offerings, which is why the sacrifice of Jesus on the cross means Christians don't have to kill animals before they can worship God?"

"Yeah," Junior added. "The Jews are going to end up in hell unless they take Jesus into their hearts. That's why they wear those funny hats, to hide their horns—they've given themselves up to Satan. We're just using them to pave the way for the Rapture."

A confusing array of images swept through Robbie's head—Soapweed's calf laid on an altar and sacrificed, with the Jews and Arnie and Pastor Nabo dancing and bowing around her; himself taking the calf and hiding her, taking her to Lara Grellier: *You have to help me hide her. They want to give her to the Jews to sacrifice.* And Lara wouldn't laugh or call him names. She'd understand how important this was and help hide the calf on the Grellier land.

Pastor Nabo drew him aside and spoke to him quietly. "You love Jesus and want Him to come again to save the world, don't you, Robbie?"

"Yes, sir." Robbie's voice came out as a whisper.

"And you know it says in the Bible that Jesus cannot come again until the Temple is rebuilt in Jerusalem. And the Jews can't rebuild the Temple until they have a perfect red heifer. As it tells us in the Book of Numbers, they require a perfect red heifer for the high priest to become pure enough to enter the Temple."

"Yes. I know that, Pastor. I just thought, I sort of thought, my calf would be standing outside the walls. I didn't know they would kill her."

"They will do it very humanely, Robbie, and it will be for the glory of God. And you, the servant of this cow, the one who helped her through her delivery of this calf, you've been picked out by God for this very special deed. You will be known throughout the Christian world!" Pastor Nabo's voice thickened with emotion. Robbie thought the pastor was imagining himself, Werner Nabo, at the center of Christian glory and praise.

Eleven

CAPPUCCINO AND ITS MAKER

IT WASN'T until a few days after Christmas that Jim finally found time to drop in on Gina Haring. An ice storm had broken the roof of one of the greenhouses where Susan planted seedlings for the X-Farm. Between fixing that and all the preparations for Christmas—Susan's baking alone was a three-day enterprise, as she tried to re-create every dish the nineteenth-century Grelliers might have eaten—he didn't have time to think about his neighbor's problems.

Jim farmed a half section down by the Wakarusa; Blitz reported that the ice storm had also damaged his levee. When he finished repairing the greenhouse, Jim drove the two miles east, past Fremantles', down to the Wakarusa. The road was nothing more than a pitted gravel track that Fremantles, Schapens, and Grelliers had used since landing in the valley. As Jim bumped from rut to rut, he cursed Arnie and Myra for their stinginess. When old Mrs. Fremantle was alive, the three families pitched in to lay down new gravel every spring: the county didn't maintain private side roads like this. After her death, Arnie refused to help pay for upkeep. Since the Grellier farm was right on the north-south county road, this hurt Arnie more than it did Jim—except when he needed to go to the river.

On his way home, he pulled into the Fremantle yard. Contrary to the custom of the country, the kitchen door was locked. New York habits, or maybe fear after someone climbed a tree to peer into her bathroom. It wasn't until the third time he pounded on the door and helloed loudly that Gina finally came and undid the lock.

She looked surprised to see him, but not stiff or unpleasant, as Lara had described her. When he explained that his wife and daughter had reported on her Peeping Tom, she asked him in for coffee.

"It's my one domestic skill, making good coffee, so you have to let me show it off."

She offered him espresso or cappuccino. Jim normally drank black coffee, but Lara had described the fancy cappuccino machine and he was curious to see what it was like. Lawrence had at least twenty cappuccino bars, but people who had to count their dimes stayed away from three-dollar coffee.

Gina twirled the knobs and the machine made noises like the Kansas City Chief roaring past the house. In a few minutes, she handed him a mug filled with foam that looked like whipped cream. The coffee tasted rich, almost sweet, under its cap of foam. He drank coffee all day out of habit, not for taste, and he said the first thing that popped into his mind, that he'd better not get used to cappuccino because he couldn't afford such a rich drink.

"It's all a matter of what's important to you. I'd rather wear two sweaters and type with gloves on than pay the utility company to warm this big drafty house." She wasn't wearing gloves, but she did have on a big sweater, the kind that somehow made you aware of the body under-neath it. When she crossed her legs in her skintight blue jeans, he had a disturbing thought of how soft her skin would feel.

He said quickly, to push the thought from his head, "We wear two sweaters and type with our gloves on and we still drink boiled coffee. But maybe you're right. I have a thing for machinery, and I do spend money on good equipment. The big workhorses, the combines, the tractors, need to last thirty years, and they will, if you take good care of them. So I fill my shop with machines that let me repair my own equipment. But a lot of times, they're things I could get by without. I just got a new jig borer. Used, I mean—it's new for me."

Jim plowed earnestly through the description of the machine, describ-ing how Blitz—Blitz Fosse—who worked for him and was a wizard with machines, had retooled it. No man who cared that much about jig borers could possibly think about soft white thighs under skintight jeans, he seemed to be telling himself, especially not a man married to a woman as amazing as Susan.

"Good heavens," Gina said, "I couldn't possibly repair this machine here; I don't even know how it works. I just like the taste of the coffee it makes for me. Would you like another?"

"No, no. I only came by to see if you were okay, to make sure you hadn't had anyone else bothering you."

"I haven't seen anyone, if that's what you mean, but I started locking all the doors," Gina said. "I called Uncle John to tell him he needs better locks on the ground-floor windows. Right now, every time I hear a noise in the night I jump up and race around to look out the windows. I never realized how many boards went into a house or that each of them creaks separately sometime during the night! Autumn—do you know her? Autumn Minsky, from Between Two Worlds in Lawrence?—she won't even stay here after dark now."

He laughed with her, but uneasily, not wanting to imagine her and Autumn together in the night. "Can you describe the person you saw in the tree?"

"It was Autumn who actually saw him. She says he looked like everyone else out here, just another—" She bit off the words in consternation.

"Yokel?" Jim suggested. "Country bumpkin?"

She gave a wry grin. "Your daughter said it sounded like a youth who lives a couple of miles from here, who's mentally handicapped."

Jim said, "Lara is fourteen. A lot of times, she leaps before she looks. It could have been Eddie Burton, but there are a few other possibilities. Did you hear an engine—car, truck, motorcycle—after he ran off?"

"Why—oh, if he was on foot it narrows the range of suspects." After narrowing her eyes in thought, Gina reluctantly shook her head. "I can't remember, and if I push at it I'll just be creating a memory."

"Eddie's pretty harmless, but if you aren't used to him he might seem threatening." Jim got to his feet. "I'm going to have a word with his dad. And I'll let Peter Ropes—he lives in that house behind you—know to keep an eye out for anyone crossing his sorghum field toward you. I'll also mention it to the sheriff."

"No, don't do that," Gina said. "The sheriff was already here, and he made me feel really uncomfortable, as if I was at fault for living here or something. He checked on Autumn's car, and when he found out who she was he lectured her about her store: he said he was keeping an eye on it to make sure she wasn't holding satanic rituals there." Her eyes turned hot with anger.

Jim remembered Susan and Lara talking about Autumn's bumper sticker, something to do with witches. "If she's doing witchcraft or something in the store, he might—"

"*Wicca,*" Gina corrected him sharply. "And it's none of his business what we do. Damned narrow-minded busybody. I lived in New York my whole life and never had a cop visit me in my home to check on my religious beliefs—let alone the sheriff. I don't even know if New York *has* a sheriff."

"Hank Drysdale's a good guy; this must have been a deputy." Jim refused to say, "Arnie Schapen, busybody, poking his nose into everyone's business, with or without a badge," as his children would have done, because while it sounded like Arnie it might have been someone else. "If you want, I'll let Hank know what's been going on, your Peeping Tom and your narrow-minded busybody."

The anger in her eyes died down, and she gave a reluctant grin, showing the crooked teeth, which seemed as charming to Jim as they had to Lara. "When you parrot my words back to me, I'm the one who sounds petty."

"I didn't mean it that way," Jim said. "I'm sure I'm as narrow-minded as anyone out here when it comes to thinking about witchcraft—I've never come in contact with it, you see. We Grelliers, we're very dull, ordinary Protestants. Not even born-again."

"Your wife makes your family sound romantic and dramatic." Gina moved over to her machine and started twirling the knobs again.

Jim opened the back door. "Maybe they were a hundred fifty years ago. But nowadays, I promise you, we are very dull."

"I don't know about you, but Susan is not dull or ordinary." Gina handed him a second foam-filled mug.

"I can't take that," he said. "When will I get the cup back to you?"

"I'll collect it when I return your wife's pie pan. Thanks for stopping by. I feel better, knowing there's a friendly person close at hand." She smiled again.

He felt himself turning red, like a teenager being singled out by a cheerleader. The mug was too big for the pickup's cup holder, but he found an empty doughnut box behind the seat and rested the cup in that. Even so, a good deal of the foam slopped out as he bounced along the rutted track to the county road. He paused at the crossroads to finish it before it all spilled out.

He stopped at the Ropes place, since it was on the way to Burtons'. Peter Ropes had grown up with Jim's father and had been one of Jim's mentors after Grandpa died and Jim was struggling to run the farm on his own. Peter, who'd turned seventy last year, farmed only a section of his acres now, leasing the rest, some to Arnie, who grazed his herd there in the summer.

Jim found Peter in the barn, where he was replacing a blade on the disk head to his tractor. Jim helped him undo some frozen bolts, and explained what had happened over at Fremantles'.

"It sounds like Eddie Burton," he told Peter. "And I wondered if you'd seen him snooping at Fremantles' or anything."

"Eddie's always wandering around," Peter Ropes said. "He should be set to some kind of job. Plenty of people with his kind of problem can do a job of work, if it's simple enough and explained clear enough to them. But Ardis is overstretched as is, and I don't suppose Clem is up to working like that with the boy."

"Probably not," Jim agreed. "My son told me Eddie hangs out with Junior Schapen. Seems kind of funny, when you think how much Clem and Arnie go after each other."

Peter Ropes grunted, tightening the bolt on the new blade. "Yep, Junior does kind of go lockstep with Arnie on who he should feud with. I reckon he and Eddie have some kind of special relationship, the way boys do sometimes. I often see them riding past on that motorcycle of Junior's, neither of them wearing helmets of course. Want me to call you if I see either of them crossing over to Fremantles'?"

Jim made a face. "You know how I feel about that, Peter, the way we all look out the corner of our eyes to see what the neighbors are up to, but I suppose in this case—if it's Eddie, I don't think he ever hurt any-one, but if he got startled or excited—I don't know that Gina, the lady who's renting Fremantles', you know, knows the country. She's from New York, probably knows what to do if she's bothered by a big-city punk, but she might overreact to someone like Eddie."

Peter leaned against the tractor and turned the spanner around in his oil-covered hands. "Eddie's not just an overgrown boy, Jim. He's got a man's body and a man's urges, but he doesn't have the brains or moral sense to know when or what to do with them. The lady ought to get a dog, if she's set on staying out here."

Jim's face brightened. "Good idea. I'll stop on my way back and sug-gest it to her. I guess I'd better try to have a word with Clem, before I lose my nerve."

Twelve

NOT RICHARD BURTON

FARMERS AREN'T HOUSEKEEPERS. Most farms have rusted-out harrows and trucks, used tractors that never found their way to a scrap-metal broker, somewhere on the property, but they're usually not right in front of the house, where you trip on them coming and going. Clem's place looked like he'd sown bolts and axles in the night, and the yard had sprouted broken-down cars and equipment.

Five cars rested on cement blocks, all missing some piece of the body. The engines lay strewn in front of them, like entrails from a deer that had been savaged by dogs. Pride of place went to a 1961 Lincoln Continental convertible. If Clem ever did restore it, he could probably name his price and move out of debt. It needed a rear passenger door, a hood, wheels, and quite a bit of engine. Every now and then, you might see Clem or his uncle Turk working on it, but most of the time it lay under a swaddling of plastic, protecting what was left of the interior.

Jim parked his pickup on the edge of the road. He moved slowly, not wanting to deal with Clem or his uncle, hoping Eddie wouldn't be around. Why did they have that old wringer washer out here? Maybe Clem had finally let Ardis get an automatic machine. He sidestepped a rusted coulter but crunched down on the head of a doll and shattered it; the eyeballs rolled around, blinking at him.

Clem didn't answer his knock, so he let himself into the kitchen. Clem's father was sitting at a table, stirring his fingers through a bowl of cereal. A cat was trying to get its head in under the old man's fingers. The table was covered with newspapers, magazines, and plates of crusted food. The sink was stacked with pots and dishes, an elaborate tower that looked as though hours of labor went into keeping it from overbalancing. Maybe the first person to drop a plate had to wash everything underneath.

The house was even colder than the Fremantle place. Jim zipped up his parka and kept his gloves on.

Mr. Burton didn't notice Jim or respond to his feeble "Good morning." Beyond the kitchen, Jim heard voices. He followed the sound to a front room, where Clem's uncle Turk was watching television—a big set, maybe thirty-six inches, that dominated the shabby space. No lights were on, but the television was pulsing with color and noise, cars whipping around a track, NASCAR in the living room.

Turk was a big, shambling man, about fifteen years older than Jim. He'd come to live with Clem and Ardis sometime back, maybe eight or nine years ago. No one knew what he'd been doing before he arrived, and no one ever heard of him working. He tinkered around the cars with Clem, and drove over to the track at Woodlands to watch the greyhound races. When he won, which wasn't often, he was generous, splashing money around both his family and Lawrence's bars.

Although it wasn't noon yet, Jim saw Turk had finished most of a quart of Colt 45. Jim cleared his throat and called out.

"Who's that?" Turk squinted across the dark room in Jim's direction. "That you, Grellier? What you want?"

"I was looking for Clem."

"Clem? He's right here. Clem!" Turk shouted, and then shook his nephew, who was dozing on the floor at his feet. "Clem, Jim Grellier's here looking for you."

Clem sat up. Jim had been afraid he was drunk, passed out, but he was just dozing. He grinned foolishly, and said he'd had too late a night. "I'm too old to keep up with Turk."

Turk grinned, and swallowed the last of the malt liquor. "You're out of practice, Clem. It's been too long since I won anything. Picked up a bundle on the dogs yesterday. Clem and me went out to celebrate."

"That's nice," Jim said. "Clem, I just want a quick word. Can we step in the next room."

Clem followed him into what was once a dining room, guessing from the furniture beneath the jumble of rusted appliances and papers that covered most of the surfaces.

Jim couldn't figure out how to approach his subject, so he asked first about the Lincoln. "Making any progress on her?"

"Nah. Too hard to track down the parts. I had a lead on a cylinder block, but it turned out to be from a 'seventy-three, wouldn't fit in this engine head. You heard something?"

"Nope. Just admired the lines as I was walking up the drive," Jim lied. "Eddie helping you out?"

"Eddie?" Clem repeated as if he didn't know anyone by that name. "Oh, Eddie. He kind of wanders around, does his own thing. Can't drive, but he gets pretty far on his feet. Got a call from someone over by Stull last week. Boy is good with numbers, memorizes hundreds of phone numbers, can add a blue streak. He ain't as dumb as some folks think, just never could learn anything out of a book. But then, we Burtons aren't readers, anyway." Clem laughed heartily.

"You ever think about getting him some kind of training so he could work?"

"What are you, Grellier, the county social worker? Since when do you care so much about my boy?"

"Sorry, Clem. I was thinking out loud, thinking if Eddie had a job it would give him something to do with his time. Someone climbed up a tree and was looking into the bathroom at the old Fremantle house, spying on the lady who's living there. From the description, it sounds like Eddie."

Clem took a step toward Jim. "You calling my boy a pervert, Grellier?"

Jim held up his hands. "Easy, Clem. Take it easy. Eddie doesn't have enough to do, that's all. And he hangs out with Junior Schapen, who might take advantage of him. That's all I'm saying."

"You saying my own boy hangs out at the Schapens'? What you do, spy on him for Deputy Arnie?" Clem was shouting—the loud, blustery shout of someone who knows he's wrong.

"Clem, am I that kind of guy, spying on people? I'm just saying, Eddie doesn't always know if he's doing the right thing or not, and if Junior wanted him to spook that city lady at Fremantles' Eddie'd do it to make Junior happy." Jim was sweating in the cold room.

Clem's mouth dropped as he thought this over. "Yeah, you're right. Arnie Schapen would be happier than a pig in mud if Eddie did something he could be arrested for. I showed Schapen up good in court, made everyone see him for the asshole he is, and he can't forgive me that. He probably sicced Junior onto Eddie, trying to get Eddie to break the law so he can arrest him."

"Could be," Jim agreed. Not that he believed it, but if Clem did it would make him more willing to keep tabs on his son.

Clem clapped him on the arm, breathing stale beer on Jim. "Sorry to lose my cool there, man, but every time I hear that Schapen name I see red, white, and blue. Turk give me twenty bucks yesterday, out of his winnings, and I have to put it on that damned fine. Schapen goes around spreading lies about my family—about my own daughter!—and I'm the one who has to pay a thousand-dollar fine, not him. If I could afford me a lawyer, I'd sue him for false witness. But everything costs money—I'm surprised they don't fine us for breathing."

Jim again agreed, wondering how the Burtons afforded that big television, or even their electric bill. He turned down an offer of a drink and made his way past Turk and the television back to the kitchen. The old man at the table had fallen asleep. The cat was eating the cereal.

Thirteen

THAT OLD HOUSE

JIM HAD THOUGHT OF stopping again at Fremantles' to suggest Gina find a dog, but as he was pulling out of Clem's yard Gina passed him, heading toward Highway 10. Just as well: he'd spent over two hours on social calls—if that's how you'd classify a visit to Burtons'.

When he got home, he paused a moment in his truck, shaking the last cold drops of the cappuccino into his mouth, carefully thinking about nothing. Inside, the house still smelled like Christmas: pine needles and cinnamon. Susan had moved on to her next project: figuring out a design for her organic-sunflower packages and logo. Jim found her in the dining room, where she'd covered the table with her work.

Susan and Lara had spent weeks arguing over the best name. Lara had wanted "SuLa," for *Su*san and *La*ra. She said it sounded Indian, and would make people think of the prairie and Native Americans, but Susan insisted on "Abigail's Organics." Lara finally gave in, and created a dozen or so designs, some from old photographs she'd found in books at flea markets, some her own drawings.

Susan was bent over the designs, her unruly hair caught up in a clip to keep it out of her eyes, exposing the line of her neck. Her skin was brown, the skin of a woman who spent most of her time outside, not like Gina's soft white face and hands. Jim bent over and kissed the nape of his wife's neck.

"What do you think?" She leaned back and looked at him. "I like this one that Lara drew of a girl in a sunbonnet, but the picture is too crude."

"Crude is going to reproduce better. Why don't you take a break before Lara gets back from basketball practice?" He lifted his eyes suggestively toward the second floor.

"I don't need a break—this is really— Oh, you mean—!" The tanned skin darkened under her freckles.

Since leaving college and moving into the farmhouse, they'd rarely made love in the daytime. First there was Gram and Grandpa, then Chip and Lulu and Curly and Blitz—everyone knowing what it meant if two people went upstairs in the middle of the day. Once, early in their marriage, they'd climbed into the hayloft. When they emerged, they'd found Grandpa in the yard on the tractor politely waiting for them to leave before he drove inside. With the house finally to themselves in the winter, they never thought of sex: too much to do, machinery to be fixed, germination trays to prepare, meals, errands, accounts.

Susan looked at the pictures in her hand, then laid them out on the table and got up to put her arms around him. "Hard time at Burtons'?"

"Yes. Let's not talk about it. I want to think about you right now." Really, of course, he meant himself, his own complicated desires to be made simple in her body. He held her tighter, then, risking his back and knees, swept her off her feet and carried her up the stairs.

Later, as they were pulling on their clothes, Jim asked where Chip was. Chip had driven Lara in for her practice. Although at fourteen she could legally drive herself to school and back, Jim didn't like her on the county roads when they were icy. Chip hadn't said anything about his own plans for the day.

"School starts again day after tomorrow. I asked him yesterday if he was ready and he bit my head off," Jim added. "What's eating him? Until this fall, he was such a happy kid, none of the moodiness boys his age often fall into."

Susan shrugged. "Maybe it's the thought of going off to college."

"But he's dragging his feet on his applications," Jim said. "When I asked him about that, he said if I was so hot on a college degree I could go in his place. You don't think—could Janice be pregnant?"

"Ask him." Susan ran her fingers through her tangled hair.

"You do it. I did safe sex and drugs, although that wasn't such a success.

Maybe he's smoking more dope than he let on—that would sure make him moody." He paused at the bedroom door, unsettled by the thought that suddenly ran through his head: he'd rather find out Chip was doing drugs than that Janice was pregnant.

Jim heard the kitchen door bang shut. Lulu had brought Kimberly Ropes home from practice. While Kimberly's folks spent the afternoon with Peter Ropes. Jim and Susan went downstairs to offer the two girls Susan's homemade mince pies and the ubiquitous overboiled country coffee.

Jim and Susan were asleep before Chip drove into the yard. In the morning, he refused to get up for church. When the family returned home following the ritual stop at the pancake house on Twenty-third Street after church, they found him in the family room with a bowl of cereal, watching the Chiefs.

Jim looked significantly at Susan, but she shook her head and went into the kitchen to check on a batch of baked beans she was preparing for supper.

"You are such a slob." Lara didn't have her parents' inhibitions. "What are you doing, lying around in your pj's at noon? Were you out drinking with Janice last night?"

"I was minding my own business, HullabaLulu," Chip said.

Using the old nickname meant he was prepared to be conciliatory, but Susan stuck her head in the family room. "Etienne, you know how destructive it is to get drunk. And I hope you aren't so upset by your private worries that you would drink and drive."

"Mom, I know what I'm doing. I'm eighteen, I don't need a babysitter. Sheesh!"

He flung the cereal bowl onto the coffee table and stomped up the stairs. Before Jim could steel himself to follow, he heard a tentative knock on the kitchen door. Susan turned around and called for the visitor to come on in. A moment later, Jim heard Gina Haring's deeper, softer voice. He went into the kitchen.

"I'm returning your pie pan," Gina was saying.

She'd put it on top of Jim's oat-crop file, which he'd left on the kitchen table in the morning, planning to work on it after church. Thinking back on the scene later, what Jim remembered most clearly, more even than Chip's anger, was his own annoyance that Gina hadn't cleaned the dish properly: a finger of caramelized sugar had dribbled down the side, making the pan stick to his spreadsheet.

She noticed his glance and peeled the paper away. "I'm sorry. I took the pie to Autumn's and I thought she'd washed the pan."

"You didn't eat any yourself?" Susan was hurt.

"I did; it was delicious. I'd put it in the freezer, actually, so I could make it my contribution for Christmas dinner—don't worry, I made sure everyone knew you baked it."

"Oh, please—" Susan made an embarrassed gesture. "I don't care about that, as I hope you know. We hadn't seen your car for a week. Did you go back to New York for the holidays?"

"New York—it's not an easy place for me to be right now." Gina made a face. "I stayed in Lawrence with Autumn Minsky—I thought I owed myself a break in a house with real heat."

Jim got up hastily and took the pie pan, which Gina was still holding, to put in the sink. He found her mug, which he had carefully washed and put aside, and handed it to her. Those slender white thighs, which he couldn't quite put out of his mind, embracing plump, pugnacious Autumn—he quickly returned to the table and busied himself with his oat-crop data.

"How do you spend your time?" Susan asked. "Are you doing any work on the house?"

"Me?" Gina laughed and looked at her slender fingers. "I think I know which end of a hammer you hold, but I'm not sure how to swing it. I worked in public relations before my marriage. I'm trying to reconnect with old clients, see if I can build up some kind of private business so I don't have to live in mold and ice forever. That isn't going too well, so I'm dabbling with writing a book. Like every other college English major, I always imagined I had a big novel in me."

"It's a pity you can't use the fireplaces," Susan said, ignoring the biting self-mockery in Gina's voice. "What's your novel about?"

"Oh, romance among the Wiccans. Nobody writes about us as if we were real people. I thought I could write a love story with Wicca as the backdrop. As if you were going to write a love story with Christianity as the backdrop."

Susan's eyes sparkled. "No, I'd make the anti-slavery days my backdrop. I'd set a romance in the Fremantle house. After all, the Victorians fell in love, just as we do."

"Why do you care so much about that house?" Gina asked. "I can see it used to be wonderful, but it's falling apart, and smells of cat pee."

Lara, attracted by the talk, came in, her iPod earpieces dangling around her neck like a stethoscope. Pee, Lara thought. Gina and her friend are obsessed by pee. That was how she would casually introduce the word into conversation with Kimberly and Melanie at lunch tomorrow.

She covertly eyed Gina's clothes. She was expensively, even exotically, dressed, in a bloodred jacket with fur trim and fringed cavalier boots. The leather was soft and clean, except for a few mud spatters Gina must have gotten walking from her car to the house. Boots like that wouldn't survive five minutes if you really walked through snow in them, Lara thought scornfully, wondering at the same time how much they cost and whether they would make her look as sophisticated as they did Gina.

"It's the pee and the mold, and everything, that makes me care about the house," Susan was saying. "Things like that don't seem repulsive to me. Just sad, the way a person who used to be, oh, maybe a great athlete, seems sad if she's falling apart."

"But why does it matter to you?" Gina repeated.

"It's the history of the time!" Susan leaned forward, with her coffee mug between her hands. "The Fremantle house is beautiful, but it's what it meant to the valley back then, that's what I feel when I walk through it. That's why I'd like to set a book there, except I can't write. Where is your story set?"

"I put it in New York, because that's what I know, but, listening to you, I'm wondering if I should write about Uncle John's house instead. After all, we're going to have an Imbolc ceremony there, which I could never have done in the city—at least, not with a real fire."

Susan, always eager for new experiences, peppered her with questions about her ritual.

"It's a fire festival. We cleanse ourselves to be ready for spring. You know the Swedish festival, where a girl wears a crown of burning candles?"

When Susan and Lara shook their heads, Gina smiled. "They do—take my word for it. It's a sort of Christianized version of the old goddess ritual. You should come see what we're all about."

"When is it?" Susan asked.

"February second. If you do decide to come, you need to bring a gift for the fire, something to burn that will bring you good luck in the harvest. Come to think of it, Imbolc was originally a farmers' holiday—they'd beg the Earth Mother for a good harvest. I'd think every farmer around here might want to do that."

"No, because then Myra Schapen would write them all up on her website," Lara put in.

"Myra Schapen?" Gina repeated. "Isn't that the family you said lived on down the road? Is Myra in school with you?"

Lara blinked, trying to imagine a teenage Myra. "She's about a hundred years old, and she's like a witch! I always expect to see her with a corncob pipe when she's out on the tractor. It's her son, Arnie, who's the sheriff's deputy. He came—probably he's the one who came over to spy on you when you moved in. Myra—Nanny Schapen, I mean—she drove his wife off, and now she and Arnie—Mr. Schapen—they live with her grandsons. Junior is the biggest bully—"

"Lara!" Susan cut her daughter off. "You cannot be talking about the Schapens like that. Just because you can't get along with Junior and Robbie doesn't mean Gina won't find a way to talk to them. And you know your father and I don't want you using Myra's and Arnie's first names."

"If Gina does a witches' bonfire, you know the only thing Myra—Nanny Schapen—will say is that Gina and her friends are going to hell!" Lara said stubbornly. "The Schapens have a website, and she's always writing up stuff about us or other people around here in a really mean way."

"But if she's a witch, as you say, she and I are kindred spirits, and she belongs at our ceremony," Gina said in the aloof, mocking voice she'd used when Lara and Susan first saw her. "Perhaps I'll call on her and issue a formal invitation."

Lara turned away, embarrassed both by her own blunder in calling Myra a witch in front of Gina and by Gina's ironic inflection.

"There's no privacy in the country," Jim said to cover the awkward moment. "You may think because you don't live near anyone that every-one minds their own business, but if you have a bonfire the whole valley, from the Kaw to Highway 10, will know what you're doing."

"I know," Gina said, laughing with real amusement. "Remember, I've already had a Peeping Tom and the witch's son calling on me."

"That reminds me," Jim answered. "I talked to Clem Burton. He's going to keep an eye on Eddie, in case it was Eddie up your tree. And I spoke to Hank—Hank Drysdale, the sheriff—casually. But it wouldn't hurt for you to have a dog over there."

"A dog?" Gina said blankly. "What would I do with it when I left?"

"Take it with you, leave it for the next tenant—I don't know."

"Since I don't know, either, I think I'd better rely on locks and bolts. But, Susan, I wish you would consider coming to our Imbolc ceremony. I think you'd enjoy it."

Jim, seeing his wife's face light up, found himself tensing. She would enjoy it. Witchcraft would become a new passion with her. Arnie and Myra would have a field day, writing about the hell-bound Grelliers. He realized that Gina was asking him something and jerked his attention back to the kitchen.

"That building that's collapsed out behind the barn," she repeated, "can I use that for the bonfire?"

Jim hesitated. "A boy was killed when that place burned down. I'm not sure if they ever brought his body out. Maybe you should leave it alone."

"Jim! They must have brought him out," Susan protested. "Liz Fremantle wouldn't have let a boy rot in there, you know that as well as I do." She turned to Gina and explained the history of the commune, the fire, the bucket brigade.

"Were you here?" Gina asked her.

"I was a schoolgirl," Susan said, "living in—I can't even remember what town we lived in then. My father never could hold a job more than two or three years; we were always moving. That's why I was so thankful to marry someone who was rooted to a single place, whose family had a long history there. No, I just used to hear Jim and Doug—Jim's brother—talk about it. And Gram and Grandpa, of course, so I feel as though I had seen it, that's all. Right before the fire, someone put weed killer on the marijuana crop. The kids were out grieving over the damage—in the moonlight, I can just picture them—when the house went up in flames."

"And you never knew who died?" Gina asked.

Jim shook his head. "I wasn't quite ten. I don't remember the details that well; I just remember forming part of the bucket brigade the night of the fire. And Myra Schapen, she always terrified me. And she came over to watch the fire, with Arnie and his dad. The Ropeses and the Wiesers, even the Burtons—everyone helped except Myra and her husband. I looked up and saw her watching the fire. The expression on Myra's face, that made a believer out of me!"

"A believer?" Gina said.

"I knew that's what would be waiting for me in hell if I died without Jesus," he said, laughing to cover his embarrassment at mentioning God to this sophisticated woman who practiced witchcraft.

Fourteen

THE COVEN GATHERS

Twice a month, Lara's church youth group helped stock the shelves and fill bags at a Lawrence food pantry. In January, after school had started up again, Lara came home from her Saturday stint and announced that Elaine Logan had been at the pantry. The rest of the family was already sitting down to lunch. Lara grabbed a bowl of soup and took it to the table, blurting out information through a mouthful of bread.

"What? Is Elaine back in town? I thought she was living with her sister or someone in Chicago," Jim said.

"Didn't I tell you? Curly said she showed up at New Year's drunk as a skunk," Chip said.

Naturally, Curly knew. Even though Curly and Blitz worked in town in the winter—Blitz as a mechanic for the school system, Curly for his cousin's construction business—Chip hung out with Curly. Lara was pretty sure Curly took Chip drinking, but she knew it would really piss off her parents if she shared that suspicion so she kept it to herself.

"Poor Elaine," Susan mourned. "What a terrible waste. She was a wonderful student, could have done anything with her life."

"*She* says she was a wonderful student," Chip corrected impatiently. "You know the kind of lies that old bag tells."

"Etienne! I will not have you using language like that, especially not about someone as unfortunate as Elaine."

"But, Mom, she really is ghastly, not unfortunate," Lara said. "Like today, I offered to carry her groceries for her, and she said, 'Aren't you Jesus' favorite little lamb,' in the nastiest way possible. And she makes stuff up, so you can't tell whether it really happened or not. Like, do you believe she really turned down a scholarship to medical school?"

People change with time, Jim thought, but his daughter was too young to know you could start out filled with promise and end up worse off than Clem Burton. It was hard to believe it of Elaine—fat, leering, drunk more often than she was sober—but maybe she really had been a student bright enough to get into medical school thirty-five years ago.

"You'd better warn Gina Haring," Chip said.

"That's right!" Susan said. "It didn't occur to me, even when we were telling Gina about the bunkhouse, because Elaine's been away for over a year now. But maybe she won't try to come out. You know, after Liz Fremantle died Elaine did stop her visits."

"All the more reason she'll do it now," Lara said. "She'll hear the gossip about Gina and want to check her out."

"And what gossip would that be?" asked Jim in his coldest voice.

"Just that someone's renting the house," Lara said hastily.

"And that she's a dyke who practices witchcraft," Chip added.

"Etienne! You're not to use that word," Susan said. "If you mean that Gina is a lesbian, say that. But you don't know—"

"Mom, I'll promise not to use the word *dyke* if you'll promise to stop calling me Etienne. You know I hate it."

"You'll grow into it," Susan said. "One of these days, you won't want a child's nickname any longer and then you'll be glad you're used to hearing your real name. Anyway, we don't know that Gina Haring is a lesbian."

"Come on, Mom, everyone knows."

"By which, I take it, Lara talked to you and you talked to Curly, and now everyone in Douglas County knows Gina and Autumn Minsky have spent a night in the same house," Jim said drily.

Chip scowled and turned his head away. Lara said, "Dad, it's not like it's some secret. She announced it right here in the kitchen, like she wanted us to know."

"She didn't announce she was a lesbian, Lulu. And if that's what you're telling everyone—"

"I didn't *tell* everyone. I asked Chip and Kimberly their *opinions,* you know, after I saw Ms. Minsky in bed that day we went over. I asked if that meant her and Autumn were—"

"*She* and Autumn," Susan corrected.

"Okay, she and Autumn. So I wondered, did that mean she was a— you know. I tried to ask you, Dad, but you got that wooden-statue look on your face you always get if I talk about anything even remotely concerned with sex, so I had to ask someone else."

"And Chip is an expert?" Jim gave a ghost of a smile, trying not to be annoyed by the criticism.

"Ask Janice Everleigh," Lara said pertly.

Chip made a violent gesture. "Dad is right. You should mind your own business for a change."

"Sor-*ree*!" Lara said. "Can't you take a joke?"

Brother and sister glared at each other as if they were four and eight, not fourteen and eighteen. Jim sighed and tried to change the subject, asking Lara if she knew where Elaine Logan was living.

"Mmm-hmm," Lara said through a mouthful of peanut butter. She swallowed. "You know, it's Ms. Carmody who takes our youth group to the pantry, and she was asking Elaine how she was settling into New Haven Manor."

"New Haven?" Jim was surprised. "How long will that last? They have a strict no-alcohol policy."

"Rachel Carmody is on the board," Susan said. "She might have persuaded them to give Elaine a trial."

"Rachel does a lot, between the youth group and being on the church's board of directors, besides teaching high school. I'm surprised she'd take on another board."

"Yes," Susan said, "but that's who people always want, someone who's shown she's responsible. Anyway, when I see Gina on Monday I'll explain who Elaine is and that she sometimes hitches a ride out to wander around the property. I do hope Gina won't mind—Elaine got into the habit when Liz Fremantle was alive."

"What are you doing with Gina?" Lara asked.

"She asked me to stop into Between Two Worlds to look at a book on the Imbolc ceremony."

"That shop is such a heap of New Age horseshit," Chip said. Then, catching his father's expression, he quickly edited himself: "Horse *doo-doo,* I mean. The girls go there to get their fortunes told off the tarot decks. I went with Janice one night, and it is so bogus. Why do girls go in for that kind of crap?"

"Why do boys go to the Storm Door and get drunk on three-two beer?" Lara demanded. "At least we don't throw up and stink after we have our fortunes told."

"Okay, you two, enough," Jim said automatically, adding to his wife, "Why are you looking at this Imblog ceremony?"

"Imbolc," Susan corrected.

"Mom, you're not going in for Gina's witch stuff, are you?" Chip demanded.

"No, of course not, but I do want to see her fire. This is the year we're getting full organic certification for the X-Farm. We could use some good luck for our sunflower crop, so some seeds will be my gift to the fire."

Jim's lips tightened. "Suze! You're on the board of directors at Riverside, remember?"

His wife smiled provocatively. "We're an open-covenant church, Jim. We start every service saying, 'Wherever you are on life's journey, we welcome you.' Of course I'm not going to become a pagan. But a party with other women, a bonfire—we'll throw in leftover evergreens from Christmas for luck, I'll add some sunflower seeds, they'll dance and have drums, I'd love to be there."

"Mom, don't do it!" Chip said. "You know it'll be in Myra's 'News' column by Monday morning. Don't get involved with that bunch of crackpots. I can't take the fallout from another one of your weird ideas."

"Just what do you mean by that, Etienne? What 'weird' ideas of mine have bothered you so much?" Susan's voice trembled.

"Come on, Mom. Don't you know everyone around here thinks you're nuts, that you're a Communist? What are they going to say if you dance around a bonfire with a bunch of dykes? Arnie and Myra and Junior will be telling the whole valley that you're a dyke, too!"

"Etienne! We just finished saying we don't want you to use that word. Beyond that, I can't believe a son of mine would be so small-minded as to care about public opinion, least of all what the Schapens think. Anyway, how can people say I'm a Communist when everyone knows how active I am at church?"

"Because of the stuff you do. The co-op market, wasn't that a Communist thing?"

"Etienne, you're making me crazy. The market wasn't some state-run outfit taking people's profits from them, it was a local initiative where everybody benefited without needing a middleman. Besides, look at all the farmers who took part in it: the Ropeses, the Longneckers, the Wiesers, even Liz Fremantle. It's only narrow-minded people like Arnie Schapen and Dennis Greynard who tried to sabotage it."

"If you hadn't named Lara for that stupid Russian movie, maybe the talk about you being a Commie wouldn't have started in the first place."

Privately, Lara agreed. But she didn't want to get involved in a fight between Chip and her mother. Anyway, Lara wasn't a weird name, at least not compared to Etienne—if Susan hadn't explained to everyone that it was Lara, not Laura, because she was named for Julie Christie's character in *Doctor Zhivago,* no one would ever have thought twice about it. Susan watched the movie about a hundred times when she was pregnant with Lara, and of course people like Arnie Schapen took it for granted that if you liked something Russian you were automatically a Communist. People were so ignorant, Lara agreed with her mother about that, but at the same time Lara wished she was a little more clued in to how they reacted to the things she did.

"Did you know," Jim asked, trying to calm down the passion at the table, "that the early Christians held all their possessions in common? That really is Communism. Imagine how Arnie Schapen would react if I suggested that to him."

"He'd be thrilled," Lara said, trying to help. "He'd take Dad's John Deere and make us drive his old Case tractor."

Jim winked at his daughter, and added, "He'd also have you up doing the five o'clock milking. One reason we don't have animals—the thought of getting you and Chip out of bed before dawn every day."

Chip and Susan were still flushed with battle, but Lara laughed loudly. Chip got up from the table and stomped upstairs. They heard the water running in the bathroom. In a few minutes, he came back down, heavily drenched in aftershave.

"Don't you have homework?" Jim called to him.

Chip's only answer was to slam the kitchen door hard enough to shake the windows. They heard his car start, the engine roaring as he gunned it, and then the wheels spinning in the icy gravel.

"What's going on with him?" Jim said.

"Etienne has always had his moods. He doesn't like to be thwarted." Susan, still angry with her son, didn't want to see his point of view.

Jim turned to Lara. "Lulu, do you know what's eating him? It's not something with Janice or at school, is it? Is she—do you know—"

"Is she pregnant?" Lara cut in as he dithered for a euphemism. "She wouldn't talk to me about it, but I don't think so. Anyway, you know Curly is the person Chip talks to, not me. Make Curly tell you, or get Blitz to make him—he's scared of Blitz but not of you."

"Scared of Blitz? What's scary about Blitz?" Jim was incredulous. Blitz was more than a farmhand, more than a crackerjack machinist—he was the closest friend Jim had.

"The way he looks at you, like he sees right through you, and doesn't think much of what he's looking at, you know, Dad."

"You make him sound like he'd be at home with Gina's witches." He stared narrowly at his daughter. "And you also make me think you know what Chip has said to Curly. I know you, Lulu, you slip in and out of places, and people don't know you're there. Come on, spill it. What is going on? It's not tattling if it helps me get things sorted out."

Lara turned scarlet but burst out: "Oh, Dad! No one wants to hurt your feelings, but Chip doesn't want to farm."

Jim blinked and sat back down. His first thought was to say automatically, if he doesn't want to farm he doesn't have to, but he realized it wasn't that simple. His own father hadn't wanted to farm; he'd gone into town and become an insurance agent. Then a Santa Fe freight, speeding around a hill to the unprotected Fifteenth Street crossing, had killed both him and his wife, leaving Jim and Doug to live with Gram and Grandpa on the farm.

From the moment he first got to drive the small tractor that summer, Jim had known that farming was his life. He couldn't imagine a different one. Knowing, too, that he was working land his family had worked for seven generations—he didn't have Susan's romantic fantasies about Abigail and the Abolitionists, but standing on land that he belonged to brought him a comfort beyond wife or children, or even, really, God.

Sitting at the table now, studying his hands while he tried to think about the future of the farm if Chip didn't want it, Jim remembered the guy who blew up the federal building in Topeka some years back because the feds were confiscating his farm. The man had been an idiot, growing marijuana on his land, selling it. Still, if the feds had merely sent him to prison he would have gone knowing he had his land to come home to, but they were taking a farm like Jim's, one his family had lived on for seven generations. When he got out of prison, his life would be gone. Jim couldn't imagine blowing up a building and killing people, but he still thought he understood how the guy must have felt.

He didn't say any of this, just looked at his daughter's scared, anxious face and put a hand to her cheek. "It's not your fault, Lulu. And it's not your problem. The worst thing I could do for Chip is to try to make him stay here when he doesn't want to be here. It'd be the worst thing for the farm, too—it's a recipe for failure. But why is it eating him now?"

"Baseball," Lara said. "Now is when people like him get to try out. He was sure he'd get to try out as a walk-on, but not even the Royals are interested. Haven't you noticed how he runs for the phone whenever it rings? And he checks his e-mail, like, every ten seconds."

"Baseball? You mean, when he went to that camp last summer and played in front of those scouts? And they won't take him? Oh, poor Etienne, no wonder he's upset, his dreams shattered like that!" All Susan's anger with her son evaporated in her distress. She looked as mournful as if it were her own dreams that had been demolished.

"Y-e-es," Jim said doubtfully, "but he was never that good."

"He was MVP in the northeast Kansas league last year," Susan flashed.

"Sweetheart, a thousand boys are MVPs every year, but not too many are good enough for the majors. I guess Chip thought baseball was big enough that if he got drafted, he wouldn't have to talk to me about the farm. He can go to college this fall, though—he should get accepted at K-State or Baldwin, don't you think, if he started on his applications right away? He'd have four years to figure out some kind of direction— maybe coaching, or sports management." Jim tried to sound hearty, as if he thought these were wonderful choices. "I'll talk to him tomorrow."

"Chip hates school," Lara said. "You know he does. He'll go to college only if you make him."

"Lara is the student in the family. We've always said so," Susan added.

Jim looked at his daughter, trying to smile. "Lulu, you'd better be careful. You're carrying a lot of parental ambitions on your curly brown head. You're the student, you're the one who likes to work the farm, you're the one who plays the trumpet and your ever-so-great-grandmother's piano."

Lara grinned. "I'll instruct a team of agriculture students out on the X-Farm while heading up a marching band and pushing a piano through the furrows. You'll see, Dad, it'll all work out."

"I know you're trying to be funny, but you could do it!" Susan's eyes glowed. "Look how Abigail ran this farm on her own, even before the first Etienne died, and she did it—"

"In twelve-pound wool skirts. I know, Mom. But could she play the trumpet at the same time?" Lara went upstairs to start her homework.

Fifteen

FIRE DANCE

"You wouldn't mind if the farm went to Lara, would you, Jim?" Susan asked later.

"Mind? What, because she's a girl? Of course not. What a ridiculous idea—I'd be ecstatic. But it's true that she's our brainy kid. I don't want her to give up doing something, oh, big in the world because she thinks we want her to stay here. Let her stretch her wings when the time comes."

He paused and took Susan's hands. "You know I don't interfere with the things you do with your friends, Suze, but this bonfire, couldn't you put that off? If Chip is this upset about his life, let's not add to his woes when we don't have to."

Susan pulled her hands away. "If I could make Etienne a baseball star by giving up my friends, I would, but it really troubles me that my own son worries so much about what small-minded people like Arnie and Myra Schapen think. He pays no attention to anything I say to him, about his course work, or his plans for his future, or the amount of time he's spending with Janice, whose only attraction I can see is between her bra straps, which, by the way, her mother should talk to her about getting fitted properly. But, anyway, Janice doesn't do anything to improve his mind or enhance his life—I know you agree with me about that! Why am I supposed to placate him by staying home this coming Thursday?"

Jim rubbed his forehead. "It makes me uncomfortable, Suze, I guess that's the point. I'm not superstitious, but—women dancing around a fire, pretending to be witches—"

"But they're not, Jim, they're not pretending to be witches. It's female bonding, it's going back to the old women's religions, when women felt powerful and comfortable in their bodies. Gina says women used to be in charge of the harvest, the planting, all the old fertility rituals. If Etienne is upset by me wanting to celebrate women's lives, I haven't done a very good job as a mother raising a son who isn't comfortable with female power."

He could tell from the glib, disjoint phrases that she was repeating what she'd heard from Gina, or Autumn Minsky at the bookstore, but it irritated him all the same. They argued about it until bedtime, and off and on again during the week, but on Thursday she left the house after supper with a bag of sunflower seeds, her "gift to the fire."

Predictably, Chip refused to eat supper with the family on Thursday. He came home from school long enough to see that his mother was intent on attending Gina's Imbolc ritual and announced he was meeting Curly in town for a burger. When Jim asked if he was keeping up in his courses, he yelled "What's the point?" and once again slammed out of the house.

Jim had tried talking to his son about how to think about a future without a professional ball career, but Chip wouldn't respond. Instead, Jim later overheard him driving Lara to tears by shouting at her that she was a tattle-telling brat who hadn't changed since she was four and told Dad it was Chip who had broken Mom's crystal vase.

Lara was excited by the thought of the bonfire and begged Susan to take her, but Jim put his foot down. The image of Gina's body entwined with her friend Autumn's hovered at the edge of his consciousness. He imagined some kind of depravity that would unnerve Lara and degrade Susan. When he tried to suggest this to his wife, she became furious, and they had the kind of shouting fight that left him hollow with helplessness.

On Thursday, Jim took a bowl of chili into the family room and doggedly watched a movie while Lara and Susan ate in the kitchen. Over the television, he heard Susan's squeaky voice and Lara's laugh. He felt hurt that they could be happy when he was upset.

A little later, the kitchen door banged shut again, the pickup engine turned over, and his jaw tightened. Had Susan taken Lara with her? If she had—but, after a minute, he heard Lara washing the dishes. He turned back to the television, trying to care about what Morgan Freeman and Clint Eastwood were doing in front of him.

He went to the kitchen. Lara had gone upstairs. He stared out the back window, but the bulk of the barn and equipment sheds blocked any view of the Fremantle house. He put his work boots on and walked out behind the outbuildings.

He was turning back to the house when he saw a shadow move in the grasses on the far side of the track. Something about the way the grasses bent told him it wasn't a coyote or fox but his daughter. Damn Lulu, anyway. He didn't want her watching the drinking or whatever else the women might do. He started through the dead grass after his daughter.

The ground was gluey from a recent freeze-thaw cycle. He never mowed near the tracks, and the head-high wild grasses and weeds had become a dumping ground for rotting fenceposts and rusty plowshares, as well as the bottles and bags that landed everywhere, even along tracks through a cornfield. Like fox droppings, he thought, with their telltale pointed ends, garbage was the recognizable excretion of the human species. He banged and stumbled his way to the tracks, barely saving himself from falling several times, roundly cursing his wife, his daughter, the whole female half of the species.

When he finally made it to the train tracks, he slopped through the muck along the ties: at least the ground was level here. In the distance, he could hear the traffic on K-10 like a faint roar of wind, but as he got closer to the Fremantle place that noise was covered by the sound of drums and singing and laughter.

He followed the sounds and the glow of the fire through the remains of the old apple orchard. Gina and Autumn had constructed their bonfire not far from the ruins of the bunkhouse. Beyond it loomed the Fremantles' main barn; they'd built it there so their hands would have easy access to it.

The fire wasn't big, but to Jim's surprise it had been carefully laid: he somehow hadn't expected that kind of skill from city women. It was burning steadily. The dozen or so women gathered around it were laughing, a few were beating drums, and someone outside his field of vision was playing a flute. The women were passing bottles around to share. Every now and then, someone would throw something into the flames. He'd see a burst of color, green or gold, now and then a flash of red, and everyone would cheer.

He made out Susan's back, her unmistakable halo of curls and the bulk of her down vest, and, near her, Gina's taller, leaner silhouette. Someone passed Gina a wine bottle; she drank from it, then handed it to Susan, who at first shook her head, but then, after Gina seemed to urge her, took a swallow and quickly passed it on. Underneath his annoyance, Jim felt a twinge of pity for his wife, who didn't much like alcohol but who wanted to be part of the group.

Staying well back from the fire, he skirted around, looking for Lara. Years of practice had made her a skilled eavesdropper—or tracker, to be charitable. He almost missed her, but she must have moved at his approach because he looked up and saw her perched on a low branch of a bur oak.

"Enjoying the show, Lulu?"

In a flash from the fire, he saw her flatten her upper lip against her teeth; she was nervous, not knowing if he was angry. He held a hand up to her, and she let him swing her down.

"Oh, Dad, don't be mad. This is so—so amazing! No one does stuff like this. It's totally awesome! I wanted to see the ceremony, and I knew you'd hate it if I went with Mom."

"Did she ask you?"

"She wouldn't let me. She said you'd expressly forbidden it. And, anyway, it was for her and her friends."

Jim felt some of his tightness ease at realizing his wife had respected his wishes, at least as far as not involving Lara in her new hobby. "So you decided to be Pocahontas Grellier and trail along?"

Lara grinned at him; the question meant he wasn't angry anymore. She snuggled up to him as she used to when she was seven or eight, although she was tall now, at eye level with him. They watched the fire ceremony together in silence for a while.

"You know, Mom wants to have a vision," she startled him by saying sometime later.

"A vision?" he echoed uncertainly.

"Like however many great-granny Abigail's. That's why she wants to be at this bonfire. She hopes she'll look into the fire and see a vision."

"Your mother didn't tell you that!" he exclaimed.

"No, but read between the lines. She talks about Abigail's vision all the time to Gina, or anyone who will listen, but she says she doesn't do anything exalted enough with her life to merit a vision. But she'd probably have to smoke dope, or something, and I don't think she'd do that. Or maybe fast for forty days. But—"

"Lulu, your imagination is working way overtime. Your mother is an enthusiastic woman, she gets passions for causes, but she's not the kind of person to lose track of the real world around her."

Lara mumbled something that Jim decided he didn't need to have repeated, and they watched a few more minutes in silence. The flute playing and the drumming became more intense, and the women started dancing around the fire. Again Jim felt a twinge of pity for his wife, trying to join in but moving awkwardly. They weren't dancers, he and Susan, not even in their college days. Susan was quick in all her motions, racing around the farm, the house, but quick wasn't necessarily rhythmic. As the women circled and the drumbeat got louder, one of the women took off her coat and her shirt, and then another one did the same.

Jim sucked in a breath, embarrassed, titillated, angry—he couldn't tell which feeling was on top. "This is where we go home, Lulu. I hope your mom leaves her clothes on. February isn't the month to prance naked around a fire."

She didn't resist, but as they walked away from the fire she kept turning her head to look. "Dad, I've been looking at naked girls for years. We don't get underneath towels to change for gym, you know. And if this is the first time you've seen— Oh!"

Before he could react, she broke off and poked him in the shoulder. He turned automatically. She wasn't pointing at Susan, as he'd feared, but beyond to the far south side of the property, where the trees stopped and the Ropeses' field started. Just visible behind the trees was Arnie Schapen, a set of binoculars pressed to his eyes.

With a rough gesture, Jim dragged Lara away from Arnie's field of vision. She wrenched away from him and darted back to the edge of the clearing, where she stood making a defiant gesture. When Jim reached her, he started to yell at her for stirring the waters but broke off at a movement in the tall grass to Arnie's right.

Jim pulled Lara down so they were both shielded by the undergrowth. After a few minutes, they saw Eddie Burton and Junior Schapen emerge. Junior's face glistened with a kind of greed Lara had never seen; Eddie was laughing in a kind of donkey's hee-haw.

Sixteen

RAMPING UP THE ARGUMENTS

http://www.schapenfarm.com/newsandnotes.html

Some of our neighbors don't seem concerned about their immortal souls. They think that drinking, dancing naked, and other abominations are benign acts that the Creator overlooks, or maybe rejoices in. Nothing could be further from the Truth! We pray for our neighbors to come to Jesus and experience a close personal relation with their Creator and Savior. Can you profess Jesus and dance before the fires that are a foretaste of Hell?? Apparently one of our neighbors sets herself on a higher plane than Jesus, thinking she can do both. Instead, she's had a glimpse into the flames that wait for her on the other side.

When Susan and Gina read the Schapens' website, they were both angry. Arnie's photos were too blurry to make out anyone's faces, or even the fact that a number of the women had been naked, but Susan resented the Schapens' attacks on her Christian commitment. Gina didn't care about that, but she was furious that Arnie had trespassed and invaded her privacy.

Susan couldn't get any sympathy at home: Jim said he'd warned her, Chip said he wished for once she'd think about someone besides herself.

"I told you your weird crap was making all of us a laughingstock, but you had to do it, anyway. Do you know the kind of stuff they're saying in school, Junior Schapen and his group of football wannabes? How you're a harlot or the whore of Babylon? They even hassle Janice for being my girlfriend, all because you had to prance naked around a fire with a bunch of other loonies! She came this close to breaking up with me over it." Chip held his thumb and forefinger together.

"Too bad she didn't," Lara muttered, but too softly for Chip to hear her.

Lara didn't know what she thought about her mother and the bonfire. She'd been excited by the spectacle, the drumming, the dancing, the wild unexpectedness of it, but that was before she saw Eddie Burton, his face glistening, licking his lips. That had made the whole evening so shameful that she couldn't think about the fire at all.

All the talk at school further upset her. Even Kimberly Ropes and Melanie Derwint said they thought Susan had gone too far. "What those women were doing is witchcraft, Lara, and my pastor says you can go to hell for it," Melanie told her. "If you want to save your mother, you should keep her away from those people." After that conversation, Lara didn't have the nerve to admit she'd watched part of it. She certainly couldn't mention Junior and Eddie.

And then Junior Schapen started taunting Lara in the hallway whenever he saw her. "Seen your mom on her broomstick lately?" he'd call, or, "Check her forehead to see if any horns are growing there?"

"Any horns around will be on you, cowman," Lara yelled back. "You spend so much time in cowshit, it's filled up your head, you and your creepy friend Eddie."

Chip happened to pass her in the hall just then, which was fortunate, because at the mention of Eddie's name Junior lunged for Lara. Chip muscled Lara out of Junior's reach and dragged her into an empty classroom. "I am not going to fight Junior or his asshole friends for you over this, Lulu, so stop stirring him up."

"Chip, he was there, him and Eddie. And Eddie, his face, I can't tell you—"

Chip said roughly, "We're not at Kaw Valley anymore, Lulu. Whatever Junior and Eddie do, we can't do anything about it. You have to do like Janice: turn the other cheek."

"Do like Janice? You mean show everyone in school my big, wobbly boobs?"

Chip grabbed her shoulders and shook her. "One moron in the family is all I can stand, so you'd better take that back."

Lara mumbled an apology that she didn't mean and ran down the hall to her geometry class. When she got home, Lara told her mother that thanks to her she and Chip were having a tough time at school. "If you find me in the emergency room after Junior breaks my neck, I hope you'll know you can only blame yourself."

"Lara, don't stoop to their level. Don't go fighting boys like Junior Schapen. It makes you look as bad as they do."

"Mom, I'm trying to stand up for you, but the way you carry on no one can support you. People say you're a witch for taking part in the bonfire, they say you're doomed to hell. What am I supposed to do? Tell them I agree?"

The next day, Robbie Schapen raced past Lara in the cafeteria and dropped a folded square of paper on her tray. She was afraid at first to pick it up, wondering what insult it might contain, but when Kimberly reached out a hand for it Lara took it herself and unfolded it.

Dear Lara, I'm sorry about everything. Would you come with me to the Christ-Teen Group at Full Bible Christian this Thursday? The group's a lot of fun, I play electric guitar and write the lyrics, Junior doesn't go.

Kimberly peered at her curiously. "What's it say?"

"Oh, all those Schapens are totally bogus!" Lara stuck the note into her social studies text. "Like I want to go hear some sermon on hellfire from his church."

Later, during Spanish, she took the note out and studied it. Was he trying to insult her by asking her to his stupid, narrow-minded church or was he asking her on a kind of date? She tried to picture going out with Robbie Schapen. He had put grasshoppers down her T-shirt in sixth grade and smashed up her diorama of Kansas during the age of dinosaurs when they were in third grade, but, really, he wasn't as bad as Junior. Of course, after the grasshoppers she'd slugged him hard enough to break his front tooth, so they were sort of even.

Still, if she went to his youth group she'd either have to get Chip or Dad to drive her—or ride with Robbie and his dad, since she and Robbie were both too young to drive alone at night. The more she imagined the evening, the more horrible it seemed. She scrawled, "Sorry, my folks won't let me," on a piece of paper and dropped it on his desk in chemistry, which they had together at the end of the day.

Susan meanwhile took refuge from her critical family with Gina Haring. Gina mocked the whole idea of religion, saying that it was no more superstitious to light a bonfire to the goddess than it was to worship bread and wine by pretending they were your god's body and blood. When Gina saw that her comments upset Susan, she put an arm around her and said, "I love you because you're so sincere," which comforted Susan since no one at the farm these days was telling Susan they loved her.

She spent most of her free time with Gina, either at the Fremantle house or with other women from the bonfire at Between Two Worlds. And it was at the store that Susan learned about K-PAW—Kansas Patriots Against the War. At supper, Susan showed Jim and Lara one of K-PAW's brochures.

"Did you have any idea what's been going on over there? Did you know we've been torturing people? Our government? Or that nearly four thousand of our soldiers have died? Why are we there?"

Jim said, "Suze, it's all I can do to get a stalk of wheat to come up out of the ground. I figure we elect people to Congress to think about whether we need to go to war or not. Anyway, I thought you and I agreed before the war started that the president and Congress were making the right decision. We shouldn't start second-guessing them now. Just because the war is going badly is all the more reason not to turn on our leaders. Saddam was a tyrant, he was threatening us—"

"But he wasn't, Jim." Susan's amber eyes widened in her intensity. "Read this and you'll see he never had any weapons like we said he did. The whole war, everything we were told about it, it was all lies."

Jim took the pamphlet from her and laid it next to his plate. "A pamphlet by a bunch of Kansas women doesn't carry weight with me. What do they know about war or foreign policy?"

"How can you belittle us without even reading the evidence? Just because we're women doesn't mean God didn't give us brains to think with. It's all documented in here, you could look at it instead of being so superior about being a man."

Jim scrunched his eyes shut for a second before answering. "Susan, if you think I feel superior to you, or any other woman, you haven't been paying attention to me for the last twenty-five years. You know darn well that's not how I look at the world or your place in it. I'm just saying, this is a group of women, well meaning, maybe even smart, but they're not involved in government, they don't have access to the information our leaders had when they made these decisions. I don't want you going out on a limb with them and getting hurt or hurting our reputation."

"Mom, you know we have to plant the lettuce and beans this week," Lara interrupted. "And I have basketball tomorrow night. It's a big game, against Shawnee Mission North, so I really really want you and Dad to be there, okay? So can we talk about that, and who's going to drive me in since Chip won't take me?"

Jim seized gratefully on the diversion. The rest of the meal was spent working out the week's schedule, who would drive Lara to the game, who would get the germination trays set up in the greenhouses for the nonorganic crops, what paperwork had to be filed with the organic-growers certification board before they could put in the sunflower crop in April, whether Jim could fix the damage to the greenhouses from last month's ice storm on his own or if he needed to hire Curly's cousin.

After dinner, when Jim dragged a reluctant Susan into the family room to watch a *Columbo* rerun, Lara took the K-PAW brochure from the kitchen table. She read it through, wondering which of her parents was right: the flyer was filled with footnotes from the *New York Times, USA Today,* and other papers, but could you trust those papers to tell the truth? All Lara knew was that she didn't want another fight to build up at home, especially over an issue where her mother would stir up more public notice.

Lara tucked the flyer into her school binder; the next day, she threw it out when she got to school, hoping that if it wasn't in the house her mother would forget about it. In the excitement of the basketball game, which they lost by one point, of working on a play for Presidents' Day with Melanie, and the rest of her life, which included band practice, choir, and putting in the seedlings, Lara forgot about K-PAW.

Susan didn't: she picked up another flyer from Gina and started going to the group's meetings. Until then, she'd paid no more attention to the war than to gasp with dismay every time a suicide bomb targeted U.S.

troops, but in short order she had mastered all the history, all the outrages K-PAW claimed Americans had committed, the numbers of dead Iraqi children, the numbers of American boys and girls with terrible injuries.

"Why does Gina Haring care so much about this war?" Chip demanded on one of his rare nights at home—he was spending more and more evenings fooling around with Janice in the back of his Nissan or meeting his buddies in town for burgers or pizza.

"We all do, Etienne, not just Gina. Our country was *founded* on principles of decency and justice. But we've murdered hundreds of thousands of innocent Iraqis with our bombs and all for what? So that the president's oil friends can get rich?"

"Says you and the *New York Times.* If you watched Fox News, you'd know those are just slanders New York Jews use to try and make the president look bad. And why is it your business, anyway?"

"Since when does anyone in this house use a negative word or tone of voice to describe people of a different religion or race? It is the tradition of this family, of *your heritage,* to take a stand against injustice." His mother's eyes flashed. She ran up to the bedroom and came back downstairs with her commonplace book.

"Here's what your father's great-great-grandmother wrote about the Civil War: 'June 17, 1862. We have always shared the Peace Testimony advocated by our brothers and sisters the Quakers, we could not sit passively by while others shed their blood on behalf of our brothers and sisters in bondage.'" Susan looked sternly at her son. "Pacifism, the peace testimony, is your heritage, Etienne, as is commitment to work on behalf of the oppressed."

"Yeah, well, even old Gramps Etienne finally saw the light and joined the Union Army," Chip reminded her.

"But only to save the oppressed," his mother insisted.

"And that's what we're doing in Iraq!"

"Killing a hundred thousand women and children to save them? Explain the logic of that to me, mister!"

Chip ignored her. "I think Gina's putting you on and you're too ignorant to tell. She'll get you all stirred up, then leave you high and dry. Just you wait."

That was one of the milder exchanges Chip had with his mother. As the winter wore on, the two had blistering arguments whenever Chip ate at home. Lara couldn't stand the tension. If Chip and Susan started in at dinner, she'd leave the table, go up to her room, plug her music into her ears, and doggedly read *The Hobbit*. One day, she made up flyers in art class, announcing the creation of PPGF—Patriots for Peace in the Grellier Farm. She brought them to the dinner table. Jim ruffled her hair, grateful to his daughter for trying to diffuse the tension, but Chip told her not to be lame, and Susan wouldn't even look at them.

Lara had her own battles with Susan, but hers concerned the X-Farm. Susan was spending so much time on K-PAW activities that she wasn't paying proper attention to the seedlings in the organic greenhouses.

The Grelliers grew lettuce, herbs, beans, and a few early vegetables in the X-Farm for sale in their own market, the one they'd reverted to when Susan shut down the co-op. The Kansas growing season for lettuce was short: between the arctic winter and the Sahara summer lay a window of about six weeks, so plants had to be ready to go into the ground when the last frost was past. Lara wheedled Curly into coming out to help her transplant the seedlings from germination trays into larger ones, where they'd grow until they were planted outside, but she was furious with Susan for treating the work so carelessly—her mother didn't even notice or thank her for taking care of the transplanting.

"I found the certification forms in your desk, too" Lara said. "You still haven't completed them, and we have to have an inspection or we might as well not bother to put the sunflower crop in because we already printed the packages saying they're certified organic."

Susan kissed her daughter's forehead. "I'm too busy right now to worry about paperwork. If you fill out the forms, I'll sign them."

Lara struggled as best she could, but there were fifteen pages that covered everything from where they stored synthetic pesticides on the main farm relative to the X-Farm to how they planned to ship the crop when it was harvested. Jim helped her, but he had, or tried to have, a serious talk with his wife about the situation.

"Lara cannot run the X-Farm. She isn't old enough or experienced enough. And, anyway, I will not have her sacrifice her education or her music and basketball to do the job you signed on for when you persuaded

me to let you have that land. I will not let Lulu plant the sunflowers. You
have to do that if you want this crop to work, Suze. And if you don't
have time or energy for the X-Farm, we should sell the land to Curly's
cousin—he's been asking for it, off and on, ever since I bought it from Mrs.
Fremantle."

"I'll take care of the crop, Jim. Don't lecture me. When have I ever
shirked a responsibility?"

Jim wanted to remind her of the co-op market and the bread oven, but
there were too many arguments in the house already so he bit the words
back. "Just remember, somewhere in the world a hundred twenty-eight
people are eating because we're growing crops. That's an important responsibility, more important than worrying about the war, because the crops
are something we're in charge of. Whether you stand on a street corner in
Lawrence handing out leaflets isn't going to make a difference to this war,
but whether you get that crop in the ground, that will make a difference to
what people eat next winter. Not to mention our bottom line."

"I said I'll take care of the crop, Jim." Susan glared at him. "Don't talk
to me as if I were Eddie Burton."

The fights between Chip and Susan got worse when K-PAW decided
to hold a protest on March 8, International Women's Day, which, Susan
said, quoting her new friends, was traditionally "dedicated to peace."
Susan announced she was taking part. Jim protested, while Chip's rage
was so extreme that he spent several nights in town with Curly until Jim
and Blitz made him go home again.

Later, Jim wondered if that had been his biggest mistake. Should he
have left Chip in town? He'd forced Chip to come home because he'd
imagined his son drifting, following Curly's aimless life, not graduating
from high school, let alone going to college, never being able to have a
real job or a real future and settling into the farm as an unwanted default.
If he'd left Chip alone, let him cool off at Curly's. If. If.

Early on the Sunday of the march, Susan painted a peace slogan on an
old sheet. She drove over to the Fremantle place with it, where she roused
Gina from bed and got her to help attach the sheet to some bamboo
poles. She left the house that morning as excited as a small child off to see
Santa. She spent the night in jail.

Seventeen

OUT OF THE TANK

From the *Douglas County Herald*
LOCAL FARMWIFE ARRESTED

An anti-war march got out of hand Sunday when some of the leaders, including local farmwife Susan Grellier, threw hog's blood on pro-war demonstrators who had gathered in South Park for an alternative event. Only about eighty people, part of a group that calls itself "Kansas Patriots Against the War," were marching against the war; about five hundred, including local military personnel, and families from as far away as Kansas City and Wichita, were in South Park, where a band was playing patriotic songs. Arnold Schapen, a farmer who is also a Douglas County sheriff's deputy, had donated two hundred pounds of hamburger for the group, who call themselves Kansas Patriots Speak Up.

Schapen says some good-natured teasing between the groups—many of whom have known each other for years—was taken the wrong way by Mrs. Grellier and others in the anti-war group. Mrs. Grellier threw blood on a contingent of local ROTC members, yelling, "Our blood is on your hands." In the resulting skirmish, Schapen handcuffed her and six other offenders: Autumn Minsky, who owns Between Two Worlds on Seventh Street; Elaine Logan of 1706 Vermont Street, Gina Haring of New York, Jonathan Schlager of 2834 Missouri Street, Oscar

Herschel of 2323 Orchard Lane, all in Lawrence, and Theodore Black of Eudora. The seven were charged with two misdemeanor accounts, of violating their parade permit terms, and creating a public nuisance, and were each fined $250.

One of K-PAW's ringleaders is from New York, Deputy Schapen pointed out. He warned that "outside agitators turned Douglas County upside down in the seventies. We're in danger of seeing that happen all over again today. The time to stop violence is before it gets out of hand. We need to send a message to sodomites and witches that they are not welcome in our community."

Gina Haring says she lives half a mile from Deputy Schapen's farm. "Apparently, Mr. Schapen considers an outsider to be any-one who doesn't live in his house and share his extremely narrow, medieval beliefs."

Ms. Haring is a niece of John Fremantle, the son of Elizabeth Fremantle, who died two years ago; Elizabeth Fremantle left money for many civic projects in Lawrence, including the Chil-dren's Theater, named for her late husband Nathan. Gina Haring is currently living in the Fremantle house five miles east of Lawrence.

Jim was in the wheat field when Susan called from the county jail to report her arrest. He'd been kneeling to feel the level of moisture in the soil and to see if the freeze line had retreated. The wheat had made it safely through the winter; right now, it looked like clumps of dead grass. It was still at least three weeks from breaking dormancy, he decided, when he heard his daughter screeching, "Dad! Dad!," at the top of her lungs as she ran into the field in her flip-flops. "It's Mom," Lara panted, handing him the phone. "She's in jail!"

"It was Arnie," Susan blurted out to him, distraught. "He was at a pro-war rally in park. He started hassling Gina and me, calling us har-lots, and worse names than that. I was carrying a plastic bag of hog's blood, we were going to pour it over a poster of the president at the end of the march, but I swung it at him to try to make him get away from me and it broke and he arrested seven of us."

"Oh, Susan," was all Jim could manage.

His concern for the winter wheat evaporated. Even though he could sense her fear from the way her voice trembled, he was angry, unable to utter even mechanical words of comfort. He had been opposed to the march, to the whole K-PAW venture in his wife's life. And see what came of it: Susan had been arrested, just like the rioters he remembered from his adolescence, the kids who turned the town and the valley upside down with drugs and anti-war violence, imagining that they were the only people on the planet with working brains.

Because it was a Sunday, Susan had to spend the night in the new jail out on Twenty-fifth Street. Despite his anger, Jim drove over to see her, but it was after hours and he wasn't allowed in. The guard, a tiny woman barely out of high school who seemed too frail for the weight of the gun and handcuffs hanging from her waist, told him that he couldn't visit a prisoner unless he was on an approved-visitors list, anyway.

"But it's my wife," he said. "She was arrested this afternoon."

The guard shook her head. "I'm sorry, sir, but I can't let you in. She was arrested at that march downtown, right? There will be a hearing at ten-thirty in the morning. You can bring your lawyer, and she'll probably be released on bail."

Jim knew some lawyers, from church and through his brother, but the only one he and Susan ever consulted helped them with their estate planning and advice on threading through the maze of government regulations affecting the farm. Those legal bills were high enough that he could well imagine what it would cost to have someone represent Susan in the courtroom. She'd have to take her chances in front of the judge, he decided, and if she had to do thirty days, well, serve her right for taking part in the blasted march. All the same, he worried about Susan spending the night in a cell. When he got home, he called his brother in Chicago.

"Schapen, huh?" Doug said. "Damned asshole. If they charge Susan with assaulting a cop, she could be in big trouble. But for this hearing tomorrow, tell her to plead not guilty and wait to see what the charges are before you hire anyone. If it's a criminal case, maybe I could fly down to represent her."

Jim was grateful, not just for the offer but for Doug not taking the opportunity to reiterate his views on Susan and her resemblance to an unguided missile.

"Call Drysdale," Doug added. "He's a good guy. He won't want to drag you through a court battle."

"I can't do that, Doug. I can't trade on your friendship with the guy."

"Jimbo, that's why we have friends—so we're not on our own when we need help."

Jim was unconvinced, but when he got to the courthouse next morning he found that Doug had played big brother behind his back: Hank Drysdale met Jim outside the courtroom.

"Jim, I'm so sorry Susan had to spend the night in jail. You should have called me yourself—I didn't even know she'd been arrested until I got Doug's message, and he didn't reach me until after midnight."

The sheriff bent forward to add confidentially, "Between you and me, Arnie got overzealous. This was a Lawrence event; Chief Furman had four Lawrence police officers posted at South Park, and Arnie was only there as a civilian taking part in a counterdemonstration. Any rowdiness, it was the LPD's call on how to respond, not an off-duty county deputy's. Chief Furman is pretty unhappy with me, letting one of my boys muscle in on his cops' jurisdiction.

"I've spoken with the DA and with the mayor. No one wants a big trial that'll bring a lot of outsiders into the town: no one wants to see those seventies riots all over again. Bad enough they've brought reporters in from Topeka and Kansas City. Someone told me there're even runners or stringers or whatever from Chicago, so we plan to keep it low-key. The DA is willing to believe it was an accident, especially since it was Susan carrying that bag of blood. We'll call it a B misdemeanor. No need to go to trial unless you want to, but then there'd be court costs and her fine might go up. Your call, though."

Jim wondered if Susan would insist on a trial. Would she think she was a martyr, like Jim's ancestors, and that a trial would be romantic? He didn't say this, just nodded at Hank, who clapped him on the shoulder.

The two men went into the courtroom together, where they separated, the sheriff joining the prosecutor's table up front, Jim looking around for a seat. The courtroom was full of people, most of whom were strangers to Jim. The only one he recognized was Rachel Carmody from church. She waved to Jim and scooted over on her bench to make room for him.

"Elaine Logan lives in New Haven Manor. I'm on their board, you know, and they needed someone to look after her in the courtroom," Rachel explained. "I'm sorry about Susan. She's such an ardent spirit. I'm sure this must be a shock to her."

"To me, too," Jim couldn't help saying, then quickly added, "How did Elaine get involved?"

"She's an old seventies peacenik, or at least she says she is—I never know if half the stuff she says is true. She claims she was involved in that commune that used to live somewhere near your farm. I'm assuming that's how she met Gina Haring. Isn't she living out there, too?"

"Yep. At the Fremantle place. That's where the commune was, too."

"I'm surprised you haven't seen Elaine, then—she hitches out there sometimes to moon over her past, and she's pretty hard to overlook. The New Haven director got an SOS from her only last week, demanding he come pick her up at the crossroads. Elaine is as proud of being arrested as if she were Joan of Arc on her way to the stake, but I have an unchristian feeling that Gina was just using her to swell her numbers—even though the country has turned against the war, you don't get too many people willing to take to the streets in this neck of the woods."

Jim smiled wryly. "I wonder if it would be any comfort to think Gina was just using Susan, too, but Susan likes big causes. Sometimes I think she's been waiting her whole life for this anti-war nonsense."

He broke off, embarrassed at having said so much about his private business, and said, to change the subject, "I see the place is full up."

"Some of them are the K-PAW members." Rachel pointed to a group across the aisle, most of them women, most in their fifties or sixties, neatly groomed, looking anxious. "The others are mostly from the other side, Kansas Patriots Speak Up. They're the ones carrying the little flags."

Jim was so rattled he hadn't even noticed the American flags a lot of the spectators were holding. For reasons he couldn't quite define, the sight upset him. It was as if the courtroom were an Olympic stadium and the spectators were all set to wave their flags and yell "USA! USA!" when the hearing started.

Rachel nudged Jim and pointed out the reporters. Jim recognized the man from the *Douglas County Herald* who'd come out to the farm when Susan was running the co-op market and a woman from the local cable channel. The others were strangers.

"I guess they're hoping we're going to reenact bleeding Kansas for them," Rachel said. "And if Elaine Logan gets close to any of the Speak Up people, that may start to happen, which is why I'm going to hustle her out of here as soon as the hearing is over."

The clerk stood and announced the judge. Jim and Rachel got to their feet with the rest of the spectators. The hearing was for everyone who'd been arrested over the weekend, not just the marchers. Jim had to wait while a man charged with beating his wife, a woman who'd broken a mirror in a fight at the Storm Door, and two teens who'd ridden their motorcycles through someone's front yard, all had their cases heard.

The protestors were then called forward as a group. They seemed bedraggled after their night in jail, especially Elaine Logan. She was a fat woman, wearing gray sweatpants and a pink sweatshirt stretched tight over an enormous bosom. Her faded blond hair stood out from her head in dirty elflocks. Her hands were shaking, but she looked pugnaciously around the courtroom, making a peace sign at the group from Kansas Patriots Speak Up, who hissed at her. She poked Gina, urging her in an audible whisper to make a stand for justice. Gina stepped back without looking at the older woman. She was holding herself aloof, looking neither at the judge nor her fellow arrestees, not even Autumn Minsky.

Susan was so white that her freckles stood out like polka dots on muslin. She, too, tried to whisper to Gina, but Gina stared forward, ignoring Susan as completely as she had Elaine. Jim felt a spurt of anger: Gina had gotten Susan and Elaine involved in her stupid march and now she was acting like they were flies she was switching off her back. For the first time since his wife called him yesterday, Jim felt the urge to wrap his arms around her, comfort her, protect her from the big bad world.

When the hearing began, Arnie Schapen testified as the arresting officer.

The Kansas Patriots waved their flags as he spoke, just as Jim had imagined they would, but the judge told them bluntly it was a courtroom, not a football field, and they would have to leave if they couldn't observe appropriate decorum.

Arnie gave his evidence without looking at Jim or Susan, but Jim could see he was smirking when he sat down. The judge gave the protestors a short, sharp lecture on civil conduct before offering them a choice of a fine or a trial. Jim waited tensely while Susan looked again at Gina, who chose the fine. Susan and the others all followed suit. It was suddenly over, no criminal charges, no trial, but two hundred fifty dollars! Where was that money going to come from?

As soon as the judge dismissed the protestors, Rachel Carmody hurried to the front of the room to collect Elaine Logan. Jim waited for Susan at the back of the courtroom. She stumbled down the center aisle, exhausted, and collapsed against him. He put an arm around her, but neither of them spoke, not while he stood in line at the cashier's window to pay her fine, not while she signed for her belongings, not while they walked out to the parking lot. The reporter from the *Herald* recognized them and hurried over, followed by a camera crew from the local television station. Jim shook his head, not saying a word, just picked up his exhausted wife and carried her to the pickup.

When they got to the farm, she looked up at him, her amber eyes painfully large. "I'm sorry, Jim. I couldn't help it."

"We've got to come up with that money somehow, Susan, so maybe you'd better pay attention to your sunflower crop for a while." In the complicated mix of tenderness and anger that he'd been feeling for twenty-four hours, it was only harshness that he felt able to express now.

She stared at him, tears forming at the corners of her eyes. "I need you to understand how it happened, Jim. I didn't mean to get you in trouble or make a spectacle of myself."

"I'm too worn out to listen right now. You go up and take a bath, get some of that jailhouse dirt off you. I have to go out to the wheat field."

She flicked her tears away; he noticed she had dried blood on her hand and on the front of her blouse. He often wondered later if he'd taken her in his arms then if things would have turned out differently.

When he turned to go to the fields, he noticed a light in the combine shed. Blitz was there, underneath the combine. He was taking apart the clutch—the bearings and gears were laid out on a tray next to the clutch housing. Blitz had the radio tuned to a country-music station and was talking to the machine in time to the music: "Yes, this bolt done left you, broke your poor old Caterpillar heart."

Jim didn't think he could stand it if Blitz offered him sympathy, or even commented on Susan's arrest, but when Blitz heard him come in all he did was pop his head out from the engine to say, "Should have done this before harvest last year. Three bearings are just about shot to hell. I don't know why Reba here didn't freeze up on us in the field."

Blitz called the combine Reba after his favorite country singer. He talked to her as if she were a horse, slapping her side when he eased her out of the shed. Lara once told him she was surprised he didn't give Reba sugar cubes to suck on, and he laughed and said, "She takes oil right from my hand, she's such a good old girl."

Blitz had shown up on the farm sixteen years ago, in the middle of a blizzard. He was driving from Abilene to Olathe, where he had a lead on a machinist's job, when his pickup got stuck in a drift. He'd seen the spotlights at the train crossing, a faint orange against the blizzard's white-out, and when he made for them he found the Grellier farm just beyond.

Jim had been in the equipment barn, trying to salvage the gearbox on his grandfather's diesel truck, when Blitz staggered in, his black beard a mass of white crystals. After he'd caught his breath, he explained that he needed a tow, but could he sleep in the barn until the storm passed? Of course, Jim and Susan put him up on the spare bed on the sunporch. In the morning, Jim found him in the barn, machining a new gear for the old diesel truck. When the snow stopped, Blitz went on to Olathe, but he returned a few weeks later. He wondered if Jim didn't need help.

It was the first winter after Jim's grandfather had died, and Jim was overwhelmed by the job of running the farm on his own: he'd welcomed Blitz like a savior. It was Chip, just learning to talk, who gave him the nickname. "Blitz, him come in blitz," he crowed, trying to say "blizzard." The memory twisted Jim in half. Why hadn't he known then that nothing was too hard to handle if your boy was shrieking with delight at the world?

Blitz handed him a long screw. "Bolt's frozen on. Can you undo it?"

The morning moved through a soothing rhythm of repairs, Jim replacing the fan belt on the tractor while Blitz machined new bearings for the combine, Jim putting new siding on the X-Farm greenhouse, where he checked on the seedlings, while Blitz hammered a bent disk on the corn-head shredder.

Jim knew Lara had been looking after the seedlings, but he hadn't paid enough attention to how they were shaping. He checked the moisture, but Lara had been keeping up with the watering. They'd joked about her taking over the place a few weeks ago, but maybe she really would want to now that Chip had made it clear he didn't: she had the knack and the patience to care for the plants.

You had to be a gambler and a conservative at the same time to be a farmer. Every time you put seed in the ground, you were betting against God Almighty and the politicians that the weather would be good, the pests controllable, the fuel prices low, the political situation overseas stable so you could sell your crop there. And you had to be conservative, willing to play by those out-of-date rules of hard work, sweat of the brow. Who would choose such a life? You only did it if the life chose you.

At noon, Blitz pulled a meat-loaf sandwich out of his lunch box for Jim. Jim ate half of it before he remembered that Blitz was a vegetarian. So Blitz had come out prepared to look after him. The thought was consoling. He punched Blitz on the arm.

By the end of the afternoon, Jim felt calm enough to go back into the house to face his wife. She was asleep, purple shadows on the delicate skin under her eyes. Jim sat on the bed, holding her hand, stroking her freckled forehead.

He heard a car door slam, then the kitchen door: Lulu was home. "Dad! Dad! Are you in the house? Where's Mom? Is she in jail? Chip got suspended from school for fighting Junior Schapen and Milt Riley."

Eighteen

ONE LAST FIGHT

From schapendairyfarm.com/newsandnotes.html

Wives, be subject to your husbands, as to the Lord. For the husband is head of the wife as Christ is head of the church. Paul wrote this in Ephesians, under the divine inspiration of Jesus Christ, which means those are the words of God, not words you can listen to or not as your mood strikes you. Some of our neighbors who profess Jesus don't seem to understand this. Their wives run around like crazed animals from a circus, not like sober Christian women. At times like this, we pity the wife but blame the husband for not filling his God-ordained role as head of the household.

God is not a pacifist! In the Bible, God repeatedly takes lives to spare His Chosen People or to make a point to His Chosen People about how far they've strayed from His Word! In Genesis, God kills everyone on earth, except Noah, his family, and the animals, because the Children of Israel have done so much evil in His sight. In Exodus, God kills every Egyptian firstborn to save the Children of Israel, and God continues to use His four dreadful judgments—sword, famine, wild beasts, and pestilence—against the sinful.

America is under a dreadful scourge right now, thanks to the liberals and their encouragement of sodomy, abortion, and idolatry. Our neighbors seem hell-bent on bringing further wrath down on all our heads. They disrupted the town by pretending that pacifism is a Christian virtue; they danced in front of idols. Maybe it's their French blood. If it is, we sure don't need cheese-eating surrender monkeys in the Kaw River Valley!

Lulu printed the file out at school and brought it home with her. Jim read it through slowly, his anger building again. The cornerstone of his philosophy: you can't farm in the valley if you're on bad terms with your neighbors. He worked hard to be a good neighbor, so why was Arnie Schapen determined to make war on him? Did he think he could drive Jim off the land or did he just like fighting, the way Junior and Chip— and Jim's brother, Doug, for that matter—seemed to like it?

Lara's face, usually round and soft with the residue of her baby fat, was pinched, her cheekbones sticking out from anxiety. "They were all laughing and talking about it at lunch, so I went to the computer lab and printed it out. Every time Junior or Milt Riley or his other friends passed me or Chip in the hall, they'd lift their shoulders up and scratch their armpits like they were monkeys."

"Monkeys?" Jim was bewildered. "Were they trying to say you and Chip are related to monkeys? I thought the Schapens' church was against evolution."

"No, Dad," Lara said with exaggerated patience. "Thanks to Mom bragging to the whole world about your ancestor coming from France, everybody knows Grellier is a French name. They were saying we were surrender monkeys."

"So Chip felt he had to fight them?" Jim asked.

"I guess." Lara hunched a shoulder. "It was in senior English, so I wasn't there."

"Where's Chip? Didn't he drive you home?"

Lara shook her head. "Mr. Meadows made Hector—he's the guard, you know—escort Chip out of the building. Melanie drove me home."

Jim started to say, "You know you're not allowed to ride with underage drivers," but bit the words off before they came out. Lara didn't need any more tension in her life today. Come to think of it, neither did he.

"Your mother's okay," he said instead. "They let her off with a fine. She's asleep right now, pretty worn-out from a night in jail. Schapen was mad that they didn't charge her with a felony, so I guess he rushed home and got his ma to put this up on their website. It's mean, it's petty, but he only did it because he felt helpless. Can you remember that and try not to fight the Schapen boys yourself?"

Lulu gave a wobbly smile. "I guess."

"You know, Lulu, I'm kind of worn-out myself—what with worrying about your mom, I didn't sleep much last night. All this anger swirling around is exhausting, too. You want to go into town, get ice cream or a pizza?"

"Everyone's staring at us, Dad, staring and talking."

"I bet the people at Chill! never heard of Arnie Schapen or Susan Grellier; they'll give you your hot-fudge sundae without even looking up from the ice-cream bins."

"Yeah, okay, I guess," she muttered: good daughter making a martyr of herself for her desperate father.

Jim pulled a wry face and went back up to the bedroom to leave a note for Susan. She was awake, roused by the noise Lulu had made shouting through the house for Jim, but not moving. She looked at him dully. When he told her about Chip, she bit her lip and turned her head away from him on the pillow.

He took her hand again, but inside he felt a hard spot of resentment toward her: Arnie was a loose cannon, but Susan had played a part in starting all this, too. "Suze, can you lay off the anti-war stuff for a while until this school thing and Arnie's vendetta both calm down? Please?"

She stiffened, but after a long pause said, "I won't go on any marches or hand out leaflets until I've worked off the fine. I'll get to work on the sunflower crop tomorrow, but I want to go to K-PAW meetings, Jim. I think that's fair."

It was fair, he supposed, but he wanted her to be generous, to say she'd leave peace work to the university people who had less to lose. He didn't know how to say that to her, though, so he finally just told her he was taking Lulu into town for ice cream.

When they got home, Lara was calmer. No one at the ice-cream parlor had shown any signs of knowing the Grelliers had the mark of the beast on them, so she'd been able to enjoy her hot fudge, and even wave at one of her classmates, who came in as she and Jim were getting ready to leave.

It was close to six when they got back. Blitz had left and Chip hadn't shown up. Jim tried to call his son, but Chip wasn't answering his cell phone. Susan had gone back to sleep and left a note asking them not to wake her. Jim challenged Lara to a game of miniature pool. She went to bed around ten, happier, but he stayed up, waiting for his son to come home.

He dozed off in the kitchen and woke with a start when Chip drove into the yard, his wheels spraying up gravel because he'd taken the turn too fast. Jim's neck and knees had frozen from sleeping sitting up; it was an effort and an agony to get to his feet. As soon as Chip came in, Jim realized he was drunk.

"Beer never solved any problems I heard of, except cash flow to the beer companies," he told his son.

"Yeah, well, write that up on Arnie's website for him, tell him the cheese-eating surrender monkey likes beer, not frog wine," Chip said.

"How come you let Junior get under your skin like that?" Jim asked.

"Jesus Christ, Dad, what planet do you live on? Here's Mom, hanging out with those dykes, letting Arnie arrest her ass because—"

"Chip, I know you're angry, and I know you're drunk, but do not talk to me in that language, and do not use it about your mother. Tell me a simple story about what happened today."

Chip flushed and swayed, clutching the refrigerator for support. "It's her fault for giving me that stupid name. I've told her my whole life I hate it, and all she says is I'd like it if *you* hadn't encouraged me to hate it. Well, nothing would make me like being called after some stupid Frenchman who was too lazy to do a lick of work on the farm and then got shot because he was off running a school he had no business at in the first place."

He raised his voice to a falsetto, mimicking his mother: "Etienne is a noble name, with a noble history in your family—the man who gave up his country to come to Kansas and fight for freedom. Chip! Chip could be a chip on your shoulder or a chip of paint, not a name you can be proud of."

Jim couldn't help smiling at Chip's mimicry. "It was Grandpa who nicknamed you Chip; he said you were a chip off the old block. I guess that made me proud, so it was what I always called you, not because I didn't like your Christian name."

"Well, I hate it. And without even talking to me, she went and registered me for school in town as Etienne, so every time I start a new course I have to tell the teacher to call me Chip, and Mottled—Ms. Motley, my English teacher—she won't. She always calls me Etienne no matter how many times I ask.

"So today Milt Riley starts yelling 'Hey, Frenchie' when I get to English class. And, honest, Dad, I tried to ignore him. But then fucking Junior Schapen says, 'Frenchie, your ma's a heroine, ain't she? Will you sign my copy of the *County Herald* pretty, pretty please?'

"And then Riley says, 'She ain't a heroine, Schapen. She's a fucking jailbird!' And I still didn't look up, until Junior says, 'Come on, Frenchie, autograph the paper for me. I never met a real celebrity before.' And I told him not to call me a Frenchie, because our family was farming in this valley when his people were still humping cows in a shack in Europe!"

Jim sighed. "You couldn't just let it go, could you? So what happened—Junior jump you?"

"No." Chip's voice was thick with resentment. "Mottled called out in that nasal voice of hers, 'Etienne, your discussion is so lively I want you and Milton to come to the front of the room to share it with the class.' And then fucking Riley says, 'Eh-ti-yen,' like making this huge point that my name is French, and he says I have such an interesting family history I should tell it to the class. And then he starts in on Mom, saying she used to be a Commie when she ran that stupid co-op market and now she's like a member of al-Qaeda, and that's when I lost it."

"I see." Jim rubbed his head, wishing he could rub one sensible idea into it, but all he felt was wool and numbness. "We're going to have to think of some way to patch this over until the school year ends."

"I'm not going back to school. I'm eighteen. You can't make me."

Jim squinted up at his son in the dim light. Chip wasn't only bigger than he was, he was angrier. Jim couldn't possibly make him do anything. "I hate to think a son of mine could be such a coward he couldn't face the consequences of his own actions."

"Think whatever you like. I'm not going back to school."

"Then you can start doing a day's work on the farm."

"And be here day in and day out, with Mom getting wackier by the minute and you pretending nothing's wrong? Thanks but no thanks."

"We're not going to figure it out in the middle of the night," Jim finally said. "But you have to think about it, son, think about a plan for your life. You can't spend your nights at the Storm Door getting drunk and your days in bed. And if you give up on your education now, it'll be that much harder to finish later on."

Chip stared at him, the night swallowing up the hot hurt in his face, then swung on his heel and went up the stairs to his room, thumping as loudly as he could in running shoes. The next day, he locked himself in, refusing to talk to anyone in the family.

On Wednesday, he got up early to drive Lara into school, not talking to Jim or Susan but telling his sister he was looking for a job. He didn't come home that night, didn't phone. On Thursday, Jim tried Curly and then Janice, but they both said they hadn't seen him—although Lulu told him from the way Janice was carrying on at school, she was sure Janice knew what Chip was doing. That made Jim try to talk to Janice again, as well as to her parents, but the Everleighs said they didn't want their daughter hanging out with a loser like Chip.

At that, Jim lost his temper. "Good. His mother and I don't think she's the right person for him, either. She's not a help in his life."

At the end of the week, when Jim and Susan were frantic enough with worry that they'd reported Chip's disappearance to Sheriff Drysdale, Blitz, who had his own sources of information, dragged Curly out to the farm and made him talk to Jim.

Lara watched them from her bedroom. She saw Blitz go into the house, leaving Curly standing in the yard, shivering in his windbreaker. Curly was a small man with a shock of blond hair that grew in a natural Mohawk, so that even at thirty-two he looked like a teenager. Alone in the yard, he looked even younger. Lara saw her father come out of the house with Blitz. The three men went to the barn.

Lara slipped out of the house through the door to the garage. She hiked across the edge of the wheat field, crossed through the combine shed, and reached the back end of the barn. There were a couple of places where boards had come loose from the concrete foundation slab. She found a gap wide enough to slide through.

When her head and shoulders were inside, she could hear the murmur of voices but couldn't make out what they were saying: the men were at the front of the barn, on the other side of the tractor heads and machining equipment. Lara slithered all the way inside.

The board made a low snapping, singing sound behind her back, but no one noticed—barns are always making noises: the wind whipping around the sides, animals crawling along the rafters. The men hadn't turned the lights on, and Lara couldn't really see, but she tiptoed slowly forward, hands out, so she'd touch a piece of equipment before she tripped over it.

She heard her father smack his hand on something. "Damn it, Curly! When I called you on Thursday, couldn't you tell I was worried sick? I haven't slept for five nights. And when the sheriff talked to you, you lied to him! I don't even know what to say to you. You've been working out here for, what, nine years now? How could you betray my trust in you?"

And then Curly's voice, thick with misery: "I promised Chip. I'm sorry, Jim, but I couldn't go back on my word. Do you want me to quit?"

A long pause, during which Lara held her breath. *Don't fire him,* she pleaded in her head. *Chip's disappeared. Don't get rid of Curly, too.* And then her hand came down on a can full of ball bearings and sent them flying around the barn, a cascade of balls that rattled and banged like a giant pinball machine. The lights came up in the barn, and she hugged herself, painfully exposed.

"Lara! What on earth—?" her father cried out.

"I'm sorry, Dad," she wailed. "I wanted to know where Chip was. Did he join the Marines?"

"Did you know?" Jim yelled. "Are you another one who knew and didn't tell me?"

"Don't, Dad. I don't know where he went, I only wondered because he used to have those recruiting pamphlets on his dresser. And I told you and Mr. Drysdale that I thought Janice knew what he was doing, but she wouldn't talk to me. Is that what Chip did? Did he join the Marines? Is he in Iraq?"

He stared at her for a minute, frightening her with the ferocious look on his face. She didn't know that he wasn't staring at her but at himself: how could he be the least knowledgeable person in Douglas County about the people closest to him? He'd never noticed any recruiting pamphlets in Chip's room, but Lara had seen them. Blitz noticed that Curly was hiding news about Chip; Lara was sure Janice knew. Only he, Jim, had spent the week stumbling around like a blind drunk at the fairgrounds.

Finally he said, in a dry, small voice, "Lulu, don't stand there in the dark. Come on over here. And, Curly, I don't want you to quit. I couldn't take it if I had to have a stranger around the place right now. Just tell me everything you know."

Curly shuffled his feet, his blond rooster's comb of hair drooping in his eyes. "I don't know much, Jim, honest, but he stopped by that apartment building out on Sixth Street on Wednesday afternoon—you know, that big complex where I been working for my cousin. He showed me his enlistment papers and said he was on his way to Fort Jackson. That's in South Carolina. He told me he'd be sleeping in his car to save money until he reports to the base. I give him a few twenties so he could get a motel room along the way. He made me promise not to tell you and Susan, said he'd call you himself when he got there."

He glanced at Lara. "He said he'd've preferred the Marines, only they make you take a bunch of tests or something first and he wanted to get going fast as he could."

"And did he call you or anything along the road?" Jim demanded.

Curly nodded miserably. "This morning. He called me from South Carolina to tell me he got there safe and sound and he starts his basic training Monday morning. He found hisself a pretty cheap room outside the fort where he's staying the night. I—I got the name wrote down someplace."

He started turning out his pockets, looking for the scrap of paper with Chip's motel written on it.

Lara felt a cold knot in her stomach. Chip was going to be a soldier. They'd make him march around in formation when he never even liked to be told to make his bed or do his homework. No more hiding in the

Fremantle house, smoking dope with Curly, or going to the Storm Door with his baseball buddies. He'd turn into a stranger, she wouldn't see him for years and years, and she'd be alone on the farm with Dad and Mom.

The loneliness terrified her. Mom was hanging out with Gina and the K-PAW people, and even Dad was acting strange, as though space aliens had come to live inside his body and make him walk in a funny, jerky way. What would she do? Who could she talk to?

Curly finally dug out the number, and Jim took it to the house so he could call Chip. Curly followed him, but Lara stood still next to the big metal planer, her teeth chattering.

Blitz came over and put his flannel shirt around her. "I know it seems frightening, but maybe it'll be a good thing for him. Boy doesn't know what he wants to do with his life. The Army might help him sort that out."

Lara clenched her teeth to stop the sound. Blitz was trying to cheer her up, which he'd never done before, so she nodded to show she understood, at least understood the gesture, even if she didn't understand what he was saying.

Nineteen

THE LONG GOOD-BYE

IN THE MIDDLE OF MAY, the Grelliers drove out to Fort Jackson to watch Chip graduate from basic training. Susan hadn't wanted to go. She told Jim she couldn't lend her presence to an activity of which she disapproved so strongly.

"You going doesn't mean you approve of Chip's choice. It means you're his mother and you love him," Jim said, so angry his knuckles showed white where he was grabbing the chair back. "I know you hate this war, but you love our son. He loves you and he needs to see your face before they send him eight thousand miles away. All those e-mails he writes, can't you see he's scared?"

Susan bit her lip but finally agreed to go. Jim left Blitz in charge of the farm. For once in a blue moon, they'd had the right mix of rain and sun; the wheat crop should be outstanding, if the weather held, and Jim knew he could trust Blitz to make the right decisions if it didn't.

They spent two nights on the road, going south through Kentucky to see the caves. Susan stayed in the truck, reading a history of pacifism, making pointed remarks about turning their son's dangerous situation into a pleasure trip. They camped out to save money, and Jim was grateful for his daughter's presence in the tent, which precluded any pretense of marital intimacy.

Lara was both nervous and excited at the prospect of seeing Chip as a soldier. Her mother was so upset by his enlisting that Lara couldn't talk about it at home, but at school she'd become something of a vicarious heroine for having a brother in the military. Of course, Janice Everleigh was milking his enlistment all she could, acting like they were married or something—she went around the halls in his baseball-letter jacket, her face radiant. Overnight, she'd gone from girlfriend of a loser who fought in school and got kicked out to the lover of an American patriot.

When they got to the fort, Lara didn't recognize Chip at first. He looked so strange, not like himself, in his uniform, with his hair shaved close to his head. Then he caught sight of them and ran through the throng of soldiers and families, his eyes wet, and Lara could see he was homesick and excited that they'd come.

"You're not mad at me, are you, Dad?"

"Just scared, son. If you're doing what's right for you, how can I be mad? And I'm proud of you for doing it in the service of our country."

Susan only said, "Oh, Etienne, I'm so sorry," which could have meant anything.

During the ceremony, Chip held himself rigidly erect, along with the other recruits, but Lara could tell from the way he licked his lips that he was scared. It was only then, glancing at her parents, that Lara saw her mother wearing a prominent button that read MOTHERS AGAINST WAR.

"How could you?" she whispered to Susan, furious. "Take it off!"

"How could *he*?" Susan whispered back. "If I have to see him carrying those dreadful weapons, with his beautiful curls shaved off, he can see me supporting him with this badge."

The next day, Chip left for advanced infantry training in Oklahoma. Lara, angry about Susan's button, refused to speak to her mother during the drive home. When they reached the farm, Susan threw herself into K-PAW work, while Lara tended the organic-sunflower seedlings in the greenhouse.

For the first time, on her fifteenth birthday, Lara was allowed to drive the combine. When she finished her part of the field, Curly grinned at her and said, "How drunk was you, Lulu, to make those big curves in the field? Or is that one of your art projects?" But Blitz clapped her on the shoulder and said she'd done well for a beginner.

Two weeks later, Gina built a new bonfire to celebrate Midsummer Eve. Susan went to the ceremony without even mentioning it to Jim, relations between the two had become so strained.

In the weeks before that fire, Lara had watched Susan growing herbs in the X-Farm greenhouse, Saint-John's-wort, heartsease, lavender. She had dried them and tied them up in bundles with red and gold thread. Lara was having her own fight with Susan, about the fate of the X-Farm. She was curious about the bundles of herbs but too angry with her mother for tying up the organic greenhouse with them and neglecting the sunflower crop—which was overdue for transplanting to the field—to talk to her about her herb bundles.

Still, at ten o'clock Lara followed her customary route along the tracks to watch Gina and Autumn set the fire alight. Hiding behind the Fremantles' big hay barn, Lara watched a parade of women file through the old apple orchard, each carrying a lantern. They were silent until they reached the fire, when they stood and faced it and began singing, the music sweet but distorted by the crackling of the fire. Lara could see her mother, her face alight with eagerness.

Elaine Logan was there as well, her gigantic bosom unmistakable in the firelight. Her breasts were so heavy that even the largest sweatshirts pulled tight across them—her "shelf," Curly called it. "Think about it, Lulu, you could rest your coffee cup on it," he said, making her blush and giggle.

Ever since Elaine had been arrested with Gina and Susan, she'd started hitching out to the Fremantles' two or three times a month. She'd pick up a ride as far as the train crossing at the county road behind the Grelliers', then waddle and puff her way up to the Fremantle place. Once, when Lara was up on the combine, she actually saw Elaine let herself into the house.

Autumn or some other Wiccan had given Elaine a ride out tonight for the midsummer fire. Elaine was already slightly drunk when she got to the Fremantles' and in a boisterous mood, hovering between hilarity and belligerence: she might do anything if she thought the other women were slighting or ignoring her. Seeing Elaine at the bonfire, face gleaming in the firelight, Lara hoped she wouldn't take off her sweatshirt. It was pink tonight, with the Pink Panther outlined in dark sequins. She had her head thrown back, laughing loudly at something one of the women near her was saying.

Before choosing a roost, Lara had scouted the area but hadn't seen any sign of Eddie Burton or the Junior Schapen. She lay in the high grass, watching the ceremony begin. Susan handed out her bundles of herbs; the women circled the fire, singing and tossing the herbs into the blaze.

Life at home had been so filled with fights lately that Lara had forgotten how exhilarating her mother could be when she was filled with enthusiasm. Seeing Susan so ardent made Lara wish she could get up and join the dance herself, but she knew she'd be self-conscious trying to move with all those naked women. Besides, if Jim came looking for her, the way he had in February, he'd be furious to find her taking part.

Lara felt these days as though she were teetering in the middle of a balance beam: keeping Jim happy meant making Susan angry. Taking Susan's part meant upsetting Jim. It was too hard to deal with, so Lara mostly retreated to practicing the trumpet or working on the X-Farm. She had a big project, too, for the county fair, monitoring pest levels in the organic-sunflower crop against state standards for chemically farmed sunflowers.

She dozed off, thinking about her sunflower project, and was roused by the sound of sirens. Flashing red lights were creating a pulsing glow like that of the bonfire. Men in fire slickers erupted through the apple trees, carrying fire extinguishers and other equipment, followed by several men in sheriff's uniforms, including Arnie Schapen. Their radios were squawking, and between that and the noise of the sirens Lara couldn't make out what anyone was saying. She saw Gina, tall and slim, trying to argue with the men. Elaine joined them. Sometime while Lara had been napping, Elaine had taken off her sweatshirt, and her huge breasts surged like the ocean as she spoke. Then Susan came up—mercifully, with all her clothes on—and apparently began putting in her two cents. What was Susan saying? Lara wondered. "Don't you know this area is the bastion of free speech in America? This is where your ancestors fought and died to keep America free."

While Gina and Susan were arguing, the men were dousing the bonfire, using extinguishers and a dump truck full of sand. The truck had driven along the road and then cut across the field where Lara was lying. She hadn't heard it coming and missed being hit by about a foot.

She backed away from the blaze and crept across the field to the road, then across the train tracks to her family's farm. She didn't want to risk being seen by Arnie or any of the other deputies.

It was while she was crossing the tracks that she saw Eddie Burton. He was standing at the edge of the field she'd just crossed, staring at her. While she looked at him, he started moving his arms and jumping around. After a few seconds, she realized he was imitating the women at the bonfire. And then he started shrieking, "They had it coming, didn't they? Firemen come. Those women had it coming to them."

She was horrified that he'd seen her, but something kept her from being able to turn away from his grotesque pantomime. Suddenly, Junior Schapen appeared next to him. He put his arms around Eddie, almost as if he were embracing him, but Eddie pointed at Lara.

Junior started across the road toward her. The sight unglued Lara's feet, and she ran through the corn. She could hear Junior pounding after her, trampling down the stalks, but she was slimmer and faster, and she knew her way through her own fields to her own farm. When she reached the main barn, she slipped inside through the loose board at the back. She waited there in the dark almost an hour, listening to rats and raccoons snuffling through the rafters, until she heard the pickup pull into the yard. She crawled back through the board, not wanting to risk running into all the machines in the barn.

When Lara finally went into the house, Susan was pouring out her woes to Jim. "I can't believe Arnie would do such a small-minded, mean-spirited thing. He claimed we were violating some county fire code or other, he got the volunteer fire departments to come out from Baldwin and Eudora and had them put out our fire."

"Susan, you can't expect me to get outraged on your behalf. I'm tired of all this witchcraft shit. You're on the board—" Jim broke off at the sight of Lara. "*Damn* it, Lulu! Did you take part in that damned fire?"

She shook her head. "I was just watching. Dad, Junior and Eddie Burton were there. They saw me, and Junior chased me home."

She couldn't bring herself to report anything else, how Eddie'd been behaving, the strange way Junior had put his arms around Eddie. Jim went out to look for Junior, but he told Lara that she had herself to thank for the episode.

"If you'd stayed home like I asked you, you wouldn't have gotten such a scare. Maybe this will teach you that I have a good reason for asking you to do things."

Lara bit her lip and went up to bed. Both she and Susan felt Jim hadn't been sympathetic to them, but when Susan tried to share her own hurt feelings with her daughter, Lara scowled at her. "I wish you wouldn't do weird stuff, Mom. That Elaine Logan, she was about the grossest thing I've ever seen. How can you want to be part of something *she's* involved with?"

The next day, she put it all in an e-mail to Chip—at least, all but the part about Elaine's giant breasts. She didn't want Chip joking about them with his Army buddies. She told him everything else, the bonfire, how she'd sneaked out to watch it, how she'd seen Junior and Eddie, and Eddie had chased her home.

Then, next morning, Mom went over to talk to Gina about getting revenge on Arnie. She had some kind of goofy plan for Sheriff Drysdale to make the Schapens go through sensitivity training on other religions!!! Like Arnie and Myra and them would ever think anyone but them was right. And Gina said, "That's an exercise in futility," in that kind of snotty voice she uses to put people down.

Chip wrote back to tell Lara to mind her own business. His enlistment seemed to have evaporated his anger with their mother.

Mom works hard, Lulu, let her play however she wants to. Believe me, I thought I knew hard work until I joined up. If this is what adult life in the big outside world is like, maybe I'll want to be a farmer after all. Whatever Gina wants to do, just ignore it because you'll only get into water over your head. If she thinks she can take on Myra and Arnie, let her get burned all by herself, okay?

And for Pete's sake, Lulu, KEEP OUT OF JUNIOR'S WAY. What him and Eddie do together is their business, unless they start setting fire to the house or trashing the fields, so don't go spreading around stories at school, promise me. Junior is about the meanest person I know. After dealing with Junior Schapen, believe me I am not afraid of any Iraqi insurgents.

Chip had five days' leave when he finished his advanced infantry training at the beginning of July. Most of his time he divided between Janice and Curly or hanging out with his friends from high school. His last night at home, though, he took Lara bowling, just her, not Curly, Janice, or his friends from the baseball team.

They had a pizza at Gianni's, and Chip said, "Remember, Lulu, you're the brainy one. Don't do like me, running away from home by joining the Army. You can make your escape by running away to college. And don't worry about me. I was the toughest guy in my unit in basic 'cause none of the others had ever spent seventeen hours on a combine under a hundred-degree sun. I know how to survive in the heat."

He hesitated before adding, "Write me, Lulu. Write me every day if you can. I need to know you guys still remember me."

It didn't even occur to Lara to tease him about Janice, who probably didn't know how to put a sentence down on paper. Instead, when his unit reached Iraq she sent him e-mails full of the ordinary news of the farm.

Twenty

TAPS

THE DAY AFTER the county fair ended, Lara e-mailed Chip:

I see it's like a hundred and twenty in Baghdad, and it's about that hot here, so the animals at the fair really suffered. Robbie Schapen camped out all night with his dairy cow; he even played his guitar to her. Pretty funny, huh? Mom's pie only came in second this year—she didn't really pay attention to her baking, but I got first place for my dress and my organic pest control project. Junior took part in the hay bale tossing contest, which was a laff riot, because he's so full of himself.

Curly, who'd taken Lara that evening, had said, "Junior and his old man are the kind of guys who love themselves so much they eat their own shit and like it." Lara added that in quotation marks, making sure Chip knew it was Curly speaking, that she wouldn't say something so dirty, even if every time she thought it she started to giggle. She knew it would make Chip laugh, although, come to think of it, Curly had probably said it to him a million times.

"Anyway, when the platform was fifteen feet high, Junior tossed the bale and it landed on his head. It knocked him out, but even Big Arnie could see it happened because Junior was hotdogging. They stopped the contest for a bit while they made sure Junior was okay, just a little concussed, but given that his head is pretty solid ear to ear they really should have checked the hay bale for damage."

She was hitting the SEND button when the doorbell rang. Lara couldn't place the sound at first, because in the country no one ever went to the front door or even rang a bell. Not just at their house, but every house in the valley, people always went in through the kitchen, and kitchens opened onto the yard—it's the way farmhouses were built.

Lara didn't even realize her house had a doorbell until that moment. When she heard the shrill sound, she thought it was the old black telephone, the one Gram used to have in her bedroom, because she couldn't abide the new, lightweight plastic ones.

Lara went down the hall toward the back bedroom and then heard the sound again coming from the front door, except, of course, the front of the house was at the back, at the bottom of the big staircase, which the family also never used. She ran down the stairs, her hand automatically caressing the eagle head carved into the newel-post at the bottom. She could see the outline of two men's bodies through the white-glass panel, but she couldn't wrestle the door open, it had been locked for so many years.

"Come around to the kitchen," she shouted through a crack along the panel.

She ran through the cold front room. It had been her parents' bedroom when Gram and Grandpa were alive, and then Gram's bedroom when she got too frail to manage the stairs, but they never used it now. She ran into the dining room and then the kitchen, where she stood waiting for the men. As soon as she saw them, in their formal chocolate jackets, covered with medals and gold buttons, she knew Chip was dead. She didn't say anything but started screaming "Dad! Dad!" and ran to the barn, to the combine shed, to the cornfield, before remembering her father had announced at breakfast he was working the oat field, two miles distant.

She was so distracted that she started to run along the train tracks that marked the south boundary of the farm, as if she could run in her flip-flops all the way to the Wakarusa River where the oat field lay, but Blitz, who'd been irrigating the corn, caught sight of her. He came after her in the small Cub tractor and scooped her up.

"It's Chip," she panted. "I need Dad, they're from the Army, they're at the house."

Blitz turned the Cub around, heading toward the house.

"No, no," she shouted, pounding his side. "We have to find Dad."

"I'm going to do that, Lulu, but I want to get the pickup.'"

When she kept pounding him and screaming, he stopped the tractor and grabbed her arms. "Listen to me, Lulu. We will get there faster in the truck than in this thing. Stop your yelling. Your dad needs you to be strong for him, you hear me?"

When they got back to the house, the two men in uniform were still standing outside the kitchen door. One of them was holding his hat, turning it around and around in his hands.

Blitz went up to them. "You here about Chip? Chip Grellier?"

And the one playing with his hat said yes, he was Captain Wesson, was Blitz Chip's father?

"Mr. Grellier is in another field, about twenty minutes from here. You sit in the kitchen and wait. This here is his daughter. We'll find him."

It was funny, in hindsight, that Lara hadn't tried to find Mom, who was just across the tracks in the X-Farm. Maybe Blitz thought of it and decided it would be better to get Dad first. It wasn't until they found Dad and were driving back in the pickup, the three of them squeezed into the front seat, that Dad asked Blitz where Susan was, did she know about Chip?

"We don't know anything yet for sure," Blitz said.

But of course that was what Captain Wesson and the other man had come to do, to say they were very sorry, that the Grelliers should be proud of their son who had given everything for the defense of his country, but he had been killed when a bomb was detonated on the road he was patrolling south of Baghdad.

Chip had been in Iraq for twenty-four days. He'd been a soldier for twenty-three weeks. He wouldn't even be nineteen until November 6. Now he was dead.

It took twelve days for his body to come home. First it went to Germany, then to Dover Air Force Base in Delaware, then to Kansas City, where the family picked up his body. The process stunned them all: they assumed he'd be in a real coffin, and that someone would be standing at attention on the tarmac to welcome his body home. Instead, he'd been stuffed into a metal box in the hold of a cargo plane, and the family had to fill out a bunch of forms and drive around to the back of the airport to collect him, picking his coffin out of a jumble of giant containers holding tractor parts and milk cartons. Fortunately, Blitz had driven over with them. Dad could never have managed everything on his own.

The Army said he could be buried in a military cemetery, but Dad and Mom wanted him to come home, to be buried next to all the other Grelliers, starting with little Lizzie, 1852 to 1855, "The Shepherd has gathered up His Lamb and carried her to His bosom," her gravestone read.

Lara had often read the faded inscription when they'd gone to put flowers on her grandparents' graves, the graves of her dad's parents. The graves didn't mean anything to her: Dad's mother and father died when he was nine, so of course Lara never knew them. Even the later graves, for Grandpa and Gram, didn't make Lara particularly sad. They'd been so old when she was little, they hardly seemed part of the same species that she and Chip belonged to.

But now Chip was going to be in the ground. For the rest of Lara's life he would be lying there, all alone in the dirt. He'd been her big brother, he'd frightened her and teased her, but he'd protected her from bullies, and given her a canary for Christmas the year she broke her heart over one of the farm cats getting run over by the tractor. And now she'd get older than him. He'd be eighteen, going on nineteen, for the rest of his life. But unless she joined the Army, and went to Iraq and got blown to bits, she'd be old someday, old like Gram. The whole thought made her insides come together, as if her heart had disappeared and her chest collapsed in on itself.

The Army provided an honor guard at the funeral but couldn't give them a bugler to play taps—there weren't enough to go around, Captain Wesson said, even though Fort Leavenworth was only thirty miles away. Captain Wesson said he'd provide a CD they could play at the graveside, but all the Grelliers, and Blitz and Curly, too, agreed that would be disrespectful of Chip to have a recording instead of real music, so Lara, wearing the blue seersucker suit that she'd made for last year's county fair, with panty hose over her scraped knees, stood above her brother's body and played taps on her trumpet.

Part Two

FALL

Twenty-One

THE QUAGMIRE OF YOUTH

Jesus wants us to be pure,
Jesus wants us for His own.
Save that burning love,
Take it to the Savior's throne!

Burn, baby, burn,
Burn with the fire of righteousness.
Burn, baby, burn,
Catch on fire with Jesus' love.
That perfect love
Everlasting love
Catch on fire
Catch on fire
Catch on fire with Jesus' love!

The sound crashed through the gym floorboards and ran up everyone's legs. Crotches tingled, ached, the dancing grew wilder, strobes chased each other faster across the walls, so that the thrusting, sweating bodies looked like parts of a machine moving so wildly the pieces would fly off.

Robbie tucked his grin behind a blank stare, nodded at Chris Greynard on drums, prolonged the chorus another three minutes. They were hot. Becoming the Archetype and Sons of Thunder couldn't match them.

"Thank you, Jesus, thank you for the shower of your love," he sang, slowing down the tempo. "Your Spirit's here, it's in us, send us out into the world to do your work!"

He softened the chords. Behind him, Chris moved from drums to xylophone, and the kids in the crowd started singing along with them. It was ten-thirty; Pastor Nabo would be turning up the lights in another minute. "Send us out into the world in love, help us do your work in love." This was the traditional farewell song for the Full Salvation Bible Church Christ-Teen Group. Robbie thought it was corny, but he loved to lose himself in the chords and the crooning harmonies.

The lights came on and the crowd gathered in a large, sweaty circle, holding hands. Pastor Nabo joined the circle, taking the hands of two unpopular girls who came every Thursday in the hopes of attracting notice, even from overweight, sweaty guys like Neal Grafton. But Neal, of course, drooled after the peppy, popular girls in the group. Pastor Nabo always went out of his way to notice the two girls, who came early to mix Kool-Aid and iced tea for the rest of them and baked cookies for everyone at Christmas.

"Jesus!" the pastor intoned. "Pour down your Spirit on these young people, keep them pure in heart, mind, and deed in the week ahead. They live in a world of great temptation, Jesus, a world filled with drugs and abortion, homosexuality and false teachers, where Satan is holding sway. Satan has come among us in person, Lord. Satan is holding orgies not five miles from here. Keep these young people from giving in to him, help them remember that a moment's pleasure here on earth is repaid by an eternity of torment in the just fires of hell."

Robbie knew that his father had made a big fuss about the women living in the old Fremantle place and that he had just about burst his deputy sheriff's uniform with pride when he got the Eudora fire department to come put out their bonfire in June. Of course it was wrong, it was wicked, to indulge in witchcraft, like Gina Haring did, but Robbie still felt angry with his father for bragging to Pastor Nabo about how he'd made fools of the witches. Why couldn't Arnie have left them alone? Lara Grellier's mother had been at the Midsummer Eve bonfire, and now there was one more reason why Lara hated him.

"At the same time, Lord, you have given us a sign," Pastor was saying. "A sign here in the heartland, where a saving remnant remains true to your Word. Your disciples questioned if any good thing could come out of Nazareth, and so it is today with Kansas. A nation of liberals and sodomites ridicules us for holding fast to the Bible, but we shall confound them, as the Nazarene confounded His disciples, because you have sent your sign to us here in Kansas, even in a manger!"

The pastor's voice choked with emotion. Robbie shifted his feet uneasily. Pastor was talking about Soapweed's calf. She was ten months old, and she was still completely red, from her forelock to her hooves, so the Jews had given her a Hebrew name, Nasya, which they said meant "miracle." Most of the kids around him knew about Nasya—or Nassie, as Robbie thought of her—it had been impossible to keep her existence secret. As soon as the elders saw the heifer, they told their wives, the talk became common around the tables of Full Salvation Bible Church members, and pretty soon everyone in the county knew about it. Robbie had even heard whispered comments at the county fair.

Right after the fair ended, the *Douglas County Herald* sent a reporter out to the Schapen farm to follow up on the rumors. Robbie knew his father had been tempted to show off the red heifer; once or twice a week, Arnie speculated out loud on how much money they'd get if the heifer was still flawless when she turned three. And if she wasn't flawless, all the more reason to start making money on her now, charging admission so folks could see her, even advertising the special quality of milk that came from her mother and the other cows on the farm.

However, the *Herald* sent out a woman reporter, and Arnie wouldn't run the risk of the woman polluting the heifer. Perhaps it was the time of her impurity, Robbie intoned to himself as his father talked it over inside the house with Myra while the reporter cautiously approached the cows grazing behind the milking barn.

Myra thought they should seize the opportunity for publicity, but Arnie disagreed. Arnie said the Jews would find out in a heartbeat that he'd let a woman not only look at Nasya but write about her.

"If God is speaking through us, as the Jews seem to think, we can't risk alienating Him."

"And since when have a bunch of Jews told a good Christian woman what to do in her own home, on her own farm? Jesus came to free us from Jewish law, and, here you are, kowtowing to it as if our Savior had never shed His blood for you. I'm starting to question your salvation, Arnold, you taking those men's word over that of your own mother," Myra snapped.

Listening to the two of them shout, Robbie realized his father was afraid of Nanny. It was a sad and humiliating thought that this big, blustering man who frightened Robbie felt small in front of Nanny.

The argument finished with Arnie, breathing hard, telling the reporter the story about the calf was just a rumor. "Some kids got hold of a wild tale and they're pulling your chain, miss."

The reporter still hung around for another half hour, photographing cows, which made Arnie happy because it would help the farm if the *Herald* ran a story on his herd. She finally left when Junior, getting bored, went out to the pasture and came back with a bucket of manure that he spilled on her shoes, apologizing with an ugly grin for his clumsiness.

The Jews, dressed in long black coats even in the middle of the July and August heat, had come every month to inspect Soapweed's calf. Robbie had finally learned their names. The short one, who seemed to be the main spokesman, was called Reb Ephraim. One of the tall, stout ones, Reb Meir, didn't speak much, but he seemed to be the leader of the trio, while Reb Gamliel did the main inspection, getting down on a rubber mat to look at Nassie's vulva. Reb Meir always questioned Arnie about who had access to the heifer, stressing that women must not be allowed near her.

Arnie loved the injunction against women. "You know, if your mother were around, that calf would have been made impure before it was twelve hours old. The Lord has a plan for everything that happens in our lives, and now I see He sent that clothes salesman to seduce Kathy because He was paving the way for our household to be worthy to receive the calf."

Arnie had said this a million or two times since the first visit by the men from the Bet HaMikdash Yeshiva in Kansas City. It was hard for Robbie to believe the Lord took Kathy away from her children just so they could make money from a calf. *Sorry, Lord, but I wish my mother still lived here. Or that she'd taken me with her.* He wondered, as he often did, what he'd done as a small boy to get his mother so angry that she up and left, abandoning him to Myra and Arnie.

The day after the *Herald* reporter came out, Robbie was working the sorghum field, across the road from the Grelliers' experimental farm. He saw Lara wandering through her sunflower crop. Robbie hadn't heard about Chip's death; he only thought Lara looked forlorn, in need of comfort. In his head, Robbie sauntered across the road, suave, cool; Lara looked up, her face alight with pleasure; he mentioned the reporter and the calf; she laughed and said she would never betray any of Robbie's secrets, not even for a chance to be on *American Idol.*

In reality, watching her, he turned the tractor too sharply. The harrow swung wide into the drainage ditch, almost toppling the tractor. Robbie leaned forward, opening the throttle and turning the wheel hard. For a hair-raising instant, he thought he was going to have to jump clear of the tottering Case and hope for the best, but after a horrible few seconds the machine righted itself, and he was able to pull the harrow out of the ditch. Beneath his sunburn, his face had been hot with mortification; he hadn't even risked a look across the road to see how Lara had reacted to his clumsiness. As it was, he had to endure a searing lecture from Myra and his father for bending a harrow blade and damaging the end of three rows of sorghum, while Junior made fun of him for days.

Robbie wondered for the first time if his mother had run off to get away from Myra, rather than because she didn't love him, Robbie, any longer. He wished he knew where she'd gone. He'd Googled her at school, but he didn't know the last name of the man she'd run off with and his searches didn't turn up any Kathy Schapens. When his dad said that God had sent the clothing salesman to seduce Kathy as part of His plan, Robbie did venture to ask the man's name, but Arnie demanded to know whether Robbie wanted to follow his mother down the road of fornication and everlasting torment.

"He's not a Schapen, you might as well face it," Myra said viciously, taking out on Robbie her anger over being barred from the heifer.

Afterward, Robbie had gone into the bathroom and stared at himself in the small, wavery mirror, wondering if the clothing salesman was really his father. It was true, he didn't look like Arnie or Junior, but when he pulled his precious pictures of Kathy from the underside of his dresser drawer he didn't seem to look like her, either.

His mother's hair was dark, like his, but curled, where his was straight and spiky. Arnie was mostly bald now, but the hair he had was tightly curled, as was Junior's, reddish gold hair that on Arnie had deepened to a rusty brown. In one photo, Kathy had scraped the curls back from her face, so Robbie was able see her round, soft cheeks. His own face was long and narrow compared to hers.

"Make these children worthy of the Lamb."

With a guilty start, Robbie came back to the present, to the big meeting room at Full Salvation Bible, the sweaty bodies around him, girls clad modestly in knee-length skirts and blouses or sweaters that didn't reveal any cleavage. He thought of Lara Grellier's nipples poking through the thin fabric of her tank top when he'd sat behind her in Chip's Nissan. It was hard to believe that Chip Grellier was in hell, although he had to be because the Grelliers weren't true Christians. But Chip had been a hero, a patriot, he hadn't just ranted about loving his country, he'd gone to Iraq and died to prove he loved America.

Make an exception for him, Jesus, he shed his blood just like you did, Robbie prayed silently while Pastor Nabo continued out loud, "Make them worthy to receive the miraculous harbinger you have given of your imminent coming. Protect them, seal them as yours, so that they may spend eternity with the blessed. We ask this, Lord, in the name of your Son, who taught us to pray—"

Robbie recited the Lord's Prayer with the kids around him, who hugged and kissed and began sorting into groups of three or four, the ones dating, the ones sharing rides home. One of the girls who'd been holding Pastor Nabo's hand had a crush on Robbie; she lingered while he and Chris went up on the stage to pack their equipment. Robbie tried to ignore her. Amber Ruesselmann was a hardworking, pious girl; Myra thought she would do him good. Amber carried her Bible with her in school and read it endlessly during study hall or break. She'd made Robbie a batch of brownies for his birthday last March.

"You don't deserve a good Christian girl like Amber, but she might save you from Satan," Myra sometimes said.

"What about Junior?" Robbie demanded. "He's never had a girlfriend and he's eighteen. Isn't it time he showed me a good example?"

But Myra said Junior was saving himself for marriage, without explaining why Robbie couldn't be doing the same thing. He sometimes wondered if she could read his thoughts, knew he was interested in Lara. He'd written a poem to Lara, or at least for her, after he learned about Chip's death, but he'd never had the courage to send it to her.

He realized Amber had been talking to him, but he had been so lost in his daydreams that he hadn't heard her.

"I thought maybe you'd like to join a prayer session at school tomorrow," Amber repeated.

"Nope," Robbie said, then, noticing Pastor Nabo was listening in, added, "My grandmother says when a man and a woman are alone together, Satan is always present as an uninvited guest. Let's not take chances, Amber."

Pastor Nabo nodded approvingly, but Amber flushed to the roots of her mousy hair, embarrassed by even the suggestion of sex. Behind her and the pastor, Chris Greynard made an obscene pumping gesture. Robbie bent quickly to tie his shoe so that neither Amber nor Pastor could see his inadvertent grin.

"Come on, Schapen," Chris called to him. "Time for cowboys to get home to beddy-bye so they can get up bright and early and milk their prize Jerseys."

Robbie wouldn't turn sixteen until next March so he couldn't drive at night, but Chris Greynard had celebrated his birthday in August and could drive both of them. Things were way better than they used to be when he had to depend on Dad or, worse, Junior, to come get him.

> *I longed to hold her,*
> *Bring her comfort in the night.*
> *I longed to hold her,*
> *Help her come into the light.*

He sang the refrain to his song for Lara under his breath as Chris turned north onto Alabama Street, heading toward Highway 10.

"She's ready and waiting for you," Chris said.

"She is?" Robbie faltered, his heart pounding. "How do you know?"

"Come on, man, why do you think she was inviting you to pray with her—the chance to wrestle with the devil for your immortal soul?"

"Oh. Amber, right." For one heart-stopping moment, somewhere between fear and desire, he'd thought Lara had talked to Chris about him.

"So who do you want to comfort in the night, man? When'd you start writing love songs, anyway?"

"It's all about love, dude," Robbie answered. "Isn't that what they've been telling us our whole lives?"

Twenty-Two

TEACHER OUT OF SCHOOL

Board Meeting Minutes,
New Haven Manor September 29

OLD BUSINESS

New Haven executive director Michael Nilsson reported to the board that Elaine Logan set fire to the building on Labor Day (see September 8 "New Business" minutes). The fire was quickly extinguished, and no one was injured, but Mr. Nilsson explained that Elaine Logan was intoxicated, in contravention of New Haven rules; she has been warned twice before that the third episode would result in expulsion.

The board discussed alternative placements, but Ms. Logan refused to go into a detoxification program, which all housing options similar to New Haven require. She collects a monthly Social Security check of $220; Rachel Carmody appealed to the Riverside United Church of Christ to supplement this with enough money to rent Ms. Logan a room in a regular rooming house. Ms. Logan stayed there for only three nights. She has been seen begging on Massachusetts Street and in South Park. After a long discussion, the board agreed that until Ms. Logan agrees to a detox program and commits to sobriety, we can't house her.

Three days ago, a Ms. Gina Haring, who is renting the old Fremantle house east of town, reported that Ms. Logan has been hanging around her property. Rachel Carmody agreed to drive out to talk to both women.

OTHER OLD BUSINESS

KU pathologist Bill Picking traced the recent shigella outbreak to a food handler, who has been fired for ignoring posted hygiene standards.

Driving between the rows of sorghum and corn, Rachel Carmody felt insubstantial. The fields were dry and the crops close to maturity, but to her untrained eye the rust-colored sorghum heads and weathered tan cornstalks appeared dead. She drove this route several times in the summer when she came out to the Grelliers' farm market, but today it looked unfamiliar, even ominous.

The sky was the color of lead. It stretched taut above the fields, like a tent covering the prairie, keeping out air. With her car windows down— the air conditioner had failed last month, and she was trying to save money by not repairing it until next summer—the roar of the wind across the plants was so loud it drowned the radio. Although it was the middle of September, the heat still had the closeness of high summer.

Rachel had a disturbing vision of the birds that hovered over the sorghum flying skyward and dashing their brains against the leaden sky. Teenage horror stories were compounding her dread of the errands she faced.

The boys in her English classes, obsessed by war and horror games, often produced phantasmagoric scenes of zombies, werewolves, and other monsters in their school writing. No matter what the topic, whether fiction or nonfiction, she could count on a dozen dramas involving wizards and demons from the boys; the girls tended to write about world peace and harmony. The year the *Lord of the Rings* dominated the movie world, she read endless accounts of Orcs and Sauron terrorizing the world until some brave Kansas boy brought them to their knees.

She'd just finished marking the first hundred fifty essays of the new school year on the topic "If I were in charge for a day" and found three that told her, "If I ran the government for a day, I would muster an army of Orcs to destroy all the Muslims."

Most kids facing that topic assumed they would be in charge of the United States, although a few wrote about running the school. Lara Grellier had turned in one sentence: "If I were in charge for a day I would oblitterate this whole sorry planet to save everyone the bother of destroying it one person at a time."

Rachel had marked it D, and added: "Lara, we both know you understand the assignment and that you can do better work. I don't object to the sentiment, but to your laziness in not working it out. See me to discuss a second chance at this topic. Also, even for a one-sentence submission, use spell-check."

Rachel pulled over to let a dump truck pass her. Its wheels spat gravel into her windshield. How did the pioneers stand it, that vast expanse of prairie, where plants grew higher than the tallest man's head, and land and sky and wind blurred into a ball of gray noise? Just driving through it, dust billowing around her, Rachel felt disoriented. But families like the Grelliers and the Schapens had built farms here when there weren't roads, the women washing clothes in tubs they filled with water obtained at great hardship.

One winter, for the church's study group, Susan Grellier had made a presentation on Jim's pioneer ancestors. She'd put up clippings from the old territorial newspapers on some of the great events of the day: how pro-slavery men poured into Kansas and threatened judges and killed settlers so that pro-slavery candidates won elections; John Brown and the Pottawatomie Massacre; Quantrill's raids. Then, to show daily life against this backdrop, Susan read from Jim's great-great-grandmother's diary, where Abigail Grellier recounted how Mrs. Fremantle checked to see if Abigail's linens were white and ironed.

Sitting at the crossroads south of the tracks, Rachel noticed a small, hand-lettered sign pointing left to the OPEN PRAIRIE DAIRY, OPEN DAILY 10 TO 4. She knew the Schapens lived close to the Grelliers, but she'd never known exactly where they were. She craned her neck, looking for the Schapen house, but the sorghum field and high grasses in the ditches blocked any of the buildings from her view. Every now and then a car came north down the county road and turned toward the dairy.

Junior Schapen had been a tiresome boy, the worst kind of student: ignorant, unprepared, and arrogant. He'd assumed that his status on the football team exempted him from classwork, and Rachel had endured more than one belligerent visit from the coach, demanding that she raise Junior's grade from an F to a C. When she compromised on a D, she'd felt filthy for betraying her own sense of integrity; even so, the coach had treated her to another tirade, as had Junior's father, dressed in his deputy's uniform, and nearly threatening her with arrest for messing with Junior's chance to go to college: even Tonganoxie Bible College, where Junior ended up, had some minimal admission standards.

When she saw another Schapen on her class roster this fall, Rachel had been dismayed, but at least at first blush Robbie seemed like a different kind of boy, skinny, shy, interested in poetry.

"If I were in charge for a day, I would make everyone stop what they were doing to sing a song, any song, not in harmony or unison, just sing. By the time they finished singing, they would be so filled with happiness, they would stop trying to hurt each other." He had appended a second page, called "A song I wrote":

Her hair shone silver
Under the prairie sun.
Her lips burned with fever
As she lay alone at night.
Her tears gleamed
Like diamonds through the mist
When they laid her poor dead soldier
Laid him in the dust

"Please tell me, is this any good? Is it okay to rhyme mist with dust?" he had added.

It was derivative, a country-and-western song, but it had some grace as well. She'd wondered idly who he was writing for, who he was too shy to show his song to. Rachel's experience of adolescents was that they wrote about the particular, people or things they knew, not abstractions.

Chip was the only Lawrence student who had died in the war. From the poem, Rachel wondered if Robbie had a secret crush on Janice Ever-leigh, Chip's old girlfriend. Janice was studying business systems, what-ever that meant, at a community college in Kansas City. She still came to the high school's football games, driving Chip Grellier's old Nissan and draped in his baseball-letter jacket.

Rachel had always thought Janice was too superficial for someone like Chip Grellier, and surely even more so for a boy like Robbie, with his hankering for poetry. Now, sitting at the crossroads with the Grelliers in front of her and the Schapens to the left, Rachel wondered if Robbie had been writing to Lara Grellier. They must have grown up together out here, gone to that boarded-up little school she'd passed at the turnoff from Highway 10.

Rachel was frankly worried about Lara. Until this fall, Lara had always been part of a crowd of kids, both in Sunday school and at high school. She'd been a leader in the church youth group, a good student in school, the kind of bright, fresh-faced girl who made adults smile. Since her brother's death, she'd dropped out of choir, didn't come to Sunday school, and was doing abysmal course work.

Lara had been working the Grellier booth at the farmers' market in town last Saturday. Rachel went up to the table just as another woman asked Lara how her mother was.

"*My* mother? Don't you mean *Chip's* mother? Susan Grellier has taken to her bed. I haven't seen her for days." Lara's face blazed with a scorching anger, the kind of anger kids use to suppress tears. "She's stopped eating. Maybe she'll starve to death."

Since the start of school, Susan had been in church only once. She'd appeared emaciated, her face white under its bridge of freckles, her red-brown mop of curls limp and unwashed. It looked to Rachel as though Jim had practically carried her into the pew.

Even the experimental farm, which Lara had shown off when Rachel came out in June to buy early tomatoes, was suffering. The sunflowers, heads all facing east, bowed under the weight of their seeds. The field was full of blackbirds, rising and swirling as they attacked the seeds, and the plants looked bedraggled, as if they weren't getting enough water.

"Your car break down? Oh, it's you, Ms. Carmody."

Rachel squawked. She'd been so lost in thought she hadn't noticed the man approaching the car. After a moment's panic, when she tried to figure out if she could drive away with him leaning into the car, she realized it was Blitz Fosse. She hardly knew him, except as the man who cleared the teachers' parking lot during heavy snowstorms. She knew he sometimes worked for the Grelliers, but she hadn't recognized him out of the context of school.

She smiled weakly, her heart still pounding. "I'm avoiding some hard errands, that's all."

"They must be hard: I watched you sit there for ten minutes, looking like a kid called to the principal's office."

"Yes, I'm a terrible coward." She knew he was teasing, but she spoke seriously. "I don't have the right skills to be a teacher. I love poetry and literature, but that's not enough—you have to be able to stand up to abuse and backbiting. I don't like having to fight people."

"Being able to hit people between the eyes is an overrated skill."

"If I were as strong as you, maybe I'd believe that."

"If you were as strong as me, you'd have a different set of problems. Every John Wayne wannabe tries to push you into a fistfight."

She finally smiled. "Okay, I can believe that. Are you spending a lot of time with the Grelliers? I'm worried about Lara."

"I work for Jim every year until we bring in the corn. Repairing equipment for the school board is something I do between harvest and planting, not the other way around. Didn't you know that?"

She shook her head, ashamed at her own ignorance. "I've lived in Lawrence for twelve years, but I've never figured out how to tap into the communal gossip spring."

He jumped back to her previous comment. "Worried about Lara how?"

"I'm her Sunday school teacher as well as her English teacher. She's not coming to church, which is between her and her parents, but she's doing close to failing work in most of her classes, and she hasn't kept her appointments with me."

"I wondered, way she's been carrying on. Of course, the whole family's in trouble—you know that if you know them from your church."

"Yes." She looked at him squarely. "Last week at the farmers' market, Lara said her mother stopped eating. How is Susan functioning out here?"

He hesitated. "It's not my business to pry into their business," he finally said. "If you want to talk to Lulu—Lara—I'm not sure she's home. I could be wrong, but I thought I saw her take off across the fields awhile back. If you want to talk to her folks about her—well, Jim's carrying a heavy load right now. If Lulu is screwing up, it'll just be one more thing he probably can't do much about."

"I like him, too," Rachel said. "I have to see Gina Haring, anyway. She's upset because a homeless woman she sort of befriended is hanging around her house."

His thick brows shot up in surprise. "Why should you drive all the way out here because of that? Let Haring sort it out—she's capable of just about anything, from where I look."

"Oh, she's sort of a problem child. Not Gina, the woman. Elaine Logan. I'm on the board of a home where Elaine was living; we had to throw her out because she was setting the place on fire. Not on purpose—passing out while smoking. We feel some responsibility for her." She mustered a smile. "Congregationalists don't support a cult of the Virgin Mary, but I'm beginning to think I was dedicated at birth to Our Lady of Perpetual Responsibility. I'm tired of it, but I agreed to talk to Gina. I'm hoping that between us, we can come up with some inspiration about Elaine. Afterward, I'll stop back by the Grelliers'. If Lara's back, I'll have a word with her about her classes."

His dark face relaxed into a grin. "No wonder you're looking like a dog facing a burning hoop. Angry teenager and an ice queen in the same afternoon. That does take courage. Even if you were as strong as me, you couldn't punch your way through those encounters. Still, you don't mind people knowing you're afraid, so you're already ahead of the game."

He stepped back into the road, hesitated again, then leaned once more through the window. "Lulu needs to know how proud Chip was of her brains."

He slapped the roof of her car and waved her on her way.

Twenty-Three

WITCHES' BREW

A BATTERED BLUE FORD stood in the Fremantles' drive, but when Rachel went to the kitchen door she didn't get an answer to her knock. She stood for several minutes, listening, thinking, at least she'd tried to see Gina, she could turn around now. But after knocking twice more, she pulled open the door and stepped into the kitchen.

The room was almost bare, as if Gina never ate or cooked. An enamel table, its white surface chipped and creased with knife scratches, stood under the window. It held only a handful of ripe tomatoes and the big cappuccino maker, which Rachel had heard about from Lara Grellier back in the spring when Lara was still a lively, engaged teenager. An old-fashioned industrial clock, dating to Mrs. Fremantle's days as a bride, seventy years ago, ticked loudly in the still room in counterpoint to a drip from the rusted kitchen faucet.

"Hello?" Rachel called. "Gina?"

There were five doors in the kitchen, two leading outdoors and three into the interior. Rachel had been in the house a few times before, most memorably when Mrs. Fremantle let Susan Grellier run a tour of its Civil War history. What stood out in Rachel's mind was not the layout of the house, but the mud-floored cellar, where Una Fremantle and her children hid from Quantrill's raiders in 1863.

Rachel started with the door farthest to her left. This led to the dining room; she stuck her head in and called hello again, more boldly this time. When no one answered, she tried the second door, which opened onto the cellar stairs, a set of planks, really, roughly nailed into steeply rising open stringers.

Rachel shut the door quickly, remembering all too well the giant spiders from the tour she'd taken. "Harmless," Susan had assured her, but Rachel didn't believe any spider the size of her palm could be harmless.

The third door led to a narrow stairwell, where chunks of plaster had disappeared from the walls, exposing the lath. Rachel heard a scrabbling sound, like papers being dropped, or mice running through leaves. She wondered if Gina were up there, sitting silent, waiting for her to leave.

Her face grew hot. How dared Gina call, demanding help from New Haven's board, and then hide from her? She turned to leave, but had a sudden vision of herself offering houseroom to Elaine Logan, not out of charity, but out of cowardice, because she hadn't been able to face Gina Haring. She laughed nervously and started up the stairs, pausing halfway to listen again.

"Hello!" she shouted. "This is Rachel Carmody, Gina. You asked me to come out here, remember?"

This time she heard a kind of thud, something being dropped. She ran the rest of the way up. The long hallway at the top offered another array of doors. She turned to her right and started flinging them open. The rooms beyond hadn't been used in months, maybe years, judging by the thick dust on the floors and furniture. A narrow-gauge model train covered the floor in one of the side rooms, but it, too, was heavy with dust. Only the master bedroom showed signs of use, the unmade bed presumably the place where Gina slept. The floor in here was more or less clean, but you'd have to dust every day to keep up with the dirt floating in from the fields and the gravel road. The house showed no signs of someone who dusted every day.

Gina had left a blue-striped nightshirt in the middle of the floor. It looked expensive, like all Gina's clothes—combed cotton, maybe, or silk—something Rachel couldn't afford. She almost bent to pick it up, then thought *Why should I be her maid* and moved on through the closet that connected to another unused room, this one stacked high with old magazines and papers. A limp tarlatan prom dress hung from the closet door. Here the dust had been disturbed by someone—Gina?—sorting through the boxes of papers. She'd dumped ones she didn't want on the floor.

Rachel left the room through a far door, past a door leading to the steep attic stairs. She called up the stairs and even climbed a few risers, but the heat up there shimmered down on her, at least twenty degrees hotter than the rest of the house, and she saw wasps at the top, like small parachutes floating on the currents of hot air. Not even Gina would hide from her up there.

As she turned away, she suddenly thought of Elaine Logan. Why hadn't that occurred to her sooner? Gina might have left the house, gone into town with some friend, which would explain why her car was in the yard and she wasn't home. Elaine could have walked in, helped herself to the house. It would be totally typical of her, and typical of her as well to think she should run off and hide when she heard Rachel calling.

Bracing herself against the heat and the wasps, Rachel forced herself to go all the way to the top of the attic stairs. She kept her hands defensively on her head and peeped underneath her arms. The attic was full of boxes, old baby furniture, the thready remnants of onions from the days when bulbs were hung from the rafters to dry. She didn't see Elaine, or anyone else, and ran thankfully down the stairs, shutting the door with a thump and brushing imaginary insects out of her scalp.

There was one last bedroom just past the attic door. This was clearly the most important room to Gina, the one where she was writing. A laptop was set up on an old side table; next to it were stacks of papers and books. She'd even piled them on a daybed that stood under the east window. In contrast to the other rooms, even the bedroom where she was sleeping, here Gina had scrubbed the walls and the floor.

Much of the faded floral wallpaper had peeled from the walls. On one bare patch of plaster, some bygone Fremantle had written differential equations in a tiny hand. Next to these, Gina had hung a poster-sized photograph of a woman with long dark hair, inscribed, "Gina, This is what a Wiccan looks like." The woman was smiling so intimately that Rachel was discomfited, as if she had walked in on someone's bedroom.

She turned away, but as she left the room movement out the east window caught her eye. Beyond the apple trees stood the heap of charred, weathered boards that had once been the Fremantle hands' bunkhouse. Someone was out there in the wreckage—Rachel could just make out a figure through the trees.

She ran back down the narrow stairs to the kitchen and out the south door. The earth was rough, untended, beneath the high grasses, and she stumbled in her low-heeled classroom shoes. She slowed down to keep from hurting her ankles.

When she reached the ruins, Rachel found Gina Haring stabbing at what was left of the roof with a long board. She turned when Rachel came up, but didn't stop what she was doing. Rachel stood well away from the overhanging beams—they looked unstable, and Gina's poking seemed singularly inept.

"I'm Rachel Carmody," she finally said as Gina kept slamming the board against the remains of the roof.

"Hang on a minute. I've almost got this piece."

Gina shoved several more times. A section of roof tumbled down, landing with a sighing thud among the weeds and charred wood inside the house. Both women jumped as a family of rabbits scurried from the rubble.

Gina dropped her long board and stood panting. She had on heavy work gloves, a T-shirt with the sleeves cut off at the armholes, and old jeans, but she still made Rachel feel dowdy. It was something in the way she held herself, perhaps, or the way her hair was cut, curling back from her face into a perfect oval at the nape of her neck. Her arms in the sleeveless tee were tanned and sinewy.

"Jim Grellier warned me not to go into the ruin of the bunkhouse because the roof was unstable," Gina said.

"So you're taking off the roof. I guess that makes sense. What do you want it for—more firewood?"

Gina looked startled. "Who are you? Have you come to lodge another complaint about the bonfires? I can't believe how much attention people out here pay to each other's every move! In New York, if I set a fire in the street no one would notice, and there'd be two million people around me."

"You wouldn't believe how little I care about anyone else's business. I only heard about your bonfires because of Susan Grellier. She was trying to explain them to me after church one Sunday—she loved the ritual, but some of the church's board thought even for an open and inclusive church, a pagan ceremonial was going too far. There was quite a debate at the meeting, and Susan was describing what went on. I've never felt free enough to experiment with New Age ceremonies, but Susan embraces change. Used to," Rachel amended sorrowfully, "until life dealt her the kind of change that no one wants to embrace."

"Her son's death, you mean. People blame me for that," Gina said.

"Blame you?" Rachel wrinkled her forehead. "You didn't encourage Chip to enlist, did you? I—I thought you were part of the anti-war movement."

"I am." Gina struck a defiant pose, gloved hands on hips. "But a couple of people have told me it was my fault that Susan got involved in the movement. They say that Etienne enlisted because of the fights they were having over it."

"Etienne—oh, yes, of course, that was Chip's formal name. I forgot. I think Susan was the only person who called him that."

"I only knew about him through Susan," Gina said, "so that's how I always think of him. Etienne Grellier. When he joined the Army, Susan said he was doing it to get back at her, because he kept trying to argue her out of her work in the movement."

"Who can possibly say what led Chip to enlist? I think a lot of things were preying on him."

Rachel's voice trailed away. It troubled her that she couldn't remember Chip clearly. He'd stopped coming to church a year or so before he enlisted, and that was where she'd chiefly known him, since he hadn't been one of her English students. Her most vivid memories stemmed from seeing him at the farmers' market, where he'd been a bright-faced, good-natured boy, bantering easily with the customers, until the last six months or so before he'd left home. He'd turned withdrawn and surly, to the point that she'd wondered if drugs had become an issue in his life. When he joined up, she'd even privately thought the Army might be good for him, by giving some structure to his life.

"Has anyone at Grelliers'—Blitz, Jim—suggested you're responsible?" Rachel asked.

Gina flushed under her tan. "Some hysterical girl came up to me after the funeral and said if it wasn't for me, Etienne would still be alive."

"Janice Everleigh. I didn't hear her accuse you. The rest of her outburst was hideous enough."

Chip's girlfriend had seen herself as the heroine of the drama, almost a widow; church gossip said Janice tried to lay claim to Chip's body, then to his life insurance, even though he had designated his parents and sister as beneficiaries of the ten thousand dollars, asking them to give five hundred to Tom Curlingford. At the interment, Janice snatched the flag as Chip's honor guard started to hand it to Susan and Jim. She draped it around herself like a cloak and ran to the open grave, leaning over it and wailing as if she were going to fling herself in. Susan stalked up to her and tore the flag from her shoulders while Janice screeched, "You don't have a right to that flag. You hate the flag, you hate America, you hated Chip being in the Army." Susan had stared at Janice for a long second, but all she said was, "Etienne. His name was Etienne, and that is how he is being buried."

Rachel shuddered in the September heat as she remembered the scene but said to Gina, "You're so sophisticated, I wouldn't think anyone could get under your skin, especially not a girl like Janice."

"Yes, I know: everyone thinks I'm some kind of shellacked, unfeeling manikin. The truth is—I'm an empty hole underneath my shellac. Anyone can fill it with anger or contempt." Gina compressed her lips, as if ashamed of revealing herself, and added quickly, "I went over to the Grelliers' to offer my condolences, but Susan was lying down, and Jim said he couldn't suggest a good time for me to come back—which sounded as though he wants me to stay away!"

"He may have been speaking out of despair. He may be afraid there won't ever come a time when she'll be—I don't know—maybe healed enough for visitors. I have to go there after I leave here, and I'm dreading it myself."

"What—are you visiting everyone in the county or just the ones who danced around the bonfire last June? Are you going to call on Arnie Schapen and his mother? Myra Schapen's the kind of person who gives witches a bad name. She and Arnie brought the fire department out to douse our midsummer fire, but you can tell them from me that I still plan to have a fire at Samhain."

Rachel felt a headache building behind her eyes. She was tired, and talking to Gina was strenuous work. "I don't have any plans to see Mr. Schapen, nor do I know what Samhain is, so it doesn't matter to me. Besides, I'm only here because you asked to see me!"

"I? I've never heard of you!"

"Elaine Logan," Rachel said, angry. "You called New Haven Manor and demanded we do something about her hanging around you, even though you invited her to your fire ceremonies."

"Oh." Gina suddenly grew quiet, deflated almost. She looked down at herself and murmured something about not realizing how dirty she'd become, poking around in the bunkhouse. "And I'm sure you're not comfortable in that pantsuit. Isn't it rayon? Rayon holds heat terribly. Who would believe it could be almost ninety on September twentieth?"

"Never mind my clothes and your dirt," Rachel snapped. "I have lessons to prepare and a ton of other things to do this evening. I came out here as a favor to you, so if you don't have anything creative to say about providing for Elaine's well-being I'm going home."

"I'm sorry. I know you're doing me a great favor. The Schapens spy on me so constantly that they've thrown me off balance. Come into the house with me for a minute so we can discuss Elaine."

Her frank apology, the wistful appeal in her eyes, the gap-toothed smile Jim and Lara both liked—all those things affected Rachel, too. She let herself be mollified, let herself be led to the kitchen, where Gina took two bottles of water out of a nearly empty refrigerator.

"There's so much iron in the Fremantle well that it's undrinkable—I have to buy bottled water in town. All the pipes are rusted out, too— I don't even like to bathe out here—it was turning my skin orange, so I joined a gym in town just to have a place to wash up."

Gina rinsed her arms under the sink tap. When she dried them, she showed Rachel the towel. Sure enough, it was faintly streaked orange.

Rachel nodded, her face grim: adolescents avoiding difficult discussions indulged in similar dramatic tactics. "Elaine Logan."

Gina flung the towel away. "I can't be responsible for her. She's too difficult."

"I don't think anyone asked you to be."

"No. But she's started coming out here almost every day, and I can't make her go away."

"When I got here, I heard noises on the second floor. I thought it might be you so I went up to see, only no one was there."

"Well, damn her, anyway! I told her two days ago she had to find some other drop-in shelter. And here she is, the second my back is turned, invading—"

"I don't think so. She's a very big woman, and she doesn't move fast. She couldn't have hidden from me, even in the middle of all the boxes and clothes and whatever else in those second-floor bedrooms. I probably just heard mice or squirrels or something." Rachel's voice trailed away uncertainly. She was sure she'd heard something drop or fall. "You don't have a cat, do you?"

"Everyone here is obsessed with animals." Gina shook her curls in irritation. "Jim thinks I need a dog, you think I need a cat—spinsters or dykes are supposed to love animals, is that it?"

"You are an Olympic medalist in the conclusion jump!" Rachel cried. "I asked because a cat might have knocked something over to make the sound I heard. How did you get from there to accusing me of the kind of homophobia that rides in your head?"

"Oh. Sorry." Gina bit her lip and looked at the floor. "Why can't Elaine go back to New Haven Manor?"

"Because they have a no-alcohol policy, which Elaine kept violating."

"And you Christians can't stand for a homeless woman to drink?" Gina looked up.

"We *Christians* turned a blind eye to that for months—everyone at New Haven knows she doesn't have a lot of choices—but Elaine has set the place on fire three times when she passed out while smoking. We can't ignore the problem because she's endangering other people's lives, not just her own. She could stay at New Haven if she joined AA or went through a detox program, but she refuses to admit that she drinks. She says the staff are lying, that they set the fires themselves."

The pain over Rachel's left eye intensified. "How does she get out here? For that matter, why did she come? You must have made her feel welcome in some special way."

Gina shook her head. "After the midsummer bonfire, she started attaching herself to me. I tried to discourage her, but she says my great-aunt let her roam around the property, which makes her think she's entitled to the use of the place. Back in the summer, back before Etienne's death, Susan Grellier told me Elaine had only come out a few times when Great-Aunt Liz was alive, but Elaine has blown it up in her head to remembering that she practically lived here. She somehow persuades people to give her a lift to the crossroads and sometimes even bullies them into dropping her at the door. I never know when she's going to show up."

"What's so special about this house that she'd go to all that effort?" Rachel asked.

"She says she was part of the Free State Commune. That was a bunch of hippies that lived in the bunkhouse—that ruin where I was working when you showed up. I don't know about the commune—I was never in this house before I moved here—I don't even know any of the Fremantles except my uncle John, who isn't even really my uncle. He married my father's sister. Anyway, I wasn't born when the bunkhouse burned down, but Elaine says her lover died in the fire."

"How terrible!" Rachel's ready empathy was engaged. "Perhaps that's why she drinks so much."

"Frankly, I don't even know if that's true," Gina said impatiently. "She enjoys drama, as you've probably noticed. She entertains herself by making up stories with herself as the heroine, so I don't know what I can believe of her memories."

"Is that why you're excavating the bunkhouse?" Rachel asked.

"What—to see if I can find any proof of her story? No." She twisted her mouth in a rueful smile. "I'm hoping to find—"

A strangled screech, the staple of horror movies, brought both women to their feet. Gina stood for a second, trying to pinpoint the noise, then strode through the dining room to the front hall. Rachel followed her. The great front door, slowly swinging on its hinges, screeched again.

Twenty-Four

WHO WAS THAT . . . INTRUDER?

THE TWO WOMEN stared at it for a frozen moment, then Gina said, "That door was bolted on the inside. I've never used it. Elaine was hiding out in here after all, damn it!"

She pushed the heavy door open and went out onto a veranda that surrounded the house on three sides. The house stood on a slight rise, man-made when it was built, to keep it above flood level when the Kaw and Wakarusa rivers spread their waters through the valley. From the top of the rise, Rachel saw a trail of bent and broken stems through the waist-high grass, showing where the intruder had fled.

The yard was filled with trees—firs, sycamore, walnut, a dozen varieties that Una Fremantle had brought with her as seedlings from Massachusetts; these had grown so huge over the centuries that they shielded the road from sight.

Rachel went down the porch stairs and made her way through the bent stalks and past the trees, but the wild prairie grasses in the drainage ditch still blocked her view of the road. She slithered into the ditch. When she made it up to the road, she couldn't see anyone in either direction.

The wind kept the high grasses in constant motion, but as she stared across the road into the twilit fields a different kind of movement caught her eye. Something like the wake a boat would make in a turbulent ocean was splitting the corn in the field to the north. She squinted, concentrating on the motion until it was lost from sight. Whoever was going through those fields was heading northwest toward the Grellier house.

Rachel limped back up the road to the Fremantle drive and slowly returned to Gina. Scrambling through ditches and grasses in her school shoes had raised blisters on her heels and toes. When she got back to the house, Gina demanded to know where Elaine was.

"It wasn't Elaine." Rachel sat on the veranda steps and took off her shoes. Blood was oozing through the stocking on her left foot. "She can't move fast. Whoever this was could run."

Gina's shoulders sagged. "Anyone could get in here who felt like it— the place has five doors. I have keys, but you can see what a sieve it is. My God, I wonder if it was Arnie Schapen or that dreadful mother of his, trying to plant some kind of evidence here so he can prance around in his deputy's uniform and arrest me."

"It's hard for me to imagine Mr. Schapen giving up his dignity by squatting down here in the hallway for half an hour or sprinting to the road with me after him—he'd be more likely to shoot me and claim self-defense." Rachel peeled off her socks and stared mournfully at her bleeding feet. "I don't know Mr. Schapen's mother, but this was someone who could move fast on foot. Unless she really is a witch, I doubt an old woman could have gotten away by the time we came out the front door."

"People have the wrong idea about witches," Gina said. "We don't do magic, we can't influence the outcome of events or violate the laws of physics any more than Christians can. However much the Schapens photograph our rituals, they won't find any sign that we fly or kill babies for their blood or any of the other crap they accuse us of."

"If Junior Schapen were still living at home, I might suspect him," Rachel said, "but the football coach, or Arnie, persuaded a local Bible school to let him play football for them, despite his abysmal grades, so he's over in Tonganoxie."

"They do have another son. I've never met him, but he passes here sometimes on his way to the Wakarusa. Hard to believe, but people eat fish out of that muddy creek." Gina flushed. "I'm as bad as everyone else out here, aren't I, keeping track of who's doing what?"

Rachel smiled, but shook her head. "That must be Robbie. He's in my sophomore English class this fall, but, Schapen though he is, he seems so engaged by poetry that I can't imagine him doing something so—so sordid."

"Eddie Burton!" Gina exclaimed. "I would have thought of him at once if Elaine hadn't been hanging around."

When Rachel said she didn't know him, Gina gave a harsh bark of a laugh. "That's because he's mentally deficient, or whatever the jargon is—couldn't even learn the alphabet, according to Lara Grellier, so it's not likely you'd have seen him in your high school. He climbed a tree outside the second-floor bathroom, spying on me the week I moved in last winter, and I know I saw him lurking around the place on Midsummer Eve, when Arnie Schapen called out the fire department against us. But Jim spoke to Eddie's father, and I haven't seen him since the last fire. I'd forgotten about him until now."

"Where does he live?"

"Down near K-10." Gina pointed south toward the highway, away from the Grelliers'. "That ramshackle place with the cars up on cement blocks."

Rachel shook her head again. "I saw movement through the field to the north. Who lives that way besides the Grelliers?"

Gina shrugged. "I don't know. A million people, all minding my business, but I don't know their names. Lara and Etienne Grellier used to come into this house when it was empty—Jim says they treated it like a kind of clubhouse. Maybe it was Lara—she slipped into the bedroom one morning right after I moved in, looking for some damned thing."

"Lara?" Rachel tensed. "I can't believe it."

"The country is a murky place. All these houses, with people doing dreadful things in them, any of them might think it was a funny idea to break in here. I can believe it of Lara or the young Schapen or Eddie or—or anyone else, if I knew their names."

"Why Lara?" Rachel demanded sharply.

"No special reason," Gina said, "except that she's one more teenager in a place where everyone seems to lead disturbed or disturbing lives."

The trouble was, Rachel realized, she, too, feared it had been Lara. The new, downward-spiraling Lara might try almost anything to get some attention from Susan. If Lara was deciding to add vandalism or housebreaking to her new hostile persona, she was heading for more serious trouble than Rachel could help with. She couldn't bear to think of the pain it would cause Jim. She made one of those meaningless prayers: *Please don't let it be Lara. Let it be someone else's child, someone else's problem. Protect Jim from more harm.*

Gina ran her hands through her hair, leaving a trail of dust across her temples. "Will you go through the house with me? I don't want to spend the night jumping up every time a board creaks—and every board in this house creaks, believe me. I can fix you up some Band-Aids for your feet," she added, seeing Rachel's pained look at her bloody socks.

Rachel rubbed the tight spot behind her eyes where her head was throbbing. She wanted to hobble to her car, bypass the Grelliers', forget life east of town, and sleep for a year or two, but then she imagined what it would feel like when she had left, when the light was gone, and Gina was alone.

With surprising patience, Gina cleaned Rachel's blisters and wrapped them in layers of bandages. She even gave Rachel a clean pair of socks. When Rachel was duly wrapped up and able to walk again, Gina took a heavy-duty flashlight from a kitchen drawer. With Rachel at her elbow, she went through each of the downstairs rooms in turn, then went up the formal front staircase to the second floor. The clutter in the bedrooms Gina wasn't using was so dense it was impossible to tell if anything had been added—or, indeed, taken away—but the black dust covering the surfaces didn't seem to have been disturbed.

It wasn't until they got to the little corner room Gina was using as a study that they found anything out of the ordinary. Gina checked her laptop, to make sure it was still there, to make sure her work files were intact, but Rachel was looking at the portrait of the dark-haired woman.

"There's a cigarette stub in her mouth," she said.

Gina glanced up from her machine, then sprang to her feet, furious. "It's a roach. How dare they? Come in here, spy, and then deface my picture!"

"A roach?" Rachel moved closer to the picture. "But it looks like a cigarette."

"You are damned naive for a high school teacher. Marijuana. The butts are called roaches, okay?" Gina blazed with anger but worked carefully on the tape holding the end of the joint to the woman's lips to make sure she didn't pull any of the paper away. "They did this so Arnie Schapen could march in, wearing his deputy sheriff's uniform, looking for drugs, and get me locked up! And then his repellent mother could write a screed about dykes who practice witchcraft and use drugs."

Rachel looked at the roach meekly, feeling there was, in fact, something amiss with her for not knowing what it was. Her roommate in college had smoked dope, but Rachel had never wanted to try it, and her adult milieu had never included drug users. Over the years, her students had used the language of the drug world in the hopes of shocking her, but she couldn't remember whether she'd ever seen *roach* in a student paper. Maybe this joint end meant it really had been one of the Schapens. If Arnie or Junior Schapen were breaking in, Rachel wouldn't want to be alone in this big house.

"Who is the woman in the picture?" she ventured, as Gina searched the room for any more drugs.

"She's someone—I treated very badly." Gina's face twisted in pain. She led Rachel abruptly from the room. On her way downstairs, she said, "I'm not up to going into that basement, are you?"

"No," Rachel agreed thankfully, "but I'd nail the door to it in the kitchen shut if I were you. That way, if someone tried to break in through the cellar they wouldn't be able to get into the house. I need to stop at the Grelliers' on my way home. Do you want me to ask Blitz Fosse to come over and do that for you?"

"Is he the big guy with the dark beard? He looks at me so disapprovingly whenever I've gone over there, I can't imagine he'd help me out."

"Don't jump to any more conclusions today, okay?" Rachel said, thinking of Blitz's encouragement to her on her way over. "You're so—so elegant, you make all the rest of us feel awkward. Most people are nervous and uncomfortable around strangers, after all, but they do want to find common ground, not look for the nearest rock to pick up and throw."

It was a talk she gave to at least one student at least once a term, but

Gina said, "Actually, I don't believe that. If it was true, we wouldn't have so many wars."

"But you're part of that peace group. If you want peace, then why not try practicing peaceful behavior? It's that old saying of Gandhi's, 'Be the change you want to see in the world.'" Rachel stopped, embarrassed to find herself preaching. "Is there someone you could stay with or someone in your group who could come out to be with you tonight?"

"Call me from the Grelliers'," Gina said. "If Blitz or Jim can come over to nail things shut, I think I'll be okay. Maybe I should let Elaine Logan move in here, after all—she could sleep in the living room, where anyone coming in through the front would trip over her."

Rachel smiled, but said seriously, "At least you wouldn't be alone in the house."

Twenty-Five

ADOLESCENT FURY

IT WAS SIX-THIRTY, the autumn twilight a hazy purple, when Rachel pulled into the Grelliers' yard. Lights were on in the kitchen and one of the upstairs rooms. When she knocked on the back door, she heard a chair scrape, and then Jim opened the screen door for her. His face was thin and drawn, but he smiled kindly at her.

"Blitz said you'd be stopping by. Come on in."

Blitz, sitting at a table in a little eating alcove, got to his feet and ambled over. The pain behind Rachel's eyes lessened, and she looked around, curious. Unlike the Spartan kitchen at the Fremantle place, this was filled with color and family artifacts: the children's clay handprints on one wall, school artwork in Lucite frames, blue ribbons from the county fair, a signed baseball in a Lucite box.

"That's George Brett," Jim explained, when he saw Rachel looking at the baseball. "Chip caught one of his foul balls when he was five, the last year Brett played. We stayed after the game and got it signed."

When she stepped closer, Rachel saw a faded snapshot of Chip standing next to his hero, grinning ecstatically. Her heart contracted at the wide, gap-toothed smile. *"Where have all the young men gone,"* she murmured under her breath.

"How did it go over at Fremantles'?" Blitz asked.

"Okay enough," Rachel said. "But something rather frightening happened." She explained about the intruder and finished with a request to help bar some of the entrances.

"Gina should come over here," Jim said. "If someone's breaking in—you say that she's there alone right now? I'll call her, she can sleep on the sunporch, it's plenty warm enough right now. Maybe—maybe Susan will get up if Gina comes over."

"She isn't getting up at all?" Rachel was aghast.

Jim shook his head. "I took her to the doctor finally. He gave her an antidepressant, but he said it could take six weeks for it to take hold, and it's hard to talk her into swallowing the pills."

"Jim, I'm so sorry." Rachel laid a hand on his arm, then jerked it away as if she had done something shameful in touching him. "Would you like me to see her before I leave?"

"You could try," he said doubtfully. "Maybe a woman . . . what can I give you to drink? Blitz and I were having a beer, but there's tea or coffee. Maybe some kind of juice, I'm not sure."

"Tea. Point me to it and I'll do it, if you want to phone Gina."

Jim showed her an assortment of boxes in one of the cupboards and turned on the gas under the teakettle before taking the phone into the dining room. Rachel heard the eager note in his voice when Gina answered and turned firmly toward the stove, her headache suddenly harsher. She noticed Blitz watching her and wondered if all her confused feelings were written on her face. If so, she'd better turn on her public face, pretend she was facing a classroom.

Blitz went to a dish cupboard and brought her a mug, choosing one from the Kansas Farm Bureau that announced A KANSAS FARMER FEEDS 128 PEOPLE PLUS ME.

Rachel put a bag of mint tea in the mug. "I didn't realize Susan was in such bad shape. I mean, I knew she looked dreadful when Jim brought her to church last week, but not getting up!"

"Yep. I don't know what it is, guilt, maybe. Grellier doesn't discuss it. If she doesn't want the rest of her family to disappear on her, she should make an effort, get her feet back on the floor. With Susan, they're never exactly on the ground."

Rachel was startled by his frankness. "Do you dislike her?"

Blitz gave his crooked, unexpected smile. "Nope. I've always liked her. She and Jim took me in when I got lost in a snowstorm sixteen years ago.

She was pregnant with Lulu. Chip was two, maybe three. He gave me my nickname," he added irrelevantly, "Blitz, for blizzard. My real name— my parents, oh, they called me Aloysius. Parents! Who wouldn't rather be a blizzard? Chip was such a happy little boy . . ."

His voice cracked. He drank from his beer can to steady himself. "Chip named Lulu, too—he couldn't pronounce his *r*s when he was little. The whole family used to be so happy. Even if she does look at the world cockeyed, it's Susan's passion that's made this farm go. I couldn't live with her, myself—too many days when you leave her in the attic and come home and find her in the basement. Or sometimes the other way around. She gets fired up, then after a while she crashes and burns. She's never gone on like this before. Usually, two, three days, a week max, and she's, well, not revved up, but ready to pick up the reins again. I'm not saying losing a son isn't a special source of loss, but if you let yourself go too far away I don't know how possible it is to come back again."

He gave a self-conscious bark of laughter. "I don't usually say that many words from the beginning of the day to the end. Must be you have a gift for listening. I'm worried because I love them all. Especially Jim."

"So Lara—it's a tougher problem than I realized. Gina suggested— not that I believe it myself, but—Lara, Gina said she and Chip used to use the Fremantle house when it was empty—" Rachel broke off in the middle of her disjoint phrases.

"That Lulu was flitting around in there, pretending to be a ghost?" Blitz supplied. "It's possible, I suppose. She was out this afternoon; showed up again about forty-five minutes ago. She probably knows a lot of ways into Fremantles', but—what would she be doing there now?"

"She—or whoever it was—taped a, a roach." Rachel stumbled over the word. "Taped a roach to the mouth of a picture Gina has on the wall in her workroom. Do you think Lara is using drugs?"

Blitz rubbed the back of his neck, considering. "If she is, not a lot. And if she is, it's probably out of some crazy sense of connecting to Chip. He and Curly, they used to do reefer over in that house when it stood empty. I don't know why the boy thought anything he did was secret, even if he was alone in the dark, but Lulu— I'll talk to Curly. Damned jackass better not be getting weed for her."

"Who's Curly?"

"Tom Curlingford, the other guy who works out here."

"I didn't actually see the intruder. Gina told me that another teen in the area, developmentally disabled—Eddie, I think she said—"

"Yes, Eddie Burton. After he climbed up a tree to peep into her bathroom, Jim talked to Clem Burton, who promised to keep tabs on Eddie. The Burtons are a ramshackle family—Eddie could easily be breaking in at Fremantles', thinking it a pretty good joke."

Rachel hesitated. "I saw, not the intruder, but someone cutting through the field across the road this side of the tracks, and Gina said the Burtons live the opposite direction."

"Yeah, but Eddie doesn't have anything to do with his time. His parents are too disorganized to get him into a group home or job training. He's a grown kid, and he covers a lot of ground during the day. Some days, he rides the boxcars up the Santa Fe tracks as far as the outskirts of K.C. Ardis—his mom—once had to pick him up in Tonganoxie, and that's a good thirty miles away."

Jim came back into the kitchen, his face brighter after talking to Gina. "She doesn't want to spend the night—says she won't give local busybodies the satisfaction of driving her out of her own bed—if we'll go over to batten down the doors and loose windows. Brave lady."

Blitz headed for the barn to collect slats and hammers. The tea and Blitz's company had eased her headache, but Rachel felt the muscles clench again as she tried to think of a way to talk to Jim. She was too tired for subtlety.

"I didn't know how badly Susan was doing. It must be a terrible worry, on top of losing your son, so I hate adding to your burdens, but I'm concerned about Lara."

The brightness faded from his face, and he sat heavily on one of the kitchen stools. "She's not in trouble in school, is she?"

"She will be if she doesn't pull herself together soon. She's a popular kid, with the teachers as well as the students, and everyone wants to help her before it gets serious, but she's not doing her course work. I've tried to talk to her, but she refuses to meet with me. It might be good to set up some appointments for her with a counselor."

"Oh, my God. Where I am going to find the money? Susan's treatment, it's already been—Never mind, not your problem." He gave a ghost of a smile, a grimace so ghastly Rachel flinched.

Rachel suggested Natalie Grimshaw, an associate at their church who was trained in pastoral counseling, or perhaps the school counselor. "He's too swamped to do individual work long-term, but if Lara could see him once or twice maybe it would help—before you have to think about paying someone to listen to her. Since she won't meet with me at school, I thought I'd stop by, try to make her talk to me at home."

Jim shrugged, tired again, and spoke to the kitchen floor. "Yeah. Go on up, see her. I'm not much good for her right now. Between Susan and Chip, I don't seem to have much 'give' left in me. Unfair to Lulu, but—Damn it, Rachel, I feel she's being unfair to me, too, right now. Does that make me a terrible father?"

He pressed the heels of his hands into his eyes. "Sorry, Rachel. I'm going to pieces, I guess. I keep thinking of my grandparents, how they handled my father's death—and he was their only child. Sometimes I wonder if there's something wrong with me, a curse even—my father is killed, my son is killed, my wife is unraveling. What's wrong with me? I know we're not supposed to think like that—look how God spoke to Job—but I can't help asking why."

He looked up at her and forced a smile. "You've gone out of your way for Lulu, coming out here and all. Believe me, I'm grateful. Maybe if I'm out of the house, she and Susan will listen to you."

Rachel nodded, tears of pity pricking the backs of her eyelids. When he left, she took her tea with her up the flight of stairs between the kitchen and the dining room. She'd never been in the Grellier house, but it was a straightforward place, without the millions of doors at the Fremantles'.

Night had settled in while she was talking to Blitz and Jim. The upper hallway was dark. She saw a sliver of light on the floor to her left and moved cautiously toward it, hands out to feel for obstacles. When she reached the door the light was shining under, she shut her eyes for a moment, took a breath, as if she were jumping off the high board, and turned the knob.

Lara was lying in bed, wearing only a T-shirt and underpants, iPod in her ears, eyes shut. She didn't move when Rachel came into the room, but from the way she tensed, her eyes squinching tight, Rachel knew Lara was aware of her. She walked to the bed and pulled out the earpieces.

Lara sat up, scrambling to pull the comforter around her. It was a rose-colored quilt, which she had made for 4-H two years ago, with emblems of her life stitched to it—sunflowers, trumpets, basketballs, even a combine, worked out piece by piece from green and yellow scraps—and its bright hopefulness seemed pathetic against the pain and anger in Lara's face.

"I thought you were Dad. What are you doing here?"

"Giving you a chance to talk."

There was a plain deal desk, homemade, painted white, against one wall. Rachel pulled out the pine chair in front of it and turned it around, facing the bed. Her blisters were throbbing; she needed to sit.

"If I wanted to talk to you, I'd do it at school. Does Dad know you're here?"

"Yes. Were you in the Fremantle house this afternoon, Lara? What particular version of your reasons for being there should I tell your dad?"

"I wasn't there. I've been here since I got home from school."

"Blitz Fosse says you were out until about an hour ago."

"So you and Blitz are a gossip team now? Call Myra Schapen and get her to put it on her website."

Only years of dealing with surly adolescents kept Rachel from giving in to the anger Lara wanted to rouse in her. "Whoever was in the Fremantle house ran through your cornfield. Blitz didn't see anyone but you go past."

"Yeah, he thinks someone died and named him God, but he doesn't know or see everything. Lots of people live out our way. Being as how the corn is higher even than his all-seeing eye, I doubt he'd know if the whole track team was running through it."

Rachel changed the subject since she clearly had taken the wrong tack with the Fremantle house. "Lara, you're a smart girl and a good student. If you fail your courses, that will affect the whole course of your life: where you go to college—whether you can even go to college—what kinds of careers are open to you, everything. Perhaps you're trying to punish your mother for abandoning you right now when you need her most, but is the satisfaction you get from punishing your mom worth the harm you're doing yourself? I haven't talked to Susan; I will before I leave. If she is so depressed that she's not getting out of bed or eating, you could damage your own life without getting any response from her. Not because she doesn't love you, but because she doesn't have the strength to help you. Lara is the one person who can help Lara right now."

"This isn't Sunday school. You don't have to preach a sermon."

"You've been in my Sunday school class for sixteen months," Rachel said, "and my English class for a month. How many sermons have you heard me preach?"

Lara turned her head away, angry at being cornered, unable to come up with an answer.

"The hardest thing about adolescence is that everything seems too big. There's no way to get context or perspective," Rachel said. "Pain and joy without limits. No one can live like that forever, so experience finally comes to our rescue. We come to know what we can endure, and also that nothing endures."

She was speaking to herself more than to Lara. After twelve years in a classroom, she knew the intensity of adolescence, and knew no cure for it except growing up. And then one has age and experience, and mourns the loss of intensity. Maybe it's why musicians and mathematicians are said to peak young—poetry needs the fire of an unbounded universe.

"My so-called mother is an adolescent, then," Lara said sulkily. "She seems able to experience pain without limits."

Rachel didn't want to get sucked into that discussion. "When did she last eat?"

"She's not a baby, and I'm not her nurse. It's not my job to make her eat."

Rachel blinked at the savagery in Lara's voice. "I don't think it is, but I bet you keep an eye on what she does. When did she last eat?"

"She gets up when no one's in the house," Lara finally said. "Sometimes I find an empty carton, or she's eaten cold soup out of a can."

"Sounds appetizing. What about you—when did you last eat a real meal?"

"You want to move in and cook, and sleep with Dad?"

"I want to smack your smart little mouth, and I would if that would have the magic effect of turning you back to the person you were six months ago. As your teacher, in Sunday school and sophomore English, as a friend of your family, I want to help you if you will let yourself be helped." Rachel kept her voice calm, but she wondered if she had some longing for Jim that showed in her words or in her tone.

Lara reddened at Rachel's remark and even mumbled something like an apology, which reassured Rachel: if the girl still had some vestiges of courtesy in her, she wasn't out of reach yet. "I eat. Dad gives me grocery money. I buy stuff on my way home. That's how I know Mom's eating when I'm away because Dad doesn't like yogurt."

"Do you have a grandmother or aunt nearby, someone you could stay with for a bit? It must be hard to live here right now."

"Dad's folks died when he was nine. My mom's mother thinks Mom is pretending to be sick to make herself the center of attention. She and my grandfather live in Salt Lake City. Whenever they come to visit, all they do is criticize Dad for being a loser and tell Mom she's going to get skin cancer from being out in the sun."

"They sound wonderful," Rachel said. "Let's find someone in your life you could talk to. What about Pastor Natalie at church? Or Mr. Gartner at school?"

"I'm not sick. I don't need a therapist, if that's what you're suggesting. My brother died, in case you hadn't noticed. I have a right to be upset!"

"Yes, he did. Would it make Chip happy to know you were doing your best to fail your classes in his memory?"

"That's not fair!"

"Blitz told me how proud Chip was of your brains. He used to brag about you and your special accomplishments. The best way to honor him is to continue to be the person he was so proud of, don't you think?"

Lara didn't say anything, just pulled the comforter up around her head and rocked herself. Teachers must not touch students, Rachel reminded herself, putting aside the impulse to gather the girl up, quilt and all, and hold her until her dry sobbing subsided. Instead, she spoke briskly to the shrouded head.

"The term is only a month old. It's not too late to pull yourself together. You owe me two essays, which I'm going to give you a chance to make up. I talked to your teachers in biology, Spanish, and math. They are willing to let you redo your first month's assignments. Today is Monday. You can turn your papers in to me this Friday."

Rachel stood. "I'm going to try to talk to your mother, but if she's decided to withdraw from life I can't make her return. Lara, if you don't have an aunt or grandmother you can live with then you need someone who cares about you to talk to. You can talk to me whenever you feel like it, but I'd like you to have someone you feel close to. Are you staying in touch with your friends?"

"All they care about these days is who's going to the homecoming dance with who. They don't want to hear about Chip, even if it's just memories about him. If I talk about him, they tell me not to be morbid. They don't want to think about the war, or people getting murdered, or even mothers who lock themselves in their bedrooms. Melanie's mother's a drunk. That doesn't stop people from being friends with her!"

The quilt muffled Lara's voice, and Rachel had to lean forward to hear her. "Robbie Schapen?" she suggested.

"Robbie Schapen?" Lara shrieked, pulling the quilt from her head. "The Schapens hate us. Mr. Schapen arrested Mom, and Nanny Schapen *gloated* about it on their website. Junior got Chip in trouble—he's why Chip ran away from school and died. Robbie Schapen is—a—a— hornworm from a whole family of vermin."

"Whatever a hornworm is. Maybe you should try talking to him. I was Junior Schapen's teacher, too, you know, and Robbie isn't the least bit like him."

Rachel put the chair back under the desk. "Your father and Blitz Fosse are over nailing the entrances to the Fremantle house shut, so if you were the person who broke in there you should know that it will be much harder to get in and out now. And if you are smoking the marijuana that was taped to Gina's photograph, don't forget that Arnie Schapen is a deputy sheriff. If he really does hate your family, he'd be happy to have the chance to arrest you for possession. You in juvie court is not something that would help anyone, least of all Chip."

Twenty-Six

THE MIDNIGHT DISEASE

WHEN SHE KNOCKED on the door of the master bedroom and no one answered, Rachel turned the knob and walked in. Lara had exaggerated only that one detail, that Susan had locked herself in. The rest of the story was much worse.

The room was dark and smelled of stale sweat, unwashed sheets, and a faint moldy odor that baffled Rachel until she fumbled her way to a light switch. The must came from the old books, stained orange with mildew, that covered much of the bed. More books were on the floor next to it.

Susan was sitting cross-legged against the headboard, wearing gray sweats that hung so loosely on her she looked like a marionette inside a sack. The clothes seemed oddly familiar. After a puzzled moment, Rachel saw they had LAWRENCE HIGH SCHOOL printed up one leg and the lion mascot on the top: Susan was wearing her dead son's workout clothes. She was surrounded by piles of paper covered with her large, round script; she was holding a pen and pad of paper in her lap.

"Do you write in the dark?" Rachel asked.

Susan stared at her blankly. "I turned off the light for privacy, but that doesn't seem to mean anything to you since you barged in anyway."

Rachel wondered where Jim was sleeping. Maybe the sunporch he'd been offering Gina, or even his son's room. No one could possibly want to sleep in this smelly room, in a bed filled with books and paper.

"What are you writing?"

"Words. Words." Susan waved her hands as if that would explain her meaning.

Rachel picked up a piece of paper at random.

War the answer to a mother's prayers. War, Peace, War, Peace. Peace you live without. Find peace, find death, find war, find life, lose all, the dice throw. Milton, Shakespeare, sin of sins.

Rachel let the page fall back onto the bed and picked up one of the musty books. It was an old journal, the entries dating to the 1850s. The book fell open to a page which Susan apparently read often, judging by the intermarginal notes in her round hand. Rachel squinted to make out the faded script, with its high curling *f*s and *s*s.

August 24, 1855

I woke alone in the middle of the night, alone save for my babe. Abigail Comfort Edwards: who are you, where are you? Only the wind rushing through the prairie grasses hears me, and it pays me no more mind than if I was one of the hundred thousand grasshoppers buzzing through those grasses all day long.

And then I laughed at myself, a shade hysteric, for I had even forgot that I am no longer Abigail Comfort Edwards but Abigail Grellier, a married lady, mother of a baby boy, and of my precious lamb who lies with Jesus.

Next to it, Susan had written, "Who is Susan Brandon Grellier? Grasshopper."

Rachel looked at Susan. "Abigail—that was Jim's great-great-grandmother, I think you told me. It sounds as though she also lost a child. What kept her going?"

"She had a vision," Susan said. "Her vision sustained her. I had no vision, only the desire for one."

"What was her vision?"

Susan beckoned to her. Rachel knelt next to her, holding her breath against the full smell of Susan's unwashed body.

"She saw the Mother of God in chains. A slave in chains, holding her broken Son, also a Negro slave," Susan whispered urgently in Rachel's ear, digging bony fingers into her shoulder. "She told no one. Congregationalists don't believe in the Madonna the way Catholics do—she thought her family would scorn her. But the Mother of God sustained her through every loss: her oldest child, her husband, and after her husband died she lost her last baby. Through it all, her vision kept her upright."

She shook Rachel's shoulder, making sure she was listening. "Pride. The angels fell because of pride. I think that's right, don't you? To be punished for too high an ambition?"

"Susan! God isn't a demon. He doesn't sit in His heaven pouring judgment out on us for being human, and He certainly doesn't start wars or send young men like Chip to fight and be killed in them because their mothers longed for visions."

"Etienne. Why can no one call him by his right name?"

"Etienne, then. God did not choose for Etienne to die, to punish you or Jim or Lara, or even Etienne himself. God knows what it's like to lose a child, after all: His own Son died a painful death, and God Himself stood by helpless while it happened."

Susan looked at her with the same blankness, as if Rachel were a stranger spouting Albanian or Hungarian, some incomprehensible language. "The empty womb. You preach about God and children from your empty womb. It's a joke—do you see?—a pun. Jesus was in the empty tomb; you're in the empty womb." She picked up the pad of paper in her lap and began writing again.

Rachel could tell her own face was scarlet, the stereotype of the old-maid schoolteacher, no knowledge of the outside world allowed except what she learned from books. She wanted to cry out, "I've loved and lost, even a pregnancy I've lost," but she only said, "I'd like to change the sheets, Susan. You'll feel more comfortable in a clean bed."

Susan didn't pause or look up. "I don't want to be comfortable."

"And Jim? And Lara? Do they need to be comfortable?"

Susan kept scribbling. "If you came here to lecture me on my duties as a wife, don't. You never married. You know nothing about it."

"You have two children, Susan. Lara is starting to fail her classes, she needs you. Do you want to lose her as well as Chip—Etienne?"

"I don't have a quotation dictionary. Who said 'the sin by which the angels fell'? I was sure it was Milton, but I tried to find it on the computer and couldn't. Didn't you study poetry in college? I did. It's how Jim and I met. He took a poetry class as an elective his junior year, in between Topics in Plant Pathology and Building a Business Plan for Your Farm. I used to know lines and lines and lines of Elizabeth Barrett Browning, but after all these years of working the land I can't remember the simplest poems. Can you give Lara a quotation dictionary to bring home for me?"

"Susan." Rachel stopped, not knowing how to go on. They didn't offer a course in managing destructive families when she was studying education. Finally, she decided to ignore the sidetrack on poetry.

"Lara has to do her homework. That's all I'm sending home with her, her homework. You must read it, you and Jim both. I'm going to tell Lara you both have to sign it before I'll look at it: I need to know you're paying attention to what she's doing."

"She's fifteen. Girls of fifteen were running households a hundred fifty years ago. Do you think we're too easy on our children? Do you see that in the classroom, Rachel? A generation of young people we haven't expected enough from? The last true measure of devotion, does any child know that anymore before they go for soldiers? I used to know the answer to that quotation but I can't think what it is anymore."

"Lincoln at Gettysburg," Rachel said helplessly. "'That from these honored dead we take increased devotion to that cause for which they gave the last full measure of devotion.' I doubt that Chip would consider you hiding up here in his dirty sweats an appropriate measure of devotion. Won't you get up, get out of bed long enough for me to wash the sheets and wash those clothes?"

At that, Susan did look full at her, eyes blazing. "I will not have you wash the last trace of my son *Etienne* from my body. Nor may you tell me what he would or wouldn't consider appropriate devotion. I am his mother. If the mother of Jesus could weep at His grave and hug Him to her, in all His blood, why can't I hug my dead son's sweat to me? They wouldn't let me see him covered with blood. I can only feel his sweat."

"What will you do if Lara turns to drugs? Or if Jim can't get in all the crops? Your organic sunflowers looked pretty withered to me."

"Don't preach to me, Rachel Carmody. You know nothing about farming and very little about children." She turned back to her pad, scribbling madly, ripping sheets of paper off and tossing them aside.

For the second time that evening, the Grellier women, divided on every other point, had accused Rachel of preaching. Was she? Had she spent so many years in front of a class that she assumed she knew better than anyone else?

Rachel picked up one of Susan's discarded pages.

Some buried Caesar bled last full measure of devotion—we the living living living are the walking mocking dead dead dead—devotion— true devotion—best friend—Jesus Jesus Jesus no gods before ME I take your sacrifice and condemn you to death. Meddling

Rachel got unsteadily to her feet. "At least take your medicine, Susan. Maybe it will help you find your way to an authentic vision."

Susan didn't answer. Rachel went back out to the dark hall and groped her way to the stairwell. Her face was ashen, her hands trembled. When she saw Blitz and Jim in the kitchen, she fought back tears with an effort. The headache had returned, making it hard for her to see.

"I'm afraid I was in over my head with both Lara and Susan. I'm sorry—I thought I could do some good, but all I did was stir them up."

"Yep. It's that kind of time. I appreciate you trying, Rachel, I truly do." Jim clasped her shoulder and let it go. "I guess I should think about some supper for Lara."

"Why don't you sit down, have a beer with Blitz? I'll think about dinner—it's the least I can do, maybe the only thing I can do."

Next to him, Blitz nodded. "Good idea, Ms. Carmody. Jim and I've been harvesting soybeans all day, and we are about as tired as is possible without actually falling down."

Rachel scrubbed out the sink, washed the stack of dirty dishes that had piled up since Jim or Lara had last felt like cleaning. The mindless housework was calming, even though her feet hurt through Gina's bandages.

She rummaged through the cupboards and refrigerator, minding Jim's warning that Blitz was a vegetarian, and settled on spaghetti with tomato sauce and cheese. There weren't any vegetables fresh enough for a salad, but she found a bag of broccoli in the freezer. All the time she was cooking, she kept thinking of Lara's snippy "You want to move in and cook, and sleep with Dad?"

Nonetheless, when she had the table set, for four, she went back up the stairs and knocked on Lara's door. A muffled sound that might have been yes or no or go away made her open the door. Lara had pulled on a pair of jeans. She was reading *The Hobbit,* earpieces in, but didn't get up when Rachel told her there was spaghetti on the table. Rachel went down the hall and gave Susan the same news, but neither mother nor daughter appeared at supper.

Rachel finally joined Blitz and Jim at the table in the alcove. The men were hungry after twelve hours in the fields and another hour sealing up the Fremantle house, but Rachel could barely bring herself to go through the motions of eating.

"We did a rough and ready job—bolted the doors, nailed slats over the ones that can't be locked from the inside, and put wooden blocks in the ground-floor windows so they can't be raised. Gina's a mighty calm and determined lady, I'll say that for her," Blitz said. "I suggested she move into town if things were too tough out there, but she said she had a right to be in the house, no one was going to budge her."

"I had her add my cell phone to her speed dial. If anyone does try to break in, I can be there in five minutes," Jim added.

"That's good," Rachel said mechanically, imagining the chaos if he bounded in and found his daughter taping roaches to Gina's pictures. "I wondered if it would be good for Lara to stay with a friend while Susan is so upset." The inadequate word made her feel all her inadequacies. She saw her own handwriting, red ink,

Use a word more appropriate to the level of emotion you are trying to convey.

"No!" The word burst from Jim. "She's my only anchor to sanity right now. I'm not going to have her go live with strangers. I lost my son. I'm not going to lose my girl."

"There's losing, and then there's *losing*, Jim," Rachel tried to keep her voice steady but couldn't manage—the day had been far too long already. "If Lara fails her classes, or starts using drugs, you will have a hard time getting her back."

"Lulu's too steady to get into that kind of trouble," Jim said. "She knows I'm counting on her. Maybe she's a little rocky right now—heck, we all are—but she'll pull through. As soon as we get the winter wheat planted, I'll talk to Glen Meadows. He knows Lulu from church, he knew Chip, he's a good man. Maybe he'll let Lara take a leave of absence or cut her course load to what she can handle right now."

"He might," Rachel agreed. The principal was a decent person, wanting his students to succeed. "Susan—" But she couldn't think of anything to say about Susan and finally asked lamely what the doctor had said.

"He said it wasn't surprising for a mom to be upset when her son was killed," Jim said flatly. "He gave her some drugs, like I told you."

"You know she's writing a lot?"

"The doctor said keeping a journal can help her work through her loss."

Rachel folded her napkin into the shape of a bird. "Have you read any of it? She's got hundreds of pages with only a few words on them."

"I'm not invading Susan's privacy. It's her way of showing grief, and I respect that."

"Lara feels you're expecting her to be Susan's minder, see that she eats or—or whatever. She resents that."

"Well, damn it, Rachel, I can't get Susan to eat. I'd think her daughter would want her mother to be healthy."

"She does, Jim. She wants her to be a mother, not an invalid. She doesn't want to have the roles reversed right now. That's why I thought it might be good for Lara to be where someone could mother her."

"If I didn't think you meant well, Rachel, I swear you and I would have a falling-out. Listen to me: my daughter is not going to live with strangers. That's final."

Rachel pushed her stool away from her uneaten food and stumbled to the door, bumping into the counter and the stove because she couldn't see through the tears she was blinking back. Absolutely the last time she would try to do good for anyone, whether student, family, or homeless drunk falling through the cracks.

Blitz, who hadn't spoken during Jim's and Rachel's conversation, got to his feet and followed her to her car. "His world's fallen apart. Don't blame him too much."

"I was probably out of line." She just managed to get the words out.

"The fact that he's too scared to listen doesn't mean you were wrong to speak. I'm going to ride into town behind you; I don't want you falling into a ditch on your way home. Or at least if you do, I'll be there to pull you out."

She smiled gratefully. The truck headlights in her rearview mirror kept her company all the way back to her tidy ranch house. Blitz stayed outside until she'd unlocked her door and flashed the porch light for him.

Twenty-Seven

NIGHT VISITORS

IN THE NIGHT, the unbearable late-year heat broke. A thunderstorm moved through the valley, waking Jim as he slept on the sunporch. He sat up on the folding bed and watched lightning fork to the ground along the river two miles away, and then rain poured on the house, pounding the uninsulated porch roof with the urgency of stampeding cattle.

The corn was close to harvest. Too much rain now and it would rot in the ground. He couldn't summon fear or worry about it. Like everything else on the farm, whether the corn rotted or came in perfectly seemed uninteresting. Losing the crop would increase his financial worries, but even that couldn't spark any emotion in him.

He looked across the fields to the east, but the angle of the house blocked any view of the Fremantle place. Was Gina asleep? Was she all right? On a restless impulse, he pulled on his jeans and a slicker and drove the pickup along the pitted road to the Fremantles'. The house was dark, its gables emerging in the sudden flashes of lightning and then disappearing again, a black blot against the fields. The rain streamed across his windshield in a thick gel.

Lightning suddenly lit the entire landscape, as if a movie crew had set up shop on the Fremantle veranda. In the blue-gray flash, he thought he saw a person outside the big front doors. He climbed down from his truck cab. The rain covered him like a shroud, pouring inside the collar of his slicker, so that in a moment he was wet inside his coat.

He put his hands over his head and stumbled to the veranda as fast as he could. The wind was whipping water across the porch floor, but the wide wooden canopy provided some protection from the wet. He scuttled to the great double doors, wondering what he'd do if Eddie Burton or even Junior Schapen were there.

It was Elaine Logan. Encased in a black trash bag, she slouched against the double doors, another black bag full of her belongings next to her, a pint bottle nestled in a crease in her lap.

She smiled up at him. "Hello, Farmer Jones. Wet enough for you and your corn?"

Even without the muzzy smile and the pint bottle, he could tell she was drunk. "You can't stay out here, Elaine. You're trespassing. Gina doesn't want you here. I'll drive you into town, find you a place to spend the night."

"It's my home more'n it's hers. I'm just a little girl. You can't beat up on me." The words came out in a high-pitched baby voice.

Jim felt the skin on his arms crawl underneath his clammy shirt. "No, Elaine, you're not a little girl. You want to be someplace dry, don't you? Up on your feet; now, there's a good woman. Let me drive you into town."

"Who are you, you big bully? You mind your own business and leave me alone, damn you. I got a right to be here, more'n you have. They told me I could stay." She began howling, so loudly her wails could be heard over the thunder.

He looked down at her angrily. Another damned woman in his landscape who didn't give a rat's ass about what he thought or wanted or needed. He wanted to howl himself.

At that moment, the front doors swung open behind Elaine. She toppled backward in a heap of trash bags and vodka. Gina stood above her, wearing a pair of jeans and loafers underneath her combed-cotton nightshirt.

She jumped to one side as Elaine fell over. "I heard the noise. What is she doing here?"

"I don't know," Jim said. "Storm woke me and I couldn't get back to sleep, so I thought I'd check up on you, and there she was."

"When I looked out and saw your truck, I thought it was Eddie Burton. My heart started pounding like—like whatever they pound like when you're frightened." Her voice was cool, but Jim saw she was carrying a carving knife and that her hand was shaking.

"Don't try taking on Eddie with a knife, not unless you know how to use it," Jim said. "He could wrestle it from you and use it against you. And don't open the door when you're alone here in the middle of the night. If I had been Eddie—" He clipped off the end of the sentence without finishing it.

In one of the blue-steel flashes of lightning, her crooked teeth showed as she smiled. "I'd be lying in a pool of arterial blood. Yes, I need to be more sensible, but Elaine's howling— Where is she, anyway?"

She moved back into the hall and found a light switch. The bronze-edged chandelier came on but with such a feeble glow that Jim that couldn't see the homeless woman, for all her great size.

"Elaine!" he called. "Elaine?"

He and Gina both turned at a sound from the stairs above them. Elaine was inching her way up the stairs on her rump, going backward like a dog crawling out of a room, hoping no one will notice he's got the family roast in his mouth. When she saw that they'd noticed her, Elaine put her fingers over her face, giggled, and squeaked, "Peekaboo!"

Jim shut his eyes. "How did you get out here, anyway, Elaine? Were you in the house this afternoon?"

"Ask me no questions, I'll tell you no lies," she said in a singsong, her fingers still covering her eyes.

"Elaine, Ms. Haring doesn't want you here. You come with me, like I already offered, and I'll drive you into town."

She pouted. "I won't go. I belong here, way more than you do, Farmer Jones. This is my home, I was born here."

"What are you talking about? I've lived here my whole life. I know all the Fremantles. You were never born out here."

"Gina isn't a Fremantle, but she gets to live here, so why can't I? I even knew Mrs. Fremantle, she let me stay, and Gina never laid eyes on her that I heard of, Farmer 'Know-It-All' Jones."

"I don't know what she's talking about," Jim said to Gina. "She showed up out here two or three times in the last ten years, but I don't think your uncle's mother ever let her spend the night in the house."

"That's a lie, Farmer Jones, and you Christians go to hell for lying. Mrs. Fremantle did too let me stay here, I have a paper to prove it."

Jim looked helplessly at Gina. "She's too big for me to budge on my own. Do you want me to call the sheriff? I'm afraid that means Arnie, but he'd be able to bring a crew. They could at least get her out of your hair."

"Call the sheriff, call the sheriff, he can start a fire like he did at midsummer, we'll all be dry and warm," Elaine crooned above him. "You wanna see my paper about my mommy and me living here before Sheriff Arnie burns me up in smoke?"

"See? You get everything backward!" Jim fumed. "He didn't start the midsummer fire, he put it out! And your mother never lived here. I hope you aren't trying to pretend you're one of Liz Fremantle's children."

Elaine started to scrabble in her bag, pulling out a brassiere whose cups looked like skillets. She dropped it negligently on the stairs, followed it with some men's boxer shorts. "I got my paper here somewhere."

Jim looked away, looked at Gina, whom he expected to mirror his own revulsion. Instead, she was looking thoughtfully at Elaine.

"I don't want Arnie Schapen to help me manage my life. Elaine can spend the night. I can put a clean blanket on one of the beds. You're soaked, Jim, and it's turned chilly. You'd better go home and get dry before you come down with something. Thank you for checking on me."

The words were thoughtful, but she hurried him out the door so fast that he felt his skin prickle with shame, as if Gina could see into his heart, could know that he had driven over out of his own loneliness and need, not because of any altruism over her. He walked back into the wet, not staying to hear whether she had pushed home the bolts he and Blitz had installed on her front door this afternoon.

He turned the truck around in the yard, but at the entrance to the road he stopped, not wanting to go home despite his wet clothes. He turned the heater up to HIGH and stared north, at his own corn, the stalks bending under the pummeling from wind and water. His crop, his wife, his daughter—all these worries he couldn't think about. He sat like that for almost an hour, not dozing, just staring frozenly at the corn. The 4:32 westbound freight finally roused him, and he pulled into the road. The surface had turned to wet clay; he had to fight to keep his truck from skidding into the drainage ditch.

At the intersection with the county road, he waited for the last freight cars to roll past. The rain had finally eased; puddles glinted black under the crossing lights. The caboose rumbled by. Jim had the truck in gear, ready to go, when he saw a slender figure jump free from the caboose ladder and land in the weeds to his left. The figure rolled a few feet and lay still.

Jim was opening his truck door to see if the man was injured when he realized it was Eddie Burton. He wasn't about to risk another rebuff tonight, especially not from one of the Burtons. Anyway, Eddie's posture made Jim think he was lying doggo until he had the road to himself.

Jim drove across the tracks and turned in to his own yard, where he killed the truck lights. He waited a minute, then drove back out to the road. He squinted up the slight rise at the tracks and saw Eddie's slim figure shambling south toward the Burtons'.

If Eddie had been the person in the Fremantle house this afternoon, he could easily have run into the Grellier corn and hunkered down, waiting for the 6:43 eastbound freight. What did he do, roaming around the county all day? And what business was it of Jim's, come to think of it?

It was almost five now, no point in returning to bed—this close to his usual rising time, he wouldn't go back to sleep. Standing in the yard, he noticed the light was on in the master bedroom. Did Susan know he'd gone out? Was she taking advantage of the cover of night to do her endless writing?

He hadn't been in his own bedroom for several days, not since he'd taken Susan to the doctor. Despite his assurances to Rachel, Susan's writing frightened him. He'd tried tidying some of the papers. Susan had watched as if he, Jim Grellier, were an intruder on his own land, in his own house, as if his wife were holding herself still until the intruder left, just as Eddie had lain in the weeds a few minutes ago, as if Jim, whose family had farmed this valley for a hundred fifty years, were the prowler, not Eddie, whose shiftless parents let him ride all over the state looking for houses to break into.

He felt a rage rise in him, against his wife for treating him like this, against Gina, against Eddie, against the world. If he went inside now, he might murder Susan, or at least violate every code of decency he lived by.

He went to the back of the barn, where Chip had cleared out space for a weight-training room. His Christmas present to his son two years ago had been a complete weight set; he'd found a used machine in Overland Park that Blitz cleaned and refitted.

Chip had been so sure building his upper body would give him the edge he needed to make it to the pros. The Royals had the worst record in baseball this season. Would they be any worse off if they'd given his boy a chance in A-ball? In his head, Jim kept writing them a letter: you could have given him a chance—would that have killed you?—could've, would've, should've, don't walk down that road. Pastor Albright had counseled Jim and Susan on that in the one session they'd attended. Good advice, if you could bring yourself to follow it.

Jim turned on the bare bulb that hung over the corkboard Chip had put on the floor. Dust and cobwebs covered everything. He got a bucket and a bottle of bleach and scrubbed the floor, the equipment, even the light fixture. He stripped off his wet clothes and turned on a space heater. By the time the area was clean, he was already sweating, but he unfastened the barbell and started lifting weights. He worked for forty-five minutes, pushing himself beyond his limits, as if daring the fates to cripple or destroy him, but all that happened was his undershorts and T-shirt got soaked through. Finally, he returned the equipment to its racks, lining everything up so that Chip would find it all in order.

He lay down on the cork floor to rest his back and fell asleep. In his dreams, he was playing catch with Chip at Royals Stadium in Kansas City. Chip was five, with his front teeth missing, but he had the coordination of an adult, and George Brett was saying, "You belong in the outfield, son," so Chip ran out on his little-boy legs, face full of joy. George Brett started hitting fungoes to him, and Chip held out his hand in its outsize glove. "Don't touch it," Jim tried to yell, but he couldn't make a sound. As he watched, frozen to the ground, the ball exploded in Chip's hands, splintering his small body into red smears that filled the stadium, so that Jim himself was suddenly chest-deep in blood.

He woke, his heart pounding, his mouth dry, his throat raw. When he sat up on the cork floor, the muscles in his shoulders and lower back ached so badly that he could hardly pull himself upright. The pain he'd been seeking in the night had filled his joints while he slept, and, now that he had it, he didn't want it. He only wanted to feel better. "Don't wish for anything too hard," his grandmother used to say, "because you won't relish it when you get it." Right as usual, Gram. He tipped an imaginary hat to her, and staggered to the sink in the far corner of the barn to sluice his head under the hose. The water was cold, and it only made him hurt worse.

His jeans had dried in front of the space heater while he slept. He pulled them on but carried his shirt and slicker. Outside, it was still raining—the soft misery rain that goes on and on, like the whimpers of a teething baby. The temperature had fallen thirty degrees in the night. By the time he'd hobbled through the rain into the house, his teeth were clacking from the cold.

He found Lara heating a frozen waffle in the microwave. It was eight o'clock. She should have been out of the house by now.

"Dad! I thought you were working the north quarter with Blitz!"

"Is that why you're pampering yourself like the Queen of the May in here instead of having your fanny in your chair over at school?" He gasped in pain and grabbed the back of a chair to support himself.

"What have you been doing? You look like a train wreck. Did the tractor fall over on you?"

"My ego fell over on me. The storm woke me, and I decided to work out with Chip's weights in the barn. I way overdid it."

He didn't tell her about driving to Fremantles', much less about seeking out pain. It wasn't the kind of thing you burdened your kid with. Besides, in the cold of the morning it seemed idiotic. He asked instead if she had any ibuprofen. Lara rummaged in her backpack; her face alight with mischief, she handed him a bottle labeled FOR RELIEF OF MEN-STRUAL CRAMPS. He shook his head but poured out a handful of tablets, chewing four and laying the rest on the kitchen counter before handing the bottle back to her.

"Gross, Dad, don't you even want some water with those?"

"I'd have to walk to the sink. I'll just stand here until they kick in."

She suddenly started fussing around him, bringing him juice, putting water on to boil for coffee, running down to the laundry room in the basement for a clean, dry shirt, tossing the wet one in the machine, then coming back up to help him fasten the buttons.

He brushed her fingers aside. "Okay, okay, knock it off. You've earned your written pass for being late."

"Thanks, Dad." She grinned at him, the old Lulu briefly showing through the new, sullen Lara.

He put his hand under her chin and tilted her head so that she had to look at him. "Sweetheart, the one thing I really need you to do for me isn't making me coffee, although this tastes better than what I boil up, but to buckle down with your classes. You hear? I don't want any more teachers making a home visit because you're not doing your work."

"Okay, Dad, okay," she muttered.

He walked to the desk in the corner of the kitchen where he and Susan kept the farm accounts and found a pad of paper in the jumble of unopened mail. The sight overwhelmed him. He was behind in everything—quarterly tax returns, bills—he hadn't even balanced the checkbook this month, although Susan usually did that. If he didn't pay the grain elevator today, he wouldn't be able to store his corn when he started harvesting.

He massaged the small of his back with his left hand while he wrote out a short note for Lulu. She kissed the top of his head and skipped out to the old pickup. After Chip enlisted last spring, Blitz had fixed the truck so that Lara could drive herself to school. It was over twenty years old, its battered body so rusty and weathered you couldn't tell it had once been blue. Blitz had taken the engine completely apart, fixed all the cylinder heads, and found four good used tires for it at Hardy's Tire Shack. Lara had scorned it at first—it looked so ratty next to Chip's Nissan or the SUVs some of her classmates drove—but, that summer, she'd fallen in love with it. Her art project for the county fair, in fact, had been to paint the sides with a history of the Grellier farm, from the days of the dinosaurs to the present. She hadn't won a ribbon, but Jim loved the pictures. Susan did, too—or had, when she was still paying attention to Lara.

After a time, when the ibuprofen started to work and he wasn't quite so sore, Jim went upstairs to change out of his dirty jeans and socks. He took a hot shower in the kids' bathroom. Then, wearing just the clean shirt Lulu had dug up for him, he stood outside his bedroom door for a long minute, praying for courage to go in for clean socks and underwear.

When he went in, Susan was sitting at the vanity table he had bought her their first Christmas together, writing on one of the pads Lara made out of old government reports by cutting them into 8½-by-11 sheets and stapling them so the blank sides faced up.

" 'Morning, Suze," he said warily, trying not to notice the smells in the room: old clothes, old sweat, old blood.

She glanced up at him but kept writing.

"Suze, we need to talk. This isn't good, for any of us, you sitting up here, writing your head off, not eating, not bathing."

When she didn't respond, he walked over to her and gently took the pen and notepad away from her. She didn't protest but started scrabbling through the heap of pages on the vanity for another pen. He took her hands and knelt in front of her, his joints giving him such a jolt he couldn't keep back a grunt of pain, but she didn't seem to notice.

"Suze, we're all going crazy here over Chip, all three of us in our unique ways. Yours is the most public and obvious, but Lulu isn't doing her schoolwork—she's deliberately courting failure, Rachel Carmody said last night. I'm not attending to the crops or the bills. I can't do it alone. I can't keep the farm going without you, don't you understand?"

"The farm has weathered troubled times before," she said, her eyes flicking anxiously to the paper he'd placed behind him on the bed.

"No, darling. The family has weathered troubled times. The farm just exists, regardless of who owns the land. But if we lose the land, how will we exist? Please, baby, please get up and help me."

"I will, Jim, I really will, as soon as I finish writing this. I can't do anything until I get it all off my chest."

"Susan, I'm begging you—if not for me, for the farm. You've always loved this place, the history has mattered so much to you. Help me preserve it so we can pass it on to Lulu."

"That's what I'm trying to write here, Jim, how history affects us, how our lives are controlled by it. When I'm done with that, I promise I'll come down and go through the bills and help you get it all sorted out."

She twitched her hands free from his loose clasp and scurried to retrieve her pen and notepad. He sat on the floor, arms over his head, and rocked in misery.

Twenty-Eight

WEIRD—REALLY WEIRD— NEIGHBORS

JIM SPENT what was left of the morning in his north quarter section, working with Blitz to dig up the soybean field. The crop had been infested with stem borers, which Jim should have seen sooner. By noon, the rain had started falling so heavily that they had to stop.

Blitz went home then, while Jim cleaned himself up for the second time that day. His back and legs still ached, but the morning's work and Lara's menstrual tablets had eased the worst of the pain. He heated the spaghetti left over from last night, tried to sort out the mess of papers on the desk in the corner, but his brain was cut in too many fragments for him to make sense of anything. He could hear Susan pacing the floor of the bedroom like a ghost, present in the house but not connected to it. The sound drove him so wild that he went into town with a check for the elevator. He lingered in the office, a bare room with a grimy cement floor that smelled of corn, to talk with Herb Longnecker and Peter Ropes, who were also using the rainy day to run errands.

No one would talk about the only things on his mind, Chip and Susan, but the weight of their pity lay heavy in the air. What they did discuss, besides the University of Kansas football team's sputtering performance and whether the school would do any better in basketball, was the story going around about Arnie Schapen's special calf.

"Did that lady reporter stop and talk to you, Jim?" Peter Ropes asked. "She came by my place, but I told her I had too much to do on my own farm to know what Arnie was doing on his."

"Lulu came home from church with some garbled story, that the Schapens had a calf they were turning into an idol, like the Israelites did, to tempt the rest of the valley, see if we'd fall down and worship it. I can't break my kids—can't stop Lulu—from gossiping about everyone around us, no matter how bizarre the story is."

"Dale, Arnie's dairy hand, he says it's some special calf the Jews need for their prayers," Herb Longnecker said. "He says these three Jews come over from Kansas City every month to check on it because if it has any flaws in it, they can't use it. There must be money in it somewhere, if the Jews are involved, so I don't see why Arnie isn't bragging about it more. Myra Schapen's mad as sin because the Jews say it'll hurt the calf's magic, or whatever it has, if a lady goes near it."

"That must be why we're not reading about it on the website," Peter chortled. "Usually, if Junior makes a tackle or Arnie blows his nose, she trumpets it all over the Internet."

"Funny how Myra never writes about the other boy," Herb said. "Our Ruth's daughter, Caroline, is in school with him—well, Lara must be, too, isn't she, Jim? Caroline says the boy is a good musician, plays lead guitar in his church's heavy-metal band. You'd think Myra would write something about him sometime. Instead, we're getting every detail of Junior's games at Tonganoxie Bible College."

"Heavy metal? What's that? Two combines falling on a guitar?" Peter Ropes laughed, and the meeting broke up.

Jim stopped at the store for some frozen pizzas. Lulu liked yogurt, but he always got the wrong kind, so he bought three different flavors just to be on the safe side. Ice cream—the two of them were keeping Wiesers Dairy in business these days, the amount of ice cream they were going through—chocolate for Lulu, strawberry for him. Vaguely thinking there should be something healthy on the menu, he added a head of lettuce and a bag of carrots, and tried not to read the total bill before running his credit card through the slot.

By the time he got home and unpacked the groceries, the rain had let up. His grandfather would have gone back out to the north quarter section. His grandmother would have somehow made Susan get out of bed and get back on an even keel.

If Gram had done like Susan and taken to her bed when Jim's father died, what would Grandpa have done? Jim couldn't imagine his grandmother behaving so extravagantly. He remembered the county fair when Susan first entered her apple pie out of Abigail's sketchy recipes in the old diaries. The judges had been dismayed and disdainful, and Susan came home weeping. Jim had tried to comfort her, but she took to her bed and lay there for two days. Gram got fed up.

"No one can be best at everything," Gram told her. "You learned a lot this year, Susan, and we're proud of you. Now you have to learn from your failures and move on. You certainly can't lie around feeling sorry for yourself, not with the hay to get in and the market to attend to. And the tomatoes need spraying—last night, Jimmy found hornworm in the west rows."

Susan had dragged herself out of bed—she never could stand up to Gram, who wouldn't cajole or tease her into feeling better, the way Jim or even Grandpa would.

Jim pictured himself going upstairs to her now. "No one can be number one at everything," he imagined saying, "not even at grieving. So learn from your loss and move on." But the thought of trying to talk to his wife again was so painful that he finally got back in the truck and drove south on the county road to Burtons'.

On the way, he couldn't help glancing at the Fremantle house. Gina's behavior last night still rankled. After he'd gone out of his way—helped her make the house secure, offered her a place to stay, driven over to check up on her in the middle of the storm—for her suddenly to act as if he wasn't there or didn't count, that made him angry. And then to let that homeless woman, that Elaine Logan, spend the night—and that was after Gina made Rachel Carmody come out because Gina claimed Elaine was more or less stalking her. Gina hadn't behaved well, by him or by Rachel: he was right to be angry. But he still looked down the road, as if he might see some kind of sign in the southeast bedroom where she'd set up her office.

"You expecting to see a banner reading COME MAKE LOVE TO ME, JIM GRELLIER?" he said aloud. He gunned the engine and hurtled down the county road toward Burtons' at seventy, jolting his sore spine in the potholes, spraying gravel into the ditches.

The beater Ardis used for getting to her job was parked along the edge of the road, maybe ready for a fast getaway, if she got so she couldn't cope with Clem and Turk and her children. Someone had flung a drop cloth over the Lincoln, but the rest of the cars on blocks were littered with branches and dead leaves from the weeping trees in the yard. Jim picked his way through the rusty parts to the back door.

Ardis answered his knock, blinking in surprise at the sight of a visitor. She had been a pretty young woman when she and Clem married, with dark hair and a firm, plump body, but the plumpness had oozed into fat during five pregnancies and life below the poverty belt. She wrinkled up her moon-shaped face in a sort of smile.

"Jim Grellier." Her voice came out in a slow, soft wheeze, as if the bellows for producing air were buried so far in her soft, fat breast that they could barely push sound to the surface. "I was sorry to hear about Chip, but you must feel real proud of him. Everybody says he was a hero."

"Thanks, Ardis. I'd rather be happy than proud, but I guess you don't get to choose, do you?"

She smiled uncertainly, not sure what he meant, but asked him to step inside. The pile of dishes in the sink he'd seen last December hadn't changed. Looking at the empty frozen-food boxes scattered on the counters and floor, he wondered if the dishes were a monument to the last time anyone had cooked a meal in the kitchen, then thought of the pizzas he'd picked up an hour ago for himself and Lara. Judge not, judge not, he reminded himself. Not so hard to see how everything could cave in around you.

"Where's Clem's father?" he asked. He'd expected to see the old man still at the kitchen table.

"Oh, last week he wandered out of the house and tripped and fell. He just doesn't know enough to watch where he's going anymore and he broke his hip, so he's in the nursing home for a bit. Until his Medicare runs out, I guess. Would you like some pop?" Her soft voice wheezed all the words together in one long breath.

"I'm fine, Ardis. I was hoping to talk to Eddie."

"He's in the living room, watching TV, with Turk and them."

Jim followed her across the cracked linoleum to the living room. Turk,

Clem, and Eddie were jumbled together on the couch, watching *Star Trek*. Eddie's sister Cindy was sprawled on the floor, eating chips; a tabby with a missing ear shared the dip container with her. The three youngest children were still in school, Ardis said. The bus would bring them home in an hour or two.

Turk was drinking out of a quart can of malt liquor, which he waved in a kind of salute when he saw Jim come into the room. "Hey, Grellier, how's it going?"

"Fine, Turk, fine," Jim said automatically. "Everything okay here?"

"Why wouldn't it be?" Clem tried to sit up, but the couch's sagging springs pulled him downward.

"No reason. I just wanted to make sure Eddie got home okay."

"Well, here he is, you can see him for yourself."

"Yep," Jim agreed. "Riding the rails, that's a hard way to get around, isn't it?"

Eddie smiled slyly and looked at his hands. With his head bent over, hiding his vacant expression, he was a nice-looking boy, almost girlishly pretty, except for his hands, which were broad and square. He resembled Ardis, the way she used to look before she cloaked herself in layers of fat—he had her dark curls and long lashes. He felt Jim's gaze and looked up; a thread of drool ran from the corner of his mouth to his sweatshirt. Eddie's shoulders were hunched over so Jim couldn't see the whole front of the shirt, but the letters ANOXIE B were visible.

"Tonganoxie," Jim said idly, filling in the missing letters.

Eddie's face changed from smirk to terror, as if Jim had accused him of blowing up the town. "I'm not in Tonganoxie, not there, no one seen me, I swear no one seen me."

"What's got into you, Eddie?" Ardis said from behind Jim. "Mr. Grellier here ain't saying he seen you, are you, Jim?"

"I saw him jumping off the westbound freight at four-thirty this morning. Way he was walking, I wondered if he'd twisted an ankle or something."

"Now, ain't that neighborly of you, Grellier." Clem spoke with heavy sarcasm. "You don't need to worry about my boy, when you couldn't take care of your own boy."

"Easy there, Clem," Turk protested. "Chip Grellier's a war hero. Jim couldn't'a saved him from a terrorist mine, no father could."

Jim's head began to swim from the strangeness of the conversation, but at least the fear died away from Eddie's face, replaced by his sly slack-jawed grin. He picked up a half-gallon bottle of cola from the floor in front of him and tilted his head back to drink. With his shoulders back, Jim could read the shirt: TONGANOXIE BIBLE COLLEGE.

"So you went to visit Junior Schapen?" Jim asked. "All the way from here by riding the rails? I didn't know the freights ran through Tonganoxie. I thought all the lines passed through Kansas City."

Eddie dropped the bottle, spilling cola over himself, the couch, and Clem, who jumped out of the sunken cushions with a curse and a smack along the side of his son's head. "Ardis! Ardis? Come and clean up after your retard son who just spilled shit all over the couch."

"I never seen Junior. Anyone who says they saw him and me, they's lying." Eddie was choking from the cola running the wrong way down his windpipe.

Ardis went over with a dirty bath towel and began dabbing at her son, and the couch, although most of the cola had run into the exposed foam rubber of the cushions.

Clem looked at his son in disgust. "What's got into you, boy? So what if you up and visited Junior Schapen? Why shouldn't you?"

"Junior don't like folks to know him and Eddie are friends." Cindy Burton spoke from the floor, startling Jim, who'd forgotten about her.

"Why not, Cindy?" Jim asked, like it was any of his business.

Turk laughed. "You went to college, Grellier. You show up on campus with a boy like Eddie, would anyone else talk to you?"

"That ain't fair, Turk," Ardis sighed, still dabbing at the foam rubber. "Eddie's a good boy, nothing to be ashamed of. If Junior Schapen thinks he's too good for Eddie, well, I say to hell with him. And to hell with Arnie, too."

"Arnie, don't say nothing to Arnie," Eddie said. "Arnie will kill me, kill Junior, we'll go to hell, not even the cow will save us."

"The cow?" Jim asked. "You can't mean Schapen really is worshipping a cow!"

"The cow is special, you can't talk about it!" Eddie cried, his eyes knuckling in his agitation.

"But—Arnie Schapen can't possibly believe a cow will save him. He goes to Full Salvation, or whatever that church is, out near Clinton Lake. It's Bible all the way through—they believe there's no salvation except through Jesus. And where do the Jews come in?"

"The Jews, they want that cow, and Arnie, he's keeping it for them, ain't that right, Eddie?" Cindy said helpfully from the floor. "When the Jews come right out and take it, then Arnie and them will be famous and richer than—than Donald Trump."

"You can't say about the cow, no one can't say," Eddie cried, thrashing his arms on the couch. To Jim's horror, his nose started to bleed.

"Eddie, Eddie," Ardis stroked his hair. "It's okay, it's all okay, baby. Come on. You come with Mommy. She'll fix you up, put ice on your nose, make you some fries in the oven, okay? Come on." She led the bleeding, snuffling Eddie from the room.

Clem turned to Jim. "Is that why you come here, Grellier? To get my boy all stirred up?"

I came here because I couldn't stand to be at home. The sentence popped into Jim's head, so upsetting him that he blurted out, "Someone was hiding out in the Fremantle house yesterday afternoon. They pasted a roach, a joint, on a picture. I wanted to make sure it wasn't Eddie."

"Eddie don't use dope, and don't you say otherwise. What are you going to do, report him to Arnie Schapen so Schapen can put on his tin star and put my boy away?"

"Yes, he does, too," Cindy said unexpectedly from the floor. "I seen him and Junior together a hunnert times, smoking and laughing and carrying on."

"So now you're a damned stool pigeon, too?" Clem demanded. "You gonna rat your own brother out to Mr. Sheriff's Deputy Schapen?"

"I know better'n talk to Mr. Schapen or any of them Schapens. I hate Junior, only him and Eddie are friends, so I have to do like they say, even when it's something dirty." Cindy's face turned red as tears of misery spurted out of her eyes.

"Oh, for chrissake, Cindy, get over it," Clem said. "And stay away from them boys if you don't want to get hurt. Jesus Christ, who is the retard in this family? Look what you started, Grellier!"

Jim began edging his way out of the room. He stepped on the cat, which yowled and spat and ran behind the couch. Turk laughed, which made Clem yell at his uncle not to treat the family like it was a TV show.

"And you, Grellier, go mind your own goddamn business. Maybe it was your wife over there yesterday, she's plenty friendly with that stuck-up dyke who won't even give me the time of day when I seen her at the food pantry. She'll talk to that drunk whore Elaine Logan, but when I offer to carry her bags for her she gets all snotty and looks at me like I'm a hole in the floor she has to step around."

Jim nodded, and backed out of the room. The bathroom was in a little room off the kitchen. As he passed it, he could hear Eddie crying still, and Ardis's wheezy voice crooning to him.

Twenty-Nine

SUICIDE TRY

WHEN JIM GOT HOME, he washed the dishes, scrubbed down the countertops, and swept and washed the floor. Since getting the news about Chip, he and Susan had let things slide around the house. He didn't want to slide down to Burton-style living.

What had he been thinking, to go over there at all? It was completely against his philosophy of not messing with the neighbors' business. All it did was set people's backs up. He'd told his kids that a thousand times if he'd told them once, and here he was a walking, talking example of how to get everyone stirred up against you. Clem Burton was a loose cannon; in the same half minute, he'd damned Arnie and Jim impartially, as if they were the same man, and who could blame him? Jim would have done the same if Clem came over claiming Lulu or Chip—claiming Lulu was breaking into someone's house.

He went up the stairs, into his bedroom. Susan was asleep. Anger was building in him. How dare she lie around like this, self-indulgent, hugging her grief while he tried to keep the farm going?

His ever-so-great-grandmother's diaries were on the bed, partially visible beneath the landfill of papers Susan had created. Papers covered the bed; more were scattered across the floor. He waded through them on his way to her side. He shook Susan's arm, lightly at first, but, when she didn't respond, more roughly.

She moaned; her eyes were puffy slits, but she didn't move. He bent down next to her. "Susan! Susan?"

He lifted her head, which lolled back on his arm. Fear chased his anger; for a long moment, he stood still. Was it her heart? Starvation? The drugs? A hoarse gasp from his wife goaded him to action. He slid through the mass of papers to the bathroom and scrabbled in the towel caddy for a washcloth. Scraps in Susan's sprawling handwriting littered the sink and bathtub; she'd even written on the wall while sitting on the toilet. As he ran cold water onto the cloth, he read "No vision, television, tell-a-vision," scrawled over so many times the letters blurred together.

He hurried back to the bed with the cold wet cloth and draped it across his wife's forehead, so that water ran down her ears and neck, but she only twitched and moaned again. Her breathing was shallow and fast.

"Lulu!" he yelled. "Lulu! Come here!"

His daughter didn't answer. He scrabbled through the wild mass of papers, looking to see if his wife had taken any pills, but he didn't see an empty bottle. He picked her up and threw her over his shoulder. He slipped and almost fell on the paper as he went to the bedroom door but managed to catch himself by grabbing the dresser handle.

Susan swayed on his shoulder like a bag of seed corn, except she wasn't as heavy. He stumbled down the hall to his daughter's room. Lara had her everlasting music stuck in her ears.

"Get those damned ear things out!" he shouted, beside himself with terror. "Your mother! When did you last see her or hear her, or anything?"

Lara stared at him, undone by his fear, by the sight of her mother's body dangling over his shoulder. She couldn't speak.

"Did you see her today?" Jim screamed.

Lara shook her head, not taking her eyes from him. He was unpredictable; he might do anything.

"Go down to the kitchen," he panted. "Look to see what she's eaten."

When she didn't move, he screamed "Now!" so ferociously that she got to her feet, sidled past him out of the room, down the back stairs to the kitchen. He took the main staircase, the one they never used because it opened onto the unused front room. It was wider than the back stairs, the risers shallower, easier for him to manage with his wife on his back.

The front room was chilly and dusty, and he moved as quickly as he could through the dining room to the kitchen. Lara was standing next to the sink, trembling so much that she had to clutch it to steady herself.

"Did you just buy blueberry yogurt? I think she ate that, and—and—" She held out her hand with the empty bottle of antidepressants in it.

"Okay, Lulu." His daughter's panic was like a slap, forcing him to steady himself, to think for all three of them. "We're going to take your mom into town to the hospital. I want you to go out and open the truck, get the front seat moved forward so I can lay her in the back, okay?"

She nodded and ran on wobbly legs out to the yard. It had started to rain again. He waited in the kitchen doorway until Lara had the truck open, then followed and laid Susan on the backseat. He didn't know whether he should elevate her torso, so that gravity would bring any drugs still in her stomach back through the esophagus, or if that might make her choke to death. He compromised by laying her flat.

"Lulu, call the emergency room to let them know we're coming in."

"Dad—I can call from the truck. I don't want to stay out here by myself." Her face was wet with rain and tears, a glossy, glassy covering that made her look as though she were a museum exhibit.

He told her to turn on the engine and get the heat on; he had to fetch blankets and their insurance documents. As he drove, she tried phoning the hospital. Whoever she was talking to wasn't helpful, kept asking questions that made Lulu more panicky and tearful. He told her to hang up and to call Sheriff Drysdale.

"It's—it's for my dad, for Jim Grellier, there's a serious problem, he needs Mr. Drysdale," Lulu gabbled to the receptionist, then handed the phone to Jim.

"Hank? Oh—can you track him down?" He knew the avidity with which everyone would greet the news once it started to spread, but he couldn't avoid telling the receptionist a guarded version of the truth: his wife's life was in danger, he needed help.

By the time the sheriff came to the phone, Jim was already in town, driving down Kentucky Street toward the hospital. Drysdale took in the facts and promised to alert the hospital.

"Where you at now, Jim?"

"Kentucky, just coming up on Seventeenth Street."

"I'll have a car at Sixth, they'll guide you into the emergency bay."

When Jim handed the phone back to Lara, he strained to hear his wife's breathing. The *hrunka-hrunka* of the windshield wipers drowned out other sounds. He turned them off, and made out Susan's slow, shallow breath underneath the drumming of rain on the truck's roof.

At Sixth Street, a sheriff's car was waiting, lights flashing. When he dipped his own headlights at it, the driver turned on the siren and led Jim through red lights, over to Fourth Street and into the hospital's emergency entrance. A couple of attendants came out, moved his wife onto a gurney, told him where to park.

By now, he, too, was trembling, barely able to control the truck. He and Lara supported each other across the parking lot back into the emergency room. A young intern, hardly older than Chip, took as much information as Jim could give, how many pills, what time, Susan's allergies, family medical history, then showed him to the room where families waited for news. Jim and Lara went in but couldn't find seats next to each other, so Jim leaned against the wall near his daughter's chair.

Since finding Susan, the need to act had carried him like flotsam in a fast-moving current. When he relinquished her to the hospital, he suddenly had nothing to do except wait. A television, perched high above the room so everyone could see it, was tuned to some drama that kept its characters in a state of feverish emotion. Jim couldn't bear the shouting on the set as a backdrop to his own anxiety and fear. His mouth was dry, and he kept going to the drinking fountain in the hall, but no matter how much water he drank his mouth still felt as though he had lined it with cotton.

Lara leaned back, with her music in her ears. Jim pulled out her earpieces and squatted next to her.

"What time did you get home this afternoon?"

"I don't know. Maybe three-thirty, maybe four."

"Had your mother eaten the yogurt?"

"Dad, I don't know. I don't keep track of what she's eating. She just sits up in the bedroom like a vulture, devouring us while she starves to death."

"Lara, that is a terrible way to talk about your mother, especially now when she may be—" He bit off the word before it came out. *No more dying right now in this family, please, Jesus, please.* "Anyway, I'm just trying to get a feel for when she might have taken those pills. The doc asked me. It matters whether they were in her bloodstream long enough to hurt her brain."

"Like it could be more damaged than it is right now," Lara muttered, just softly enough that Jim could pretend he hadn't heard her.

Jim pushed his palms against his eyes. "Please, Lulu. Help out here. Did you get a snack when you came in?"

"I had some ice cream. I didn't notice the pill bottle in the garbage, but I wasn't looking. Anyway, I don't think she ate the yogurt before I got home, because blueberry is my favorite flavor, which she knows, so I think I would've noticed if the carton was in the garbage. Where were you? Out in the north quarter section?"

"I had to run an errand when I got back from town with the food."

"Over to Fremantles'? Checking to see if anyone pried your barricades off while Gina was out of the house?"

He felt his cheeks grow hot. He'd been fretting over Gina Haring while Susan was feeling abandoned and desperate enough to take her own life. An *accident,* he corrected himself. She was depressed; it was an accident. She was trying to take enough of the pills to cheer herself up, get back to her everyday life.

"You weren't over there yourself this afternoon, were you?" he demanded. "To see if you could get past Blitz's and my barriers?"

She reddened, but before she came up with an answer a nurse summoned him to a counter in the emergency room. Jim asked one anxious question after another—how was Susan? could he see her? was she going to be okay?—but the nurse just kept repeating that the doctor would talk to him in a minute.

After a quarter hour, while doctors and nurses passed without looking at Jim and Lara, the young intern reemerged with an older woman in a gray gown. She was Dr. Somebody. Was he Mr. Grellier? They were going to keep Mrs. Grellier for a few days for observation.

"Her brain, does she have brain damage?" Jim's voice was tight and high, like it had been when he was thirteen and it first started to break. "Can I see her?"

"We'll have to do some brain scans to make sure there are no lesions. She's lucid. She knows her name and where she lives. But she's a little shaky on the date—at first, she thought it was 1856."

"She's, like, obsessed with these old diaries about Kansas," Lara whispered. "Maybe she went to sleep thinking she was living back then."

"I see." Dr. Somebody looked as though she might say something else but changed her mind. "The main worry is whether she is a further danger to herself, so we're going to put her in the psychiatry ward for a few days and try to get a sense of her mental state. Very often, after a suicide attempt fails, people develop a newfound desire for living. That may well happen to your wife. Do you know if anything particular was weighing on her these last few weeks?"

"Our son. Our boy, Chip, he was killed in Iraq. She—it's hit her pretty hard."

"She was protesting the war," Lara put in. "Chip was mad at her, so he went and joined. And now she thinks maybe she killed him, although she's still against the war."

Dr. Somebody wrote a note on her chart. The intern took Lara and Jim into a curtained cubicle where Susan was propped up on a gurney, wearing a hospital gown. Her arms stuck out of the sleeves like a stick doll's. Bags of fluids were attached to her arms, which were strapped to the table so that she couldn't take out the needles. She looked at Jim and Lara and looked away.

Jim bent over her and kissed her forehead. "Hi, honey. How are you feeling?"

"Tired. I'm tired. I thought I could sleep for a hundred thousand years. Why did you let them wake me up?" Her voice came out in a raspy whisper, the result of the tubes the doctors had stuck down her throat into her stomach.

Jim bit his lips. He'd been hoping for a miracle—a sudden zest for living, not an attack for saving her life. Words of love, of concern, died on his lips.

He said dully, "They're going to keep you here for a few days while you get stronger. I'll come every day, but do you want anyone from the church to visit? Or any of your friends, like Gina?"

She shut her eyes without answering. Jim went over to Lara and whispered to her fiercely to kiss her mother, to say "I love you," something, anything, to make Susan feel better.

Lara gave him a murderous look but went to her mother's side. "I'm here, Mom. Your child, Lara, remember me? Any chance you feel like you're my mother, too?"

Thirty

SUNFLOWER CROP

http://www.schapenfarm.com/newsandnotes.html

Jesus said to the devil, "It is written, Thou shalt not tempt the Lord thy God." Some of our neighbors don't understand that message. They spent the summer dancing around shrines built to Astarte, even though it is said, "Whosoever would not seek the Lord God of Israel should be put to death, whether man or woman." When the Lord took their son, they repented not. Will the remnant of this family repent now that the Lord has seen fit to remove the wits from the wife, so much that she tried to take her own life?

Every Wednesday, teens at Salvation Bible Church were supposed to blanket downtown Lawrence to bring people to Jesus. Teen Witness, it was called, and Pastor Nabo said it was among their most important work.

"When they see bright, happy young people like you who've given your lives to Jesus, you will be an example to other young people. University students who come down to the bars on Massachusetts Street don't realize they are thirsting not for beer but for the Word that will make them whole. You can bring them that life-giving Word."

The teens, wearing modest clothes—calf-length skirts for the girls, jackets and ties for the boys—handed out flyers with Bible verses on one side and a schedule of services at Salvation Bible on the other. The most ardent, like Amber Ruesselmann, tried to seize strangers' hands and force them to pray with her for the Holy Spirit.

Robbie hated Teen Witness. People laughed at him enough because of his weird clothes, his cow milking, his angry father, and Nanny, who posted all her neighbors' problems on the Web. She had made Robbie teach her to use the Internet, then was always coming to him for help in putting photos and stuff on the Schapen Web page. If he tried to argue with her, she and Arnie both got on his ass about the Fifth Commandment.

Most weeks, Robbie avoided Teen Witness because of the farm's milking schedule, but, for some reason, this fall Nanny had decided that Robbie wasn't showing his faith strongly enough. It was something complicated, something to do with her anger at the Jews' not letting her near Soapweed's special calf, or her anger with Robbie for not being a muscular blond clone of Junior, whom she missed, even though she drove over to Tonganoxie Bible every Saturday to watch him play football. Or maybe she was just getting senile. Ever since school started, she had forced Robbie to race home on Wednesdays to do his share of the evening milking, then drive back to town for Teen Witness.

"Junior never had to do this," Robbie said to her.

"Junior had football practice." Myra's false teeth clacked like a snapping turtle, as if she wanted to stick out her neck and snap off Robbie's head.

"I have band practice."

"You spend enough time making that racket. You're doing Teen Witness for Jesus and you're doing it so the valley can see we're a Christian family, not like some out here. Jesus is showing the Grelliers the error of their ways, all right."

"Isn't it enough that you wrote it up and put it out on the Web?" Robbie shouted. "How do you think Lara feels having you point a finger? Didn't Jesus say, 'Judge not, that ye be not judged'?"

Myra hit him so hard across the mouth that his lip split.

"Don't you try quoting Scripture to me. You're this close to the pit, Robbie Schapen. If Jesus returned this minute, with your disrespect fresh in your mouth, you'd be left behind with those Grellier heathen you're so fond of."

Robbie recoiled, not so much from the blow but from the fear that she'd divined his longing for Lara. He was so careful with the songs he wrote for her, to keep them taped inside his biology notes, between two pages of formulas for carbon derivatives. When he went upstairs to change, he double-checked the notebook. The pages seemed secure. Anyway, Myra wasn't subtle: if she'd found his love poems, she would have been screeching about them.

He took a quick shower, and put on a jacket and tie, but stood in his room for a time, staring out at the fields. Too many trees and barns lay between his house and the Grelliers' for him to know what Lara was doing.

The day after they took Mrs. Grellier to the hospital, Lara had stayed out of school. She'd been coming the two weeks since then, although in the classes they had together, biology and Spanish, she hardly seemed to be doing any homework. Robbie worried that she might start failing her classes. He imagined offering to have study sessions with her. The one time he'd tried to approach her, she'd looked at him with so much contempt that his blood froze and he backed away without speaking.

Of course, that was because of Arnie and Myra. Naturally, Arnie had learned about Mrs. Grellier taking a drug overdose when he went on duty at the sheriff's office that night. He'd been ecstatic at more bad luck befalling Jim Grellier, gloating that now Jim would know what it felt like to try running a farm without a wife to help him out.

"And that daughter of his he's always been so proud of, mark my word, she'll be next, drugs or pregnant, or maybe both. Grellier has always looked down on me, but when he sees Nasya—sees this miracle calf the Lord sent me—and when he sees how my boy is making a success over there at Tonganoxie Bible while his own son is burning in hell, he'll be eating my shit and wishing it was his. Like the Bible tells us, 'Pride goeth before destruction.'"

No wonder Lara looked at Robbie like he was a plague of kafir ants. He turned gloomily from the window and went back down the stairs.

Myra came out of the kitchen to look him over, to make sure he wasn't wearing his BECOMING THE ARCHETYPE T-shirt. "I called over to Amber Ruesselmann's mother and told her you'd be by for Amber in twenty minutes. So, mind you, step lively now. And remember, Amber's a good Christian girl, so don't try any nastiness with her."

Since you think I'm a faggot, Robbie thought, *why do you imagine I'd try any nastiness with a girl, especially one as butt-ugly as Amber. And how dare you set up a date for me without talking to me first?* But he kept that, and the rest of his rage, to himself, too scared of his grandmother to risk another confrontation this afternoon. Instead, he slammed the door as hard as he could, ignoring her clacking and hissing behind him about the sin of using objects to do his swearing for him—that will send you to hell just as sure as taking the Lord's name in vain. He knew the litany by heart.

Robbie drove slowly down the long side road that connected the farm with the county road. Arnie had stopped maintaining their end when old Mrs. Fremantle died, and it was as rutted and hole-filled as the Fremantles' side. When Robbie asked why they couldn't get a load of gravel, at least for their side, his father answered incomprehensibly, "I won't give Jim Grellier the satisfaction."

Robbie turned south toward the highway but stopped to look at Mrs. Grellier's experimental farm. He had joined Junior and Chris Greynard in making fun of her and teasing Lara when Mrs. Grellier had started the farm four years ago. Now he felt ashamed, especially since no one was looking after it. The dying organic-sunflower crop was one more thing Arnie was gloating over.

Blackbirds and meadowlarks were helping themselves to the seeds. As he watched, he spied Lara. She had draped herself in a sheet and was running down the rows, flapping her arms. The birds rose and squawked as she approached but settled back down on the flower heads as soon as she moved to the next row. They bent the sunflowers almost to the ground as they helped themselves to the seeds.

Robbie pulled his truck as close to the ditch as he could and climbed down from the cab. By the time he had picked his way through the ditch, on the east side of the road, and reached the field, Lara had disappeared.

He felt a sharp contraction under his ribs. She had seen him coming and taken off for home. Just as he turned to leave the field, though, he caught sight of her: she was sitting in the middle of the field, her white-draped arms over her head like a tent.

He walked up to her slowly. "Lara? Lulu?" His voice came out in an embarrassing squawk, as if it were still breaking in the dreadful way it had done all last year.

"Go away!" Her own voice was muffled by the sheet.

He squatted next to her, his right hand out, palm up, as if she were a meadowlark herself that he was trying to coax. "Lara, it's me, Robbie. I was driving by, and I—uh, I saw you here. Do you need some help? With the birds, I mean?"

"What, so you can laugh at me, and put it on your family's website? 'Some of our neighbors have grandiose ideas, but God hates them and is punishing them by letting the blackbirds eat their crop while their mother tries to kill herself'?"

He turned crimson. "I wouldn't ever do that, Lara, honest. It's my nanny, her and my dad. I tried to make them stop, but they don't listen to anything I say."

She finally pulled the sheet free of her head and looked at him suspiciously. She'd been crying so hard that the dirt on her cheeks had turned to mud. Somehow that made her look all the more vulnerable, all the more appealing. He leaned over and put his arms around her. She smelled of dirt and sweat, not fresh grass as she had when he was crouched behind her in Chip's Nissan last winter. He didn't care. He couldn't believe it, she was in his arms, she wasn't fighting him off or calling him "cowpoke," or "milkboy." She was leaning against him.

"You're all dressed up," she said. "Now your good clothes are dirty. Will your gram be pissed off?"

"Probably. I'm supposed to be—" He broke off, reddening again, ashamed to tell her about Teen Witness.

"Supposed to be what? Going to church?"

"Sort of," he muttered. "We're supposed to do this witness thing, you know—"

"Oh! You're part of *that* group!" She pulled away from him.

"Not really. I mean, really, yes, I am. I go to Salvation Bible, and it's part of the youth ministry. But, well, I hate Teen Witness. Only my grandmother, she's on me like my underwear. Sorry, I mean she's always nagging at me, like I'll go to hell if I don't do what she says. Of course, she thinks I'm hell-bound, anyway, because of my music and me not playing football. I don't know why she thinks Teen Witness will save me."

Lara giggled. "So you'll be there with me and my mom and—and Chip, because she says us Grelliers are hell-bound, too."

"But—but I don't think Chip is in hell," Robbie stammered.

"Of course he isn't!" Lara's face turned round and red with anger. "Only an ignorant—dickhead—would believe something so mean and stupid."

"Don't be mad at me, Lara," Robbie begged. "I can't stand you to be mad at me."

And then, without knowing exactly how it happened, they were lying on the ground, wrapped up in Lara's dirty sheet, and she was crying and telling him how angry Jim was with her, how he told her she wasn't carrying her weight on the farm.

"He acts like I'm this total loser because I don't look after my mom. But how can I look after someone who doesn't talk to me or eat or—or even take a bath?" She laughed nervously, thinking the idea of Susan not bathing was so gross he'd run away in disgust.

But Robbie was kissing her teary eyes, and she was letting him kiss her mouth, letting him put his hands underneath her sweatshirt and feel her skin, which was softer than anything he had ever imagined. She didn't wear a bra. He couldn't imagine any of the girls in Teen Witness going out of the house without a bra on: it was part of being a modest Christian girl. The thought made him even more excited. He cautiously touched one of her nipples. She moved her breast away from him but let him keep his hands on her back. He found himself telling her how his grandmother thought *he* was a total loser because he didn't like sports and wasn't big and blond like Junior and Arnie.

"But you look interesting, like—like one of the old Delaware Indians, who used to live north of the river." In the midst of all Abigail Grellier's papers were some old photographs of leaders of the Delaware Indians who came to the aid of the anti-slavery pioneers.

"Yeah, my mom's mom was part Indian—Munsee, I think it was—but I don't really even look like my mom. At least, I just have three pictures of her. Nanny and Dad burned all the others when she ran off—I don't remember her face after all this time. I know your mom is kind of, well, not doing too good right now, but—but at least she's still here."

"Maybe. But it's like Chip was her only child," Lara burst out with all the hurt and anger she'd been feeling since Susan retreated to her room. "And even before Chip died, she was already abandoning the X-Farm. I had to do all the work with the organic-certification board. And now, now Dad won't help me with the crop because he's bringing in the corn and the sorghum, so I can't use the combine. And, anyway, how are we going to pay Mom's hospital bills? He might even sell the X-Farm."

Robbie held her tighter. He wanted to say he'd help her bring in her crop, but he couldn't quite imagine telling his father he was using the Schapens' combine to help out the Grelliers.

The October twilight was closing in around them; the birds had stopped eating the sunflowers and gone off to their nests. Lara's cell phone rang. She looked at the screen: it was her father.

She didn't answer it. "He wants to know where I am—he's afraid I'm breaking into the old Fremantle house."

The phone call silenced them both. Robbie started to wonder what he could say to Nanny—why hadn't he picked up Amber Ruesselmann? why hadn't he been to Teen Witness? why were his clothes dirty?

"You're supposed to be going out with Amber?" Lara giggled again.

"Nanny thinks she's a good Christian girl for me, that if I start praying with her I won't go to hell," Robbie said gloomily. "If she knew about you—I mean, about how I feel about you—she'd be furious, because you're a Grellier. And, anyway, she'd never believe someone as pretty as you could ever like me."

Lara didn't say anything. As pretty as she? As pretty as someone with tiny breasts and a pimple on her chin, with mousy hair, covered in dirt? Susan thought worrying about appearance was a ridiculous waste of time, maybe because Susan's mom spent all her spare time, and money, on skin treatment and makeup; she'd even had eyeliner tattooed on her eyelids. If Lara worried about her mousy hair or her pimpled skin, Mom would say, or at least she used to say, "It's the content of your character that counts, Lara, as Dr. King said, not your hair or your skin."

"Why not tell your gram you got a flat tire?" Lara suggested.

Robbie was appalled at the thought of out-and-out making up a story, but when Lara reminded him of all the lies his grandmother had told him—about his mom, about him, about the Grelliers—he felt a thrill almost as pleasurable as the excitement of being with Lara herself.

It was completely dark when they finally got to their feet. "I—when can I see you again, Lulu?"

"In biology, tomorrow," she teased.

"No, I mean, well—"

"After school," she suggested. "We could go to that park in town down by the river. No one we know ever goes there."

He started to agree, eagerly, then remembered that tomorrow was when the Jews were coming to look at the calf.

"You mean there really is a magic calf on your place?" she demanded. "I thought it was just the way people talk around here."

"It's not magic," Robbie said. "It's just special. It's all red, see, and the Jews need a perfect red heifer if they're ever going to build the Temple again in Jerusalem. And Jesus can't come again unless the Temple is standing, and—"

"Robbie, you can't make Jesus come by doing stuff!" Lara cried.

"No, of course not. But God won't rebuild the Temple, the Jews have to do it themselves. And if we can help them do it, then the end of days will be that much closer."

Lara shivered and pulled away from Robbie. Pastor Albright at Riverside United Church of Christ didn't preach about the end of days. Vague images of devastation flitted through her head. The X-Farm, its sad rows of sunflowers, would look like the photographs of Iraq she studied on her computer where the bombs had torn big holes in everything. "Serves you right," she would whisper through the screen to the Iraqis, "serves you right for blowing up my brother."

In the cold gray light of the new moon, the field already looked desolate. Did God really want that, to destroy the whole farm, just so people like Robbie's grandmother could be in heaven?

"I don't want the end of days," she said.

"Not want the end of days? But—don't you want to be with Jesus in glory?"

"Oh, Robbie, it's—it's—" She spread her arms so that the dirty sheet billowed around her like the feathers of a bedraggled peacock. "I'm living in the end of days right now. I want the farm alive, I want my mom out of the hospital, I want my brother alive, I don't want any more people dead and the farm burned down."

Her phone rang again: still her father trying to track her down. She again stuck it back in her jeans without answering it.

"But don't you want to be with Jesus?" Was Nanny right, were the Grelliers already damned? How could you not long for the end of days?

"Maybe you should have gone to Teen Witness with Amber," Lara said, trying her best to be hurtful. "I don't want a sermon from you or anyone in your family, telling me how my brother and my mother are damned. You and Amber can pray over me to your heart's content."

"Lara, no!" Thoughts of the end of days, the building of the Temple so Jesus could come in glory and kill all the Jews, along with people who pretended to be Christians, people who worshipped with their lips but not their hearts, vanished. Instead, he thought of Amber's pasty, acne-scarred face and the soft skin of Lara's back underneath her sweatshirt. He grabbed her and pulled her to him, but she pushed him away.

"I have to go home," she said. "My dad is freaking. The next thing you know, he and Blitz will be out looking for me, and then they'll see your truck."

As if to prove her point, her phone rang again. This time, she answered it. "I'm in the X-Farm . . . Yeah, I heard it ring, but I was trying to stop the birds from eating all the seeds . . . Yeah, I'm on my way . . . No, don't. I'll walk."

She headed toward the road, wrapping the sheet tightly about herself. Robbie jogged after her.

"But Lara—Lulu—I want to see you again."

"I'll be in biology tomorrow."

"But I want to see you alone, be with you alone. Would you come to my youth group tomorrow night? We could go out for a Coke or something after."

"After you've finished worshipping your cow?" Her words were still mean, but her tone was softer, more provocative.

"Well, after these Jews from Kansas City leave we have supper and then I go back to town for youth night."

"Let me come and see the golden calf with you, and I'll ride along to your youth group," she said.

"No, you can't, the Jews say not to let any women near it, not even Nanny is allowed."

"Robbie! What is with you and all this stuff? If you think women are so evil they'll destroy your stupid calf, then I'm so evil you can't be alone with me."

"Oh, Lara, I don't think that, please. I don't even want them to use the calf, and she's so lonely, shut up all by herself, it's cruel. But even if I said you could come, my dad would be there, he wouldn't let you anywhere near the calf, and if I tried to show her to you by myself my nanny is always checking on me. It just isn't possible."

They had reached the train tracks. Just over the ridge, Robbie could see the lights of the Grellier house. Even though he knew Lara's mother was ill and her father upset with her, the house still looked warm and cozy to him. Arnie and Myra did nothing to fix up the Schapen house, except keep the roof shingled and the gutters cleaned, but they never even painted it, while, inside, they still used the old lights and furniture Robbie's grandfather had grown up with in the 1930s.

Even from the outside, you could see that the Grelliers cared about making the house look inviting. It was painted a soft cream—although, of course, you couldn't tell that in the moonlight—and the shutters were a dark, rich green, and when he'd sneaked into the yard in the dark early one morning after milking, trying to guess which room was Lara's, he'd seen the modern lamps in the family room, and the kitchen, with its bright-painted cupboards. Jim Grellier had come to the window that morning, coffee cup in hand, staring at the sky as he tried to guess the weather, but Robbie had felt sure Jim had seen him. He'd backed away, run home, and never tried spying on Lara again.

Robbie ached with so many desires he didn't know which was uppermost in his mind—to be part of Lara's family, to be inside the Grellier house, to kiss Lara, to touch her again, to make her respect him and his music. If Lara walked across the tracks without kissing him, she would disappear from his life forever. He put a tentative hand on her sheet-draped arm.

She stood rigid for a heartbeat, then turned to look at him. "What time do the Jews come?"

"They get there around four-thirty and stay for about an hour. Does this mean—"

"I'll be here by the tracks at six-thirty." She brushed his cheek with her lips and darted into the yard around her house.

Thirty-One
PENNED IN

CARS BEGAN ARRIVING around four while Robbie and Dale were starting the afternoon milking: first Pastor Nabo with three of the elders, then some dedicated, avid church members, all male. They went into the house through the front door, not the kitchen.

From her perch in the crotch of the oak tree, Lara could see Myra Schapen through the kitchen window. Arms folded across her chest, she was walking back and forth, her jaw snapping up and down, as if she were biting holes in the air. Lara pulled her legs up underneath her. Myra's wild face was frightening. If she went to the window, if she saw Lara dangling there— Lara pictured Myra with a pitchfork, a shotgun, a backhoe, knocking Lara out of the tree, mutilating Lara, Myra snapping her jaw all the while.

As soon as she got home from school, Lara had run into Chip's room to rummage through his box of effects. When the Army sent them back, Susan had taken Chip's sweats, and Jim his iPod. He liked listening to his son's music while he was alone on the tractor. Songs he'd hated when Chip was alive now made him feel close to his dead son. Jim had let Curly help himself to whatever he wanted, even though it meant he took the fielder's glove Chip had carried with him to Iraq. Lara hadn't even wanted to go near the box before, but this afternoon she rummaged through it until she found Chip's desert fatigues.

The uniform was miles too big on her. Just as she had her fabric shears poised over the pant legs, ready to slash four inches off the bottoms, she realized it would be a desecration to cut them. Instead, she made a deep hem, and basted a series of tucks into the waistband. Even so, she had to cinch a belt pretty tightly to keep the pants from sliding down her hips. The shirt was also big on her, but that meant she could wear a sweatshirt underneath to keep warm. She pulled her hair back on her head with a clip, then tucked it inside Chip's camouflage cap.

The clothes still smelled of Chip, his sweat, the aftershave Janice Everleigh had put into the first and only care package the family had sent. Lara paused at the top of the stairs, suddenly feeling queer, putting on her brother's clothes to sneak up on Robbie's house. Then she thought of the night three years ago when Chip had slithered through the ditch and into Arnie's barn, draping all the cows in toilet paper because of some fight he'd had with Junior.

Lara giggled, remembering Myra's fury. She'd been sure it was Chip who did it. She'd come to the Grelliers' kitchen, screaming bloody murder at Jim and Susan, who only stared at her in bewilderment. Susan had even said, "Myra, you'll damage your heart if you keep getting this exercised." Lara and Chip had had to run to the barn before they exploded with laughter and gave away the whole story. Chip would approve of her mission; he would send her luck. "From up in *heaven*, you snot-filled Schapens," Lara hissed.

Jim had started bringing in the corn, which meant he was with Blitz and Curly in the field closest to the house. Lara watched them from the window on the landing. It was almost four. The light would hold for two more hours, so they weren't likely to take a break anytime soon. Even so, she crouched low to the ground as she left the house, sticking up an arm to open the door to her pickup, then sliding into the driver's seat—she didn't care if they saw her leave, but there'd be buckets of questions if they saw her in Chip's uniform.

She parked her truck on the service track that ran between the X-Farm and the Ropeses' sorghum field, out of sight of the road and her own house. Mr. Ropes had cut his sorghum. He might see her truck from his back window, but he would just think she was working the X-Farm.

The October sky was a dull gray, an iron sky pressing down on the earth. It didn't hold rain, just a chilly dreariness. The blackbirds and meadowlarks were still working furiously at the sunflowers. As Lara walked along, she swung Chip's cap at them. The sight broke her heart, all that hard work disappearing into their greedy little bellies, but she didn't take extra time to try to chase the birds away.

"An exercise in futility, anyway," she said under her breath, repeating the phrase she'd heard Gina use last summer.

Thinking of Gina made her wonder how she'd get back into the Fremantle house now that Jim and Blitz had nailed shut the door between basement and kitchen. "Where there's a will, there's a way," she whistled. "Tomorrow the sun may be shining, although it is cloudy today."

Her mission this afternoon was easier, since she only had to sneak onto the Schapen land, not break into the house. It was also riskier. If Gina found her at Fremantles', she would be cold and nasty but not frightening. If Myra or Arnie Schapen found her on their land, they'd hurt her. Physically, probably, while grinning and saying they were beating the devil out of her. They'd go after Jim, too, maybe sue him for trespassing or some shit.

"So be careful," she admonished herself when she reached the county road.

She knelt in the ditch until she was sure no one was around in the fields or on the road, then crossed the road and dropped down into the ditch on the far side. She'd worried that Chip's light fatigues would stand out against the dark autumn landscape, but, once in the ditch, she saw that they blended perfectly with the dead grasses and leaves around her. When she reached the Schapen buildings, she stuck her head up cautiously. She saw Robbie in the distance, calling up the cows from the south pasture.

She poked a hole in the ground with her finger. Her feelings about yesterday were too complicated for her to understand. The pleasure of having someone care about what she was thinking and feeling, that had been a balm to her sore spirits. The physical thrill of being touched in that way, that was new to her. Oh, yes, her own hands on her own body. But not a boy's hands. Huddled in the ditch, watching Robbie, she ran her fingers lightly over her arms and shivered from the memory of his touch.

But he was a Schapen. Even if he was obviously different from Junior and Arnie and Myra, he still was one of them, went to that bizarro church where they thought they could make Jesus come again by breeding a red calf. And because he was a Schapen, did she want to spend more time with him really? Was that why she was sneaking over here really? To spy on his golden calf just because he'd said she couldn't, was that a way of saying she didn't care what he thought or said?

Robbie disappeared from her field of vision, but he'd be back soon with the cows. She'd have to move now. She picked out a big bur oak near the driveway as her spy's perch, double-checked the outbuildings for any sign of Arnie or Myra, then crawled across the rough-cut grass to the tree. Arnie came out of the house, and she froze against the ground, but he was heading for the new enclosure, the little round house he'd built for his golden calf. Lara couldn't actually see the special pen from here, but she'd watched Arnie building it last winter, before the corn and sorghum grew high enough to block the view across his fields from Highway 10.

Lara jumped up, grabbed a big overhanging branch, and hoisted herself up, quickly, smoothly, no mistakes allowed here. A second later, she was in the tree crotch, shielded by the branch from house, barn, and road.

Pocahontas Grellier, champion tracker. Too bad 4-H didn't have a category in that at the county fair; she'd take the grand prize every year.

She'd gotten to her roost in the nick of time: Robbie's pastor drove up seconds after she'd found a place flat enough that she could sit. After him and the four cars with other church members—or so she guessed the men to be; except for Chris Greynard's dad, they were strangers to her—there wasn't any action on the road. She watched Robbie and the Schapens' hired hand working the cows in and out of the milk barn; she saw Arnie leave the circular enclosure and go back into the house.

She could see the details of the kitchen, the industrial clock on one wall, the corner of the old-fashioned range, its enamel chipped, and then Arnie and Myra talking. Arnie disappeared and Myra turned to the window, but only to fill a teakettle, Lara realized after a nervous moment: the sink was probably under the window where Lara couldn't see it.

She began to understand how isolated Robbie's life was. The county road running past her own house carried traffic all day long. She could see the Ropeses' from her bedroom, and even bits of the Fremantle place. But the side road dead-ended here at the Schapen farm. People only drove up this way if they were going to Schapens', and Arnie and Myra were so mean no one ever just dropped in on them the way they did Jim and Susan.

Poor Robbie! How could he stand it, cows for friends, a witch and a warlock running his house, a bully for a big brother? Maybe in the hospital the nurses had made a mistake, given his mother an Indian woman's baby. Maybe over on the reservation, there was some big blond lunk who thought he was a Pottawatomie. Lara almost giggled out loud at the image.

Another car was coming up the road now. A dusty Dodge van turned in to the Schapen yard. Lara stretched out along the branch to get a better look as three men climbed stiffly down. These must be the Jews. There were Jewish teachers at Lara's high school and a number of Jewish kids in her class, but they were all like Lara's friends, worrying about how they looked, what people thought of them, who was going out with who, how they were doing in their classes. These three men were exotic, not just foreign in space but in time as well. Like Robbie, when he first saw them last winter, she recognized the strange clothes from pictures in her history book. They were wearing the round, hard black hats, the long black frock coats, the corkscrew curls—like the men from the Lodz Ghetto who were killed in the Holocaust.

Arnie came out from the front of the house with the pastor from Salvation Bible Church. Lara couldn't hear any of the conversation, but she could see Arnie strutting, as if he were trying to prove that he, not these strange, bearded men, was in charge. After another minute, the other men joined them, and they headed toward the special calf's round enclosure.

The Schapens' hand emerged from the milk barn and got into his beat-up Chevy. A few minutes later, Robbie came out and headed to the house. He passed through the kitchen, where Myra snapped her jaw at him. He seemed to be ignoring her—he passed on through a swinging door without stopping to look at her.

A light came on upstairs. After a time, Robbie reappeared in the kitchen, his hair wet, wearing his sports jacket. At this distance, Lara couldn't tell if he'd been able to get yesterday's dirt out of it.

When he opened the back door, Lara heard Myra screeching, "Did you hear me, young man? I told you to fetch the coffee cups from the parlor. You're not a man or a church elder, you don't belong out there in Junior's place. I'm not here to wait on you hand and foot. You do as I say."

In the dull twilight, Lara could see Robbie slump over, as if Myra's words were rocks hitting his shoulders. She stifled an impulse to jump down from the tree and race over to him, to put her arms around him and console him.

Robbie slouched his way across the yard, passed the milking shed and other outbuildings, and disappeared from Lara's view. Myra stood in the back door, hands on hips. Probably her jaw was still snapping even now that she'd shut up. She finally returned to the house, pausing at the window that overlooked Lara's tree, but, after a time, she went through the swinging door into the room beyond.

Lara took a breath, tightened her stomach muscles, swung over the branch, and dropped into the yard. Keeping low to the ground, she moved around behind the milking shed, hopping around the cow patties that were splattered everywhere. In the gray half-light, she couldn't avoid them all. "Sorry, Chip," she muttered to her brother, "I got your brand-new fatigues all stinko."

On the far side of the milking shed stood equipment sheds. Beyond them, the lagoon for collecting wastewater glimmered purply black in the fading light. She paused at the main barn, where Arnie kept his combine and his tractor. The golden calf's special pen lay another hundred yards beyond it. The troop of visitors was so big they couldn't all fit into the enclosure; a half-dozen men shoved for position in the open doorway, craning to see what was going on inside. Lara could hear their voices, raised in excitement, but could not make out the words.

The ground between the main barn and new pen was rough, open terrain. The only possible cover was a set of small sheds, about eight in all, where new calves were tied up. She didn't know anything about dairy farming, and couldn't understand what the calves and sheds were doing there, but they were her only way of getting close to the golden calf's enclosure.

It wouldn't be dark for another hour, so she had to hold her breath and get close to the ground, inevitably putting hands and knees both smack into cow shit. She swallowed a gag and got behind the nearest of the little sheds. The calf bawled in misery when it saw her. Its hair was wet and tufted, like a newborn kitten's; it couldn't be very old. Lara wiped one filthy hand in the dirt and petted the calf.

"You poor little thing, where's your mom? She take an overdose of drugs and end up in the ER, that you have to be tied up like this all alone, crying?" she murmured, stroking it.

The calf tried to suck on her fingers, and she saw there was a bucket of milk at its feet. She dipped her fingers into it, momentarily forgetting her main goal, and let the calf suck the milk from her fingers. A louder cry from the men startled her. Lara glanced over at them, but they were still looking into the enclosure; they hadn't seen her. Still, she was pretty exposed out here. She patted the calf's rump and darted behind the next shed, working her way toward the golden calf.

She felt triumphant when she reached the last shed in the row without detection. This one didn't have a calf tied to it; she backed into the dank, musty straw covering the ground inside and studied the closed pen. It wasn't sealed, the way it had appeared in the distance: the roof was raised about a yard from the walls so that air could blow through. The wall was also six inches or so from the ground to make it easy to sluice out the pen. Arnie had put in a series of skylights in the roof, which Lara could see because the interior lights were on, but the sides didn't have any windows. Poor calf, Lara thought. No mom, no fresh air, no buddies to talk to.

She was only fifteen feet away now and she could hear the excited voices of the men crowded into the doorway: "It said what?" "How can they tell?" "What does it mean?" "Shut up so we can hear for ourselves!"

At that moment, her cell phone rang. Her heart almost stopped, so great was her fear, but the men were too intent on what was happening at the pen.

She looked at the screen. Her father. Oh, *no*! Not checking up on her now! She backed into the empty shed again and answered.

"Lulu, where are you?"

"Just out, Dad, I'll be home pretty soon."

"Where is 'out,' young lady?"

"I'm at a friend's house. I'll call you in a minute. Got to go!"

"Don't hang up! I'm going into town to see your mother, and I want you to come with me. Tell me where you are!"

She hung up and turned her phone to VIBRATE, which she should have done before she left the house. If she told Dad what she was doing, he'd have ten fits. Besides which, she didn't want to see Mom. Anyway, she had a date with Robbie—sort of a date. Seeing Robbie would be way better than looking at her mother's dead-alive face and listening to a lecture from Dad.

She could feel the phone vibrating. Her father called her three times while she stared at the phone face. It was six o'clock. She should go home and wash up so she'd be on time to see Robbie, but—then she'd get sucked into going into town. And, besides, she was this close—she had to see the calf.

Thirty-Two
PHOTO OP

LARA SCUTTLED AWAY from the empty shed. She made a wide circle around the miracle calf's pen, moving so close to the waste lagoon that she heard the frogs and insects chirping at its edge, then crawled through the field to the back of the pen. She lay flat on the ground, which was wet and smelly from a recent sluicing, and peered under the raised wall. The men inside the pen were shouting now, some yelling at the others to shut up, but all of them creating so much racket that Lara couldn't make out individual words.

She couldn't see much: straw on a raised platform with large black stones beneath it, Arnie's overalls and the black pants of the three Jews and Pastor Nabo to her right, unidentifiable legs of two men in front of her so close that she could have reached a hand in and untied their shoes. Robbie's legs, which would be skinnier than any of the others, weren't visible—he must be lost in the crush at the door. She could see nothing of the calf but heard its anxious bleating over the men's voices.

"What a gift, what a blessing." Pastor Nabo choked on the words. "Brother Arnie—I can't believe—here, in your manger— Let us pray!"

Nabo intoned Jesus' name, and started to thank Him, but one of the Jews interrupted. "You may mean well, my friend, but this calf is speaking the sacred Name of *Ha-Shem* in Hebrew. She is calling on the Holy One in language so ancient and so sacred, it would be a sacri—it would be a mistake to invoke your Christ's name on her. She is set aside for the rebuilding of the Holy Temple, and, as such, she must not have her mission compromised by other gods."

The man's voice, as thick with emotion as Pastor Nabo's, briefly silenced the others. Lara heard someone directly in front of her mutter, "Damned Jews, trying to tell us how to worship." Another voice said, "Later, Kurt, later."

The men started filing out. As the crowd thinned, Lara could see the calf's red legs dancing uneasily around her raised pen and then Robbie's jeans as he climbed up on the platform next to the heifer. All the visitors were gone. Robbie and Arnie were alone in the building.

"Don't you do *anything* to that calf!" Arnie shouted. "That calf is set apart, she's sacred. You cannot touch her or spoil her the way I know you've been doing. You come along with me now, boy."

"But, Dad, do you think she was really saying the secret name of God? To me, it sounded like ordinary bleating, you know, the noise they all make when they're nervous. And this girl, she's so lonely, it's made her act—"

"And you know better than the Jews what ancient Hebrew sounds like, I suppose?" his father said. "Don't go talking like that: this heifer is going to make our fortune. You come along now."

Robbie's legs turned around and stepped down again from the platform. He was moving slowly. Lara pictured him slumped over, the way he'd been when Myra was yelling at him.

The work lights that had brightened the pen went out, and the calf bleated again, "Yeh-heh, yeh-heh," as Arnie shut the door. Lara heard him cry, "See, there it is again. She's repeating God's secret name. She's bound for glory!"

The gap between the ground and the wall was narrower than Lara's shoulders, but the dirt was soft from all the sluicing the Schapens gave the pen; it didn't take Lara long to scoop out a shallow trough with her filthy fingers. She stretched her arm under the wall. Her fingers closed on one of the black stones; grabbing it, she pulled herself all the way inside.

The day had almost spent itself while she'd been watching and waiting. Without the work lights on, she could barely make out the heifer on her raised platform. The dimness turned the heifer's red-orange hide to black. The animal heard her and moved restively.

Lara wished she could turn on the lights, but they'd show through the skylights and bring Arnie on the double. She got to her feet, stubbing her toes against the boulders that surrounded it. As her eyes adjusted to the murky pen, she saw the railing around the platform and the calf's manger full of hay.

"Hey, girl, it's okay," she whispered to the heifer, reaching an arm up through the railing to scratch her flank. "I know you're not supposed to have any females near you, but, dang it, you're a female yourself, you must miss all the other girls in the herd, not to mention your mom."

The calf bleated again, the "yeh-heh, yeh-heh" that had so amazed the men, but then lowered her head and rubbed against Lara's outstretched hand. Lara grabbed the railing and hoisted herself up to the platform. She swung a leg over the rail and climbed inside the enclosure.

Her heart was racing. If Arnie found her here, she was worse than dead. The thought only made her want to raise the stakes. Arnie thought he was everyone's boss, he thought he could gloat over her mother's illness, over Chip's death, but she, Lara, could destroy his precious heifer, bring him down to earth in a hurry.

What if she stole the heifer? She could hide it in the X-Farm, feed her sunflowers. She swung back over the enclosure rail. Using the pale light from the screen on her cell phone, she tried the door. It was padlocked on the outside. If she was going to take the calf, she'd have to come back with a screwdriver to undo the padlock.

The cell phone gave her a new idea. She scrambled back into the pen, tucked Chip's cap into one of the back pockets of his pants she was wearing so her face would be recognizable, and took a picture of herself with her left arm draped around the heifer's neck. Holding the phone at arm's length, she turned and kissed the calf on the nose and snapped the shutter again.

The calf butted her in the chest, sending her sprawling into the straw. Lara laughed with excitement. "Want to play football, do you, missy?" She got up, grabbed the heifer's shoulder, and had flung a leg up over her back when she heard voices outside the enclosure and the sound of a key in the padlock.

She froze with terror. She couldn't get out of the pen and under the wall before the men came in. She dove into the manger and pulled the hay over her head. It was a tight fit. She was terrified her shoes were showing, but she couldn't afford to sit up to check. In another second, the lights came on inside the room.

The heifer was bucking and snorting around her small pen. Lara had alarmed her by trying to climb onto her back, and she was further startled by the return of the men. Lara heard Pastor Nabo cry in ecstasy, "She's full of the Holy Spirit!"

The hay was tickling Lara's nose; she sneezed several times before she could work a trembling hand through the grasses to squeeze her nostrils together, but it seemed that the calf was making enough noise to muffle the sound.

Through gaps in the manger slats, she could see a little bit of what was going on. Arnie unfastened a gate in the calf's enclosure and the men climbed onto the calf's platform. Lara couldn't tell how many there were, especially when a couple of them leaned back onto the manger. If she goosed them, maybe they'd think the Holy Spirit was descending on them.

"Now that the Jews have gone, we can invoke the God they have ignored to bless this holy animal." The pastor's voice shook with emotion.

"Pastor, we don't want to jinx her in any way." Arnie's voice was uneasy. "Until the Temple is rebuilt and the Temple sacrifices begin again, she's kind of a Jewish calf. If we baptize her, maybe something will go wrong with her."

"Brother Schapen, I respect your fears, your concerns, but the Lord is not controlled by superstitions. We can't 'jinx' a calf He's put His special mark on any more than we can create her ourselves. The Lord Himself knew the Jews were a stiff-necked people. We've seen this time and again in our dealings with these men from Kansas City. They won't accept Jesus as their Savior. They only want to rebuild the Temple for their own worship, not to hasten the Lord's return."

"Yeah, Arnie, Jews or no Jews, since when do we let a bunch of guys from Kansas City tell us how to run a farm or raise a calf?" Chris Greynard's father said.

"But they were the ones who knew what the calf was saying. None of us would have known it was repeating the sacred name of God."

"*Secret* name," Pastor Nabo corrected. "The secret name of God. The Jews have special knowledge that comes from dedicating their lives to the Law instead of the salvation that comes through Christ Jesus. The Lord spoke to them first through the Law. Since they refuse the salvation that could be theirs, they only know half the story. And the half they refuse, the cornerstone that they reject, is our Savior Jesus Christ. We cannot reject Christ. We must invoke His blessing. If you're afraid of the presence of the Lord, Brother Schapen, maybe Brother Greynard should take charge of this calf."

Arnie said sulkily that the calf had been given to him, to his farm, and he didn't need anyone else to take care of it. "But if we're willing to disobey the Jews over this prayer, maybe we should let women into Nasya's pen. You know my mother is a holy woman, Pastor, and it seems hard that she can't go near a calf on the farm she's looked after for over sixty years."

"I think we all know the answer to that, Brother Schapen," Pastor Nabo said. "We know that when Jesus spoke to us through His apostle Paul, He told women that they were to be subservient to men. We don't allow women to preach in our churches, and we don't want them desecrating this heifer. Let's invoke the Holy Spirit on this animal, my brothers in Christ."

The men on the platform knelt. The poor calf was trembling in distress at having so many men close to her. All the while the pastor prayed, she moved anxiously around, bleating her pitiful "yeh-heh, yeh-heh." Every time she made the noise, the men around her cried, "Praise Jesus!" and "Hallelujah."

The pastor's prayer went on and on. He beseeched the calf to bring the day of the Lord, the day of Rapture, close to them. He besought her to go willingly to her solemn sacrifice, and recounted the Temple sacrifices from the Bible. He praised the calf for her holy virginity.

Lara's left leg was cramping. She wanted to scream in pain, and in annoyance with the pastor for being so full of himself that he couldn't shut up. She needed to get home. Robbie would be waiting for her at the tracks and think she'd stood him up. Dad would be so pissed off; she didn't even want to think about that. Behind those thoughts was something deeper, scarier, that revolved around the calf itself and the way Pastor Nabo was praying. Temple sacrifices, purity, the virginal cow—the words evoked images of blood and rape that sickened her.

Lara felt her face wet with tears but knew she couldn't cry out or even move. She clamped her teeth down on a mouthful of straw and held onto it for life. When the pastor finally finished, when the men climbed to their feet and left the enclosure and Arnie turned out the lights, Lara slid from the manger as quickly as her cramped and shaking legs would take her. She flung herself under the depression in the ground and crawled past Arnie's milking barn, then ran across his sorghum field to the road. She'd get her truck tomorrow. She couldn't face going into the dark sunflower field now.

Lara trudged slowly to the train tracks. Robbie had said he would meet her there at six-thirty. It was a little after seven, and there wasn't any sign of his truck. He must have gotten tired of waiting. She walked on into the house on leaden legs.

It was only after she'd stood under the shower long enough to use all the hot water, as she tried to flush not just the cow shit but Pastor Nabo's hot, blood-filled words away, and after she'd put Chip's fatigues into the washer with a double cup of soap and another of bleach, that Lara realized she was missing her cell phone. She remembered now: she'd been holding it when the men came into the pen. She must have dropped it in the golden calf's manger.

Thirty-Three

A SHOT IN THE DARK

WHEN JIM GOT HOME, the kitchen light was on, but his daughter's truck wasn't in the yard. He could hear the washer working through a spin cycle, so she must not have been gone long. He called her name, and then dialed her cell phone for what seemed like the twentieth time in the last hour only to get her voice message, the perky voice she reserved for her friends. Her own father didn't get that happy, lively Lara these days.

Susan was coming home. When he went in to visit her this evening, the doctor said they would discharge her on Saturday. That should be making him happy, his wife under his roof instead of in the hospital, but instead he felt scared.

He needed his daughter in the house to keep him from feeling so alone, so overwhelmed. Even though the hospital bills frightened him because their insurance plan didn't cover psychiatric care, he was more terrified still of how his wife might act when she returned. The drugs and whatever they'd been doing with her in therapy had made her more coherent, but she talked to him, her husband of twenty-three years, in dull monosyllables, and her eyes were dead in her gaunt face.

He went up the stairs and looked into the master bedroom. He hadn't gone into it since he took Susan to the hospital two weeks ago. The mass of papers was still strewn across the room, and everywhere he looked he saw where she'd scrawled words onto walls and furniture, words about peace and war and death that didn't fit together in any way he could make sense of.

He would have to get all that cleaned up, the walls scrubbed, fit all that into the next two days while bringing in the corn. The ball of tension between his shoulder blades grew. Lara would have to suck up her resentment against him and Susan and help out.

He went back down the stairs to the front room. He and Susan had used it as their bedroom when they got married, and then, when Gram got too old to manage the stairs, they'd moved her in here and taken over the main bedroom upstairs. Since Gram died, they used the front room only at Christmas, to set up the tree and open presents.

He found the bottle of bourbon Chip had given him last Christmas and poured two inches into one of his ever-so-great-grandmother's crystal glasses, which stood in an old-fashioned breakfront in the corner. It was cold in the room, because he kept the doors closed and the heat shut off to save on fuel, but he sat down at Abigail's walnut folding table. He lifted the glass and offered a toast to his son, then drank the bourbon quickly as if it were medicine. He gasped from the burn in his gut—he almost never drank, and never that much that fast.

He nodded at the bottle as if it had confirmed something he'd said to it and poured out another inch. He tried to remember Chip's face as he'd been on his last home leave, but all Jim could see was his son's eager grin in the picture with George Brett. He tried to remember his own parents, who'd been dead for almost forty years now, but he couldn't even say what color his mother's hair had been. It was as if his parents and grandparents, and now his son, lived in the country of the dead, while the country of the living moved further and further away from them. And yet someday he'd move to that country, too, so it couldn't be all that distant.

He'd been brought up to believe the dead were with Jesus, who wiped away all their tears, but it was hard to imagine. Hard to think that Jesus was any more real than the hobbits and gremlins Lara liked to read about. *If you really exist, Lord Jesus,* Jim prayed to himself, *and if the dead are in your arms, take me to them now. I need my grandfather. I need someone who cares about me and the farm. I want my boy with me. Don't leave me here with this sick wife and troubled daughter and our farm falling deeper and deeper into debt. Please, please.*

The cold began seeping through his clothes. He took the bottle with him into the family room and stretched out on the couch, not bothering to take off his shoes even though his feet hurt. He lay there, holding the bottle, but not drinking any more, just staring bleakly at the ceiling.

After a time, he became aware of his daughter standing over him. He didn't notice how pale she was or the tearstains on her face but sat upright, anger flooding him.

"Where in Jesus' name have you been, Lara Grellier? I have called and called your phone and you have been acting like you're the queen of England, too high and mighty to talk to me. If you can't answer your phone when I'm calling you, then I am stopping the service on it tonight."

"I lost it," she whispered.

"Goddamn it, Lulu, I will not have you lying to me!" He slammed the bottle against the coffee table.

"I'm not lying. I—I dropped it after you called me. I mean, after the time I answered, and—and it was dark, so—so I couldn't find it."

He got to his feet and looked her in the eye. "Where were you? At the Fremantle house?"

"No."

He drew his hand back to slap her and put it down in the nick of time. No matter how angry you were, you did not hit people, especially not your wife or daughter. Nothing could ever justify that. But Lara had seen his hand and seen the murderous fury in his face.

She backed away from him and hugged her arms around herself. "You're drunk, aren't you?"

He looked down at the bottle of Old Grand-Dad and made an effort to swallow his rage, his fear, all the emotions that were pummeling him to the point that he didn't know who he was anymore. "No, I'm not drunk. Can you please tell me where you were this afternoon? You weren't with Kimberly or Melanie. I know—I called their mothers."

She tried to speak but couldn't choke out any words.

"Do you have a boyfriend I don't know about?"

The thought of Robbie made her blush despite herself, but she shook her head. Jim saw the blush and said wearily, "Lulu, please just tell me the truth. If you're sleeping with some boy, I won't be happy, but I can deal with it better than I can you lying to me, okay?"

"I—Dad, I went over to see the Schapens' special calf."

This was so unexpected that he burst out laughing. "And did it perform a miracle while you were watching?"

"Dad, it isn't funny. These Jews came from Kansas City. They come every month to inspect the cow—Robbie says she'll lose her special power or whatever if she isn't red all over or if there's some kind of nick or anything wrong in her skin—and all these men from Arnie's church were there. Dad, they got down on their knees to pray to the calf. They said they were praying to Jesus, but Robbie's pastor, he went on and on, all about blood and stuff. I was hiding in the manger, and that's when—"

"You mean you sneaked into Arnie's farm uninvited?"

"Yes, yes. They don't let any women come near the calf, Robbie told me, not even Myra—I mean, Ms. Schapen. And Myra and Arnie, they've put so many lies on their website, about Mom and Chip— you know, they say Chip is in hell! So I thought it would serve them right if I went right up and kissed their stupid calf and put a picture of it out on YouTube. Only, they came in, Arnie and the pastor and all these men."

When she finished her tale, Jim didn't know whether he was proud of Lara for her nerve or angry with her for her spying. In the end, all he did was take her hands and bring her over to sit next to him on the couch.

"Sweetheart, I think we'll leave your phone in Arnie's manger and chalk it up as part of the worst year of our lives. They'll find it sometime when they're cleaning, but they'll just think one of the men out there dropped it."

"But, Dad, I took pictures with it, a picture of me with the calf. They'll know it's mine. And Arnie, he's a deputy, he can probably trace our phone number on it through some police database."

"We'll have to go over, then, and tell Arnie the truth."

"Dad, no! You know how mean he is! He'll sue you for trespass or me for ruining his calf, or something. He thinks the calf is going to make him rich. Can't you and Blitz go over and talk to him and Myra about something else, keep them in the house? Then I could crawl back into the pen and get my phone back."

"Baby, you know I don't like you sneaking into places. And now you see one reason why. You need to learn to face up to the consequences of your actions and one of those consequences is telling Arnie the truth. Maybe that will cure you of trying to spy on people."

"No, Dad, no!" Her voice rose, trembling near the breaking point.

He was tired, too tired to try to reason with her or think of any other solution to the problem. "Okay, Lulu, okay. We'll talk about it more tomorrow; I'm too tired to think right now. And that's because I've been bringing in the corn all day, not because I had two shots of bourbon. Now I have some good news for you: the doctor says your mom can come home on Saturday."

"Oh," she said blankly. "I mean, good, I guess. Is she eating?"

"Yes, she's put on six pounds, they said. And she's taking her medicine, so she's starting to feel better."

Father and daughter stared bleakly at each other, each imagining how much harder their lives would be with Susan back in the house.

"Which reminds me," Jim said, as if they'd both spoken the shared thought, "I could really use your help cleaning out the bedroom, Lulu."

She opened her mouth to protest, then remembered how much trouble she was in and how much she needed his help. She mumbled something that passed for agreement.

Jim clasped her to him. "Lulu, we'll get through all this. I don't know how, but we will."

She clung to him briefly, despite the smell of bourbon, which she found disgusting. For a moment, she forgot all the hurtful words he'd said to her since Chip's death. For a moment, she felt like little Lara, whose daddy could cure anything that was wrong in her world, from her despair at her mother's abandoning the co-op market to her hurt feelings when Chip beheaded all her dolls.

Then she remembered her cell phone and how Jim wouldn't help her find it. And how Robbie hadn't waited for her at the crossroads. Even though it was her own fault for being late, he might have cut her some slack. After all, yesterday he seemed to want to be with her. She turned from her father and went to put Chip's clothes in the dryer.

There wasn't any way for Lara to know that Myra Schapen had forced Robbie to wait in the kitchen with her until the men were through in the heifer's pen, since Robbie refused to go back out to pray with them. The calf's fear and loneliness made him miserable. Even though it felt like sacrilege, to go against Pastor Nabo and the Jews, Robbie couldn't believe the heifer was speaking ancient Hebrew. She sounded too much like a frightened, lonely calf to him.

At six-thirty, hoping to see Lara, he started for the kitchen door. When Nanny demanded to know where he thought he was going, he said to town, to set up his music for Teen Youth Night.

"You'll ride in with Pastor Nabo, young man. And if you're not going to go pray like a Christian man and take your responsibilities seriously, then you can work in here with me like a woman and help me get all these coffee cups cleaned up. I'm not having you disappear on the pastor like you did last night. I'll be ashamed to hold my head up at the women's Bible class tomorrow, when Gail Ruesselmann asks me how you could leave poor little Amber in the lurch. Flat tire, indeed. Tonight it'll be trouble with the carburetor, no doubt!"

Robbie could only be grateful that Myra hadn't guessed he'd spent the whole evening right across the road with Lara Grellier—that would really have fried her eggs! She thought he was out doing drugs or getting drunk.

"But, Nanny, Pastor can't drive me home after Teen Youth Night!"

He'd been afraid she'd snarl that he could walk home, but he was startled when she said Junior would pick him up.

"Junior?" he cried in dismay. "He's over in Tonganoxie."

"He's coming home. I called to tell him how this calf was speaking Hebrew and about to make us all famous, and he decided he'd best come home and see for himself. His first class isn't until ten tomorrow. He'll be able to drive back in the morning. It'll do you good to spend time with your brother, instead of drinking and carrying on like a sodomite in some Lawrence back alley!"

"Nanny, I'm a better student than Junior ever was, I work hard at Teen Youth. Why can't you trust me to get myself to church and back?"

"I trusted you last night and look where you ended up. And don't you go comparing yourself with Junior. If you had his abilities, you wouldn't need to boast about your grades. Pride goeth before destruction, young man, and don't you forget it! And if you think I'm calling that cup clean just because you ran water over it, think again."

While the men were still praying over the calf, Robbie finally found a chance to slip out and walk the quarter mile to the crossroads. There was no sign of Lara. His depression deepened. Why had he ever believed someone as beautiful, as unusual, as Lara Grellier would seriously think of going out with him, especially to a lame event like a church-youth meeting? If he was honest, he'd have to admit he'd just wanted a chance to show off to her how good a musician he was. He'd imagined her eyes shining at him on the way home, telling him how special his music was, so he'd have a chance to sing one of the songs he'd written to her.

He waited until a quarter of seven, then turned back to the farm, shoulders hunched over, kicking rocks. He got to the yard just as the men were starting to get into their cars and Myra was shouting his name loud enough for God and all the angels to hear it.

Thirty-Four

ACTION IN THE HEIFER'S BARN

JIM HAD GONE to bed as soon as the nine o'clock news finished. Lara went through the motions of her homework while picking at a pizza, but she was too tense to eat, let alone study.

Now that the weather had turned chilly, the uninsulated sunporch was too cold at night for sleeping and Jim had moved into Chip's room. Lara listened to her father's heavy breathing; the bourbon he'd drunk was making him snore. The raw noise was oddly comforting—it made her feel at least she wasn't alone in the house.

She tiptoed past Chip's door to the sunporch, where she had a view of the road, wondering what time Robbie's youth group ended and when he'd be coming home. She had a half-formed notion of stopping his truck, telling him what had happened, and seeing if he'd retrieve her cell phone. Maybe he'd be so mad at her for coming near his precious calf he'd never speak to her again. And why should that bother her? What did she care if a loser Schapen turned his back on her? She'd be better off. Lonelier off.

She must have stood at the window for close to an hour, but all she saw were cars and pickups racing down the county road between Highway 10 and Fifteenth Street. A few minutes before eleven, a jeep turned off the county road, heading toward Schapens'. That was Junior's: Arnie had bought it for him when Junior left for college so he wouldn't have to ride his motorcycle in bad weather.

Lara's stomach tightened. Junior hadn't been home once since he'd started over at Tonganoxie in August. Arnie must have found her cell phone in the manger. He'd called Junior. The two of them would come over and arrest her or beat up Dad and burn down the house.

She thought about waking her father, but she imagined what he'd say: we'll face Arnie if he comes here, and, meanwhile, think twice the next time you want to pull a stunt like sneaking into the special heifer's enclosure.

She'd done it once, she could do it again. She went down to the utility room and took Chip's fatigues out of the dryer. "Sorry, Chip," she murmured, "I got your uniform stinko once already today, and now I'm going to do it again. But just in case Arnie hasn't found my phone yet, I'm going back for it. Remember me, your stupid little sister? Look after me if you're not too busy playing your harp, okay?"

Lara giggled with nerves—she couldn't picture Chip playing a harp. If he was with Jesus and the saints, he'd be so holy she wouldn't recognize him. But if she got to heaven herself maybe she'd be holy, too. Only, would Jesus even let in someone like her, who messed up in school and got her dad in trouble with the meanest man in the Kaw Valley?

"Help me get my cell phone back and I promise I'll scrub all that garbage off the walls in Mom's bedroom," she pleaded, not with the Lord—too remote, too busy to bother with Kansas farm girls—but to her brother.

Lara slipped out through the garage, taking care not to wake her father by banging the door shut. Once she was outside in the cold October night, she felt so frightened she almost turned around. Only the thought of Arnie's and Myra's gloating over one more screwup by her family, of what Arnie might do to her if he had found her phone, made Lara move forward.

She had just reached the county road when she heard Junior's jeep coming back down the road from Schapens'. She dropped into the ditch, terrified that he was heading into her yard, but he turned south toward Highway 10. She waited until his taillights had turned into little red dots before getting out of the ditch. She dashed across the intersection and into the bushes that Arnie never bothered to cut back.

The yard lights were on around the Schapen house; two shone near the cow barns. Another was set up near the sheds for the baby calves. Lara could see Robbie's truck in the same place it had been when she came over in the afternoon. It was parked on the verge so the visitors would have room on the gravel drive. Maybe he'd never gone out at all. Maybe Myra had wormed out the truth about him and Lara and forced him to stay home. The idea brought a little calm to her jumbled thoughts.

The kitchen light was on, but Lara didn't risk getting spotted by climbing the oak tree to peer in. If the Schapens all rose at four-thirty or five to do the milking, she couldn't believe anyone in the family would be up now. However, the Grelliers and the Schapens were so at odds she knew nothing about their habits, the way she did for Mr. Ropes, or used to for old Mrs. Fremantle—Lara had known when Mrs. Fremantle liked to go to bed, what shows she stayed up to watch, what she did when she couldn't sleep. Same for the Ropeses, after all the sleepovers she had done with Kimberly when they were little. She could believe Myra would stand in the kitchen all night brewing witch's potions, but maybe she was just staying up because her prize creep grandson Junior had come home.

Lara sank to the ground and crawled around behind the cow sheds. The cows lowed as she passed, but the sound of their munching, the hard jets of their urine hitting the floor, the soft plops of cow patties dropping, sounded normal and soothing.

She repeated her maneuver of the afternoon, swinging in a wide arc away from the cow barns so she could come to the heifer's pen from behind. The lagoon seemed enormous now, its inky water alive with menace. She got to her feet and ran. In the stubble of Arnie's sorghum, Lara heard the night creatures moving away from her, alarmed by so big a beast in their midst: at this hour, voles, possums, and deer mice owned the fields. An owl swooped past her, hunting, and the scream from the small being it caught made Lara scream herself and drop back to the ground.

She had studied all these field animals for 4-H projects, had even identified those eaten by owls from the bones in owl pellets. That had been an impersonal science project, but tonight she felt like one of those little animals herself, helpless in front of Myra Schapen's claws.

She crawled the rest of the way to the pen, again lying flat, and rolling underneath the outer wall through the depression she'd dug earlier. The heifer danced uneasily in her enclosure when she heard Lara come in, and bleated her nervous "yeh-heh, yeh-heh."

"It's okay, girl, it's okay," Lara said, her voice shaking. "It's just me, the heathen Grellier girl."

She crept up to the platform and started digging through the hay in the manger. Standing on the floor, she couldn't reach all the way to the bottom. Once again, she swung a leg over the enclosure fence. The calf started bucking and running around the small space.

"Easy, girl, easy." Lara backed into the manger and stuck her left arm in. "I hope if you found my phone, you left it alone, okay? I don't want to have to dig through all your poop—"

She broke off at the sound of voices outside the barn door: Junior and another man. She froze with fear and then dove once more into the manger, wildly covering herself with hay, praying for obliteration. In another instant, the door opened, and the calf started dancing in earnest, crying out at the top of her lungs.

Junior laughed. "So that's the Holy Spirit at work. Look at her go— what a gal! We ought to try to ride her."

Peeping through a gap in the manger slats, Lara watched as Junior and the man with him tried to corner the calf. The poor animal was already so frightened that she reared up and tried attacking them with her front hooves. "You *go,* girl!" Lara mouthed encouragement. "Knock him out. Put a hoof through his idiot skull."

The calf's frenzy was getting Junior angry or excited—Lara couldn't tell which, but he was trying to grab the calf's head and wrestle her to the ground. He looked as though he'd put on another fifty pounds since he'd gone off to college. Next to him, the calf, who probably weighed five hundred pounds, didn't seem all that big.

"Don't hurt her," the other man said. "Arnie be very, very mad if she's hurt."

Lara almost cried out—that was Eddie Burton! So Junior had been heading to the Burton place when he passed her on the road. She felt a dizzying wave of relief. They didn't know about her; they weren't thinking about her at all.

"Yo, dude, don't tell me what I can and can't do on my own farm."

"No, Junior. But Arnie, he come around with his gun, he wants my daddy in jail. You know, if he seed you and me he'd shoot me. I'm scared of Arnie."

"Be better if you were scared of me, boy." Junior's voice combined a caress and a threat in the same breath.

Lara's relief turned to nausea. She remembered the wildness in Junior's and Eddie's faces at the midsummer bonfire, and she knew what was going to happen next. *Don't, don't, don't,* she begged Junior in her head. *Stop him,* she prayed to Jesus or Chip, or even the calf if she were listening. Lara felt Chip's fatigues turn wet with her own urine, but that humiliation wasn't as great as the revulsion that made her whole body shake with shock.

Junior grabbed Eddie, who laughed excitedly and halfheartedly punched at Junior's arms until Junior pinned his hands and undid the snaps on Eddie's jeans. When he pulled down Eddie's underpants, Lara squeezed her eyes shut, but she couldn't close her ears to the sounds, Junior grunting, Eddie squeaking, then a loud cry from Junior which made the calf bellow in turn. Junior roared in laughter at that and said the calf was blessing their union.

"It's her first holy deed," he said, and Eddie said oh, yes, the calf was very holy.

Lara opened her eyes, hoping that she would see them leaving the enclosure. Junior's naked buttocks, as large as a prize hog at the fair, were almost under her nose. They were pallid, the color of lard, with coarse hairs down his spine like hog bristles. He wasn't pulling on his pants but getting up on his knees to straddle Eddie. Lara shut her eyes again. She couldn't help whimpering aloud, but mercifully the calf was still bellowing and Junior and Eddie were laughing so they didn't hear her.

Junior's laugh stopped abruptly. Lara heard him scrambling upright and then say roughly, "What are you doing in here, twerp?"

"Dad's home from patrol." It was Robbie. "I thought you'd want to know. You don't have to thank me—he'll be real proud that you're admiring his perfect heifer. She *is* still a heifer, isn't she?"

"Knock it off, choirboy, or I'll break your nose and tell Nanny that I caught you being naughty with the family prize." He zipped his jeans and yanked Eddie roughly to his feet.

"Oh, for God's sake, Eddie—he's not going to do anything to you," Junior added, because Eddie was shaking too much at the thought of facing Arnie to be able to pull on his clothes.

A few seconds later, Arnie appeared. "What's going on out here? Robbie, what are you doing to the—Junior! Well, well, Junior, what brings you home?"

Lara couldn't see Arnie's face, but the change in his voice was profound—anger at Robbie for disturbing the calf turned into something like thick cream at the sight of Junior. Poor Robbie! He saved his brother from being caught by Arnie and instead of thanking him Junior was going to blame him for hurting the calf. It was so wrong she wanted to sit up and denounce Junior.

"Nanny called me—she told me this calf of yours was performing miracles. I hopped right in my ride to come see for myself. And me and Eddie, we saw her in action, didn't we, buddy?"

"What did she do?" Arnie demanded eagerly.

"Miracle," Eddie volunteered in a husky gulp. "She made a miracle for me and Junior."

"Eddie Burton?" Arnie seemed to notice him for the first time. "Burtons don't belong on my property, I thought I made that crystal clear to Clem."

Junior laughed. "Take it easy, Dad. Me and Eddie are buddies, nothing to do with Clem—he don't know Eddie's here instead of tucked into his crib for the night. And he won't blab, will you, Eddie?"

"No, Arnie, no sir, I won't say nothing to anyone about the calf or Junior or nothing."

"See you don't," Arnie said, his voice ripe with menace. His tone changed back to milk and honey when he reiterated his demand to know what miracle the calf had performed.

"Just that noise that Nanny said you told her about," Junior said easily. "She sounded like a cow to me, but, hey, if the Jews think she's spouting magic I say let's cash in on it."

The calf came to rest by the manger. Her flanks were wet with sweat, and she was breathing hard.

"Robbie," Arnie barked, "her water trough's empty. What were you doing out here to get her so wild? And her feed, it's all over the place. Get this manger cleaned out and put sweetgrass in, you hear me, boy? Don't forget, you have to be up in four hours to start milking, so maybe you'll think twice before you come out here getting the calf all wound up with your music or whatever the fuck you were doing."

Junior snickered and Eddie gave a falsetto laugh. Arnie slapped Junior on the back and led him out of the enclosure. He stopped at the door to warn Robbie he'd be back to check on the calf in fifteen minutes, so Robbie needed to step lively.

The door shut behind the trio. Robbie put his arms around the calf and stroked her softly, wiping her wet flanks with his shirttails. Any minute, he would start putting fresh hay in the manger; he'd find Lara, find her in Chip's fatigues, covered with cow shit and wet with her own urine.

Scarlet with shame, Lara sat up. "Robbie? Robbie, it's me."

He stared at her in disbelief, not recognizing her in Chip's fatigues and with straw in her hair.

"It's Lara Grellier. Don't be mad at me, Robbie."

Part Three

MIRACLE

Thirty-Five

TALES FROM THE CRYPT

IN SOMEWHAT MULISH compliance with an order from Jim, Lara was on hand to greet her mother when Susan came home from the hospital on Saturday afternoon. She put her arms around Susan, trying not to flinch from her mother's drawn face and dull eyes, and pecked her cheek, muttering, "Welcome home, Mom."

"Yes, it's good to come home," Susan said stiffly, in the formal tones of a foreigner practicing English.

The doctor had told Jim not to be surprised if Susan was nervous for the first few days: she'd been living in a sheltered environment, so the outside world was bound to seem frightening at first.

"Try to behave as normally as you can around her, even though I know you're worried about how she may react. She truly is stronger than she was when she arrived. Going to a grief support group with other parents whose children died has been a help to her." The doctor looked at Jim's tight-drawn face. "It might be a help for you, too: the next meeting is Wednesday evening."

Jim nodded, but he was too nervous to pay much attention to the doctor's words, only thanking her with a mechanical courtesy, before going with the nurse and the orderly to help Susan pack up her things. Besides the small suitcase Jim had brought in when she was admitted, Susan had a shopping bag of medications, along with a list of emergency phone numbers for support staff, and a six-month calendar of appointments for group therapy, the grief group, and private therapy.

The social worker who met with the Grelliers before they left stressed the importance of Susan's attending all these sessions. Jim tried not to see dollar signs when he looked at the schedule. Nothing was more important than Susan's health, after all.

When they got home and Lara had greeted Susan, Jim asked about lunch.

"I waited for you two, even though I'm *starving*," Lara announced, gamely trying to keep up the pretense of a happy family gathering. "We had band practice this morning and then basketball, and I'm hungry enough to swallow an alligator stuffed with goat. Where do you want to eat? Kitchen or dining room?"

"I'm not hungry," Susan said. "Just very tired. I'll go up and lie down."

"Suze, you need to eat something." Jim tried to keep a note of panic from his voice. "Lulu will bring lunch into the family room, where you can be cozy on the couch."

He nodded at his daughter, who made a face, but busied herself with making up the kind of tray they created in 4-H, everything attractively laid out for an invalid.

Rachel Carmody and a few of the other women from Riverside United Church had come out to help clean this morning. They'd also brought food for the family. Rachel's dish was the best, an eggplant lasagna with a romaine salad, so Lara chose that, eating a large spoonful of noodles out of the pan while she fixed the plates.

She was arranging a flower display, using foam core and wires so it would be truly artistic, when a van from Global Entertainment Television pulled into the yard. A reporter wearing heavy makeup and a vivid blue jacket hopped out of the passenger's seat. Lara watched in anger as the woman walked toward the front of the house.

Right after Chip's death, the *Douglas County Herald* and several area TV stations had tried to do stories on Susan. How did it feel to be an anti-war protester whose only son had died in the war? Susan had been upset by the question, by the microphone thrust in front of her face, and Jim had pulled her into the house, with a stern reproof to the reporters.

The sight of the woman striding toward the house made Lara burn hotly. What were they doing, getting a police report from Arnie on every move Susan made so they knew to the minute when she arrived home? Lara ran through the dining room to the front hall, shouting for her father.

She wrestled open the heavy door and glared at the woman. "Who are you and what do you want?"

"I'm Ashley Fornello with Channel 10 in Kansas City. I'd like to come in for a minute and talk to you about your special visitation." She thrust out a hand and a wide smile.

"She's not a visitor. She lives here."

The reporter's smile broadened, if that was possible. "Not visitor, honey, *visitation.* I understand she's very shy, but we wouldn't put a mike on her, and we'd film her with a remote camera."

"That's creepy!" Lara said. "And you can't spy on her. It's against the law."

Jim came up behind Lara and put a hand on her shoulder. "We don't have anything to say to reporters, miss, so why don't you just be on your way and let us keep on doing what we're doing."

"But this is *news.* People will want to know about it. This kind of exposure could get you the attention you deserve."

"I've had more attention than anyone deserves, miss," Jim said. "What would help me most about now is peace and quiet. Come on, Lulu."

"If you're not up to talking, I can understand that." Ashley Fornello nodded sympathetically, her shoulder inside the open door. "If I promise to be *very* respectful, would you let me just take a peek inside the barn?"

"To see the combine?" Lara was bewildered.

After a startled moment, Jim gave a shout of laughter. "No, Lulu. She wants—I think she wants—well, you tell us what you're looking for, miss."

"Aren't you Arnie Schapen?" Ashley Fornello asked.

"No, ma'am. You're on the wrong side of the tracks and then some. You go on south toward Highway 10. About half a mile up, you'll see a house on the left with a bunch of old cars in the yard. They'll be glad to help you."

When he'd shut the door, Lara's eyes were round with wonder. "Dad, you sent her to Burtons'."

"Clem deserves a little excitement," Jim said. "Anyway, it'll do the lady good to work for her story. But how did she find out about Arnie's calf?"

"Oh, Dad, everyone in Douglas County knows. They were all talking about it in school yesterday, because Chris Greynard's dad was out on Thursday when, you know, they prayed to the calf, and so was Mr. Ruesselmann, so they all heard Nasya say this secret name of God. The men talked about it at home, so naturally Amber Ruesselmann brought the story to school. Of course, all she wanted was for everyone to look at her like she was something special. Then the women's group at Robbie's church— they meet on Friday—so Nanny Schapen talked about it there, although the other ladies knew already. It's not like the calf was a secret or anything before Thursday, but after that they couldn't keep the miracle to themselves."

Jim put his hands on his daughter's shoulders. "It wasn't you? You swear you weren't responsible for spreading the news about what you overheard on Thursday?"

"No, Dad, honest. I— No!"

The events in the calf's enclosure were still too raw in Lara's mind for her to want to talk to anyone about them. She'd only told her father the vaguest details of what she'd seen on her second trip—it was all too horrible. Junior and Eddie in the middle of the cow's straw and manure, Eddie's sly laugh, got mixed in her head with her own shame at soiling her clothes so that she felt as though she'd somehow been part of that scene on the floor, the grunting, the cow bellowing, the filth of it all.

She'd been soothed only partially by Robbie's joy on seeing her emerge from the manger. He hadn't minded her clothes—Chip's clothes— covered in cow shit, or the dirt on her face, but clung to her, disbelieving his good fortune at seeing her emerge like this, Venus from an ocean of muck. His own misery at his brother's swagger, his father's unfair accusations, vanished as he held her. That swagger, those accusations, also made him ignore the strictures against women in the shed.

He helped Lara dig her cell phone out of the manger. While he dried off poor, sweaty Nasya, Lara filled the calf's water trough and helped Robbie replenish the manger. Then, just in the nick of time, before Arnie came back with a grudging approval of his work, Robbie smuggled Lara out of the enclosure the same way she'd come in—as soon as he could, while Junior was driving Eddie someplace else and Arnie and Myra went to bed, sneaking back out of his house and escorting Lara home across the sorghum field.

They hadn't discussed Junior and Eddie, beyond Robbie saying, "Sorry about my brother," while Lara shivered and held on to him, despite her embarrassment over her clothes. They'd lingered in her yard only long enough to make a whispered date for Sunday afternoon before Lara ran inside and flung herself under the shower again.

Friday morning, when Jim went into her room to rouse her for school, Lara clung to him, her eyes sticky with tears she'd shed in her sleep. Jim couldn't get her to tell him exactly what she'd seen, but the details she did let out—Junior there with Eddie, getting the cow upset—alarmed him. He worried, too, about what Robbie might report to Arnie, despite Lara's belief that Robbie wouldn't say anything.

Jim cradled his daughter until the worst of her distress had passed. He wanted to take her into town, for a movie or a sundae, those cures for her childhood woes. Unfortunately, weather, equipment rental, and Susan's imminent return meant he had to make the corn harvest his priority.

He sent Lara to school, again with a note to excuse her tardiness—this time on account of the harvest—but told her she was to come straight home afterward. "Sugar, I hate to ask it, but I need you to help me clean out your mother's room."

Later Friday morning, while Curly was at the far end of the field emptying the grain wagon into the big truck Jim rented for the harvest, Jim reported part of Lara's escapade to Blitz. "Trouble is, she went back for her damned phone after I fell asleep. She says Junior came out from Tonganoxie Bible and brought Eddie into the shed with him. She wouldn't say what they did, but—whatever they got up to, it shook her pretty hard."

Blitz grunted. He knew, or at least suspected, Junior's relationship with Eddie, but he didn't talk about the things he knew or guessed, either on the farms or in the Lawrence schools. Curly picked up the most extraordinary details about people's private lives while working on his cousin's building projects; he happily shared them with everyone he met. As a result, Blitz kept his own counsel whenever he and Curly were together. Jim, of course, was the last to know ill of anyone, even Junior

Schapen, so Blitz didn't embroider on the situation, just agreed it was more than a fifteen-year-old girl should have seen.

"Although if she'd paid attention to me to begin with and cut out this wretched habit she has of sneaking in on people, she wouldn't have seen whatever it was to begin with," Jim added, exasperated.

Blitz only grunted again, but when Jim said he'd told Lara to clean up the mess Susan had left behind Blitz took matters into his own hands. He didn't say anything to Jim, but he didn't think a girl who'd just witnessed some pretty raw sex, with or without a heifer—given what he knew about Junior, neither would have surprised him—needed to be cleaning up after her mother. When he was alone in the combine, he called Rachel Carmody.

"I know you shouldn't try to bribe a teacher, ma'am," he said, "but Susan Grellier is coming home tomorrow afternoon. Could I take you to that fancy French restaurant in Prairie Village if you'll organize some of your church ladies to clean out that bedroom tomorrow morning before Susan gets home? Grellier says he's siccing Lulu on it, but it's too big a job for a kid. I'd help, but we'll be in the field until midnight tonight getting the corn in and I'll be back on the combine tomorrow while Grellier's fetching Susan."

Rachel had seen the room and she shared Blitz's unspoken commentary on the appropriateness of giving the job to Lara. She did a quick phone-around and on Saturday morning arrived with a team carrying brooms, buckets, and casseroles.

The women sent Lara into town to her band and basketball practice. They cleaned and did laundry. At eleven, when the men broke from harvesting for lunch, Jim carried the great pile of Susan's scribblings out to the yard and burned them. Blitz and Curly returned to the cornfield, but Jim went upstairs to shower and make himself tidy for his wife. As a last act, before driving into the hospital, he carried his ever-so-great-grandmother's diaries up the ladder to their tin trunk in the attic.

Thirty-Six

MAN IN THE MIDDLE

GLOBAL ENTERTAINMENT WAS merely the first of the news crews to ride out Saturday afternoon in search of the calf. CNN came next, followed by Fox and a stringer out of Kansas City for some of the Chicago and St. Louis papers. Most of them stopped at the Grelliers' for directions. Lara and Jim took turns answering the door and sending them on to the Burtons' to sink or swim as best they could.

A few sightseers were arriving, too, mostly area families who'd been hearing rumors of the calf for months, but a few from farther afield, picking up rumors out of the ether. Lara watched the parade from the family-room window. She tried to interest Susan in the drama, even telling her about the way the men had prayed to the calf on Thursday and showing her the pictures she'd taken with her cell phone. The old Susan would have objected as loudly as Jim about Lara trying to stir up gossip about the Schapens; the new, drugged Susan only nodded and said in a languid, uncaring voice, "How nice, Lara."

"Mom! It wasn't nice; it was gross. First of all, I was covered in cowshi— cow poop, and, second, all these creepy guys were kneeling on these rocks and praying to the heifer. I bet when Moses came down from Sinai and found the children of Israel worshipping the golden calf, it was exactly like that, and the poor calf was crying for its mother, and—"

"Lara, can I see you a minute?" Jim took his daughter into the kitchen. "Sweetheart, I can see you're upset with how lethargic your mother is. I am, too. But don't poke at her as if she were an anthill. When she feels strong enough to start responding to us, she will. That's what the doctor says, anyway. And, in the meantime, we need to give her as much support as we can."

"I'm trying to help her see there's a world outside her head! Why do I have to always be the one who's wrong? Why can't *she* be the one who's wrong?"

"It's not about right or wrong," Jim said. "It's about what she's strong enough for. You're stronger than she is these days."

"That's so unfair!" Lara cried and fled from the house.

Jim sighed and went back to the family room. He stood at the window, watching his daughter as she ran across the yard toward the road until the trees blocked her from his view. The knot of tension between his shoulders was so big he felt as though he had a basketball glued to his neck. Mute wife behind him, distraught daughter in front of him, him in the middle.

"I hope she's not going back to Schapens'," he said aloud, hoping Susan might respond, but she said nothing.

He turned to look at her, but she was pleating the plaid blanket he'd put across her lap. "I'm just going out to see—I—we can't afford her courting disaster with Arnie. Do you agree?"

"I don't know, Jim. I don't know anything, except I'm tired and my head is filled with fog. Please, let me go to bed."

Jim wanted to burst into tears himself, but he said quietly, "Of course. Go on up to bed. I'll tuck you in after I check on Lulu."

When he went outside, he found his daughter perched on an upper branch of the elm near the road, watching the people heading toward the Schapen place. He went back into the house long enough to fetch windbreakers for them both, then pulled himself up to the branch below hers, groaning out loud—the muscles he'd strained working out with Chip's weights last week had been further stressed by his stretch of sixteen-hour days in the fields.

"Hope you're not turning into an old man, Dad," Lara said from the branch above him.

"Hope I'm not, too, Lulu. That'd make you about forty, way too old to still be living in a tree at home."

Harmony restored between them, they watched together in silence. During the time Jim stayed with her, he figured at least twenty people passed them. Some came into his yard, hoping for directions, but Jim didn't feel like climbing down from the tree to help them, and Susan ignored the doorbell. He'd never been a tree climber as a boy, but he began to see why Lulu liked it. It was peaceful to sit suspended above the ground, even if the dust from the procession on the road below made him cough.

"How much do you reckon Arnie's charging folks for looking at his calf?" he asked.

"Do you think he would?" She was surprised.

"Stands to reason. He's been telling enough people that heifer was going to make his fortune. Unless he thinks he can sell her for some astronomical amount."

"Dad, you know they plan to burn her."

"You mean they're going through all this to have a barbecue?" He thought she was pulling his leg.

"No. Burn her up into ashes so she can be used in sacrifices, if the Jews rebuild the Temple in Jerusalem. It seems horrible, she's such a lonely, scared calf. How can Jesus want people to kill a calf?"

"Oh, baby, Jesus doesn't want us to hurt each other, let alone some poor heifer, but we seem to do it, anyway. When you think of all the people who've been slaughtered because someone told them God or Jesus or Allah wanted them to do it, it's enough to make a grown man cry. It's a good thing God is the one who's really in charge of our sorry lives, not all these priests and pastors and rabbis who think they know best."

"I thought maybe I could rescue Nassie and hide her in the sunflower field," Lara blurted.

"Lulu! Please, please un-think that thought. I can't even imagine what Arnie would do to you when he found her. And if you think you could keep her secret for thirty seconds around here, you've never listened to Curly share the news of the world." He paused a moment, trying to keep his voice neutral, not wanting to accuse her of eavesdropping, "How do you know they want to burn her?"

"Robbie told me."

"So you and he are starting to get along, even though he's a Schapen?" Jim quizzed her.

"He's not so bad. Not like Junior and their evil grandmother."

Jim squeezed the leg that was dangling over the branch above him. "I'm going to go check on your mom. You stay out of trouble, okay?"

"I'm not going over to Schapens', if that's what you mean," she said stiffly.

He stood up on his branch and hugged her, then swung to the ground, his trapezius protesting so that he couldn't keep back a bark of pain when he landed.

Back in the house, he went straight up the stairs so that he wouldn't have time to think, worry, dawdle. Susan was lying in bed, her breath short and shallow. Real sleep, he thought, kneeling next to her, not faking it in the hope he'd leave. He couldn't help patting the covers and the floor underneath for scraps of paper or a pen, but he didn't find anything, even when he stuck his hand between the box spring and mattress.

He knelt there, holding her hand, hoping she might wake up and smile at him. When she didn't stir, he found himself praying, not to Jesus but, as Lara had on Thursday, to his dead son. He didn't expect much help or understanding from the Lord. Maybe God had lost a son, like Pastor Albright had said, but Jesus didn't know anything about that kind of loss, didn't even know the grief Mary felt when she laid His own broken body in the tomb. Maybe Jesus knew about human sin and suffering, but He didn't know human grief: even when He wept over His dead friend Lazarus, the next second He brought Lazarus back to life.

"Give me a hand here, boy," he said to Chip. "Your mother went off the deep end this past year. You were the heart and center of her life, so give me a hand now, pull her back to the country of the living. We'll all be with you soon enough. Help us make it through this time, son."

He knelt so long that he lost all feeling in his legs. He lay flat on the bedroom floor, waiting for the numbness to wear off. He couldn't remember ever feeling this alone. Even the winter after Grandpa died, he had Gram and Chip and Susan. Now Gram and Chip were dead; and Susan, if she didn't return soon, he didn't know what he'd do.

Blitz had been working in the combine shed all afternoon, putting the combine to bed for the winter; Jim heard him give a couple of sharp honks, saying good-bye, as he drove out of the yard. A few minutes later, the back door banged: Lara coming back inside. That was one relief.

By and by, he got back to his feet and went downstairs to eat supper with his daughter. They took another one of the casseroles the church women had baked into the living room and watched reruns of *I Love Lucy* until bedtime. Jim lingered on the landing, but he finally went into his bedroom and climbed under the covers next to his wife. He lay there stiffly for a long time, listening to her breathing. But, finally, around one in the morning, he slipped into a fitful sleep.

Thirty-Seven

MANGER WARS

From the *Douglas County Herald*
AWAY IN A MANGER?

When Jesus returns in glory, it just may be due to local farmer Arnie Schapen. Several hundred people were herded into his dairy farm east of town this past weekend, some from as far away as Texas, all eager for the sight, or at least the sound, of a red heifer who—some believe—speaks Hebrew.

"She could be the perfect red heifer the Book of Numbers tells us is required for Temple sacrifices," explained Werner Nabo, pastor of the Salvation Through the Blood of Jesus Full Bible Church, where Schapen worships.

Three men from the ultraorthodox Jewish yeshiva Bet HaMikdash, in Kansas City, come out every month to examine the calf and make sure she remains without blemish.

I spoke with Reb Meir and Reb Ephraim from the yeshiva. They said it would be a major act of blasphemy to reproduce the sacred name of God in a newspaper, so I won't try to print what the calf has allegedly been saying. You'll have to go out and hear her for yourself—if you're prepared to shell out five dollars for twenty-three seconds in the calf's pen (I timed it!) and if the calf is performing. Like all artists, she's temperamental.

Reb Meir and Reb Ephraim are concerned that the crowds may harm the heifer. They also told me that women are not allowed near her, in case their menstrual cycles affect the heifer's development. This stricture led to several altercations between Schapen, who's a Douglas County sheriff's deputy, and women who had come to see the calf. Most of them were resolved peaceably, if not happily, although Schapen threatened to have one woman taken away in handcuffs.

"This is one place in America where the liberal lesbian agenda is not in charge," Myra Schapen, the deputy's octogenarian mother, told me. "No one can force affirmative action down our throats on our own farm." In time-honored tradition, she and the other women organized refreshments that they carried to the men and boys waiting in line for a brief glimpse of the calf, which Schapen is calling Nasya, the Hebrew word for "miracle."

When the first reporters arrived, Arnie and Myra were at Tonganoxie Bible watching Junior play football. Robbie was taking advantage of being home alone to practice guitar in the house, so he didn't even notice the Global Entertainment van when it pulled into the yard or hear Ashley Fornello ring the front doorbell. It wasn't until he glanced out the window and saw her bright blue jacket disappear around the milking shed that he realized someone was on the property.

His first thought was that Lara had come looking for him. He knew her mother was coming home today—it was why they weren't trying to meet until Sunday—but maybe she missed him as much as he missed her. He put down his guitar and hurried out to the back of the work buildings. When he realized it was a grown-up, and a stranger, he felt let down but tried to be polite.

It had taken Ashley Fornello so long to get a coherent story out of the Burtons that she'd lost some of her high-gloss reporting veneer. She told Robbie that she needed to see the miracle heifer and tried to bribe him with fifty dollars to let her into the enclosure.

"No, ma'am, I'm sorry, but ladies aren't allowed near the calf. The rabbis made it real clear." When he said this, he wasn't thinking about Lara being in the calf's pen—she was separate from the rabbis, his father, the pastor. Her hiding in the manger didn't count as a female being near the heifer. But if he let a reporter with a camera in—the hair on the back of his neck stood up, imagining Arnie's reaction. "My dad will be home around five. You can talk to him, but he'll say the same thing."

Ashley wheedled, flattered, bribed, tried to get him to point out the calf's special pen so she could take a picture from the outside. She asked him if he could repeat what the calf was saying. He kept saying "No, ma'am" as the easiest way to avoid trouble until she wondered if everyone in the valley was mentally deficient.

Before long, her rivals showed up, and then the stream of pilgrims began, initially people from Robbie's church, then the larger county community, as word spread via text messages. At first, Ashley and the other camera crews were content with interviewing the would-be sightseers, but pretty soon they got impatient and started going into the different barns and milking sheds.

Over in Tonganoxie, one of Myra's cronies in the parents' section got a text message from her daughter saying that her boyfriend's mother had gone to see the magic cow. The woman showed the message to Myra at halftime, and she and Arnie did the unthinkable: they left partway through one of Junior's games. He'd been doing so well, too, Myra mourned in the truck going home—three solo tackles and part of a sack in the first half alone.

By the time they reached the farm, there were twenty or thirty people milling around the back buildings. Arnie grabbed his deputy's megaphone from the trunk and ran across the rutted lot to the heifer's pen. Robbie was standing outside the door, barring people from breaking in, but the more enterprising camera crews were climbing up to take shots through the skylights.

Arnie turned on his megaphone. "I'm Arnie Schapen, and this is my property you're trespassing on. If you have business here, talk to me and we'll sort it out."

As the news crews shoved for position around Arnie, their mikes outthrust, Myra started to snarl at Robbie for letting all these people on the property. Arnie interrupted his remarks to Ashley Fornello from Global to pull Robbie into the center of the group of reporters. He clapped Robbie's shoulder. The boy might look weedy, but he'd stood up to all these people. Maybe underneath that hippie getup and long hair, he really was a Schapen.

All he said out loud was, "Robbie here bred Nasya, our special heifer. Of course, he was looking for a good milk bearer, not a miracle, but God doesn't send us miracles when we're arrogant enough to try to create them ourselves. We don't know what the future of this heifer is. We don't know if she'll make it to three years old without a blemish. But what we do know is, the Jews who are paying attention to Nasya for us think she's pretty special."

"I heard from one of your neighbors that she's performing miracles," Ashley Fornello said, thinking of Eddie Burton's disjoint comments, that the calf had blessed him and told him he was doing the right thing.

"I haven't seen any myself," Arnie said, "but, well, she's started speaking ancient Hebrew."

There was a ripple of disbelieving laughter among the television people. "What's she saying? Give me more grass?"

Arnie's lips tightened. "If you came out here to make fun of me—or, worse, make fun of the Lord—there's no need for you to hang around. According to the Jews, she's begun saying the sacred name for God that no one has spoken out loud since the last of their high priests was murdered two thousand years ago."

"So how do they know?" the man from Fox demanded.

"You'd have to ask them," Arnie said. "I'm just a simple Kansas farmer. I figure the Jews know more than I do about ancient Hebrew and the Old Testament, but if you guys are up on your biblical Hebrew I'll be glad to learn from you."

The crowd laughed at that, with him this time, so Arnie went on to say that the Jews warned them against letting women into the enclosure. "Not even my mother has been allowed in to see Nasya. Most of you here are like me, believing and hoping for the risen Lord to come again in glory. And even if you don't share all my beliefs, I know you'll respect them, and respect this heifer. So I'm going to ask the ladies to be patient, to remember what the Bible says, that they should 'learn in quietness and full submission,' and to honor my commitment to look after this precious gift the Lord has trusted to me."

"Too bad for you, Ashley," the Fox reporter said to Ashley Fornello. "But if you're quiet and fully submissive, we'll let you borrow some of our footage."

"Sorry, boys," Arnie said. "I can't allow cameras in the special enclosure. They may disturb or overly excite Nasya. And because of the wear and tear on the place, if you want to see the calf I'm going to ask you to pay a little something for the privilege."

"Five dollars," Myra snapped.

"Five dollars," Arnie agreed. "My mother will set up a table near the house, and you can line up there to pay. We'll let six people in at a time. Of course, members of my church, they get a special rate of three bucks. If you want to join, I can give you the pastor's cell phone number."

No one knew if he was joking or serious, so everyone laughed uneasily. Myra, ordering Robbie to fetch her a card table and a jar she could use to hold the money, moved the crowd to the gravel yard outside the kitchen door. At five, when Robbie went off to start the evening milking, everyone had left, including the television people.

Sunday turned into a different story. The clips that the Kansas City stations ran, using pictures of Nasya taken surreptitiously with cell phone cameras, got picked up on YouTube and the national networks. Even the *New York Times* sent its own reporter instead of relying on a local stringer to talk to Arnie. By Sunday afternoon, the crowds grew so large that managing them turned into a headache for the family.

At three, when Robbie had planned to meet Lara at her truck at the X-Farm so they could drive somewhere private, he could see he'd never make it out of the farm on time. The cowman, Dale, had come over, and some of the church elders were helping out. Junior, drawn home by the excitement of seeing his father on television, was enjoying the chance to shove people into place in the line, but Myra was keeping a bony hand and malevolent eye on her younger grandson.

She had planted Robbie at the card table, collecting cash from people and giving them numbers so they'd have a secured place in line. When

Myra went into the kitchen to oversee preparation of another batch of cider—a dollar a cup, no refills—Robbie sent a text message to Lara. Since Myra always examined the phone bill and catechized him about any text messages he sent or received, it was a bold and desperate move.

It was at three that Reb Meir, Reb Ephraim, and a van full of yeshiva students and teachers arrived from Kansas City. Reb Meir was furious with Arnie for allowing so much publicity to escape about the heifer. He banished everyone from her enclosure, lining his students—who looked more like street toughs than a religious community, despite their fringed shawls and long frock coats—in front of the entrance.

Myra squawked in outrage. Junior, always eager for a fight, ran over to confront the yeshiva boys. Arnie pushed past Junior, his hand on his gun belt, his nose an inch from the enclosure door.

"You're on private property, and this is my calf. She's sanctified to the living God, to the Lord Jesus Christ, not to the dead letter of the law, so get away from that door."

"Fine." Reb Meir came up next to Arnie. "Do as you please with her. If you don't wish our help in ensuring her ritual cleanness, I will make it clear that she is so deeply flawed, under the 'dead letter of the law,' as you call it, that no one will want to use her for any sanctified purpose."

"You can't go around telling lies about my heifer!" Arnie shouted.

"If you won't let me examine her alone, and in quiet, I can only assume that she has been violated and you are ashamed to let me see her for myself." Reb Meir shrugged and called to his students in Yiddish. They laughed and started back to their van.

"Chickens," Junior called as they passed him. "Piglets."

"You've eaten so much pork, your brains have turned to lard," one of the students responded.

Junior jumped him, knocking him to the muddy ground and grabbing him by the throat. The other yeshiva boys began punching Junior but couldn't make a dent in him. Shouting to each other in Yiddish, they grouped themselves on Junior's left side and pushed, as if rolling a log—or tipping a cow. In a moment, they'd flipped him onto his back.

The cameras were rolling. For the journalists who'd been hanging around hoping for some kind of action, the altercation was a miraculous answer to their prayers. The yeshiva boys were punching Junior in the face. He roared. Pushing them aside, he got to his feet, picked up the ringleader of the students, and threw him to the ground. Some teens from Salvation Bible joined in, kicking or picking up larger pieces of gravel to gouge with. The yeshiva boys fought back with equal savagery.

Of course, the crowd quickly formed a raggedy ring around the fight. Some of the parents were even cheering their sons, applauding when they scored direct hits on the opposing boys.

Robbie slipped into the front of the crowd, near Chris Greynard's father, to see how much damage Junior was doing. He hadn't been involved in a fight himself since his Kaw Valley Eagle days, and he wasn't going to start now, either for or against his brother. Junior was dangerous when he was mad. Robbie hoped someone could stop him before he paralyzed one of the yeshiva students, although they were fighting as aggressively as the Salvation Bible crowd. One of them even seemed to have some kind of weapon, knuckles or maybe a knife—Robbie saw a flash of light on metal, but the boy was moving too fast for Robbie to tell.

As he stood in the circle of onlookers, nervously chewing a hangnail, Robbie heard one of the reporters say, "This is what life is going to be like all day, every day, if these crackpots actually try to rebuild the damned Temple." Another answered, "No, it'll be worse, because they'll be using bombs and grenades instead of just fists."

"Why?" Robbie couldn't help asking the men.

"Don't you know where they want to put up the Temple?" The first man was smoking. He talked out of the side of his mouth, like Clark Gable in an old western.

"Yes, of course," Robbie stammered. "In Jerusalem, in the place where the old one was."

"And you know that's a holy site for the Moslems, right?" The reporter pinched off his cigarette just below the glowing end and stuck it in his windbreaker pocket. "So if these nutcases start building on the Dome of the Rock, the next thing you'll see is World War Three in the Middle East. This here is just the first skirmish."

Junior or Arnie would have pointed out that they themselves were among the so-called nutcases the reporter was condemning, but Robbie only flushed and turned away. Pastor Nabo often proclaimed that God was not a pacifist, especially when he was talking about Lara's mother and other anti-war protesters. Pastor would rub his hands in glee over the coming fight of Good versus Evil. Just this morning, he had preached on one of his favorite themes, how the coming war with Islam would destroy half the people of the earth.

Was that really what God wanted? Robbie wondered. For World War III to break out over rebuilding the Temple? Would that herald Jesus' return in glory or would it just mean more misery, with people like Chip Grellier getting killed and people like Lara breaking their hearts over the dead?

Look at Junior right now. If you asked him, Junior would say he was fighting for the glory of Jesus' name, when Robbie knew his brother only ever fought because he loved beating people up.

The yeshiva boys were fighting hard, but the Christians were definitely winning this skirmish in the war of salvation. Reb Meir and the other yeshiva teachers seemed to realize this because they called out to their students in Yiddish. None of the onlookers knew what they said, but the Jewish youths, their clothes torn, their faces cut and bruised, pulled themselves unwillingly out of the melee and slouched over to stand next to their teachers.

Junior and his cohorts yelled abuse at them, but when the yeshiva students started to shout back Reb Meir and Reb Ephraim silenced them with raised hands.

"It's good for the Jews to learn how disciples of the Prince of Peace behave in public," Reb Meir said to one of the reporters. "Now that we see what they want to do with their calf, we can't be involved."

The reporters surged around Reb Meir. "Does this mean you don't think she's the perfect red heifer you need for the Temple?"

"I think if the Schapens are this violent, there is every reason to suspect they have abused the heifer and that she is no longer sanctified, or pure enough, to use in ritual sacrifice."

Robbie could see his father's face register first fury, then worry: he was counting on Nasya to make their fortune. If the rabbis said she was blemished, the crowds would evaporate, along with the money he was taking in, as well as the recognition the heifer was starting to bring him.

Arnie never found it easy to be conciliatory, but he walked over now to Reb Meir and said, "Look, boys will be boys, whether they're Jews or Christians. They all got carried away, but I promise you this kind of behavior has never taken place in Nasya's presence. We have respected her in every way, even making sure we put obsidian under her pen the way you told us to."

Reb Meir nodded slowly. "I'm willing to treat this as an aberration, but you must let me examine the heifer to make sure the crowds haven't molested her."

The two men shook hands, both looking as though they were swallowing live beetles, but the television cameras caught the clasped hands and fake smiles: that's what would matter tomorrow morning. The reporters began bombarding the pair with questions.

"Have the crowds hurt Nasya, Reb Meir?" "Arnie, what do you mean by 'the dead letter of the law'?" "Does your church say the Jews are going to hell?" "Why does it hurt Nasya for people to look at her?" And from the women, fuming over their lack of access: "She's female. You're men. You'll do her more damage than we could."

Reb Meir held up a hand. "We don't know what shape the calf is in; we haven't seen her since all this disturbance began. Of course, yesterday was the Sabbath—it was impossible for us to drive over to keep an eye on her."

The reporters also wanted to know whether having a red heifer meant the Jews were ready to start rebuilding the Temple in Jerusalem. "She'll be three before you know it. Will the Temple be ready by then?"

"No," Reb Meir said. "Assuming she's still unblemished in three years, we can sacrifice her according to Torah precepts and store her ashes in an appropriate container—which we have already created, in accordance with Torah precepts—until the Temple can be rebuilt."

"And when the Temple is rebuilt, then Jesus will come again and destroy it, isn't that right, Mr. Schapen? He'll cast the Jews and Muslims, and even Christians who don't believe the same way you do, into outer darkness while whisking you to heaven, isn't that right?" Ashley Fornello was feeling aggressive after spending two days in a barnyard, getting her story secondhand from the men around her.

Arnie shifted uncomfortably. He didn't like having these things spelled out so plainly in public, not while he still needed Reb Meir to help him look after the calf. "I'm not any kind of theologian," he finally managed. "I'm just a simple Kansas farmer God entrusted this special calf to. So I think I'd better let Reb Meir look at her, make sure she's doing okay with all this excitement. If he gives us the go-ahead, we'll start letting people back into the enclosure."

The excitement died down while Reb Meir and his colleagues examined the heifer from stem to stern, so to speak. Nasya moved restlessly around her pen, worn-out by so many strangers and unhappy—or so it seemed to Robbie—with the way they were touching her to make sure her virginity was intact. When Reb Meir finally gave Nasya a clean bill of health, Robbie relaxed. He'd been afraid of what Junior might have gotten up to with Eddie when they were in the enclosure Thursday night.

He went back out to the yard, hoping to make his escape, but Myra was there and jumped on him, dragging him back to the money table. He thought they were acting like the money changers Jesus had driven from the Temple, but when he mentioned this Myra's face turned mahogany.

"And the damage to the pen, and to the yard, you're going to repair that yourself, Robbie? If you're too squeamish to touch money, you can go inside and heat up another five gallons of cider."

"Nanny, I need a break. I have to start milking in another hour."

"Your brother was standing up for the farm while you gawked like a girl on the sidelines, afraid to get your hands dirty. You go in the kitchen with the other girls, and I'll take care of the money you're too pious to touch."

Robbie went into the kitchen, into the crowd of church women washing cups and gossiping. "Nanny says could you please heat up some more cider?" He was astonished to hear the words coming from his mouth, and even more surprised when he found himself moving quickly to the front of the house, out the unused front door, and down to the road. He started to run, jumping out of the way of the cars heading to the farm, praying as he went. Not for the Second Coming or the sanctity of the heifer, but for something more simple: that Jesus would keep Lara in the X-Farm until he reached her.

Thirty-Eight
COLD COMFORT FARM

BETWEEN TELEVISION, YouTube, and text messaging, the Schapen heifer quickly turned into global entertainment. As pictures of Nassie flooded the Net, Islamic leaders threatened jihads that would "make Iraq look like a kindergarten picnic" if anyone, Jew or Christian, tried rebuilding the Temple on the Temple Mount. The Israeli consul general for the Midwest held a press conference to assure the world that rebuilding the Temple was not part of Israeli government policy. He added that Reb Meir and his yeshiva were an extremist fringe of Judaism that misunderstood Torah. Reb Meir startled his Christian supporters by replying that Israel should not even be recognized as a country because a state of Israel could not exist in the absence of the Temple.

Dashiell Goode, professor of Near Eastern languages and literature at the University of Kansas, explained that the sacrifice of the red heifer mentioned in Numbers didn't have anything to do with cleansing people from sin. "The passage is obscure and hard to interpret, but it seems to treat a class of impurities connected to handling dead bodies. It's only recently that a small group of would-be millenarians have started conflating the sacrifice in Numbers with Christian teaching about Jesus' blood sacrifice on the cross. Raising and slaughtering a perfect red heifer serves no textually grounded religious purpose today."

Professor Goode also pooh-poohed Reb Meir's claim that Nasya was speaking ancient Hebrew. "No one knows how to pronounce the secret name of God. It was an oral tradition among the high priests, who passed it on to their successors in private. The Name was too holy for ordinary people to use in ordinary discourse. When the last of the high priests was killed during the great rebellion against Rome in 70 C.E., the pronunciation of the secret Name died with Phannias ben Samuel."

Arnie, Pastor Nabo, and various authorities from Full Bible Christian seminaries countered Professor Goode's "blasphemous, atheistic beliefs." Other scholars weighed in on every aspect of the debate, from how you knew a heifer was perfect—itself a subject of debate: could she have three white hairs, five, or none?—to whether the Second Coming of Jesus would even be noticed by most people. As a result of all these arguments, sightseers flocked in ever-larger numbers to the Schapen farm to get their own view of the calf.

Arnie was so proud of his heifer that he gave Robbie fifty dollars to spend however he wanted—"Even on more of that catcall music you like, son"—an act of generosity that made Myra fume.

Robbie was touched by the gift, but it was the only pleasure he had out of the calf's popularity. Just as his dreams of Lara had miraculously turned into reality, he had no time to see her. They couldn't get together at school, not if they wanted to keep their relationship hidden from their families. And now, on top of his work with the cows, Robbie had to help Myra tend to the visitors. He would grab a few feverish moments with Lara, slipping away to the X-Farm when he finished the afternoon milking, only to endure his grandmother's relentless bitterness when he reached home again.

"Where have you been, young man?" she would demand. "I was looking for you all over to take charge of the cash receipts so I could make a bit of dinner for your father. And for you, I might add, although why we bother to feed someone who doesn't pull his own weight around here—"

Arnie astounded Robbie by sticking up for him—really, twice in one week, if you counted the fifty dollars. "Now, then, Mother, you know he does two milkings a day as well as keeping up with his studies and the church youth group. And we wouldn't have the calf at all if Robbie hadn't bred the mother."

"All the more reason for him to stick around and do his share." Myra glowered.

Robbie reported his woes to Lara Thursday evening, as they huddled among the drooping sunflowers at the X-Farm. "And then she went on and on, the way she always does, about what a loser I am."

"I'd think your gram would be happy as a pig in mud right now with all the attention your farm is getting in the news."

"Yeah, but nothing makes her happy. Except maybe Junior beating up people. It was practically like Jesus coming again in glory to hear her talk about Junior pounding those Jewish boys from Kansas City on Sunday. 'And what about you, Robbie? You were sitting around like a schoolgirl in tears not helping your brother at all. Just what I'd expect from Kathy Sheldon's son.' Then came the usual earful about how my mom was a harlot and I was a harlot's son, and it was practically like Junior didn't even have the same mother as me."

"Your gram sure has a thing about mothers—she hates mine and yours both. Maybe she's really a space alien. Maybe she brought Junior with her from outer space, so she hates human women who can have babies."

Robbie laughed dutifully but burst out, the darkness a shelter behind which he could speak: "I keep wondering what's wrong with me. Why would my own mom go off like that? She—I always thought she loved me. We played games, we named the cows together, and then—whammo!—she disappeared without a word, not even a birthday card."

"But she did want to take you with her," Lara said. "Don't you remember the day she left? She came out for you, but your dad forced her off the land."

"I was there when she drove out," Robbie said angrily. "Nanny said she came to pick up her clothes and never even asked about me."

"Robbie, that's not true!" Lara sat up in the twilit field. "I was only nine, but I remember her driving over to our house and crying for, like, an hour because your dad locked you and Junior in the barn. And when she tried to get into the barn, he shot at her. And Mom and Dad even tried to talk to your father, but he wouldn't listen. You know my father, he doesn't talk about stuff much, so he won't talk about Arnie—I mean, your dad—so I don't know what happened when my folks went over. But, cross my heart, your mom really wanted to take you with her."

"Then why did she disappear? Why didn't she ever write?" Robbie wanted to believe Lara, but six years of Myra dinning at him that his mother was a harlot who thought more of her clothes than she did her own children was hard to overcome.

Lara stroked his hair. "Have you ever tried to track her down? She grew up in Lawrence, didn't she? My dad says he went out with her a few times in high school, before she married your dad, so don't you have another grandmother in Lawrence?"

"No, her people moved away years ago, and I can't find them. Even though my mom's family went to Salvation Bible, no one at church will talk about her. It's like they're so afraid of Nanny that they won't even tell me they ever heard of my own mother's family. I've tried Google, but their last name was Sheldon, and there are a zillion Sheldons in America. Of course, I've Googled her, too—Kathy Sheldon and Kathy Schapen both—but if she married the man she ran off with, her name would be different. That still doesn't explain why she never writes or anything."

"Maybe she does and your nanny burns her letters," Lara suggested. "Your mom is the one person who knows how scary your nanny is, so she probably doesn't try to phone."

"You're so lucky," Robbie said wistfully. "You have both your parents with you, and they don't pretend the crappy stuff they do is for your own good."

"You wouldn't say that if you were living with the Zombie Queen," Lara said. "My mom might as well have run off with someone. Her body sits around the house all day working on some stupid project for occupational therapy while her face is blank, like a turnip.

"These ladies from Riverside Church came out this afternoon, including Ms. Carmody—you know, she belongs to our church—and Turnip Grellier sat staring out the window like they weren't there. Dad wanted me to make tea, but I couldn't take it, not the way she sat without saying a single word. I know this is a terrible thing to say but sometimes I look at her and wish my dad hadn't—hadn't found her in time."

She let out a hiccupy sob. Robbie pulled her close, the refrain of a new song flitting through his head: *I longed to wash all those heartsick tears away.* He could hear the chords, but it would sound better with a fiddle than a guitar.

After a long embrace, when they both knew they needed to go home, Lara said, "You know, Robbie, if it was me I'd look to see if your gram is hiding letters from your mother in her room."

"Lara! I can't go into her room. Do you know what she'd do?" Visions of whippings, both verbal and physical, of being thrown out of the house, his guitar smashed to pieces, all the violence and threats of violence that had descended on him since his mother disappeared washed through him and he trembled.

"Not while she's home," Lara said. "But maybe your mom left a note or something and your gram is hoarding it and gloating over it. Wouldn't it be worth some risk to find that out? I'd do it for you if I could get to your house without anyone seeing me."

"Oh, Jesus, no, Lara," Robbie said. "Don't try coming near our place. My dad would probably burn down your house if he saw you going into ours."

Lara's cell phone rang: Kimberly, checking on algebra homework. Lara said she'd call her back and hung up, but a second later her father phoned, demanding that she get home for supper.

Robbie scrambled to his feet and ran down the track to the road: if it was time for the Grellier's supper, it was way past mealtime in his house.

When Lara got home, Ms. Carmody and the other church ladies had left. Jim was in the kitchen, trying to read, Susan in the family room, where she'd taken possession of the long couch, filling it with an afghan she was endlessly crocheting as occupational therapy. Jim looked bleakly at his daughter but didn't ask where she'd been: he didn't think he could cope with an evasive answer from her. Instead, he forced a smile, told her there was chili on the stove, and asked if she had done her homework.

"When she was out here this afternoon, Ms. Carmody reminded me that your mother and I both have to sign off on your homework assignments. You still have two problem sets to do before you're caught up in algebra. And she said you owe her a book report on *The Red Badge of Courage* compared to *The Things They Carried*."

Lara pinched her lips together. "She only assigned those to me because of Chip."

"Yes, and because she thinks you have the maturity to read and respond to them. She hopes they'll help you understand what may have been going through Chip's mind when he went to Iraq. Come on, sweetheart, *please.*" The last sentence came out as an anguished plea; he hadn't intended it, his voice cracking from fear.

Lara turned from the stove to stare at him. The idea that her own actions might make her father cry—she'd never imagined she had that much power. She spooned out the chili and brought a bowl to him, nudging him to move over in his chair. She wedged her tall, skinny body next to him, and they ate together in silence.

In the morning, Jim drove Susan to town for her appointment with a social worker. The social worker was a man, which seemed odd to Jim, but the guy was experienced and easy to talk to—at least, easy for Jim to talk to. Susan wasn't saying much to anyone.

The social worker pulled Jim in for a few words at the end of Susan's session: he wanted Jim's perspective on how Susan was functioning at home. Jim said things weren't as bad as they'd been in the first month after Chip's death. Susan hadn't started writing again and she was eating, but she wouldn't talk to him. It wasn't the way it had been before, when his wife was inhabiting some remote place where she didn't hear him. She just didn't care about anything.

"She needs an occupation, she needs her friends to visit her," the social worker suggested.

When they got home, Jim tried getting Susan to look at the farm accounts. She had always maintained the books, had known down to a penny what their cost per acre was, and how to decide when it was better to bet on soybeans, when on corn, but now she just looked at him and said, "Oh, Jim, it's too much for me right now. You got the corn in, you can take the time now to add up these numbers. Or maybe Lara . . ." Her voice trailed away; she started picking apart the threads on her sweater.

Lara was angrier than Jim and therefore more ruthless with her mother. When she got home from school, and her father reported on the social worker's comment, Lara dragged her mother to the X-Farm.

"Look at this field: the birds have wrecked it, but there's still something here to harvest. We could do it together. I can clean out the hopper on the combine so it meets the organic-certification standards, and I'll drive the wagon if you'll run the combine."

Susan looked at the sunflowers, then turned without speaking and slouched back to the house. Lara, beside herself with fury, followed her, shouting, "The X-Farm and the sunflowers were your idea, but it was me who made them come true! I put in the crop and saw we got certified while you were dancing around bonfires with Gina Haring and Elaine Logan. So get off your butt and help me save the seeds. Even if you wish it was me over in the cemetery and Chip standing here, you can pay attention to the crop."

Susan stopped and turned to look at her daughter. "Lara, it's me I want over in the cemetery, not you, so leave me alone."

Lara watched her mother move on her dead legs back to the house. So enormous was her rage that she went out to the supply shed and found the crates with the packages she'd designed.

"Abigail's Organics, Abigail's Orgasms, Abigail's Colonics," she shouted, thinking of as many hateful words as she could. She dragged the crates into the middle of the drive and set fire to them. But they were packed too densely and wouldn't burn.

Jim had seen the drama develop from the equipment barn, where he was straightening a disk that he'd bent when he drove the harrow over a tree root down by the river. He ran out as the yard grew thick with smoke. Looking from his daughter's tight, angry face to the crates, which he himself had marked FOR THE X-FARM last June, he finally said, "If you want to burn them, you need more oxygen on your fire. But if you think you might want to use them next year, I'll put out the fire and help you salvage them."

"You said you were going to sell the X-Farm to pay Mom's medical bills!" Lara screamed. "This was my only chance for a crop, and it's too late, it's ruined, and she doesn't give a rat's tailbone."

"I'm sorry, baby." Jim put his hands on his daughter's shaking shoulders. "I should have let you have the combine for a day, but all I was thinking about was the corn crop and how you'd need Curly to help you clean the rasp bars and the hopper up to the organic board's standards. I wish I could promise you I'd make it right next year, but I'm not sure I can. I'll have to run the numbers in a month when I have a chance to see—"

He broke off the sentence without finishing it—*when I have a chance to see if Susan is ever going to recover.* To see whether I have to sell my acres to a developer. Peter Ropes might want to buy, but a developer would pay five times as much. There were plenty of builders, Curly's cousin among them, who coveted land out here for mansions, as Kansas City's commuters moved farther and farther afield.

Curly's cousin had come around one morning, offering Jim a price on the X-Farm that would just about cover Susan's medical bills. Which meant Curly had been gossiping to his cousin, and the whole county by extension, about Susan's condition and Jim's finances. Jim was angry and chewed out Curly. When Blitz heard about it, he came so close to beating the younger man to a pulp that he went home to cool off. Curly prudently lay low for several days.

If Jim sold to Curly's cousin, Peter Ropes would hate it, having city people living out here; they'd start wanting to zone the place to keep noise down. And Arnie would be furious, because the first thing city people did was shut down animal operations—too much smell too close to them. They moved to the country for peace and quiet, by which they meant golf courses around their houses, not working farms.

Friday afternoon, after helping Lara put out the fire and telling Curly to see how many of the packages were still usable, Jim walked over to the X-Farm; he hadn't been there since Chip died. Despair, fear, anger with his wife, all these had turned him against the organic farm.

As he lifted the drooping sunflower heads and saw the damage the birds had done, he wondered if his impulse to sell the X-Farm stemmed more from anger with Susan than a need for money. Not that her medical bills weren't a huge and mounting worry—but he could sell the half section he farmed down by the Wakarusa. It would be good pasturage for Arnie's cows, for instance, and easier to maintain as a grazing pasture than a crop field. Assuming Arnie would even buy Grellier land; he'd be sure there was some hitch to it if Jim offered it to him. Maybe Jim could set up some elaborate scheme where Arnie would think Jim was cutting him out of the picture—then he'd want to buy.

Arnie was so sure this calf of his would make him rich—even Jim had heard that talk, down at the grain elevator, or at the coffee bar in town where he went sometimes to talk with other men his age. Not that he ordered their expensive cappuccinos and whatever, any old java of the day would do him fine. He'd nurse one cup for half an hour while he caught up with people from church, or Peter Ropes and Herb Long-necker, who also stopped in there.

The thought of cappuccino made him walk to the east edge of the sunflower field to stare at the Fremantle house. Gina, bundling him out of the way as if he were a tiresome two-year-old and letting that horren-dous Elaine Logan move in. Surely, they weren't—his stomach turned at the thought—it was hard enough to accept Gina with Autumn Minsky from the bookstore. Riverside was an open and accepting church, but sometimes he thought they went too far.

Thirty-Nine

MURDER ABOUT

IT MIGHT HAVE CONSOLED Jim to know that relations between the women at the Fremantle house were strained if not downright cold. Gina had asked Elaine to stay on an impulse: the naked longing on Jim's face was more than she could take. It was the look her husband used to wear, hoping against all odds she might be in love with him, and she didn't like the reminder of the life she used to lead, when she'd buried herself deep in the closet so she could have access to beautiful clothes, rare art, splendid travel.

When her uncle offered her the use of the house while she got back on her feet, Gina thought she'd have some welcome privacy in the country, time to recover from the pity or scorn of the people she'd lived around in the six years of her marriage. She'd imagined exploring her interest in Wicca, coming to terms with her lesbian self, all in a remote but comfortable home.

Privacy, comfort—both had been fantasies—and if she'd been able to celebrate Wiccan holidays and sleep openly with other women, she'd also done so in the middle of mold, cold, and open warfare from the neighbors. She'd arrived in Kansas full of good resolutions: she'd rebuild her old career in public relations. She'd try to write a novel, a long-standing fantasy that had faded in her years of marriage. Instead, although she busied herself with Wicca, with lovers, and with the anti-war movement, the isolation made it hard for her to organize herself.

Networking via the Net was possible in theory, but of course the

Fremantle house didn't have a broadband connection and the old phone wires were too uncertain for dial-up. She had to do her business via BlackBerry, which cost a fortune, or go into town to an Internet café. Both made it hard for her to restart a career that seemed more remote every week.

In the summer, she started work on a novel—romance and social commentary, about the upscale closeted women of New York. She managed to write eight pages in the month of August, and when she read them over the language felt brittle and phony. Perhaps she was choosing the wrong setting; perhaps she needed to write about the people around her right now.

When Elaine Logan had come out for Midsummer Eve, she kept prattling about her baby who died in the fire. Elaine was such a mix of fantasy and fabrication that Gina hadn't believed her. While the Grelliers had told her about the fire, all those years ago, and the youth who had died in it, they'd never mentioned a baby.

In fact, at the midsummer fire Elaine had a fit when Susan Grellier said there'd been no babies in the bunkhouse. "And you were there, Missy Know-It-All? You think because you know the War Between the States, you know the Civil War, too. But you don't. And I do. Because I lived through the real Civil War."

Arnie had arrived with his fire truck a short time later, putting an end to any squabbling among the Wiccans, but the tale began to worry Gina. She wanted to see what lay inside the ruined bunkhouse. If a baby had died there that no one knew about, maybe it would explain why Elaine had become the tiresome drunk she was today. Maybe that would be Gina's book, *Murder on the Plains.* She could visualize the cover and the reviews. The book would be unusual; it would let her reclaim her dead Manhattan life.

The day that Rachel Carmody came out to see her about Elaine, Gina had decided to dismantle the old bunkhouse, to see whether she could find any relics from the fire. When Elaine showed up during the storm later that night, Gina thought Elaine might be able to give her more details about the baby or the fire. She also thought Elaine would provide company of a sort, a buffer against the intruding eyes of the Schapens,

Burtons, and Goddess Knew-Who-Else. She'd been afraid, too, after see-ing the roach taped to her poster. Even with the bolts and bars Jim and Blitz screwed to the windows and doors, the house was too isolated, too easy to break into. Gina had thought another human in the place, even one as strange as Elaine Logan, might make her feel safer.

The decision proved as confused and fruitless as all the other choices Gina had made this past year. When Gina asked about the baby, Elaine would put a finger along her nose, like a caricature of a movie spy, and say, "Dead men tell no tales," or whine that no one believed her.

She wouldn't help out, even with the minimal housework Gina required, and Gina had to hide her wine, which made Elaine snarl abuse. She bewildered Gina by her rapid swings, from hurling ugly insults at her to clinging to her, as if Gina were her own mother. One morning, Elaine fumbled in her trash bag of belongings and pulled out a crumpled copy of her college transcript.

"You're writing a book, aren't you? I read some of your pages. You're not making much progress, are you? And you're trying to write about my old commune. You should let me help. I got A's in English, see?" She thrust the transcript at Gina, who was furious that Elaine had been snooping into her papers and embarrassed that this drunken homeless woman could so easily recognize the bare bones of her story.

Gina called Rachel Carmody to see if the church could help find another placement, but that proved a vain hope. Gina certainly wasn't going to call the sheriff for help, not when it was his deputy who'd caused most of her problems, so she settled into a kind of cold coexistence with the older woman.

Most days, unless it was raining, Elaine walked the quarter mile to the county road and hitched a ride into town. All the people flocking out to see the Schapen calf made it easy for her to get a lift. In Lawrence, she'd make a circuit of her usual haunts, finishing at Raider's Bar if she'd been able to panhandle enough money for liquor. Most nights, she found some-one, often Turk Burton, to take her back out as far as the crossroads.

Gina refused to give her a key to the house. If Elaine returned after Gina had gone to bed, she wouldn't get up to let the older woman in. Elaine screamed venom up at Gina's window: "If some farmer you want to impress comes by, then you'll get up, but not when it's me, a helpless little girl!"

Whether Gina even heard her, Elaine didn't know, but she spent one cold, wet night in the Fremantle barn. Elaine had hated it, because of the rats and the fact that the roof leaked, so the next time she got drunk and lost track of time she stayed at a drop-in shelter in town.

Gina hoped that meant she was gone for good, but later that afternoon Elaine returned, pouting and grumbling. The next morning, she announced she was going over to see the Schapens' calf.

"Everyone's talking about it in Lawrence. Why don't you come with me? A cow that speaks Hebrew. That'd give your book something no one else is writing about."

"Arnie Schapen may choose to involve himself in my affairs, but I have zero interest in his. Besides, haven't you seen that women aren't allowed in the calf's enclosure?"

"Can't you at least give me a lift? No one ever helps me out, and I'm such a tired little girl."

"Because you're hungover," Gina snapped.

Pouting, grumbling, Elaine set out for Schapens' on foot. She had to rest half a dozen times, leaning against trees or fence posts since it was a major effort to get up from the ground. At the county road she hoped someone would stop and give her a lift, but it was the middle of a weekday, the slowest time for traffic going out to see the calf. She waited twenty minutes at the intersection, before finally puffing her way up the rutted track to the farm.

Arnie and Myra were going about the usual business of the farm; Arnie was disking his sorghum field, Myra had driven over to Wiesers' with the midweek milk delivery. Dale, the cowman, was tied up with extra work for the calf. Arnie had told him to knock together some benches for visitors to sit on, and to put up fencing to keep them out of the main milking and grazing sections of the farm.

Myra's spreadsheet for the calf began to include expenses she hadn't anticipated for wear and tear on the land. She wanted to up admission to $7.50, but Arnie was afraid people would accuse them of caring more about money than the Lord's anointed.

As it was, they needed volunteers from Salvation Bible to help with the pilgrims. Weekdays, when traffic was light, one of the church elders who was a retired heating contractor waited outside Nasya's pen to let in any men and boys who wanted to see her. Gail Ruesselmann took care of collecting admission.

On the morning Elaine showed up, Gail was sitting in her SUV, doing needlepoint, ready to hop out to direct traffic. Only ten cars had arrived that morning. Gail had sent the men and boys to look at the calf, while the women went to the kitchen for cider, or at least some warmth.

Pastor Nabo was in the kitchen. He drove out to the farm most days, hoping for more television cameras—he had new points on his side of the red heifer debate that he wanted to project to a worldwide audience. However, the big entertainment companies had moved on to newer stories. Only the reporter from the *Douglas County Herald* was there, and she had already heard everything the pastor had to say thirty or forty times. The reporter moved into the chilly front room, leaving the female pilgrims to study photographs of Temple artifacts, all created according to biblical precepts, that the pastor had loaded onto his laptop. These included a vessel for collecting Nasya's blood, when the day came to sacrifice her, a picture that always roused an appreciative squeal of horror from Nabo's audience.

When Gail Ruesselmann saw Elaine stagger into the yard, in her bright pink sweatshirt with the Pink Panther outlined in sequins, she climbed down from her SUV and asked if she could help.

"I want to see this cow everyone's talking about," Elaine puffed.

"We all do," Gail smiled brightly. "But we women are not allowed near the calf."

"Why not?"

"It's one of those mysteries that we don't question. Why don't you sit down for a minute"—Gail pointed at a rough bench that Dale had just finished hammering together—"and I'll get you a cup of cider. Where did you park your car?"

"I don't have one. I walked. I'm entitled to see this cow. If she's going to bring about the end of the world, the way they're saying on TV, I have a right to see the cause of my doom."

"If you believe in the Lord Jesus Christ, His love and His sacrifice will take you straight to His bosom in heaven. You won't have to worry about your 'doom,' as you put it," Gail said. "Have you accepted Jesus as your personal Savior?"

"Oh, fuck all that religious shit," Elaine said. "You holy hens and your everlasting preaching make me want to puke. If God made this world, He did a sorry-ass job of it. Now, let me see this one perfect thing you claim He created."

"Even if I wanted to let a woman break the Law of God, it wouldn't be someone who's taking His name in vain," Gail said. "Women are not allowed into the enclosure with the animal. There's no argument about it."

"Bull piss, there's no argument about it. We're going to argue plenty, you and me."

Gail turned pink with outrage. "Can't you open your mouth without spewing forth dirt?"

"*Me* spew out dirt? Yours is the dirty mouth, spouting all that hypocritical crap. Did they tie you up and beat you to make you believe you're a baby who can't think for yourself? I was here when the February Sisters took over the university, and I don't let any man tell me what to do." With a militant gesture borrowed from the seventies, Elaine clomped across the yard toward the barns.

Gail ran after her, grabbing her arm and yelling, "No, you don't. You can't go back there."

Elaine ignored her. Gail tried to stop her, but even though Elaine couldn't walk fast she was too massive to hold back once she'd started moving. Gail kept step with her, pulling out her cell phone to call the pastor in the kitchen.

"Pastor! There's a horrible woman—a harlot, a Jezebel! She wants to get into the enclosure, and I can't make her listen to reason!"

They had reached the milking shed. Beyond it, Nasya's teepee-shaped enclosure was visible at the end of the row of huts for the new calves. Elaine put her shoulders down like a football player and headed toward it, her arms swinging like sides of beef. One flailing arm smacked Gail in the diaphragm hard enough to make her double over in pain.

The church elder guarding the enclosure saw the women but assumed they were bringing him a message of some kind from the house, or perhaps a sandwich. He'd escorted the last of the most recent group of men out of Nasya's pen half an hour earlier and was feeling both hungry and bored. It wasn't until Elaine came straight to the door and started to pull it open that he realized he had trouble on his hands. He leaned into the door, trying to hook the padlock in the latch, while Elaine yanked on his arm.

Gail had gotten her wind back. She wanted to help the elder push the door shut, but Elaine grabbed her by the shoulders and pulled her from the entrance.

In response to Gail's call—*Weak woman panicking*, he thought— Pastor Nabo walked out from the house across the lot, taking his time. When he saw the tussle at the enclosure, he realized it was more serious. *Weak woman seeking strength from the male.* He took a minute to call Arnie on his tractor in the sorghum field, warning him trouble was brewing at the sacred enclosure, then put all his strength into moving Elaine away from the door. With the elder and Gail Ruesselmann pushing, they were able to keep the door shut long enough for the elder to snap the padlock into place.

"Woman, whoever you are I command you in Jesus' name to get away from that door," Pastor Nabo thundered.

Elaine turned and spat. "I am not part of your stupid church with its sexist rules. I don't believe women are supposed to sit around twiddling their twats while men tell them what to do, so unlock that door, buster."

Arnie rolled up on his tractor in time to see Elaine spit. He jumped down, not even bothering to turn off the engine, and ran to the enclosure. "Has she been inside? Has she spoiled the heifer?"

"No, Brother Schapen. It took three of us, but we managed to keep her out." The elder was panting, wiping sweat from his face with a tissue.

"You're on private property, you drunken slut!" Arnie recognized Elaine from all the years she'd been hanging around the bars in the county. He'd even run her in more than once himself for disorderly conduct. "I have the right to admit whoever I want to see my calf, and no drunk liberal feminazi is going to come on my land, insulting my faith and violating my rules. If you don't want to be arrested for trespass, you'd better leave right now."

"Nazi yourself," Elaine shouted. "You little tin-pot Hitler, don't you go telling me what to do."

She lay down in the mud in front of the door, knocking the elder out of the way as she toppled over. All of the people who'd been in the kitchen with Pastor Nabo were surrounding the calf's enclosure now. There were around two dozen of them, about a third men, and a number of teens with their ubiquitous cell phones. The kids began taking pictures of Elaine, roaring with laughter at the sight of her giant thighs sinking into the mud, and e-mailing them to their friends.

"This is a *lie-in*, for all you kiddies who weren't yet born in the sixties. It's how we protested injustice back then, and it's how I'm protesting it now. You can't bar women from this calf. Join me! Let's get our rights out here."

Arnie was turning purple with fury. He started to scream at Elaine, then bit off the words. He got back on his tractor and drove across the lot to his SUV, where he stored his deputy sheriff's gear.

Myra, returning from delivering raw milk to the Wieser farm, saw Arnie pull his handcuffs from the back of the SUV. She hurried to his side.

"It's this damned drunk," Arnie fumed to his mother. "I've run her in a dozen times over the years, but the liberals at Grelliers' church encourage her to drink and carry on, just so she can thumb her nose at law and order in this county and make me look like I'm the bad guy. I've had it! This is my land, and she follows my rules or she gets her fat ass slung into jail!"

He ran back to the calf's enclosure, Myra following as fast as she could. When Arnie reached the teepee, he could hear Elaine singing "We Shall Overcome," off-key and missing some of the main phrases. He shoved through the circle of onlookers and knelt next to her to put the cuffs on her.

"Brother Schapen!" Pastor Nabo spoke so commandingly that Arnie looked up. The pastor jerked his head significantly toward the rear of the crowd. Arnie, lips tight with fury, stepped away from the onlookers.

"Brother Schapen, people are taking pictures, e-mailing them, and there's a reporter here for the *County Herald* besides. I don't think it will do our cause good to spread a picture of you arresting this—this creature—around the world. My advice is to let her lie there, ignore her. She'll get tired of being cold and dirty soon enough if no one pays attention to her."

"But, Pastor, she's been living over with that lesbian witch the last few weeks. And I know she took part in their bonfires. Having her this close to Nasya—she's completely committed to Satan's cause! She could do permanent harm to the calf!"

"Arresting her will give fuel to our enemies," Nabo objected. "At least while these visitors are here. Wait for them to leave. We can do what we want if no one's recording it, but if the Jews think we've done something to put Nasya at risk who knows what they might do."

Arnie slapped the handcuffs against his thigh, trying to make up his mind. His mother arrived and pushed her way through the gaping visitors. Myra was decisive and commanding. Maybe she'd figure out some way to get that disgusting woman off their land.

He followed his mother back to the door of the enclosure and heard her start to harangue Elaine. Elaine had shut her eyes and was singing, *"Jesus loves me, this I know, / He makes my brown shit white as snow."*

"Don't add to your problems by taking the Lord's name in vain," Myra clacked.

Elaine opened her eyes and looked up. She started to say something, and then suddenly seemed to recognize Myra.

"Murderess! Get away from me. Don't try to preach to me, you murdering whore. You killed my baby. I saw you dancing around the fire, laughing your head off!"

Forty

A GIRL'S "FRIEND"

As the pilgrimages to the heifer showed no signs of letup, most area churches began discussing what Nasya meant. Was she a miracle, a portent, or an abused animal? Even Pastor Albright, at Riverside United Church of Christ, preached about her at the eleven o'clock service:

> The Word of God according to the prophet Hosea: "I desire goodness, not sacrifice; Obedience to God, rather than burnt offerings . . . They have made them molten images, idols, by their skill, from their silver, wholly the work of craftsmen. Yet for these they appoint men to sacrifice. They are wont to kiss calves!"
>
> When I was preparing today's sermon, I had to keep reminding myself that Jesus was telling me that I could only cast the first stone if I was without sin myself. And if you in the congregation don't know it, my wife can surely tell you that I am definitely not free of sin!

A ripple of laughter ran through the congregation at Riverside United as Pastor Albright continued:

> So I'm not going to stand here and tell you that our Christian brothers and sisters are kissing calves out at the Schapen farm, or acting like harlots, or any of the other abominations that Hosea spells out. You know, when I read the Book of Hosea I am uncomfortably aware that the Bible is not suitable reading for young children.

The congregation laughed again, and Pastor Albright went on in his conversational style to talk about sacrifice, and what it meant.

We believe with Paul that when Jesus sacrificed Himself on the cross, it was once and for all time a complete sacrifice for mankind. It means we no longer have to offer literal burnt animals to the Lord, because Jesus shed His blood for all of us. But He also left us some pretty stern commandments. He told us that the most important commandment was to worship God with all our hearts, and, right behind that, to love our neighbor as ourselves. And I can't help wondering how much of that neighborly love is going on in our community these days.

Jim, sitting next to Lara near the back of the church, let the words flow over him without registering them. He couldn't seem to notice anything around him these days. Even the crowds that continued to chew up the gravel on the county road, spreading dust into the Grellier house as they raced to Schapens', scarcely existed for him as he struggled with his silent, withdrawn wife.

The worry churned round in Jim's head as Pastor Albright spoke on the hubris of supposing we know what's in God's mind. "Does God want war? Does He want us to rebuild the Temple? We can only study Scripture and pray for guidance. We can't presume to say with certainty, 'We are doing exactly what God wants.'"

Jim didn't know anymore if he agreed or disagreed with Pastor Albright and the board of directors on anything. He'd been opposed to Riverside's war resolution, when the directors prayerfully announced the church's opposition to the war in Iraq, but it was clear now that they'd been right and he'd been wrong. Would Chip still be alive if Jim had agreed with Susan, if he'd opposed the war, too?

Lara nudged him: the collection plate was being passed in front of him. The sermon had ended, and he hadn't noticed.

A dozen times in the last week, he'd picked up the phone to call Gina: "This is Jim Grellier. You doing okay? Susan's home from the hospital, and the social worker says it would do her good for her friends to visit her. Could you stop by?" He kept rehearsing his careful words, because what he really wished was that Gina would come visit him. Each time he pressed the SPEED DIAL button, he put the phone down before it started ringing, afraid he wouldn't be able to mask his neediness if Gina answered.

He knew Elaine Logan was still camping out at Fremantles', because most days he saw her standing by the train tracks, thumbing a ride into town. With all the people driving to Schapens', it seemed someone was usually willing to stop for her. Jim couldn't bring himself to talk to her, let alone give her a lift—the shame and anger he'd felt the night he found Elaine on Gina's doorstep still felt like a physical pain around his heart.

Curly, back at work, told Jim about the scene at Schapens' farm, when Elaine accused Myra of killing her baby. Curly said it took six men to get Elaine to her feet. He said the *Herald* reporter had coaxed Elaine to ride into town, promising the paper would investigate if Elaine gave them all the details. The reporter had gone through all the unsolved child murders for the last forty years but hadn't found any that might plausibly connect Myra and Elaine and a baby.

Jim had been ashamed with himself for listening to the whole story, knowing that all he really wanted was for Curly to mention Gina's name. But of course Gina hadn't played any role in Elaine's drama. And not even Curly knew what Gina was up to, although he did report that she kept poking around in the ruins of the old bunkhouse.

"They're getting ready for another bonfire, you know," he'd told Jim. "For Halloween. Maybe Susan would like to take part in it, give her something to be interested in."

Blitz had silenced Curly with a ferocious glare, but in a moment of gallows humor Jim had thought maybe it wasn't a bad idea. He could drive Susan over. It would be something more fun for her than farm accounts.

Even though Gina didn't come, or even call, several members of K-PAW did drive out one evening after their weekly meeting. Susan couldn't seem to remember who they were or what the protest was about. They finally left, with little chirping admonitions of "Peace," like the hippies used to say back in the sixties. Jim asked them if Gina was still part of their anti-war movement, and Oscar Herschel, the ringleader, said, "Oh, yes. She doesn't make it to meetings very often, but she's still committed to the cause."

Jim was trying hard not to take his anxieties out on his daughter the way he had earlier in the fall when Susan was collapsing, but he couldn't cope with the way she kept vanishing. He worried that she was sneaking into the heifer's pen, trying to jeopardize Arnie's big success. And even though she swore she hadn't crawled into the enclosure again, he could tell she was lying, or at any rate concealing something. At least she had stopped failing her classes at school. She wasn't doing well, not the honor-roll work she'd produced her freshman year, but Rachel Carmody had assured him that at least Lara was going through the motions these days.

His daughter poked him again; once more, he returned to the present with a jolt. The service had ended, and everyone was getting up. Jim might as well have stayed in bed, for all the attention he'd paid. Low-pitched laughter and conversation floated around him. Pastor Natalie, the associate who was trained in pastoral counseling, came over, as the other clergy took up their posts by the door.

"When can I visit Susan?" she asked Jim.

"She's not doing well with visitors right now, Natalie."

"That's what I hear. If you don't mind, I'd like to see her. We miss her around here. Is Wednesday afternoon good for you? You're out near that miracle calf, aren't you?"

"The miracle calf is near *us*," Lara said. "I want to charge Arnie Schapen a dollar for every car that goes by because I'm the one cleaning off the dust they spread all over our house."

"Have you seen it?" Pastor Natalie asked.

Lara clasped her hands and assumed an expression of total sanctity. "Girls aren't allowed in. Didn't you know our menstrual blood might make the calf start hemorrhaging or something?"

"Lulu! Enough."

Jim felt his face burning, embarrassed at his daughter's language, despite Pastor Natalie's spurt of laughter. Natalie looked at him, her laughter turning to sorrow and pity. Rachel Carmody had given him a similar look when he came into church this morning. He was a Grellier, damn it all, not an object of pity. If this was how people were going to treat him, he'd stop coming to church.

"You do what you think you need to do, Natalie." He turned away. "Lulu—pancakes today?"

It was their old Sunday ritual, which they hadn't followed since Chip's death, pancakes after church. Jim waited tensely, afraid Lara would turn him down and disappear on her mysterious errands, but after a brief hesitation, when he saw her look at her watch, she agreed.

They walked over to the river before getting into Jim's truck. The church had originally been built during a drought cycle; it wasn't until the first time the Kaw overflowed its banks that the settlers realized their mistake. The second building was set back from the river's bank; the church planted a peace garden between the new building and the river.

Lara ran her fingers through the dry lavender flowers. "Dad, you know it'll be a good thing for Pastor Natalie to see Mom. One of these days, someone is going to say the right thing to Mom, the thing that will make her come back to life. Like the prince in 'Sleeping Beauty.'"

"So I'm not really a prince—is that what you're saying?—because my kisses don't have any magic to them?"

Lara blushed and snapped off a piece of lavender. It was when she bent over the plant that Jim noticed the hickey on her neck. So someone was kissing her, that was where she was flitting off to. He felt a further abandonment as well as worry. Who could she be seeing that she didn't want to tell him about?

All through lunch, he tried to summon up the language to talk to her about it. It wasn't until they were heading back to the farm that Jim said, "Lulu, you're too young for sex. I'm afraid if I ask you, you'll lie to me. So I'm just going to say—if that's become part of your life, will you *promise* to be responsible?" He kept his eyes on the road but was aware of her looking at him, her dark eyes large, her cheeks crimson. "You know what that means, right? You—you take steps to see that you're—" He stumbled over the words. "Safe sex. You know what that means, don't you?"

"Dad, please. I can't. It isn't like that. We just hang out," she whispered. "How did you know I was—"

"I didn't just fall off a turnip truck, baby," he said when she couldn't finish the sentence. "Why don't you want me to know his name? Is it someone— Oh! Robbie Schapen, of course. That's why Arnie didn't skin your ass when you were in his manger!"

"Dad! Mr. Schapen doesn't know. He'll kill Robbie if he finds out. You can't tell him. Promise you won't tell him!"

"You two are playing with fire, if you think someone won't see you and rat on you. But, of course, I won't talk to Arnie. Maybe as long as these crowds keep up, he won't notice anything. Bring Robbie to the house, though: don't go sneaking off with him in your pickup."

They'd reached home. She dashed inside, still scarlet around the ears. Robbie Schapen. He wasn't Jim's first choice for his daughter, not that family with their violent religion, their dislike of women, not to mention their hatred for Jim himself. But he couldn't forbid Lara from seeing Robbie. Then she'd become even more secretive. And, anyway, he couldn't face any more friction in his family. As long as there were no pregnancies, no bad diseases. If she made it to twenty-one without those, without getting killed on the Kansas highways, or fleeing to a distant war—

If, God, if, if, if. Keep her safe for me. Can't you do this one thing, Jesus, or are you really not omnipotent after all?

Forty-One

COLLAPSE

Jim followed Lara into the house on lagging feet. His wife was in the family room. She had taken all the farm accounts from the filing cabinet in the kitchen and spread them on the low table in front of the couch, but she was staring sightlessly at a cooking show on television.

"Pastor Albright and Pastor Natalie both asked after you," Jim said with the kind of fake heartiness he couldn't turn off when he spoke to Susan. "Pastor Natalie wants to visit you Wednesday afternoon."

Susan didn't look at him. "I wish you'd stop arranging my life as if I were a chess piece you could move around wherever you felt like."

Jim's head filled with a familiar fog, the mask of anger that took over more and more of his brain. "Susan, if I could move you around wherever I felt like, I'd move you back to where you were a year ago. I wish you'd make some kind of effort instead of sitting like a zombie day and night."

"I am a zombie, Jim. That's why I act like one. You saved my life, so now you have to accept having an undead person in your house. You should have thought of that before you took me to the hospital."

The bitterness in her voice made him furious. "Save this drama for your therapist. If you really want to die, there are a thousand ways on a farm to make that happen. If you don't, then pull yourself together and start paying attention to the farm and your daughter even if you resent me too much to pay attention to me. Did you know Lara's been sneaking off to make out with Robbie Schapen? For all I know, she's sleeping with him!"

"Robbie Schapen?" she repeated. "How can she do that to me?"

"Do that to you?" Jim said blankly. "She's doing it to herself, or with him, not to you."

"How much she must hate me, to start sleeping with the boy whose brother drove her own brother to his death." Spots of color burned in Susan's cheeks, the first real emotion she'd shown in months.

"Maybe she's lonely and he's available," Jim shouted. "Maybe it doesn't have anything to do with you at all!"

"How can she be so disloyal to Chip's memory?" Susan's voice trembled.

"She's lost her brother, she's lost you, she's lost the sunflower crop she worked on so hard. Is she supposed to give up on life, join a convent or something, until you've decided it's time to return to the world? Instead of thinking this is about you, or Chip, try to see that it's about her. How much does she know about sex? Safe sex, I mean. Have you had that talk with her? I don't want her having sex, not at fifteen, and not with Robbie, but she needs to know he has to wear a rubber. Does she know that much?"

"They cover that in school."

"It will mean more if it comes from you," he cried. "I tried in the car coming home, but—help me here, Suze, please—you know how hard it is for me to talk to Lulu about sex."

"She doesn't listen to me." Susan started picking at the skin around her fingernails.

"Because you've stopped talking to her! Think about what it would mean if she got pregnant."

"What difference would it make, in the end?"

"When it was Chip with Janice Everleigh, you thought it would be the end of the world if she started a baby, and I talked pretty forthrightly with Chip. It's your turn to step up to the plate."

Susan's lips quivered and tears seeped from the corners of her eyes. "That's below the belt, Jim, it really is."

Time was when he would have picked her up, kissed those tears away, but now they only increased his annoyance. Jim looked at the papers Susan had strewn across the table. "You know, Curly's cousin would pay twenty-seven hundred an acre for the X-Farm. Think about that as you study these bills."

"What difference does that make? X-Farm, K-PAW, the co-op market, why did I imagine anything I said or did would matter for one minute, let alone a whole lifetime?"

She picked up a handful of papers and tossed them, as if they were a fistful of wheat she was throwing up to winnow. It was too much. He went into the kitchen, where he found a beer buried in the refrigerator, and took it upstairs, to watch the Chiefs game on the set in the bedroom.

After an hour or so, Susan came up to lie down. She looked pointedly at the beer, at the television, but Jim didn't move. Finally, she climbed into bed, not bothering to take off her clothes, not even her slippers. Jim turned up the volume on the television. When the game ended, he gave up on the silent struggle for control of the room and went back downstairs.

He looked at the farm accounts, strewn every which way on the table and floor, feeling a hollowness under his rib cage. Now that the corn was in, he needed to plant the winter wheat. He'd never decided how many acres to put into wheat on his own before, and he'd never waited until the day before planting to figure it out. First with his grandfather, and then with Gram and Susan, they would discuss the rotation schedule, the number of acres, and the varieties weeks before Labor Day. And now?

Four weeks ago, under Blitz's prodding, he'd ordered seed, changing the varieties based on last year's crop. He hadn't run the numbers to decide on how much acreage to put into wheat or which fields to rotate, and here he was at the tag end of the planting season. With less thought than Lulu was putting into sex with Robbie Schapen, he would go out in the morning and spread nitrogen in the no-till fields he was going to use this year so that he could plant next week.

The beer in the middle of the day had left him with a sour taste in his mouth and a headache, but he grimly pulled all the accounts together. If Gram were still alive, she wouldn't tolerate dramatics in Susan, or in him, either. The farm had to come first. He turned on the computer and opened his farm spreadsheet folder.

After a time, the familiar calculations began to soothe him. He stopped thinking about the wreck of his family and concentrated on the University of Illinois's advice on nitrogen. Would it be better to bet on lower prices from foreign producers next year and get the rest of what he needed then or buy it all now and know he had it? That was the kind of question Susan helped answer. She was a risk taker. She would have said bet on Venezuela and Iran, even though the risk of interrupted supplies was greater. He pulled a quarter from his pocket and flipped it. Heads. He went with Susan's imaginary advice and lowered his fertilizer order.

At five, he heard his daughter tiptoe down the front stairs, trying to slip out the front door. On impulse, he called to her to wait and ran up the stairs to forage through the box of Chip's effects.

"Lulu, these were Chip's. I don't want the situation to arise, but if it does, use them, promise?" he folded her fingers over a packet of Hot Rods. Both of them were blushing, but Lara thrust them into her jeans pocket.

"And you be home by nine, you hear? Or I'll get Blitz to hunt you down."

"Dad!" She gasped in a high, uncertain voice and ran out the door.

She had showered and washed her hair since church, he noticed, and smelled of sweet lemongrass. His heart turned over.

Oh, be kind to her, Robbie Schapen. Be good to her or I'll kill you.

After a time, he returned to his calculations, marking off fields on the computer crop by crop: winter wheat in the northeast section that had lain fallow this year and in the section where he'd grown oats. Soy by the river? Maybe. He didn't need to decide that today, especially if he decided to sell those acres. Corn? He hated using the same fields twice running for corn. It was too expensive, both in chemical inputs and stress on the land. Alfalfa there, and corn in this year's wheat fields?

He was so wrapped in his calculations that he worked the afternoon away. When he stood to turn on the lights, he suddenly remembered his daughter. Where was she? What was she doing? Was Robbie feeding her? Arnie didn't pay his sons for time on the farm, as Jim had always paid Chip and now Lulu, so if Lulu and Robbie were sneaking off someplace to eat would Lulu be paying for the meal? For some reason, this made him angry again.

He debated trying to track her down. *Come on, kids, let's go into town for a pizza.* Before Arnie, patrolling the county in his deputy sheriff's uniform, surprised them in a lay-by and shot them both.

He was standing in the kitchen, staring into the refrigerator, while these confused thoughts chased through his head, when someone pounded on the back door hard enough to shake it in its frame. So vivid had his imaginings about his daughter been that he sprinted to the door, expecting to find Arnie on the other side. When he saw Elaine Logan, he stared at her in the blankest bewilderment.

"I thought you were Farmer Jones, but she says your name is Jim." She blew beery breath on him, and he stepped back. "She told me to come find you."

"She?" His mind was still on Lulu, arrested or shot or both.

"Gina. She's trapped in that old bunkhouse and can't get out."

He shook his head, trying to change gears, and looked past Elaine to the darkening sky. "What's she doing out there this time of night?"

"She isn't. I mean, she is, but she was there for a while until I got back from town. Good thing for her I came home early. And good thing I heard her screaming for help."

"Does she need an ambulance?"

"I'm not a doctor, and I'm not an archaeopteryx. I can't dig her out, and I can't tell if she's hurt. That's why you'd better come along."

Archaeopteryx, an old dinosaur. She meant archaeologist, but he couldn't stop picturing the wingspan it would take to give Elaine lift. The other part of his head was ticking off what he would need. Work lights, chains, the big tractor, attach the small supply cart in case Gina had broken a leg or arm or something and needed to lie flat.

He took the plaid wool comforter from the living-room couch and ran to the barn. Behind him, Elaine called in a horrible, high-pitched voice, "You can't leave me here, I'm afraid of the dark."

He ignored her, hefting chains and a work lamp into the supply cart, adding a roll of foam rubber and splint-sized pieces of wood. A wood saw, two shovels. A gallon of water. He drove the load back to the house, where Elaine was sitting on the stoop, snuffling through her fingers.

"Come on, climb up!" he shouted at her over the tractor engine.

"I can't. Can't climb so high. You lift me, Farmer Jim."

"If you can't climb up on the tractor, get in the cart," he yelled.

She pushed herself to her feet and lumbered over to the cart. "It's cold; it's dirty. Elaine will get sick."

"It's the cart, the tractor, or walk back," he said, exasperated.

"No need to be rude. Didn't your mommy teach you any manners?"

She grabbed the cart and managed to swing a leg over the side. Her foot caught in the chains, and, with a loud howl, she pitched over backward onto the foam rubber. Jim hoped she hadn't broken anything. That would be the last straw, going off to rescue Gina and having to run Elaine into the hospital with a busted hip.

He drove at the tractor's top speed, almost thirty miles an hour. Over the loud *kerchunk* of the engine, he could hear Elaine's howls, screaming that he was trying to murder her. He stopped outside the Fremantle house long enough to ask her if she wanted to get out there and then saw he'd have to take out the coil of chains, which had bounced up onto her leg. He drove on to the back of the lot, slowing down to avoid the apple trees: the tractor was too big to navigate this area easily.

By the time he reached the bunkhouse, night had enveloped the land. Little pricks of light showed around him, his own house, the Ropeses', the modest lights of Eudora two miles distant.

He placed the tractor so that its headlights shone onto the bunkhouse and jumped down. "Gina! It's Jim Grellier. Are you okay in there?"

"I think so. I'm buried under part of the roof, and I can't move it."

Her voice had lost its usual coolness, but he could tell she was trying not to panic. Under the tractor lights, he studied the wreck of the building. The main support beam of the roof, which had stayed in place all these years, had come down, bringing the rest of the roof with it. If he started pulling the roof away with his chains, he ran the risk of the rest of the structure falling in and crushing her.

He explained the problem to her. "What I think I can do is pull away the front of the building: it isn't connected to the roof anymore. Then maybe I can burrow underneath what's left of the floor and reach you."

He set up the work lamp so he could see more clearly where he needed to fasten his chains. "When did this happen?"

"Around four. I tried to call for help, but I couldn't get a signal on my phone in here."

"What were you doing, anyway?"

"She thinks she's an ickyologist." Elaine had managed to dislodge herself from the cart and waddle over to the bunkhouse. "Will she die in there? People do die here, you know. The Schapens burn them up."

"Hi, Elaine," Gina said. "I am an ickyologist; I dabble in icky stuff. Thanks for finding Jim for me."

"He was mean to me. He bounced me in the cart and hurt my poor little tushie."

Jim thought he could see which boards he could pull clear without bringing more of the house down onto the place where Gina was lying. He unhooked the cart from the tractor, backed up close to the house, and attached his chains to several pieces of board. He drove forward just far enough to put a small amount of tension on the chains, and then jumped down to check that he was moving the right pieces. The wood had softened and rotted with time; the piece of siding he'd attached his chains to broke up as he was moving away instead of pulling the front with it.

"It's going to take longer than I thought," he called to Gina. "This wood's too rotten for easy handling. Anything fall in on you?"

"Just more rotting things. I don't want to imagine what they are; it's hard enough to lie here without screaming from claustrophobia. I'm going to look like a chimney sweep by the time you find me."

"That's okay. I look like a prairie dog, from grubbing in the ground."

He unwound the chains from the rotted boards and tried to find a sturdier place to attach them. Again only a small amount of wood held as he pulled away from the bunkhouse. He had to repeat the process half a dozen times before he cleared enough of the front to take a shot at the back room where Gina was pinned. At that point, he took his shovel and started digging away thirty years' worth of dirt, animal droppings, and rotted wood.

While he worked, he kept up a cheery conversation with Gina. Elaine kept interrupting, insisting that the Schapens burned children in the old bunkhouse.

"Gina will find the bones, and then they'll go to prison, bad, nasty people, with their calf. Do you know, Farmer Jim, you have to have a penis to see that calf? *You* could go look at it, but I can't. And then I tried to show them how we used to do protests back in the sixties, and they dragged me away, and Gina wouldn't even give me a drink. I'm thirsty now, and she won't let me have her wine. That's selfish and mean."

When Jim offered her his water jug, she said, in her horrid, little-girl voice, "He's teasing Baby Elaine. He wants her to drink nastiness."

He'd drunk most of the gallon of water himself by the time he'd cleared away enough of the dirt that he could wriggle into the back area, where Gina was pinned. He'd had to use a trowel for the last few feet. He played his flashlight around and saw Gina lying about four feet from him, the main beam of the roof perched on more of the decomposing siding about three inches from her head.

"Hi, Jim," she called when she saw him emerge through his tunnel.

"Hey, Gina, hang in there." He whistled through his teeth, trying to figure out how to approach her. "I can't get a hold on anything to pull that wood away. It's all so soft that if I try to move the sides, the beam will fall on you. I'm going to shovel this dirt away, make you a little tunnel so you can crawl out from underneath."

In another forty minutes, he'd dug a deep enough trench that Gina was able to crawl to him. He pushed her ahead of him through the first tunnel. When they reached the outside, she tried to stand, but shock and exposure made her tremble too violently to get up. He carried her to the cart and looked doubtfully at Elaine.

"I'm going to get you inside, get you warm, and then I'll figure out what to do with her."

Gina's teeth were chattering but she managed to grin. "Thanks, Superman. I know you'll think of something."

Forty-Two

HAUNTED BY THE DEAD

IT WAS AFTER TEN by the time he'd returned all his equipment to the cart. Elaine was lying on the ground nearby, snoring loudly. When she didn't respond to her name or a sharp shake of her shoulder, he poured the remains of his water jug on her. She looked up at him blindly in the tractor headlights and then swore at him with a startling viciousness. She called him names he'd never heard. When he tried to get her into the cart, she accused him of trying to kill her.

"Then you can walk to the house."

He was so exhausted he could hardly bring himself to climb up on the tractor, let alone behave with reasonable civility. When he'd crawled up into the seat, he turned around and saw Elaine trying to scramble into the cart. He waited, his skin itching with fatigue, until she toppled in, then drove back to the house, trying to hit every hole he could find.

He left the tractor, with Elaine still in the cart, in the drive while he went inside to say good-night to Gina. If Elaine hadn't emerged from the cart when he went back out, he'd unhitch it and leave it in the Fremantle yard until tomorrow.

Gina had taken a shower and was sitting at the kitchen table, nursing a hot drink. Her dark hair was springing up in little ringlets around her face. She had on a severe dressing gown that zipped up to a high collar and covered her down to her toes, but when she moved the lines of her body were unmistakable. Jim squeezed his eyes shut, not wanting to think, not wanting to imagine.

She got to her feet. "Jim, I can't begin to thank you properly. I'd be dead if not for you."

He managed a smile, swaying slightly in the doorway. "Life in the country, Gina. We help each other if we can."

"You're going to fall over in another second!" she cried. "Why don't you spend the night here? You can clean up, if you don't mind smelling like blood—sorry, that's the way the rusty water smells to me. I'll make you a drink, and you can crash on the daybed in my study."

Jim thought about riding home. It was only five minutes away, but it meant returning to Susan's angry, inert presence, to his daughter— Lara! How could he have forgotten her, out somewhere with Robbie Schapen?

He had to get back, he was starting to say, when Lara phoned him. She was frantic because the truck and car were both in the yard but he had disappeared.

"Lulu, you okay? Gina Haring got herself trapped in the wreck of the old bunkhouse. I've just finished digging her out . . . No, I don't know what she was doing there . . . She's fine, just shaken up . . . Did you get dinner? . . . Okay. I may have a drink before I come home, so you get to bed, sweetheart."

When he hung up, he collapsed in the other kitchen chair. "I should go home. Susan isn't in great shape, and I don't like to leave Lulu alone with her."

Gina stood without speaking and steamed a mug of milk for him at her espresso machine, then poured brandy in it. "I have to hide all the alcohol from Elaine, which makes it hard to have a drink when I need one. What did you do with her?"

"She's in the cart." He gulped down the hot, sweet milk. He hadn't eaten since the pancakes he'd had with Lara at noon; the brandy hit him almost at once, making his eyelids thick but soothing his itching skin. "I'd still like to know what you were doing in that bunkhouse, but not tonight, not when I'm one inch from falling asleep."

He finished the drink, but when he stood he realized he wasn't in any shape to drive the tractor, even the half mile to his farmyard. He let Gina find him a pair of old Mr. Fremantle's pajamas and a towel.

If he hadn't been so very tired and so very filthy, he couldn't have brought himself to stand under the shower. The glass door and the shower floor were thick with orange scum and rust had dug deep grooves in the metal walls. How had Liz Fremantle lived with this all those years? And how did Gina, so fastidious in her appearance, tolerate it?

Even so, the physical pleasure of hot water on his dirty head and arms felt so good that he stood there until the water began running cold. When he got out of the bathroom, Gina was sitting on the bottom of the stairs outside the door.

She stood with an effort. "I'm dead on my feet, too."

She led him up the stairs, past the bare laths where the plaster had fallen out, to the back bedroom where she tried to write. "I'm sorry about Susan, Jim. I've been a bad friend, but I'll come over this week to see her, truly I will."

He couldn't muster the strength to answer, just stumbled around her small worktable and fell onto the daybed. He didn't even ask about Elaine, although his last conscious thought was to wonder if she had passed out in his cart.

When he woke, the room was dark. He stretched a hand out for the bedside clock and panicked as his fingers closed on air. For a moment, as his hand flailed, he couldn't think where he was or why his joints ached so. And then he remembered: Gina Haring.

In the dark room, he felt desire lick up his legs. Get your clothes on, Farmer Jones, get your clothes on and go home where you belong.

He found the lamp on Gina's worktable and looked at his watch, which he'd dropped on the floor with his clothes last night. It was five in the morning: his mind said that was time to get up, even after a night of heavy work, even in a strange room. Which was good. He could get home before Lara woke and save himself the embarrassment of trying to explain why he'd been gone all night.

He stood, trying to stretch the kinks from his tired body. He was supposed to spread fertilizer on his wheat fields today—he hoped he didn't fall asleep on the tractor. He picked up his clothes from the chair where he'd flung them last night. They were too foul to contemplate wearing again. He instead zipped his jacket over Mr. Fremantle's pajamas and rolled his jeans into a ball. He'd managed to shove one of his socks all the way under the daybed; his knees protested loudly as he knelt to fish it out.

As he brushed away the dust bunnies clinging to his sock, he found a small photograph, a yellowing black-and-white shot of a youth with a thin, dark face and a mop of thick hair, almost an Afro. He stared at the picture, puzzled. He thought he recognized the wide, sensitive mouth, but it wasn't one of the Fremantles.

He was too tired; he couldn't put his own name to his own face this morning let alone some thirty-year-old photograph. He laid it on Gina's worktable. As he bent to pull on his socks, though, the memory came to him: Jim himself as a boy, sitting in front of Grandpa on the big tractor. They were harrowing corn—at least, he had a vivid picture of the bright green stalks. And then Grandpa got angry: *"Not in my field, young man."* Grandpa set the brake on the tractor and jumped down. The youth had been angry, but the young woman he was with had laughed at Grandpa in a saucy way. She'd had hair the same color as cornsilk, and it hung down over her like a waterfall.

It was this man, Jim thought. He was using the cornfield as a place to have sex. At the time, Jim couldn't make sense of the scene, nor of Grandpa's anger: *"In front of the boy,"* he spat at Gram over lunch. *"How could they do that in front of the boy?"*

That made Jim think it was wicked to have your clothes off in front of a child, or out of doors, even though Gram said, "Now, Nathan, they couldn't have known you'd be harrowing there today with Jimmy. They're bone ignorant about farming. Just don't tell Myra—she's trying to get the sheriff to arrest that whole bunkhouse, and throw in Liz Fremantle for good measure."

Right after that, someone had killed all the marijuana plants the hippies were growing behind the barn. Jim and Doug had always assumed Myra did that—but what if it had been Grandpa, angry about sex in the cornfield? And then had come the fire in the bunkhouse, which had driven away all the hippies, including this one.

Jim had never known the name of the boy who died in the fire. Maybe it had even been this one, the one in the picture. The boy probably hadn't been much older than Chip. And Jim didn't even know his name!

He was sitting on the bed, lost in space, holding his socks, when Gina appeared, still wearing her green dressing gown.

"I thought I'd sleep round the clock, but I kept jumping awake, thinking the ceiling was collapsing on me. I saw the light and figured you couldn't sleep, either."

"I'm always awake around five; my body doesn't know any better." He gestured at her worktable. "I found this picture under the bed. I think maybe it was one of the hippies in the bunkhouse."

Gina looked at it, but shook her head. "I've never seen it—unless— Elaine gave me her college transcript, trying to prove to me she was smart enough to help me write a novel—maybe this picture was with it?"

She picked up a crumpled document from her worktable and handed it to Jim. The seal of the University of Kansas's registrar announced it as the "Official Record of Elaine Logan." In the spring and fall of 1969— the end of her sophomore and beginning of her junior years—Elaine had received A's in the Victorian Novel and the Honors English Seminar, B's in all her other subjects. In the spring of 1970, she'd failed one class and dropped the others. In the fall of 1970, she'd withdrawn.

"I didn't know she'd been a student at the university—it's hard to picture."

Gina's shoulders sagged. "She's going to drive me into an insane asylum. Some days she'll quote reams of nineteenth-century poetry: she knows 'Barbara Frietchie' by heart, and I'll hear her declaiming, '"Shoot, if you must, this old gray head, / But spare your country's flag,"' or, 'Christ! What are patterns for?' A minute later, she'll start talking baby talk, and want to pretend I'm her mother."

Jim laughed softly. When Gina said crossly that it wasn't funny, he apologized. "It's just life I'm laughing at. I don't want to go home because Susan won't talk to me, and you don't want to be here because Elaine won't stop talking."

Gina made a face. "You can say that again. Elaine says she lived in the bunkhouse when it was a commune. Is that true?"

Jim shrugged. "That's what Liz Fremantle said. I guess Elaine left Lawrence after the fire. Whatever she did in between didn't do her a whole lot of good. A mental hospital, where they kept her in restraints, gave her all those drugs. That's what I did hear from Curly—Tom Curlingford—who works for me, but I never know if what he reports is true or not."

"I don't think Elaine's psychotic, just addled," Gina said.

"Is that why you were excavating the bunkhouse? To find out if she really lived there or not? I wouldn't think there'd be any evidence after all this time." Jim smiled.

Gina flushed. "You and Susan told me about the boy who was killed in the bunkhouse. Elaine keeps talking about him, too, but she also says her baby died in the fire. Maybe it sounds ghoulish, but I wanted to see."

"Excavating for bones?" Jim's amusement fled. "It does sound ghoulish. Don't you have anything better to do with your time?"

Gina stiffened. "I am so tired of every mortal soul in this county sitting in judgment on me. My New York friends warned me that people out here were narrow-minded. I should have listened to them."

"We're no more narrow-minded than city people who sit in judgment on us for thinking differently than they do," Jim objected.

Gina smiled brittlely. "Arnie Schapen sicced the fire department on our midsummer fire. He also was pretty crude in the response he organized to our K-PAW march last winter, as you should remember."

"I certainly do remember," Jim said with a spurt of anger. "How can you say we're narrow-minded after that, after my wife danced around your bonfires, and even got arrested taking part in a group you drew her into? And then— Oh, my God, Gina, is it all a game with you? The fact that my wife turned her energy to the anti-war movement, that my son went to Iraq and was killed. Did that matter to you at all, or were you just playacting, trying to pretend you were some sixties hippie?"

"It's not playacting, Jim. My own life is in turmoil. Not on the scale yours is, maybe, but I keep screwing around trying to figure out how to make a living and getting more and more stultified out here by myself. I thought I could write a book about the dead boy in the bunkhouse, that it would be a way of using this time here productively."

She came to sit next to him. "The only thing I will apologize for is neglecting Susan, and that's because I haven't known what to say to her. It's cowardice that's kept me away, not malice, or—or because I think her life is a game. Do you honestly believe I'm responsible for your son's death? I know your man Blitz does—he treats me as if I were every plague ever visited on the land of Egypt."

"Blitz isn't my man, or anyone else's," Jim said irritably. "I don't hold you responsible for my son's decisions, but Susan must have told you how hard your anti-war group was on her relationship with him."

"Of course, but I only heard it from her side. She felt he was trying to dictate to her what she could do, who her friends should be. I agreed that no man should dictate her political beliefs or actions, especially not her son. No woman, for that matter. Anyway, even if I were a fairy-tale witch and could have foretold the future, seen your son's death in a crystal ball, how could I have stopped Susan from participating in the anti-war movement or my bonfires?"

Jim thought of all the fights in the family last winter. No one could have stopped Susan once she had her mind made up, that was true. No one could stop Chip, either, come to that. He had always been more like his mother, more passionate, more intense, than Lulu.

"Still," Jim said, "I'd like to know what's real and what's fake. The bonfires—were you doing that to see what kind of rise you'd get out of us, checking how narrow-minded we actually are?"

She sighed. "I've been a Wiccan for, oh, since I was in college, but I've never lived where I could try some of the rituals on a bigger scale. I met Wiccans in Lawrence, the way everyone meets people who share their beliefs. The bonfires grew out of that. We all were longing to have real bonfires, do the full ceremonials. One of the women had taken part in them in Massachusetts and showed us how to set up the fires.

"They are meaningful to me, these rituals, as much as church and communion are to a Christian. We will have our Samhain festival at the end of October, when the world celebrates Halloween." She stared at him as if daring him to condemn her religion.

"Fine. Burn down the whole property, as long as it doesn't cross the tracks and get into my cornfield. Are you really trying to write a book about the kids in the bunkhouse?"

"I don't know." She played with one of the gold studs in her ears. "I've started reading what I can find about them—there isn't much. They called themselves the 'Free State Commune.' They grew dope, of course. Susan told me how Myra Schapen killed the crop."

"We don't know who did that," Jim corrected her. "My brother and my wife assume it was Myra, but no one saw her do it."

Gina picked up a stack of paper by her laptop. "The Free State ringleader wrote for an old underground newspaper in Lawrence. His name was Dante Sirota—he's the kid who was killed in the bunkhouse. He was pretty inflammatory about the Vietnam war, and on the collusion of townspeople in violence against Indians and African-Americans in the area. I can imagine how Myra Schapen would have reacted to him. I can't help wondering if she set the fire in the bunkhouse."

"The sheriff concluded at the time that the fire was started accidentally. The kids burned a lot of candles, and the wiring in the bunkhouse was pretty ancient, so—"

"Naturally the sheriff said that!" Gina cried. "The law-and-order man wouldn't challenge the local power structure, especially not when the communards were urging the abolition of private property."

Jim thought with longing of his fields and the winter wheat. How safe and reliable the land was, not filling your head with romances about dead revolutionaries and great-great-grandmothers and visions—just land that might or might not give you the crop you wanted but wouldn't pretend to be something it wasn't.

"Maybe. Maybe. But I don't think Myra Schapen set that bunkhouse on fire." He got to his feet again.

"But Elaine saw her the night the bunkhouse burned," Gina argued. "She went over to look at that miracle calf, or whatever the Schapens are so puffed up about, and she recognized Myra Schapen. She told me when she got back here."

"It's true Myra was at the bunkhouse the night of the fire. I saw her myself when my brother, Doug, and I were helping with a bucket brigade. Mr. Schapen—Myra's husband, who died a few years later—was there, too. But just because Myra wasn't helping put out the fire doesn't prove she set it. Why don't you talk to Hank Drysdale, Gina? He's the sheriff now, and he's a decent man. He can look in the files at the county building and tell you what the investigation showed."

"Oh, Jim! I bet you were the last guy in your school to give up on Santa Claus and the tooth fairy, weren't you?"

"What's that supposed to mean?" He was nettled. "That I'm too naive or too bone ignorant to make reliable judgments about people?"

"I'm sorry—I wasn't trying to insult you. You're such a decent person, Jim, basically, you can't believe there's bad in anyone, can you, not even Myra Schapen, let alone a sheriff who's supposed to uphold law and order?" She put a hand on his sleeve, white hand, long fingers.

Even annoyed with her, disliking her dogmatic opinions, he couldn't stop flashes of fantasy. "And what if I can't? Is that such a bad thing? Myra is a pain in the butt, I'll give you that any day of the week, even Sunday, but I will not believe she put a torch to a bunkhouse when she knew people were inside of it."

He removed her hand from his arm. "I have to go, Gina. I need to get Lulu up, make sure she gets to school, and I have to fertilize twelve hundred acres today."

She moved around him to face him in the doorway. "Promise me you won't say a word to anyone about my looking for those—those bones in the bunkhouse. Please! I can't stand for people to make fun of me."

He smiled faintly. "I don't believe in minding other people's business for them. You'll come see Susan sometime soon?"

"A trade, you mean. I'll visit Susan and you'll keep quiet?"

She gave him a saucy smile of her own; once again, he saw the young woman in the cornfield and felt a breath of hot July air on his neck. He took Gina's face between his hands and kissed her, expecting her to back away, slap him, or say something cold and cutting, that she might do it with Susan but not Jim. Instead, she slipped her hands under the top to Mr. Fremantle's pajamas and ran her fingers up his back. They were as soft as he'd imagined, whispers on his wind-roughened skin. He knew he should draw away, return home to face his responsibilities: daughter, wife, wheat. Instead, he pulled Gina closer, wishing he hadn't given all of Chip's Hot Rods to Lara.

Forty-Three

MORNING AFTER

THE SKY WAS still dark when Jim left the house an hour later. This was usually the hardest hour of the day for him, the long wait for sunrise after the autumn equinox, but today he was grateful for the protection from his neighbors. The Schapens would have finished milking by now; Myra or Dale were often leaving with milk deliveries about this time, and Arnie might well be returning home from his sheriff's deputy shift.

Gina had made Jim a cappuccino before he left, and between the richness of the coffee, the pleasure of her body, the guilt of lying with her, he felt light—light-headed and light on his feet. He jumped onto the tractor, so light that not even his dirty boots dragged him down.

He had put his own dirty clothes back on. In case either Lara or Susan was up when he got home, he didn't want to compound his guilt by making up a story about Mr. Fremantle's pajamas. He had the engine going and was bouncing down the drive, singing *"Froggy went a-courtin' and he did ride,"* when he thought he heard someone cry out. He braked hard, sure it was Gina, and turned around.

It was still too dark to see, but he heard the cry again over the tractor engine and swung down from the high platform. It wasn't Gina at all but Elaine Logan.

"What do you think you're doing, Farmer Jones?" she snarled. "Trying to break every bone in my body? Why don't you ask people if they want to get yanked all over the country before you drive off with them?"

She was struggling to push herself upright, but a piece of chain had come loose and was lying across her stomach, as Jim realized when he got close enough to see her in his taillights. He burst out laughing, which made her even angrier.

"I could sue you, you and every rotten motherfucker out here. That Schapen and his calf that he won't let anybody see, his murderer of a mother, all of you, getting together to destroy my life."

"When you put it that way, I can see we're a bad bunch," Jim said, still laughing but lifting the piece of chain from her and trying to help her out of the cart. She had wrapped herself in the plaid comforter and lain down in the middle of the foam rubber he'd brought along; her weight had wedged the foam so tightly into the cart that he couldn't get underneath her or the foam. He was beginning to think he'd need to drive her back to his barn and use his crane to hoist her out when she grabbed his arms and managed to free her own shoulders. He quickly knelt, got his hands under her, and shoved. She fell onto her left side but was finally able to push herself upright.

"You're going to hear from my lawyer, Farmer Jones, leaving me outside all night, laughing your head off while you molest me. I'll go to the sheriff, I'll talk to that Sunday school teacher, the one who's in love with you, you'll see what trouble I can cause when I put my mind to it."

"I'm sure you can," Jim said. "Can you also find your way back to the house?"

"Without help from you." She turned and waddled up the drive, very much on her dignity.

The Sunday school teacher who was in love with him, he thought as he climbed back on the tractor. She must mean Rachel Carmody. He started to laugh again, thinking how embarrassed Rachel would be by such an accusation. He was a molester, Myra Schapen a murderer, and Rachel a would-be adulterer—unlike Jim himself, who was the real thing.

He was still laughing when he pulled into his own yard. Lara was up, leaning against the counter, eating blueberry yogurt out of a carton. Susan never allowed that kind of sloppy habit, but Jim didn't feel like correcting her, especially not this morning when he'd been so incorrect himself.

"What's so funny?" his daughter demanded.

"Oh, Elaine Logan. I told you last night how I went over to dig Gina out of the bunkhouse. Turns out Elaine crawled into my cart and slept there. When I started up the tractor just now, she woke up and began hurling insults at me. I was afraid I was going to have to get the crane to pry her off the tractor. She thinks Myra Schapen murdered her baby, and a bunch of other stuff. And she kept calling me Farmer Jones."

"It doesn't sound very funny to me," Lara said coldly. "And it's wrong to make fun of Elaine just because she's fat. You told me that yourself."

"I know, I know. I can't help it, sweetie. I don't know what's got into me." And he gave way to another loud burst of laughter, collapsing onto one of the kitchen chairs.

Lara stared down at him, her lips pinched in disapproval, looking as forbidding as the sepia photograph of ever-so-great-grandmother Abigail in the front room. "Are you drunk, at seven in the morning?"

He forced the laughter down his throat. "No, Lulu, just light-headed from too little sleep. Is your homework done? Are you taking off? What do you have on today?"

"I have basketball practice until four-thirty. Then me and Kimberly are going to work on our science project."

"Which is what?" Jim asked, not wanting a meeting with Kimberly to be a cover-up for a date with Robbie Schapen.

"We're taking swabs from doorknobs in the girls' and boys' bathrooms and culturing them. Then we'll compare them to see if one has more germs than the other."

"You don't need a science project to do that. You can write up the results here in the kitchen. Boys are filthy creatures who should keep their hands in their pockets at all times. You certainly don't want one of them touching you."

"You are acting really strange this morning!" she cried. "What happened over at Fremantles'? Did Gina put a spell on you?"

"She was too tired and beat-up to do much witchcraft—she was trapped in the bunkhouse for about two hours before Elaine wandered by and heard her yelling for help. Elaine walked all the way here to find me, so you're right, it's very bad to laugh. Elaine's the real hero in this story. Gina was darned lucky that Elaine came out to the bunkhouse and that I was home. That center beam missed killing her by about an inch."

"What was Gina doing there, anyway?" Lara demanded.

"She's decided to write a book about the kids who used to live in the bunkhouse. She was hoping they left something unusual behind. Ludicrous, really—there's nothing there but rotting furniture. The old enamel kitchen table was still there but all rusted out. I cut my shin pretty good on it when I was crawling in after her. Those hippies had a name, which I never knew. They called themselves the Free State Commune."

Jim didn't think Lara needed to know Gina was really searching for human remains. He went over to the counter and started the coffeemaker just for something to do, something that wouldn't betray him when he talked about Gina. "Your mom up?"

"You know she never is, this time of day. Are you going to stay home tonight? Should I count on eating here? Because if you leave me with the zombie again, I'll spend the night at Kimberly's."

Her crudeness told him she was worried that he'd slept with Gina. He wasn't going to lie to her, swear he hadn't done what he had, so he settled for a partial truth.

"Lulu, by the time I got Gina out of that wreck I was so beat I couldn't move. I have to confess that she gave me a drink, and after that brandy hit my empty stomach I was too woozy to drive the tractor home, so she let me sleep on the couch."

"Oh. That one in her study?"

He forgot his own embarrassment. "And how do you know about that couch, missy? When were you in Gina Haring's study?"

She fiddled with her yogurt carton. "Uh, when Mom and I—"

"Lulu, were you the person who taped a roach to that poster on the wall?"

"She was so mean to Mom, getting her all stirred up against the war, then not even coming over to say she was sorry Chip died! I figured she could suffer a little."

Jim suddenly felt the ache in every muscle he'd strained last night. "You were breaking into the house when I expressly told you to stay away, and you promised you would."

"I never promised!"

He took her shoulders. "Lara. No more of this. If Junior had found you when you hid in the Schapens' manger, he'd have beaten you so hard you might not ever see again or walk again! What will it take for you to stop sneaking into people's private spaces?"

She scowled, fighting back tears, then broke away from him. "I'll be late for school, and we can't have any more of that, either, can we? Tardiness and making up excuses and not doing homework. Are you like Mom? Do you wish it was me who died in Iraq and Chip who was here?"

He grabbed her again. "You're out of line here, Lara Abigail. I wish Chip was alive but he's not. And I'm glad you're here, you're the bright spot in my heart, which is why I don't want you making mistakes so big that you can't correct or undo them. You hear?"

She muttered an apology and started for the door, but Jim blocked her path. "One last thing, Lulu: where did that roach come from that you put on Gina's poster?"

"I'm not smoking dope. That was one that Chip left behind. I found it in the piano—Gina hasn't touched anything in the parlor, you know—it's all thick with dust."

Jim sighed, his light mood evaporated, but he let her pass. He didn't know if he could believe her or not, and he hated that more even than the idea of her smoking. If he'd so alienated his daughter that she wouldn't tell him the truth, what was he going to do? He watched her climb into her old pickup, the dinosaurs on the side too covered with mud for him to make them out.

When she'd taken off in a great spray of gravel, he poured a cup of thin, watery coffee and took it upstairs to Susan, who was lying awake in the dark.

"Come on, Suze," he coaxed. "Get up, have breakfast with me. I'm laying down nitrogen for the winter wheat today. I'd love it if you'd go over the field charts with me, make sure I'm choosing the right varieties and the right acreage."

She turned over. "Not today, Jim. I'll look at them later. I'm not ready to get up."

He sat down next to her in his dirty clothes. "I went over last night to rescue Gina Haring from the bunkhouse. Silly woman had been poking around in there looking for bones from the hippie who died in the fire there."

"That was noble of you," she said, not moving. "Was she hurt?"

He recounted the rescue, trying to make a drama of it, trying to make a comedy of Elaine's behavior, but he'd never been much of a storyteller, and his wife's passive back made his voice peter out. He sat looking at her unkempt hair, again feeling Gina's soft white hands on his back, her silken skin next to him in the Fremantles' creaking bed. No stretch marks from childbirth, no roughness from too many days in the sun.

"Will I see you again?" he'd asked at the door. She'd only smiled, brushed a hand across his cheek, and said, *"Thank you for helping me last night, Jim. You saved my life, and I'm truly grateful."* Which he took to mean that this morning was a thank-you gift, that he shouldn't expect to go back for seconds. The thought produced an ache beneath his ribs sharper than the soreness in his muscles.

Finally, he went downstairs, not bothering to change. His clothes were unbearably filthy, but he was going to spend the day in the fields, so why put on something clean now? He fixed himself peanut butter sandwiches to eat later, filled a thermos with the watery coffee, and scrambled four eggs, which he ate out of the pan.

Lulu and I, we're reverting to a state of nature, not bothering with plates and sitting down at the table. Pretty soon, if he wasn't careful, the house was going to look like the Burton place. Tonight he would make a proper dinner. Even if Susan lolled apathetically in the family room, he would shower, would sit down at the dining-room table with his daughter and eat like a human being.

He took his lunch box and drove the tractor to the equipment shed, so he could unpack the cart and attach the spreader to the tractor. Grandpa had taught him that you halved your workload if you put everything away as soon as you finished using it. That way your equipment was ready when you needed it. If it needed repairing, as it inevitably would if you hadn't put it away, you could fix it now.

He dragged the chains to the far wall and slung them over giant hooks. He folded the plaid comforter and left it by the door so he'd remember to take it back to the house. As he hung it over a sawhorse, a square of paper dropped from the blanket. It was a photocopy of an old newspaper clipping so folded and faded that it was practically illegible.

Jim held it directly under the light, trying to make it out. It had been cut from the *Douglas County Herald,* but the date wasn't clear. The headline was melodramatic:

TRAGEDY TAKES SECOND LIFE

Lawrence, Kans. Last week, the violence that has rocked Douglas County for the past eighteen months took the life of one of the hippies who have been squatting on empty farms in the area. We reported on the fire that killed a boy who had been living in a bunkhouse on the Fremantle land, five miles east of town. The other youths in the commune managed to flee, but the dead boy had apparently passed out and didn't wake when the others cried out to him.

Neighbors are divided as to whether the hippies were part of the Weather Underground and blew themselves up in a homemade bomb; the sheriff says it was an accident from too many candles and too much dope. Sheriff Delano assured us that the fire was a pure accident. He says there is no evidence the hippies in the bunkhouse had firearms or were toying with explosives. Delano also says there is no evidence of arson. Nonetheless, University of Kansas students poured into the streets claiming that local right-wing groups actually set the fire.

Yesterday, that fire claimed a second life. The shock of last week's fire sent one of the girls living in the bunkhouse into premature labor; she miscarried and came close to bleeding to death herself.

"We put all the girls into the back bedroom to spend the rest of the night," Mrs. Fremantle explained, "but we didn't even realize one of them was pregnant until one of the girls came to get me, worried by how badly her friend was bleeding."

The Fremantle house is a historic mansion, with a Tiffany chandelier, silver drinking fountains, and all kinds of hiding places where runaway slaves hid in the decade before the Civil War.

Liz Fremantle, 67, and her husband Walter, 78, had outraged a number of area farmers when they let seven hippies move into an unused tenant house behind their mansion.

See our editorial, "Where Will the Violence End?" on p. 21.

Jim sat down on one of the sawhorses. Elaine Logan was saying her baby had died in the fire; he had to assume that this was what she meant. She must have been the girl who miscarried in the Fremantles' back bedroom. Why else would she carry the article around with her?

He'd have to take the clipping back to the Fremantles'. If it was this precious to her, she'd be missing it. Unspoken, in the back of his mind, was the thought of Gina. If he took Elaine's clipping back, Gina would come to the door. They would—do nothing.

His watch beeped. Jesus Christ! Nine in the morning, and he hadn't even put the nitrogen in the spreader. Enough of all these women: his wife, nursing her grief like an old sock; his daughter, gambling with sex and missing school; and his—not his lover, not after a single embrace— call her his neighbor. And that damned drunk Elaine. Enough of all of them. He put the cart away, hitched the spreader to the tractor, and began filling it with sacks of fertilizer.

Forty-Four

PUPPY LOVE?

WHEN HE REALIZED how much media attention circled around the calf, Junior Schapen started coming home more often. He was thinking partly of his future. The pros didn't scout Tonganoxie Bible, and someone with connections in the NFL might see him here on national television. At least, that was one of Junior's excuses to Myra—that, along with his pious duty to help her and Arnie with their sacred charge.

"He's so bogus," Robbie complained to Lara. "How come Dad and Nanny don't see through that whole pious bullshit line he feeds them?"

Robbie figured his brother's real reason for coming home so often was the chance to bully people visiting the farm. One Thursday, the animal rights group ARK—Animals R Kin—were picketing, as they had each day since learning the Schapens were raising an animal just to slaughter her. Junior had attacked them as though they were the opposing line, or even the anti-Christ. He'd actually given one woman a concussion and broken her arm.

The woman had threatened to sue, but Arnie said the people from ARK were trespassers who'd been asked to leave more than once. He, his mother, and Gail Ruesselmann were all witnesses to the fact that the ARK people had acted as though they were about to attack Junior first.

"Junior loved the whole event," Robbie told Lara, "and Nanny was as proud as if he'd saved America from Osama bin Laden. Then she was on my butt about where had I been. Of course I didn't tell her that!"

Lara giggled, because he'd been with her, as they were this evening, in their new hideout: the loft of the old Fremantle barn.

In the beginning, starting with the Sunday the crowds first swarmed to the Schapen farm, they met in Lara's truck; she parked it on the track in the X-Farm and they sneaked away from their separate homes to meet. They sat in the cab, sheltered from any prying eyes by the towering sunflowers, grabbing hungrily at each other, exchanging bits of news about their discordant families in breathless whispers.

That refuge lasted only a short time. After Lara tried burning the sunflower packages, her father felt so stricken that he asked Curly to salvage what he could of the seeds. Curly cleaned the hopper, combined the field, and disked under the stalks. When Lara got home from school, Jim showed her the yield: only sixteen hundred pounds, less than ten percent of what they would have gotten if they'd harvested on time! Lara was so upset by the small crop that it was easy to hide her dismay at the loss of her secret place.

That evening, she and Robbie embraced furtively in the open field and then sped home before anyone spotted them. Lara spent that night putting the meager harvest into what remained of Abigail's Organics bags. She could sell these at the farmers' market, even if the harvest was too small to market on the scale she and Susan had envisioned when they put the crop in. Then next year, unless Dad had to sell the X-Farm, people would at least recognize the name.

Robbie spent that same evening in the barn, ignoring Myra's criticism and Junior's bullying while he worked out chords on his guitar.

Love your neighbor
As you love yourself.
Jesus taught us this.
Jesus taught us this.

I love my neighbor.
Her hair is like bronze,
Soft bronze,
Living bronze.

It moves in the breeze,
Shines in the sun.

I love my neighbor.
Her breasts are like pomegranates.
It says in the Song of Songs
My love's breasts are small and perfect
Like twin—

Like twin what? He couldn't come up with an image beautiful enough to describe Lara's breasts. And then Junior grabbed his guitar and threatened to break it if Robbie didn't get in the house to help Myra with the washing-up.

"Aren't you supposed to be at college?" Robbie demanded, uselessly trying to pull his guitar away from Junior.

Junior punched him in the gut. "Aren't you supposed to mind your elders, twerp? Get in there or I'll snap this little piece of junk in half."

Robbie went sullenly inside, where Nanny lectured him for half an hour on his bad attitude. On the weekend, he couldn't get away from her until late on Sunday. This was partly due to the crowds. Even though Global Entertainment and Fox and the rest of big media had lost interest in the story, Nasya the miracle calf was still hot news on fundamentalist Christian and Jewish blogs. This meant there were long lines at Nasya's enclosure every Saturday and Sunday; Nanny figured they cleared almost twenty-five hundred on the weekends, after you subtracted the expenses of maintaining the property.

When Robbie finally got away, he and Lara drove her truck into town. They went to the park on the north side of the Kaw River, with its bike trail that ran the seventy miles between Kansas City and Topeka. To their dismay, it seemed as though everyone in Douglas County was there—the kids making out, the adults walking their dogs. Even Kimberly Ropes, Lara's best friend, was there; the girls smiled weakly at each other, each chagrined to be caught with a boy who she'd never mentioned to the other.

At school the next day, Kimberly asked Lara what she'd been doing with Robbie. "Winding him up," Lara grinned. "I thought it might be fun to see how far the milkman would go if he thought he had a chance, but he was completely pathetic, as you might imagine. What were you doing with Kevin?"

"We—I think we're going to the homecoming dance together. Want to double-date?"

"Who with?" Lara hooted. "Not the milkman, that's for sure!"

That seemed to satisfy Kimberly, to Lara's relief: she and Robbie couldn't afford for whispers around the high school to filter back to Robbie's family. In the halls, the two acted as though they barely knew each other, and in the two classes they shared, biology and Spanish, they sat as far away from each other as possible, so aware of one another that they heard nothing of the class around them.

Desire made Lara inventive. The old Fremantle barn stood in back of the apple trees, about a hundred yards from the ruin of the bunkhouse. During the two years that she and Chip had treated the place as their private clubhouse, Lara had always hated the barn because of the spiders. There were snakes up there, too, but she had never minded them; they chased away the rats who scrabbled for old bits of grain wedged in cracks along the floor joists.

After school, she drove her truck past Fremantles', pretending she was heading to Jim's river acres, and scanned their yard. Gina's battered Escort stood near the door. Lara waited until six, but Gina never emerged. The next day, Lara was luckier: when she got home from school, Gina was gone. There was no sign of Elaine, either.

Robbie was doing the afternoon milking, so Lara worked alone. She drove her truck through the apple orchard to park behind the barn. If Gina came home before she finished, Lara would just have to trust to her luck to get off the property unseen.

The Fremantles had never turned off the water tap in the barn, and there were working electric outlets. Lara hooked up a length of flex cord and brought up a work light and a big push broom. Using a leaf blower, she forced most of the spiders out of the rafters. In October, snakes were giving birth; a garter snake had left a family in a corner that she tried not to disturb. The rest of the loft she swept and scrubbed. It was a drag, carrying water up and down the ladder, but by the end of the afternoon she had it pretty well cleaned.

She brought up Chip's sleeping bag, provisions like juice and Fig Newtons in a rat-proof metal hamper, and a flashlight, and still managed to leave before Gina returned. Susan was in the family room, staring into space. Jim was busy somewhere on the land.

On an impulse, Lara ran up to the second floor. She pulled on the rope that opened the hatch to the attic, bringing down the stairs folded up inside it, and fetched down the old tin trunk that held Abigail's diaries. She tiptoed down the stairs, hoping to avoid her mother, but she needn't have worried, she realized bitterly: Susan acted as though Lara didn't exist. *Fuck you, fuck you, fuck you!* she yelled inside her head.

Lara drove back to the Fremantle house. Gina's car was still gone. She didn't want to put the trunk in the barn, where rain might leak onto it. She surveyed the locked house. The second-floor bathroom offered her best chance for entry. She put the trunk by the kitchen door and shinnied up one of the pillars on the veranda that circled the house. Yes, Pocahontas Grellier, mistress of the mountains and the plains, has no trouble scaling this cliff, which daunts the white settlers like Eddie Burton!

The bathroom window was unlocked. Careless, Gina, very careless, Lara mouthed, slipping inside. She ran down the back stairs, unlocked the kitchen door, and brought in the trunk. It was too big to fit into the niche in the fireplace where she used to stow her own diary. She went through the connecting closet to the northeast bedroom and stowed Abigail's trunk in the bedroom closet, under the limp graying prom dress that hung on the door. She was just pulling out of the Fremantle drive when Gina's Escort turned east from the county road. She waved at Gina as they passed: perky farm girl, on her way home from the river.

On Wednesday afternoon, when Myra ordered him to go to town for Teen Witness, Robbie and Lara finally met in the Fremantles' hayloft. It was a tough trek for both of them. Since all the crops were down, if they'd gone across fields someone would have spotted them; Myra would have heard three seconds later and come after Robbie with a large-gauge shotgun. By the same token, they couldn't drive their pickups down the road and park—Jim might choose that very moment to inspect his river-bottom acres.

Instead, they hiked through the rough undergrowth in the drainage ditches, where the prairie grasses stood higher than the tallest man's head. The ditch bottoms were muddy and filled with every kind of garbage that humans could think to toss, from car parts to condoms. They had to go past the bunkhouse and approach the barn from behind, slipping in through a board that Robbie had loosened, and then quickly climbing up the old ladder to the hayloft. At least for Lara, half the pleasure of meeting in the loft was the excitement of evading detection as they came and went.

She didn't tell Robbie that. Nor did she reveal another part of her reason for meeting at Fremantles': she wanted to check up on her father. She and Robbie were exchanging almost every secret their families had, but she couldn't put into words, even to herself, her suspicion, her fear, that her father had slept with Gina after rescuing her from the bunkhouse.

Lara wanted to keep Jim under her eye to make sure he didn't do anything dreadful—although what she would do if she saw his truck pull into the yard she hadn't imagined. The stroking, touching, moaning she and Robbie did didn't count as sex, in her mind. Sex would mean pulling Chip's packet of Hot Rods out of her jeans pocket and persuading Robbie to put one on. She wasn't ready for that, and neither was Robbie, not after all the mauling he'd seen his brother and Eddie go through.

She and Robbie could never stay together very long. Jim would start phoning Lara around six-thirty, but more worrying was the effort Myra Schapen was putting into finding out where Robbie was going. And it took them so long to hike through the ditches and out to the barn that in the end they only spent a short hour together.

"Nanny can't be happy with success, she can only be happy if she finds out I'm a fuckup." Robbie's language became coarser when he was with Lara; it was part of the sense of freedom he had when he was with her, breaking all of Myra's taboos in one delicious outing.

"I mean, we're getting so much free publicity from all the news stories, plus YouTube and blogs and everything, that we're getting milk orders from Christian wholesalers all over the country," he went on. "We don't have a big enough herd, or a big enough plant, to pasteurize and ship milk to those places, but Nanny and Dad upped our per-gallon price by almost five percent anyway, even for our oldest customers.

"Of course, Mrs. Wieser was really upset. She came over to meet with Nanny and Dad, and said her cheese business was what had kept us afloat all these years, that she should get to keep her old rate. And she's right. Nanny told her to take it or leave it. Mrs. Wieser took it, but I think she's looking for another supplier—there's a guy near Topeka who can supply her with raw organic milk, same as us. But if Nassie turns out to be a dud, we'll be totally screwed. I tried to say to Nanny that we ought to honor our commitment to the Wiesers, but Nanny whacked me on the head and told me I wasn't a true Schapen and all the rest of that crap."

Lara nodded soberly, not at Myra's insult but the economic worry. Like Robbie, she couldn't remember a time when she hadn't known to a penny what it cost to run the family farm.

"Anyway," Robbie added, "Nanny is desperate to find out where I'm going after the afternoon milking. Not to mention how she is so on my case about going to Teen Witness with Amber."

Lara giggled again and bit Robbie in the neck. "Tell her you're with a vampire. Tell her you have too much respect for Amber to infect her with vampire blood."

She bit him again. He yelped, and they scuffled happily for several minutes.

"Lucky for me it's football season or she'd have Junior chained to me like a prison guard," Robbie said a little later. "He tried to follow me this afternoon, but I was too fast for him, and he had to get back to the school—he missed football practice yesterday, and his grades aren't good enough that they'll let him keep his scholarship if he keeps missing practice. But I think he told Eddie to spy for him. So, Lulu, we really have to be careful."

Lara agreed, more readily than Robbie thought she would. She was more courageous than him, or at least more willing to take risks, but Junior and Eddie in the heifer's shed had frightened her badly enough that she didn't want to court the disaster of them coming on her and Robbie.

"We can cool it for a day or two," Robbie said. "I'll go to my youth group tomorrow. Maybe we could get together Saturday: I think Nanny's going to leave Mrs. Ruesselmann in charge so Dad and her can drive over to Tonganoxie Bible to watch Junior play."

"Three days," Lara said.

They clung to each other, trying to ward off the impending separation. And then it turned out Robbie couldn't even get away on Saturday because Arnie kept him hopping all afternoon. They didn't meet again until Monday evening. After four days' separation, they melted together. They clung to each other in Chip's sleeping bag, whispering, stroking, not caring how late they were.

When she got home at eight, after ignoring Jim's calls to her cell phone, Jim told Lara she was grounded for two weeks and that he was going to enforce it.

As for Robbie, even though he always left the Schapen farm on foot when he slipped off to see Lara, Myra was so furious at his late arrival home that she took away his truck keys. She gave them to him in the morning so he could drive to school and then took them away when he was doing the afternoon milking. Since Myra monitored all the phone bills so closely, he and Lara were reduced to using e-mail. At night, when they were supposedly doing homework, or at study hall during the day, they sent each other longing messages, Robbie's filled with the songs he was writing to her, Lara's with pictures she had drawn of him or the two of them together. Robbie saved her messages on a flash drive that he kept in his jeans pocket, making sure he erased them from the family machine each night.

Forty-Five

VISITING HOURS

THE ONLY GOOD THING about her and Robbie's two-week separation, at least in Lara's mind, was that if Jim had to keep an eye on her, to make sure she was out after school only to go to basketball or band practice, she could keep an eye on him, too. No trips over to Gina's, at least not after school.

Jim embarrassed her by driving her to and from school; the winter wheat was in, and he wasn't nearly so busy during the day as he had been all fall. She told her friends that her truck was in the shop and sat sullenly at her father's side all the way into town. Secretly, she enjoyed the time alone with him, especially after school when they might stop for a coffee at Z's or at the store, where he let her choose the dinner menu. She'd done a cooking course at 4-H and amused her father with her lectures on nutrition and balanced meals.

One afternoon at Z's, she asked him, point-blank, if he had been visiting Gina. When he froze before answering, she looked at him from under her lashes as if inviting him to confide in her. "I mean, did she have any terrible aftereffects from the bunkhouse falling on her?"

"Not that I know of, Lulu. You could have asked her yourself when she came over to see your mother."

Jim tried to speak naturally, but Gina's visit, which he had longed for, had not been a success, for him or for either of the women. Gina had treated him with the coolness of a stranger when he answered the door, while Susan insisted on receiving Gina in the front room, dressing as if she were a Victorian widow in deep mourning with the Gold Star pin the Army had sent her at her throat.

After letting Gina in through the kitchen, Jim busied himself with farm accounts in the family room. He knew Lara was eavesdropping: he'd seen her crack open the door that connected the parlor to the unused front staircase. Instead of admonishing his daughter, Jim wished he had the nerve to join her.

When Gina said she was sorry for everything Susan had been through, Lara, peering through the crack in the door, watched her mother bow her head like a queen, saying nothing.

"I'm sorry I haven't been to see you sooner," Gina said. "I guess I've felt helpless."

"Then you know exactly how I feel," Susan said.

"We'll be celebrating Samhain at the end of the month," Gina said after a pause. "That's the original Celtic ceremony the Christians took over and turned into Halloween. We'll make a fire and show Arnie Schapen that he can't frighten us out of the valley."

Susan didn't answer, just sat with her hands folded in her lap.

Gina ploughed on, desperate. "We hope you can join us, Susan. You brought so much good energy to our earlier ceremonies. Even though it marks the end of summer, Samhain is a festival of new beginnings. If you came, perhaps it could be a time for you to make a new beginning as well."

"Did Jim tell you to deliver this message?" Susan asked.

"No!" Gina was startled. Even from behind the door, Lara could sense her wariness. "But you're hovering between life and death, and Samhain is the time when the world itself is balanced between life and death. If you come to the festival, you might find yourself ready to choose life again."

"I see." Susan's voice held the dryness of old leaves or old paper. "You've done your duty. You've visited the sick, and apologized for whatever you imagine your own sins are. You can go now."

Lara scrambled to her feet and was waiting in the kitchen when Gina left. She watched her father suspiciously for any signs of passion, but he merely came into the kitchen to thank Gina for being neighborly.

The sight of her had brought desire to the surface, like a sore tooth. Only the awareness of Lara's sharp gaze made him behave as remotely as Gina did herself. But he drove over to Fremantles' the next day, after delivering Lara to school, while Susan worked on the endless afghan that her occupational therapist thought would do her good.

Gina met him at the door, gave him her crooked gap-toothed smile, but told him it wasn't a good idea for him to visit her. "I don't want to do any more harm to Susan than I already have. And the one thing I've learned in my short stay in the home where the buffalo roam is that everyone for miles around is watching the deer and the antelope play. If you keep visiting me, people will notice. Inevitably, one of them will say something to Susan."

She looked down at her hands, at the long white fingers that roused Jim more than the idea of her body. "I ran into Clem Burton at the drug-store this morning, and he said he'd be glad to come out the next time I was trapped inside a falling building. Elaine probably blabbed it all out at Raider's Bar—Clem's uncle Turk drinks there, which means everyone out here knows at least that you pulled me out of the bunkhouse. Let's not have them start telling each other that you're neglecting your wife and your farm by visiting the local witch."

His face burned. He couldn't say anything because he knew Gina was right, but he pulled her to him, anyway. She let him kiss her but drew away almost at once. As he turned to leave, he saw Elaine Logan in the kitchen, her face alive with malevolence.

After that, Jim was just as glad he'd grounded Lara: driving her back and forth to school gave some shape to his time. That, of course, and taking Susan to her therapy appointments. Settling the bills for September, Jim tried to believe Susan's therapy was helping her.

He studied his wife for any encouraging sign. She was bathing regularly. She ate enough to keep her weight steady. Those were the good signs. But, on the minus side, Susan wouldn't go to church or the farmers' market. Nor would she talk to people, not even Rachel Carmody, who faithfully phoned every few days. Besides the afghan, now about ten feet long, Jim didn't know how his wife filled the hours when he was in town or working on the repairs that farm buildings and machinery always needed.

When Pastor Natalie came over on her promised visit, Susan received her, as she had Gina, in the formal parlor in her black dress with the Gold Star pinned at her throat.

"Susan, I'm so very sorry for the loss you have suffered," Natalie said.

"Our family is used to the senseless shedding of blood in the name of some higher good," Susan said. "Some *alleged* higher good. Abigail's brother Michael died at Peach Tree Creek."

Natalie blinked uncertainly, and Jim mumbled, "That was a battle in the Civil War."

"July twentieth, 1864, just outside Atlanta," Susan said. "Mr. Grellier had been murdered the previous August, in the great slaughter committed by Quantrill here in Lawrence. Mr. Grellier was teaching in a school for freedmen, and this, of course, was gall and wormwood to a slaveholder like Quantrill. Abigail said of Mr. Grellier's death, 'It is what we came into the Kansas Territory to do. Not to be murdered, but we were called by God to take up His yoke, and we were to count no cost.' I don't remember her words more exactly, but Jim, or perhaps my daughter, has hidden her diaries away from me, so I can't check them for you. They used to be in our attic, but who knows where they are now. The invalid must be protected at all costs from her personal desires."

So she had been looking for the diaries. Jim had thought, or hoped, that Susan had forgotten them. If they weren't in the attic any longer, then Lulu must have moved them. He felt so tense he thought his skin would turn inside out on him, while Lara, dragooned into sitting in on the visit with him, froze: if she told her father what she'd done with the trunk, he'd ground her forever!

Jim didn't think he could endure more of the conversation. "I'm going to make some tea, Natalie. Do you want any, or a soft drink?"

Natalie gratefully accepted the offer of tea, but Susan, sitting pointedly under the portrait of Abigail—dressed, like herself, in black, with a cameo at her throat rather than a Gold Star—shook her head.

"Is that Abigail?" Natalie asked, looking from Susan to the portrait. "What did she do after she lost her husband and her brother?"

Susan fingered her pin. "She went on. She had to. She kept this farm going and raised her surviving children."

"What kept her going, do you know? Or what's your guess?"

"Do you want me to say it was her faith in Jesus?" Susan said with a bark of laughter.

Natalie shook her head. "I want you to say what you think kept her going."

"She'd had a vision," Susan said listlessly. "She came out here because she'd had a vision. And her faith in her vision helped. Also, she was very close to one of the neighbors, Mr. Schapen, and his mother, and their love sustained her."

Lara pinched her lips together. Her mother was behaving in a shocking way—she was playacting at being in mourning. She pretended she didn't want visitors, but, really, whether it was Gina or Pastor Natalie, or even poor Ms. Carmody on the phone, Susan was enjoying the chance to show off how depressed she was.

For instance, when Pastor Natalie said, "We miss you. We need you at Riverside Church," Susan said, "To do what? Show you what happens when the blind lead the blind?"

"Bogus," Lara said under her breath. Bogus. She got to her feet and went to the kitchen to help Jim make tea and to tell him what she thought of Susan.

"I bet if we left Mom totally alone, she'd come around, because she wants an audience."

"You think? You an expert now on human psychology as well as nutrition?" He handed her the tea to take into Pastor Natalie so that he wouldn't have to go himself. "Lulu, where are those diaries? And don't tell me you don't know."

"Do I have to tell?" she whispered. "I'm taking good care of them, I promise."

Jim felt the hair crawling on his scalp. "Don't tell me you put them in the miracle calf's manger!"

"No, Dad, honest—I haven't been near the calf again. The trunk is safe, okay? I just couldn't stand it if Mom started going through those old papers again, scribbling notes like she was some clone of Abigail's."

"Oh, Lulu—" He threw up his hands, not knowing what to say, finally finishing weakly, "They should go to the university library. The archivist there has been asking for them, and the library would take better care of them than we can. Bring them home, okay? We'll take them in together to the archivist."

Lara nodded and scurried to the front room with Pastor Natalie's tea. The pastor didn't stay much longer. When she'd left, Lara leveled her scorn on Susan.

"You want us to think you're teetering on the brink of death because you're so overwhelmed by losing Chip, but then you dress up as if you were in a play and sit underneath Abigail's portrait so everyone will see what a martyr you are. You never even wore that Gold Star to Chip's funeral, or anything, so I *know* you're just showing off!"

Susan looked at her. "Perhaps you're right, Lara. My feelings are so far away from me that I don't know what they are anymore, and drama seems a way of at least pretending to have feelings. Do you know where Abigail's diaries are? You are so alert about what everyone in the family is doing, I'm sure you know where your father put them."

It was Lara's turn to be discomposed, but she said hotly, "Even if I did know, I wouldn't tell you. I couldn't bear it if you locked yourself in your room again, studying those old books and writing crap all over the walls. Do you know how long it took Ms. Carmody and the other ladies to clean up after you? Do you even care?"

After a long pause, Susan said, "I don't like you shouting at me, Lara. You're my daughter, not my mother or my drill sergeant."

Lara bit her lip and fell silent. Susan undid the Gold Star from her throat and pinned it to Lara's sweatshirt.

"I'll share my loss with you," Susan said. "We're a Gold Star family. They tell me in therapy to remember that I'm not the only mourner in the house."

Forty-Six

TALK, TALK, TALK . . . NO ACTION

From Pastor Albright's Sermon

Hope that is seen is not hope, Paul tells us. What was he saying to the Church in Rome? When we say "Our hope is in the Lord, who made Heaven and Earth," we certainly see the earth, and now, thanks to the Hubble telescope, we see heaven upon heaven, but these don't take away our hope in the Lord.

Paul is talking in part about Jesus' return. Every Christian for two thousand years has been hoping to see Christ come again in glory. We're like small children whose parents have left us for the day. We fear that they will never return, and the day seems unbearably long. Grandma or Uncle John or whatever unfortunate adult has to look after us hears us whining and panics. Maybe Grandma says, "If you're extra special good, Mom will bring you a present when she gets home," or, "If you clean up your room and wash the dishes, Mom will come home." By the end of the day, we've done all our chores, we've been as good as we know how to be, and Mom still hasn't come back. We haven't been able to influence her behavior. And yet, all the time she's away Mom is thinking of us. Her love for us never wavers.

We Christians are like that. It's hard to believe we can't *make* Christ appear in glory. If we go through every prophecy in Revelation, and Isaiah and Hosea and Micah, if we sacrifice that red heifer and rebuild the Temple, surely that will prove how good we are and make Him come home in a hurry. It's hard to believe we can do all that and still not make God do anything that isn't in the Holy One's own good time. It's hard to believe Jesus still loves us when He seems so distant. And yet we are obliged to live in hope.

"Oh, yeah, mothers always come back for their children, don't they?" Elaine Logan muttered. "Pious hypocrite. As bad as all the other Christians. 'Whited sepulchers,' just like the Bible says."

Her voice carried to the people in the pews closest to her. One or two giggled, but most of them shifted uneasily in their seats, not wanting to be near someone who was unstable but mindful as Christians that it was their duty to love and respond to her.

Elaine had hitched a ride into town with Jim and Lara Grellier. When they saw Elaine waving her arms at the crossroads, her face sullen, Lara had urged Jim to drive right on past—certainly, his own inclination as well. But he saw Arnie's truck approaching from the Schapen farm: Myra, Robbie, and Arnie on their way to Salvation Bible. If they picked up Elaine, she might well tell them everything she knew about Jim, and then he'd supplant news of the miracle heifer on Myra's website. He told Lara to climb into the back and let Elaine have the passenger's seat.

"Farmer Jones, Farmer Jones," Elaine crooned as she hoisted herself onto the running board. "So you do know how to treat a lady. And is this Mrs. Jones?"

"No! I'm his daughter, and his name isn't Jones," Lara cried, angry with Jim and disgusted by Elaine, whose breath smelt sour. How could Gina stand to have someone so foul on the premises?

" 'All the animals are very hungry, but where is Farmer Jones?' " Elaine quoted from the children's book. "Why, he's rolling in the hay, just like his lovely daughter, isn't that right? All those old tales, they knew what they were talking about."

When books said a character's "head swam," it was the literal truth, Lara realized. Shame and anger nearly suffocated her, and the gray fields disappeared in a hazy mist in front of her eyes.

"If you weren't such a drunk, you wouldn't make up stuff and start telling people it was true," Lara said.

"You're so pure, like all good Christians, where what you say matters more than what you do. But something is happening, and *I* know what it is, don't I, Mr. Jones?"

"Where do you want me to drop you?" Jim asked hastily, as embarrassed as Lara and therefore not paying attention to Elaine's revelations about his daughter.

Elaine said she'd get out wherever they stopped, so they drove her to the church with them. Jim lost track of her then: he wandered into the church hall for a cup of coffee while Lara went off to Rachel Carmody's Sunday school class with Kimberly Ropes.

Jim assumed that Elaine had taken off, but between Sunday school and church she popped up again. He was talking to Rachel at the back of the nave when Elaine rolled in from the porch. She'd found someone to give her a drink in the last forty-five minutes, or maybe she kept a bottle in the cloth bag she carried that proclaimed, in faded letters, WOMEN'S LIBERATION UNION.

"I'll be your chaperone, Rachel." Elaine leered. "You don't want to be alone with Farmer Jones. He's a bold man, the farmer. And his daughter's just as bad."

Rachel and Jim both flushed. Jim remembered Elaine's earlier crack about Rachel being in love with him. Surely, that couldn't be true? Rachel was such a solid, reliable woman. Jim couldn't imagine that she'd indulge in a foolish fantasy about a married man—forgetting for a moment that that same married man had a foolish fantasy about a different unmarried woman.

Fortunately, other members of the congregation were coming in to worship, asking Jim about Susan, talking to Rachel about parish matters. The organ began to play the voluntary. Jim wasn't sure how it happened, perhaps through Elaine's maneuvering, but he found himself wedged in a pew with Rachel and Elaine. Lara was sitting farther back, with a group of other teens from Sunday school. At least she was doing better, that was one comfort, to see her with her old friends again.

"Now you two can be cozy together, and I'll watch over you," Elaine said, breathing gin over them.

As the service progressed, Elaine became more sullen and more belligerent. At first, she grumbled about bad mothers, and then how Jim was a whited sepulcher, but when Pastor Albright spoke about the red heifer and how to think about the prophecies in Revelation Elaine's grievances turned to Arnie.

"He thinks he's the boss of everyone. He's not the boss of me, not him, and not his murdering mother. They'll be sorry. They think I'm not good enough for their calf, they'll see if that calf is good enough for them. *Them that takes cakes / Which the Parsee-man bakes / Makes dreadful mistakes.* High and mighty Sheriff Arnie will see, just you watch!"

At that point, Elaine became so loud that Rachel tried to get her to leave the service. Elaine stood and shouted, "You call yourselves Christians, but you can't wait for the service to end so you can go on with your gossip and your fucking and your drinking. I'm saying out loud what you're thinking, so you want to throw me out. Well, I'm not going!"

Congregation and minister were momentarily silent, then he said, "We acknowledge that we are less inclusive than we are called to be. We acknowledge that we sometimes find it difficult to accept the gifts that others bring. Lord, teach us to accept the words this woman brings as gifts, and to learn from them. As all our gifts come from you, help us to give back to you that which you have loaned to us."

The congregation took this as an invitation for the offering. Servers leaped up with collection plates, and the organist began a prelude to the offertory anthem at such a volume that Elaine found herself drowned out. Uttering general curses against Rachel, Jim, Arnie, and all Christians everywhere, Elaine strode out of church as fast as her bulk allowed.

Of course, her outburst was the subject of conversation at the coffee hour. Since Rachel and Jim seemed to be the pair attached to Elaine, they found themselves called on as experts by everyone who wanted to discuss the situation, until Jim, exhausted by the ordeal, grabbed Lara and fled with her to the House of Pancakes.

The next day, when he came to school to collect Lara, Jim sought out Rachel in the teachers' lounge first. He apologized for leaving her in the middle of the coffee hour.

She smiled. "I don't have your allergy to conversation—or what you always call gossip. Elaine's situation is troubling, though. I'm glad Gina

Haring is offering her a home, but if Gina moves back to New York I don't know what we'll do with Elaine. She's such a strange mix, too. The things she knows or half knows, like quoting from Kipling's *Just So Stories*."

Jim shook his head, puzzled, so Rachel said, "Those lines about *'cakes / Which the Parsee-man bakes'*—that's from Kipling. She was clearly an educated woman before she became, well, what she is today."

Jim thought of the transcript he'd seen in Gina's study. "Yes, I guess she was."

Rachel smiled at him. "As long as you're here on school property, Jim, let's do a little school business. Lara is performing better in most of her classes, but her work in biology and Spanish is very marginal, and the rest of her work is only at a C level. Except for social studies, where she's doing a major report on Iraq—history, religion, the works."

Jim was startled. Lara hadn't said a word to him about it.

"She seems happier these days," Rachel added. "Which is good. But I'd like to see her putting the muscle into her work that she gave it last year. And I don't want any F's or D's on her permanent record, so maybe it's time for another fatherly chat. I did try talking to Susan about this last week, but she didn't seem interested. I'm afraid it's all falling on you."

Jim looked around the lounge to see how many people were in earshot. "I— Lara's spending a lot of time with one of the boys in her class. She's been grounded for two weeks—this is the start of her second week—so I was hoping she'd pay more attention to her schoolwork."

"Do you know who the boy is?"

Jim leaned forward and whispered Robbie's name, so that no eavesdropper could pick it up and spread it around.

Rachel nodded. "That would have been my guess. I understand why he wouldn't be your first choice, but he's a good kid, even a good student, not like Junior. Melissa Austin—she's in charge of the music program—she thinks he's a pretty good musician, too. We all imagine Mr. Schapen is an ogre, but he's supported Robbie's music, even buying him a good guitar and seeing he has the lessons he needs."

Jim was surprised—he wouldn't have expected that of Arnie—just one more proof of how wrong it was to sit in judgment of your neighbors. "Maybe that's why Lulu's started playing her trumpet again."

Right after Susan's hospitalization, she'd thrown it down the cellar stairs, saying she never wanted to see it again. Jim had retrieved it and put it in her room. Three weeks ago, she'd started practicing—she was at band rehearsal right now. He left Rachel to listen to his daughter play.

On his way to the music room, he ran into Blitz, who was doing his winter stint for the school board. They talked for a couple of minutes, about the winter wheat, about when Blitz might come look at the planter, which hadn't spread evenly when Jim was putting in the crop, and then Rachel emerged, and Blitz's face lit up. Rachel smiled, too, not with Blitz's warmth but friendly enough, Jim saw.

Jim felt let down, then laughed at himself. "Serve you right, you old porker," he said under his breath. "You wanted Elaine to be wrong about Rachel being in love with you, then you wanted her to be right. You want a harem, boy, become a Mormon. Otherwise, stay loyal to the one wife you've got."

On the drive home, he talked to Lara about her school performance. "I'm happy that you're paying better attention, baby, although I wish you were working up to your real abilities. Rachel—Ms. Carmody—says you're doing outstanding work on some report you're preparing on Iraq, which proves that you can do better. I don't want to nag. I know you're having a tough time, between losing Chip and the way your mom's acting, but I can't have you failing any courses. Will you buckle down in science and Spanish?"

She was looking out the window, not at him, but she nodded grudgingly.

"Maybe next semester you'll feel like picking up the reins again, hmm? I don't want you to wreck your chance for a college education, Lulu. You have the brains to go to a good school." He paused, then said, "You and Robbie Schapen still seeing each other?"

She gasped, then whispered, "Sort of."

"And you're being careful?"

About sex? About stirring up talk in the valley? The unspoken end of the sentence. He looked over at her. Her head was bent down, so that her brown curls fell forward, exposing the long white line of her neck. She looked so fragile that he could hardly stand it. He repeated the question until she gave him back a muffled assurance.

Part Four

HALLOWEEN

August 29, 1863

My dearest Mother,

How can I find the words to recount our horrors? I sit among the charred ruins of my home, my children clutching my skirts and crying. They want their papa. They look for him on the road, but he will never come home again.

All last week, the air was hot and still, as if the prairie itself were Nebuchadnezzar's furnace, seeking to burn us to a cinder. The corn shimmered under the sun, so that from the doorway of the house my eyes were nigh blinded by the glare, and I fancied myself standing outside Grandmother Peabody's neat frame dwelling in Lynn, shading my eyes from the sun striking the green waters of the Atlantic.

Oh, Mother, if you knew the ravages of my guilt in the midst of my grief! How many times did I let the sun go down on my anger with M. Grellier. His noble ideals were too great to be encompassed in the body of a farmer. When he set off for his school, how I did inveigh for his leaving me alone to deal with the homestead and the children. When he was going on an errand of special grace, instead of praising him I whined as if I were Baby, grizzling over her new teeth.

How my shame at my harsh words now threatens to strike me to the ground. Why did I not rejoice in my good fortune, to be married to a man of such lofty principles? Instead, I cried out bitterly. I had broke the sod alone, save for the help of our kind neighbor, Mr. Schapen. I had planted and harvested nigh on my own for eight years. Now, when blackbirds threatened the crop, could he not stay?

No, he replied, in his patient way. For this hot weather means that the freedmen, who have lately moved into our free state of Kansas from

Missouri, escaping the vile slavery under which they toiled, are free from their labors—for you must know that many hire themselves out as farmhands to earn money for purchasing a stake of their own. And as many are eager to learn to read and write, my husband must needs teach them. The school meets—met—close to the homes where the freedmen and their families live, some fifteen miles distant, and M. Grellier deemed it kindest to our horse not to drive him back and forth in this dreadful heat each day but to bunk with one of the freedmen.

On the morning of 21 August, the children and I slept badly on account of the heat. All the windows, covered by mosquito netting, stood open, as I prayed for some stirring in the wet heavy air. Around four in the morning, the clopping of many horses on the main road, which is a scant half mile south of our homestead, roused me. I stole out of the house and saw, against the predawn sky, the silhouette of many men on horseback. I feared at once that it was the demon Quantrill, who had vowed to raze the town of Lawrence, out of his hatred toward us for making Kansas a free state.

Scarce knowing what I did, I flung on a few garments. Helen and Nathaniel I dragged wailing to the cellar and told they must make no sound, that they must answer to no voice but Mother's. Tucking Baby under my arm, I raced on foot to rouse our neighbors, first the Schapens, then the Fremantles. Mr. Schapen rode to the town as fast as he could to sound an alarm, but, alas, he arrived too late. They had already begun their rapine—burning, slaughtering—oh, the murder of Judge Carpenter while his wife lay covering his wounded body with her own! They lifted her arms and shot him in the head. God, have you no mercy? And yet she had this mercy, that she was with her husband as his soul left this world.

All day Friday, the children and I huddled in our cellar. As the rebels returned drunk on that which makes men madder than all the rum in the Indies—drunk on the blood of their fellow men—we heard them yelling and carousing. They came into our yard—even now I can hardly write for the shaking that fills my entire body! I lay across Baby to smother her cries, nigh suffocating her, while Helen and Nathaniel shivered under my shawl, frozen so by fear that the thermometer might stand at 120 degrees and not warm them. The

Ruffians, laughing the whole time, set fire to our house, my little house that took five years' hard work to build.

When we finally rose from our hiding place, our house lay in cinders around us. We had naught but the few things I had brought to the cellar in my old tin trunk. Our only blessing was that Blossom and her calf had escaped notice, for the corn where I hid them is now eight feet high. The smoke and turmoil distressed her sadly, and she gives little milk, but enough that my babes have something for their evening meal.

By and by, Mr. Schapen and his mother came to see how we fared. The reports were of the gravest, he said, many slaughtered, many Negroes murdered. Did I have the strength to go with him? When Mrs. Schapen offered to take the little ones home with her—their homestead had escaped the rebels' attentions—I said I must see for myself.

We arrived at my husband's school in a few hours' time, hours in which we passed through such scenes of destruction, fires still smoldering, bodies lying in ditches! I pray your eyes never look on such terrible sights. And there, just outside the shanty walls, lay my husband's body, among those of the men whose children he had gone to teach. Their wives and babes stood round, as desolate as I—more, for they must needs witness these cold-blooded murders. We fell into one another's arms, sobbing and praying. One woman begged for my pardon for bringing my husband into harm's way, and those were the only words that could possibly have brought me strength.

"It is what we came into Kansas to do," replied I. Not to be murdered, to be sure, but we were called by God to take up His yoke, the yoke that our countrymen had laid on the bondsman, and we were to count no cost. "Greater love hath no man than this, that a man lay down his life for his friends." The heroes of Shiloh and of Gettysburg played their noble roles in the conflict that consumes our nation, but my children's father was a greater hero still, for he laid down his life for his friends.

I can write no more, dearest Mother. Don't fear for our safety, for our good neighbors watch over us.

Ever your loving daughter,
Abigail Comfort Grellier

Forty-Seven

HIDEAWAY UNCOVERED

HALLOWEEN FELL on a Wednesday that year. The Monday before, Lara's grounding was finally over, and she and Robbie were blissfully reunited in the Fremantle barn. After a time, they looked up, still holding each other, but ready to take part in the larger world.

Gina and her friends from town were laying the bonfire for their Samhain festival, pulling boards from the bunkhouse and gathering brush from the apple orchard and other trees on the property. They were also picking apples from the trees that still bore fruit. It was part of the ritual that the harvest all be in or fairies would blight the crops, Gina said.

Some of the group were placing buckets of sand around the perimeter of the bonfire. The fall had been so dry that area farmers were being warned not to burn off any fields, and, in town, they were considering banning barbecues.

Elaine Logan was tagging along after the other women, picking up small sticks and adding them to the pile. She stopped frequently, sometimes looking toward the barn, almost as if she knew Robbie and Lara were up there. It was Robbie who first noticed her staring at the loft.

"How could she know?" Lara whispered. "She's too big to climb the ladder, and we'd see her if she was trying to hide behind a bush or something. Can you imagine her climbing down into the ditches? She'd never get out again."

They both laughed quietly but soon fell silent, uneasy about whether they'd been found out.

When Elaine thought no one was looking, she pulled a half-pint from her sweatpants and took a quick swig. Lara mimicked her, mockingly, which shocked Robbie. His church prohibited alcohol altogether, as Lara knew.

"Oh, come on, Robbie, everyone knows Junior was drinking Mogen David in the parking lot as soon as he started high school, and Chip used to see him after football games over at the Storm Door."

"Just because Junior gets drunk even while he makes Nanny believe he's the most pious boy in the whole county doesn't make drinking right. And Elaine Logan, she's been homeless all these years. I wouldn't think you'd find it a joke to see her getting drunk."

"She came to my church last Sunday, and she'd already been drinking before the service started. She stood up and called us all whited sepulchres. And she made a creepy remark to my dad, kind of suggesting she'd seen you and me together," Lara whispered in a hot undervoice.

"All the more reason to take her drinking as a serious problem instead of making fun of it," Robbie said doggedly.

"Maybe you'd better go to your church Halloween party with Amber," Lara said. "You can tell her how dreadful alcohol is and how terrible I am because my parents sometimes have a drink on their anniversary or my dad shares a beer with Blitz and Curly. Amber can pat your arm and say, 'Oh, Robbie, I've been so worried about your immortal soul, but now I know you've returned from the brink of the pit.'"

"Don't, Lulu! You know I don't talk like that about you, so why do you make fun of me when I'm trying to stand up for what I think is right?"

"I won't if you won't preach at me." She made a face, somewhere between a pout and a kiss, and held out her hands to him. They came together again.

It wasn't the only issue they disagreed over. Salvation Bible Church was opposed to evolution and to birth control; Riverside Church actively supported both. Because Robbie was lonelier than Lara, he struggled more to understand her point of view than she did his. Everyone at Salvation Bible when they turned thirteen took a pledge of abstinence until marriage. At least once a month, Pastor Nabo preached on how people who used artificial contraception or had abortions, or who disputed the creation of the universe as described in the inerrant Word of God, would be writhing in torment someday. It was hard for Robbie to think that the Grelliers really were Christians, when they believed that the earth was billions of years old, or that Cindy Burton wasn't damned for having an abortion.

"But you told me it was Junior who raped her," Lara said.

"Junior came back and bragged that he and Eddie had done it together," Robbie said. "But it was Cindy who took the innocent life of her baby."

"If anyone is going to hell, it should be Junior and Eddie. They're the ones who hurt an innocent girl," Lara argued. "And it wasn't a baby. It was a little fetus as big as my thumbnail."

"And you don't think that was wrong?"

"Robbie, I don't. Especially when her own brother— Don't you see how gross that is? The baby would have had horrible problems if it had been born. Don't send me to the Salvation Through the Blood of Jesus Full Bible Church's hell, please. I mean, not unless Chip is there, and Gram and Grandpa. Anyway, how can we speak for God, deciding who is damned and who is saved? God is so much bigger than us, so much bigger than our hates and fears."

Lara was unconsciously quoting Pastor Natalie and Pastor Albright. Like Robbie with Pastor Nabo, she had listened to her church's theology every week her whole life and believed it to be the truth.

"Only God knows what is in our hearts and souls," she added. "And He knows that in my heart and soul, against all my best judgment, I'm in love with you."

And the argument ended, as theirs always did, in each other's arms, fumbling hotly in the sleeping bag, Robbie tormenting himself with the question of whether he'd be doubly damned if he, a., let himself get inside Lara and, b., used one of Chip's condoms to go there.

It was after that particular argument that he first asked Lara to go to his church's Halloween celebration. "We don't do a hell house—you know, those setups some churches use to show us what happens to the damned. But Pastor Nabo preaches about the godly life, and then we have kind of a dance. Chris and me are going to play this year."

"Can I wear a costume?"

He shifted uncomfortably. "Pastor Nabo discourages them because they're part of the satanic version of Halloween. No, don't jump down my throat. I'm only telling you what *he* calls it."

"If I can't wear a costume, then everyone would know it was me," Lara said. "And, pretty soon, our private business would be everyone's supper conversation."

"But a lot of kids come from the community because their parents like them to be in a safe place on Halloween," Robbie urged. "And I want you to hear me play—I mean, really play, not just listen to my lame podcast that I had to record myself. Oh, why can't we see each other publicly?"

Lara hunched a shoulder. "My dad already knows—or, at least, he's guessed—so it's just a question of your father."

"And Nanny and Junior. Oh, Lulu, maybe we could run away together."

"To a cave by the river!" Lara was enthusiastic. "We could live on what we stole, or maybe Kimberly Ropes would bring us care packages. In the spring, I'd plant sunflower seeds and tomatoes. You could sneak over to your place and get us milk!"

"I was thinking of Nashville, so I could try out my music for a real audience and see what they think."

For a moment, they both got carried away by the fantasy: Robbie a star, singing on Grand Ole Opry, Lara famous for her album-cover designs. No more getting up every day at five to milk, no more Nanny criticizing every move Robbie made, no more Susan sitting like the original Immovable Object, sucking all the air out of the Grellier house.

Lara's cell phone rang. It was Jim. The grounding still fresh in her mind, she answered at once. Her father told her she had fifteen minutes to get home.

"If we aren't going to run away together tonight, we'd better get home now or he'll ground me for a whole month instead of two weeks," she reported.

Reluctantly, they untangled their arms and legs and slipped down the ladder to the barn floor.

Elaine Logan was standing at the bottom. "I caught you, I caught you, I knew you were up there! Mean children, not letting me play with you. What will you give me not to tell?"

The two stood frozen for a moment and then dove through the loose board in the back of the barn and ran for their lives through the field to the road.

"Spies inside, spies inside!" they could hear Elaine screaming to Gina and the other Wiccans. "Myra the murderess has her spies looking at you!"

Robbie and Lara crossed the road and landed in the drainage ditch, waiting for the pursuit to begin in earnest. A minute later, they heard the eastbound freight approaching. They scrambled out of the ditch and jumped across the tracks. Shielded by the train, they ran on the grading until they reached the county road, where they laughed triumphantly.

"Still," Robbie said after a final kiss, "we'd better find a different place to meet."

"How about Nassie's manger?" Lara teased.

"Don't joke about it, Lulu," Robbie begged. "Junior's started lurking around Nassie's pen at night. He had so much fun beating up the lady from Animals R Kin, he can't wait for someone else to try to break in. He's carrying Dad's second gun, the Colt. He even talks about training an armed militia, but Dad won't agree to that."

"Doesn't he have to go to class or anything over at that Bible college?" Lara asked.

"Yeah, like Junior ever cared about class, even in high school," Robbie said. "He got the football coach to give him some special pass or something for the holy or sacred or whatever work he said he was doing, guarding Nassie, because curfew over there is supposed to be eleven o'clock for all the good Christian boys and girls."

Headlights appeared on the Schapen road. Lara fled for her own home; Robbie dropped into the ditch.

Forty-Eight

WORD STORM

LARA REACHED HOME, breathless, as Jim was taking lasagna—another gift from the church women—out of the oven. He looked meaningfully at the clock, but all he said was, "Bring plates over to the oven and get yourself washed up. You've been mining coal or drilling for oil, judging by your looks."

Lara ran up to the bathroom to clean up the worst of the dirt; she'd have to wash her hair after supper. She helped Jim set up trays in the family room, where Susan was ensconced in her corner of the couch, the afghan making a handy barrier between herself and her family.

Over supper, Lara tried again to interest her mother in the Halloween bonfire. "They'll be dancing, and everything, like they always do. They don't call it Halloween, you know, but Samhain, which is some ancient word meaning 'summer's end'—I looked it up at school. Gina's picking apples from the old Fremantle trees to roast in the bonfire—"

Lara broke off nervously, afraid that Susan would ask how she knew, but Susan only stared at her dully and said, "That's nice," in the dead voice that made Lara want to pick up a knitting needle and skewer her mother. Jim raised his eyebrows but said nothing—not for the reasons Lara feared, that he guessed she'd been on the Fremantle land overhearing Gina—but because he wanted to know what Gina had been doing and saying, and he could hardly ask his daughter. Lara stopped trying to make conversation. She gulped down the rest of the lasagna, hurried into the kitchen with the dishes, and ran upstairs, muttering, "Homework."

"I hope that's what she's doing," Jim said to Susan. "Rachel says her schoolwork is marginally better. But she's spending too much time with Robbie. I'd like to know where! I don't want her having sex in a ditch with a boy. Could she have found someplace over on the Fremantle land? Do you think we should talk to her about it?"

Susan shrugged. "If you think it's the right thing to do, go ahead."

"She's your daughter, too, Susan. I don't want her destroying her long-term happiness just because she's feeling lonely and abandoned right now."

"Maybe Etienne would still be alive if I hadn't argued with him about his life choices. I'm not going to kill our other child by arguing with her."

Jim, like his daughter, wanted to scream with fury, but he picked up the remote and turned on the football game. Susan stared vacantly at a recent issue of *Farm Family Living*.

They were both startled to hear Elaine Logan yelling from the kitchen, "Farmer Jones? Farmer Jones, I know you're around here someplace."

"Elaine Logan." Jim got to his feet, wondering if—hoping—Gina had gotten into trouble again.

"Farmer Jones, don't think you can hide. I've seen the spies you and Myra Schapen set on me, murdering bitch. Don't think I haven't. And don't think I'll put up with it for one second longer!"

Elaine appeared in the doorway between the kitchen and the family room. Burrs covered the legs of her turquoise polyester pants; her faded yellow hair was matted with leaves she'd picked up resting on her way from the Fremantles' to the Grellier farm. Her appearance startled even Susan, who dropped her magazine.

"What are you talking about?" Jim demanded.

"I need to sit down, and you could give me something to drink. Just because I'm not ready to take off my pants and wave them in your face doesn't mean I don't deserve to be treated as politely as Gina."

Jim looked nervously at his wife, wondering what she would make of Elaine's comment, but Susan only said, "Sit down. You are as welcome as any other visitor to our home."

Her cold, languid voice didn't sound especially welcoming, but Elaine went to the couch, sinking into a heap of afghan. Susan exclaimed angrily and tried to extract her handiwork, but the burrs on Elaine's pants stuck to it. Elaine made no offer to help Susan clean the blanket but reiterated her demand for a drink. When Jim offered tea, coffee, or juice, Elaine gave him a sour look, but said juice would do.

She swallowed the orange juice in one long, loud gurgle, slammed the glass down on the coffee table, and announced, "I'm tired of your daughter and her lovebird boyfriend spying on my home. I have a birthright to that house, Myra Schapen only has a death right to it. The farmer's daughter and the murderess's grandson better get used to it."

Jim looked at her in blank bewilderment. A birthright to the Fremantle house? Did Elaine have some delusion about being a secret Fremantle heir? Then he thought of the newspaper clipping Elaine had dropped in his cart. If she had miscarried in the Fremantles' back bedroom, maybe that's what made her think she had a *birth*right to the house.

Jim went back to the kitchen and found the clipping buried in his printout of planting charts. "Is this what you're talking about?"

Elaine snatched the paper from him. "How did you get that? Did your lying, whoring daughter steal it for you?"

"Elaine, you can't come in here calling everyone in my family names and hope to get any support from us," Jim said. "You dropped it in my cart when you slept in it two weeks back. I've been too busy to return it."

Elaine kissed the article but stared at him belligerently. "Where is my picture?"

"What picture?" Jim said.

"Don't act naive with me, Farmer Jones. I kept them together, my baby's picture and my story. Now, where is it?"

Jim shook his head. "I don't have it. You can come out to the barn with me to see for yourself."

"No you don't, mister. You don't go dragging me off to your barn and shut me in that cart overnight again. You produce that photograph now!"

"What does it look like?" Susan asked, interested despite herself. "If we knew what you were looking for, it would be easier to find."

"Oh no you don't," Elaine said. "If you knew what I was looking for, you'd use it against me. I bet your butter-won't-melt-in-her-mouth Sunday-school daughter knows what I'm talking about."

"My daughter doesn't steal people's private papers," Jim said stiffly.

"Of course you'd stand up for her against me. But you ask your darling daughter what she's doing in that old barn, her and that boy from the murdering Schapens. If she's hiding my papers up in that loft, you tell her I won't put up with it. I'll call Sheriff Drysdale and get her arrested for trespassing. Then we'll see what kind of song you sing."

"Are they hiding in the Fremantle barn?" Susan asked. "Did you interrupt them in the middle of fucking?"

Jim winced at the coarseness of his wife's language, but Elaine hissed, "They were up the ladder, spying. They think because I can't climb up after them, I don't know what they're doing, but they're wrong."

"I'll talk to Lara," Jim said quietly, "and let her know she's upsetting you. Now, why don't I drive you home."

"Not in the back of that tractor. Don't think I'm stupid enough to do that twice."

Jim couldn't help laughing. "No, we'll go in the pickup."

He helped hoist Elaine into the truck, but when he turned left at the crossroads, toward the Fremantle house, Elaine demanded that he take her to the Schapen farm.

When he refused, she said, "You want to take off all of Gina's clothes and get in bed with her again, don't you? But one of her girlfriends is doing that tonight, so you're shit out of luck, buster."

Did every woman talk like a field hand these days? First Susan and now this monstrous woman. "I'm not taking you to the Schapens', Elaine. If you don't want to go back to Gina's, I'll take you into town."

She started to harangue him, but he cut her off. "If you go to Schapens', remember that Arnie is a sheriff's deputy and he's not afraid to use his power. They won't invite you inside for orange juice and a chat."

"I know what Arnie likes to do, beat up women, or get his son—the big thug, not the skinny spy—to beat us up for him. No women allowed near their heifer, but he doesn't care what men do. And that mother of his, setting fires, she murdered my baby."

"You had a baby in the Fremantle house, and you think Myra murdered it?" Jim said, trying hard to sort out Elaine's disjoint accusations.

She was quiet for a moment, then said, as if surprised by the thought, "That's right. There were two of them. I lost them both. Myra burned him, too. 'Fire within fire.' I used to know that whole poem by heart because it was by Dante. I met him in Mr. Patterson's class on Victorian poetry. He was the most beautiful boy in the world."

"Dante?" Jim's head was spinning. "You're out of your mind. Even I know he's been dead for a thousand years."

"Not that one!" Elaine was scornful. "*My* Dante. And then Myra burned him to death. And now that she thinks I'm collecting evidence, she's siccing that grandson of hers to spy on me, him and your darling daughter both."

"Get out. Get out here, Elaine. I've had enough."

"I can't get out of this great big truck alone," she whimpered.

"Then I'll drive you back to Gina's."

She gave him a bitter look but clambered down to the road, reciting curses under her breath. He turned the truck around. But when he reached his own yard, he didn't think he could bear to see his wife, or even his daughter, again tonight. He drove into town, to the coffee bar where he usually met Peter Ropes or some other friend. His insurance broker was there tonight. Jim sat talking with him about the Kansas football team until the place shut down at midnight.

It was only when he was driving home that he thought again of Elaine and her outburst. *Her* Dante. And Gina had said the ringleader of the kids in the bunkhouse had been named Dante something. Her lover, her father, she'd said tonight. Had Elaine Logan been the young woman Jim saw in the cornfield all those years ago? He couldn't remember her face, only the waterfall of pale hair and the provocative smile.

Forty-Nine
GRAFFITI ARTIST

As HE SCURRIED home in the dark, Robbie wondered about all the sarcastic ways he described not just Junior but even the students at Tonganoxie Bible College when he talked to Lara. Maybe she really was a bad influence on him. Thanks to her, he was questioning everything he'd been taught all these years, by Nanny and his pastors at Salvation Bible Church.

At first, he kept telling Lara that what they were doing didn't count as sex because he wasn't inside her, but he had to admit it was pretty hard to believe he was truly being abstinent. Besides which, she showed him websites that proved she could get pregnant even if—well, he didn't like to put it into words—so she was using a gel, which was messy and nasty, and that meant he was encouraging her to use artificial contraception, which was against Jesus. But Lara claimed that Jesus never talked about contraception, and when Robbie searched his Bible at home he had to agree. So maybe she was right when she said it was just something his church had made up, to mess with his mind.

If Nanny had been different—well, even if she'd been the same angry person but had treated him like she treated Junior—he might have stood up more strongly for his church's teachings to Lara. Come to think of it, Salvation Through the Blood of Jesus Full Bible Church wasn't really the Schapens' church: they'd always been Methodists, up until Nanny married Robbie's grandfather. Maybe *true Schapens,* to use the phrase Nanny was so fond of, really were Methodists.

If he became a Methodist, or even joined Riverside Church with Lara, would he start thinking the Universe was billions of years old? Trying to imagine the big bang, dinosaurs, the earth going back billions and billions of years without any people on it, made him feel dizzy. How could you believe that and still believe in God?

Even so, as Robbie ran up the road into his family's yard he couldn't help laughing at what Nanny would do if he said, "Dad and Junior aren't true Schapens, because they belong to your church, but as soon as I leave here I'm going back to the Schapens' real religion."

He could see Myra in the kitchen. He could only stand up to her in his head, not in the flesh, certainly not with Lara's kisses on him: he was sure Myra would be able to smell Lara's lemongrass shampoo on his skin.

He went around to the back of the house, where he crawled in through a window that he kept unlocked just for such occasions. The window opened into the old parlor, where the family Bible sat on a carved wooden stand.

On impulse, he opened the Bible to the genealogy page. He had never been interested in it before, except to see his own birth date and that he was named for that first Robert, Robert Cady Schapen, *b.* 1826. Now he wanted to find some sign that he was the true Schapen, Junior the imposter. With Junior gone, Arnie would love him best, the unspoken fantasy of every younger brother.

After his mother ran off, Myra had put a heavy black line through her name, so that it appeared as though he and Junior—Arnold Taylor Schapen, Jr.—had sprung from Arnie's body without any womanly help. He studied the history of marriages and births. Schapens had married Wiesers, Longneckers, and Fremantles, and his great-great-grandfather had even married one of the Grellier daughters. That meant he and Lara were cousins of some kind. The thought made him laugh again.

The noise brought Myra from the kitchen into the front room. "And just what do you have to laugh about, young man, missing dinner without a by-your-leave? Since when do you get to pick and choose when you'll be here?"

Robbie ignored her complaint. "I was looking at the family tree, Nanny. It says here we're cousins of the Grelliers'."

She glowered but bent over the page. "Hmm. Must be where you come from, then. Or maybe your ma fooled around with Jim Grellier, and told my son you were really his. Kathy Sheldon dated Jim in—"

"I'm tired of you talking that way, about me and about my mom. I am Arnie's son!" Robbie shouted. "If you're so sure I'm not related to him, get our DNA tested."

"DNA," she cried, as if he'd suggested her running naked down the county road. "You know Pastor says DNA stands for 'Devil *Noes* All.' Are you being infected by evolution talk now? Is that what you're doing when you waltz off to get away from the crowds? Studying evolution?"

Robbie started to say "DNA isn't about evolution," but it was a waste of breath to argue with Nanny. And, anyway, he had an uneasy feeling, from what his biology teacher said, that DNA *did* have something to do with evolution.

"What did you do with my mom's letters to me?" he demanded, made suddenly bold in front of Myra.

"How did you know—" She bit off the words.

"So she *did* write me, and you never let me know. I want to see my letters."

"I'm trying to save your immortal soul all the time you're trying to sink back down into the pit. Ever since your father told Pastor Nabo you bred that calf, you've been getting a swelled head. Well, I am here to bring it back to normal size! You think you can come and go from this house as if it was a Holiday Inn, but you'll think twice about that from now on. This is a working farm. Your *father* does double duty, working for that liberal, Commie-loving so-called sheriff, besides carrying his load here. I cook three meals a day that you don't think you have to show up for. Your brother cares enough about the farm to come all the way from Tonganoxie to guard the calf, even though he's a college student and a football star, while you wander around the countryside as if you were the prince of Douglas County."

"That's so unfair," Robbie said. "I milk a hundred twenty-two cows every day, sometimes twice a day. I clean out the barn. I'm in school, too—and, unlike Junior, I actually study."

"Junior doesn't need to study," Myra said loftily. Which was true,

Robbie thought, when you considered the free pass instructors at the high school and now at the Bible college gave their football star.

His grandmother added, "Your *father* is on the four-to-midnight shift tonight. You can relieve Junior until your father gets home. And when you get up at four-thirty tomorrow morning to do the milking, we'll see how big your mouth is then."

"I have homework. Anyway, Junior loves guard duty. You know he's hoping to shoot someone, or break heads or something."

Robbie brushed past Myra and went into the kitchen. His grandmother had thrown his supper into the garbage, so he started to make himself a peanut butter sandwich. Myra stormed in after him and snatched the bread away, so that he ended up spreading a knife full of peanut butter onto the countertop.

"You will respect me, you—you vermin. I told you to get out there and relieve Junior!"

Robbie's hands were shaking, but he took another piece of bread from the bag and put peanut butter on it. The knowledge that his mother hadn't forgotten him, that she had written to him—written him letters his grandmother had kept from him—brought him a small glow of comfort as well as courage. "You know, Nanny, if Arnie isn't my father that means you're not my grandmother, either, which means I don't have to listen to you for one nanosecond. Which is what scientists call a billionth of a second."

"Don't you dare bring science into this household and pretend it means something. If you won't respect me out of your own conscience, your brother will make you do so. Junior!" she shouted, but of course he couldn't hear her, all the way at the back of the lot, so she stumped her way out past the old hay barn, the milk and cow barns, and the sheds for the new calves to the red heifer's enclosure.

When Myra reached the enclosure, she expected to see Junior patrolling the perimeter. The padlock was off, and light was seeping around the edge of the door. What if someone had jumped Junior and was making off with the calf? She'd better go in to see.

It was wrong that a boy like Robbie, who talked back to his own grandmother and even dreamed about DNA testing, could get in to see the calf while she, Myra Schapen, who had rebuilt this farm and raised Junior and Robbie when that worthless Kathy ran off, was barred from it. On top of which, since when did a good Christian like herself take direction from a bunch of Jews with greasy coats and long, dirty beards?

She pushed open the door to the heifer's pen and heard a loud howl. She blinked, her eyes adjusting to the lights, and saw the calf, her grandson, and Eddie Burton in a great whirl of motion. The calf was bleating unhappily, its "yeh-heh, yeh-heh" drowning the noise that Eddie and Junior were making. Eddie Burton had his jeans down to his ankles. That was what she focused on. Not on her beloved older grandson, whom she hadn't seen naked since she changed his last diaper seventeen years earlier.

"Eddie Burton! Eddie Burton, have you been peeing on this calf?" Myra said. "Get your clothes on this minute and get home! What are you doing in this sacred place?"

The calf continued its uneasy lowing, but Junior was laughing. "He didn't hurt the calf, Nanny. Don't get your undies in a bundle."

Robbie appeared in the doorway behind Myra. "Junior! You and Eddie better not have been touching the heifer. The Jews are coming tomorrow and they look at everything about her—and I mean *everything*!"

"You think a couple of Christ killers with long hair should be telling me what to do? Think again, shrimp."

"You shouldn't be in here with Eddie," Robbie said, trying to stand his ground.

"I seen you," Eddie said to Robbie. "I seen you at Fremantles'."

Robbie's stomach went cold.

"Oh yeah?" Junior was interested. "When was that, Eddie?"

"Today. Lots of times. Yesterday, maybe, too."

"You're a retard, Eddie," Robbie said crudely. "I was here all day yesterday."

"What was he doing, Eddie?" Junior had a fatherly arm around Eddie's shoulders.

"Him and that girl, you know, that Grellier girl, her and Robbie, they hide in the old barn at Fremantles'."

"You're making stuff up to change the subject," Robbie said wildly. "Lara Grellier calls me names all over school, ask anyone."

"I *seen* you," Eddie repeated. "And I ain't a retard just because I can't learn my letters. It's a—a illness, my ma explained, in my brain—"

"You've been hiding at the witch's den with Lara Grellier?" Myra cried, glad to bury what she'd seen in the calf's enclosure under renewed anger with Robbie. "You've been seeing the daughter of your father's worst enemy and lying, telling me the boldest lies that ever came from Satan's mouth, with a straight face. And you've been doing it at Fremantles', with the help of Gina Haring, who flaunts her perversions in public and boasts that she's a witch! She's getting her Halloween bonfire ready. And, if she has her way, you'll be roasting with her in fires like that for all eternity."

"Nanny, listen to me: I have never in my life done anything with Gina Haring. So what if she is building her Halloween bonfire, that's nothing to do with me. Eddie, you should learn not to spread lies around or, before you know it, I'll be spreading some truth around."

"Like what, you shit-eating dirtbag?" Junior's voice was heavy with menace.

Robbie had had enough experience with his brother to recognize that tone as the prelude to violence. He took off for the old hay barn, where he'd been keeping his guitar since Arnie had banned it from the house. Junior and Eddie ran after him. Junior's size made him slower on the rough ground, and Robbie reached the barn just ahead of his brother. Robbie scrambled up to the loft, pulled up the ladder, and swung the trapdoor shut. He shoved everything in the loft on top of the trap and sat on it.

Junior menaced him from below, so Robbie started playing his guitar, singing loudly, *"Yes, he's heavy—he's my brother,"* which wound Junior into a greater frenzy. Cheered on by Myra and Eddie, Junior found a ladder and tried to push up on the trap, but the weight of a couple of hay bales, Robbie's amplifier, and Robbie himself kept it shut. Junior climbed down and found an ax. He started hacking at the door.

He'd been at it for about ten minutes when Arnie drove into the yard;

he was stopping at home so he could use his supper break to take a look at the calf. The commotion from the old barn made Arnie detour to it on his way to Nasya's enclosure. When he got there, he couldn't make sense of what he was seeing—Junior on a ladder with an ax, Eddie Burton's mouth bubbling saliva in excitement.

"What's going on?" Arnie demanded.

Eddie Burton jumped up and down gleefully. "Junior's gonna kill Robbie with the ax. Nanny Schapen told him to."

Junior stopped chopping. "Sheesh, Eddie, you get everything backward. I'm just trying to get the brat to come down here and eat his words."

"That's right. I won't tolerate him disrespecting me the way he does," Myra snapped. "He sneaks off every night after he finishes milking. He doesn't go to Teen Witness. He's been lying to me, and to you, too. You won't believe it when I tell you who he's been seeing—"

"Fremantles'," Eddie hooted. "He goes to Fremantles'. The witch put a spell on him."

"What are you talking about?" Arnie turned on Eddie.

"I seen him, I seen him," Eddie insisted. "Crawling through the ditch with the witch."

"That's a lie," Robbie yelled, his voice muffled through the trapdoor. "I've never been anywhere with any witch. And I've seen you, too, Eddie Burton. I've seen you in the calf's pen—"

"You haven't seen anything!" Junior roared.

"Enough!" Arnie shouted. "Junior, you're nineteen years old and in college. And Robbie, you're supposed to have a brain, that's what your teachers tell me. Can you two act your age and stop this bickering? Robbie, open this trapdoor and come down."

"Not if Junior's going to hit me," Robbie said.

"I'd rather wrestle every drunk in the valley than deal with my own sons. Junior, take Eddie home and keep him away from Nasya. The Jews are coming tomorrow, and I don't want there to be any question about her, you hear me?"

"All right, all right," Junior grumbled.

"And you, Robbie, come on down, and don't be such a crybaby."

Robbie moved everything away from the trapdoor and lowered the ladder. Arnie stood watching, breathing hard through his nose, his face as red as the heifer's. Junior took a swipe at Robbie with the ax as he reached the floor, but it was a only a token, a promise of things to come, not a full swing. Arnie decided his sons could be left with Myra while he looked at the calf.

The brothers were still hissing insults at each other when they heard Arnie. His outraged howl carried all the way across the calf pens and equipment sheds to where they were standing in the yard. Robbie and Junior took off for the heifer's pen with Eddie, Myra huffing behind them as fast as she could.

Inside Nasya's enclosure, they found Arnie struggling with Elaine Logan, who had a can and was spraying paint over Arnie, the calf, and the pen. Junior gave a happy cry. Lowering his head, he rammed Elaine with his shoulder, knocking her to the ground. He sat on her while Arnie clamped his cuffs around her fat wrists.

"You're under arrest," Arnie panted. "For defacing private property and for animal endangerment. And public drunkenness."

It was only then that Robbie saw the calf. Elaine had painted MYRA = MURDERER in white across Nasya's left side.

Fifty

HEIFER CLEANING

TUESDAY MORNING, Jim waylaid Lara before she could leave for school. He'd wanted Susan to join the discussion; she did get out of bed and put on a pair of jeans, but she sat at the breakfast table staring at her coffee cup, making it hard for Jim to stay focused on the issues he had with his daughter.

"Lara, I don't want to ground you again, but I want you to stop sneaking into other people's houses."

"I didn't, Dad. I haven't been in the Fremantle house since—" She broke off. She'd been about to say, since she taped the roach to Gina's poster, but then she remembered taking Abigail's diaries into the house three weeks ago, when she fixed up the hayloft.

"Since when?"

"It's been three weeks, and I only went in and out—I haven't been spying on Gina, if that's what you're worried about—but Robbie and I need a place to be private. I fixed up the old hayloft, and I can't even see the house from there, so it's not spying, it's just being private."

"Sweetheart, you haven't been private: Elaine Logan knows, which means the Burtons will know, because she drinks with Turk at Raider's Bar. If Arnie doesn't already know, he will soon enough."

"At least it won't be on their website," Lara grumbled. "Myra—Mrs. Schapen—she'd never be able to hold her head up at Salvation Bible if the world knew someone in her family was joining a hell-bent bunch of atheists like us."

"We're not atheists," Susan broke into speech, "although, after a decade in the wilderness, even a believing Christian is entitled to ask where God is hiding Himself."

"But Myra thinks we are," Lara said. "She wants Robbie to date Amber Ruesselmann because Amber can save his soul. Do you know, at gym class she won't undress in the locker room? No one can look at her body, not even the rest of us girls. And she never takes off her panty hose, even to play basketball. She told Kimberly to save herself for marriage after she heard Kimberly talk about how she and Kevin Sawyer had, well, done it, you know. Which makes me wonder what Amber is saving—"

"Enough, Lara!" Jim said sternly. "The Ruesselmann girl has an unhappy enough life without you poisoning it further with your chatter. And since you're making your own self the subject of chatter, I think you'd have a little more compassion for someone else. Here's the deal. If you want to be with Robbie, you do it here at home, where your mother or I can see you from time to time. If you don't come home promptly from school, I'm going to tell Blitz to monitor you at school. I would hate to do that, hate to have to make him party to your private life, but this has to stop now, this sneaking into other people's homes, or barns or mangers. Do you understand?"

Lara's lower lip stuck out: defiance, unhappiness, in one look, but she mumbled, "Yes."

"And do you promise?"

She shut her eyes tightly but finally promised, leaving for school with a great clatter of her book bag banging walls, doors slamming, truck gears grinding, and finally a spray of gravel smacking the yard.

At school, she looked for Robbie, to tell him the unfair edict that had been handed down. She didn't see him all day, and, finally, before sixth period, even waylaid Chris Greynard. They'd known each other at Kaw Valley Eagle, when Chris had ganged up on her with Robbie, but he didn't seem so awful now that they were in high school. Or maybe it was because he was Robbie's friend that he seemed nicer.

"If I ask you something, will you promise not to tell?" Lara said.

"Tell who?"

"Your folks, the people at your church."

"Maybe."

She grabbed his sleeve and pulled him to one side. "I need to know about Robbie— He and I— It's a secret, his dad and his nanny will murder him if they know— Where is he?"

Chris grinned. "So that's who he's been writing all those love songs to. I knew it couldn't be Amber Ruesselmann. Well, well, Lara Grellier, who would have thought."

"But where is he today?" she cried.

He shook his head. "Haven't heard from him. But he'd better pop up by tomorrow because we have our big gig for the Christ-Teen party at church. You coming?"

"Maybe." Wednesday was Susan's therapy night. Both her parents would be gone at least until nine. Lara could drive into town, go to the party for an hour or two, and be back before they returned. After all, she had only promised not to sneak into people's houses; she hadn't promised to stay away from Robbie's youth-group party.

She finally sent Robbie an e-mail, hoping he could see it without his grandmother or dad snooping.

From: meadowlark21 @freestateserve.com
Date: October 30
To: heavymetal@chiefsworld.net

Are you okay? Did Elaine get you in trouble big-time? She's such an interfering bitch!!!! She came around our place and now my dad made me promise if you and me want to see each other we have to do it at my house, not in the barn. Dad says she was heading to your place after she left here. Can you call me or are you under house arrest?

❤❤❤❤❤❤

Lulu

Lara was scared about what Arnie and Myra might do to Robbie, but, in fact, it was the damage to the calf that worried the Schapens at the moment, not Robbie's liaison with one of the Grelliers.

Arnie made Robbie spend Monday night and much of Tuesday morning cleaning the paint off Nasya and her stall. Robbie removed all the straw, hosed down the obsidian underneath the platform as well as the pen itself, before slowly and carefully working an industrial skin cleanser into Nasya's hide. The heifer bleated the whole time.

When he finished, not only did she smell of lanolin and evergreen, there was a raw spot on her side that Arnie knew the Jews would easily find. Arnie decided that a lie in Christ's service didn't count. They would tell the Jews that the heifer had rubbed herself raw against the slats of her pen.

Robbie was collapsing on his feet. Arnie sent him into the house for a nap. Myra, who seemed to Arnie to be getting angrier by the day, had actually tried to lock the boy out at breakfast time on the grounds that he'd been the cause of all their problems with the heifer, and he didn't get to eat until he'd cleaned it all up.

"But I wasn't," Robbie protested. "It was Junior who let Eddie into Nassie's enclosure, and then ran off and left it unlocked. Why don't you make Junior clean up?"

"If you'd stayed home, doing your Christian duty instead of rutting around those Grelliers, Junior wouldn't have needed to chase after you. I want to see real repentance in your life, Robbie, before I let you eat my food again."

"I always learn from your Christian example, Nanny," Robbie said with heavy sarcasm.

Arnie gave Robbie a sharp reproof but told his mother not to be vindictive, that Robbie more than pulled his weight on the farm and he needed to eat.

"I have to go into town for Elaine Logan's bond hearing. I'm not going to have her let loose on her own recognizance. In fact, when I called Pastor this morning to tell him what happened to Nasya, he suggested we try to get her released to the church's oversight. Anyway, while I'm in town I'll stop at the store for some padded strips to put on the slats around her pen. That'll show the Jews that we're already on top of the problem. So, Mother, while I'm in town I want Robbie to sleep. I'll need his help soon enough with the five o'clock milking."

Robbie felt tears pricking his eyelids, he was so grateful to his father for this rare intervention. He knew if he started to cry, he'd only earn another round of blisters from Myra, on what a sissy he was, so he gulped out a "Thanks, Dad," before slapping three cold fried eggs between four slices of bread and wolfing them down on his way up the stairs to bed.

The court hearing went as Arnie had hoped. The presiding judge was predisposed against Elaine: she'd appeared before him a few times over the years on disorderly conduct charges, and she was always combative. At Tuesday's hearing, she was even more obstructive. She kept repeating her claim that Myra had committed murder, and that she was within her rights to stop Myra and Arnie from spying on her.

Elaine's overworked public defender protested Arnie's suggestion that Elaine be remanded to Salvation Bible to do community service under their guidance and asked for a recess to find another alternative. The judge agreed, to Arnie's annoyance, but the recess only delayed the outcome he wanted.

The public defender tracked Rachel Carmody down in the teachers' lounge at the high school and persuaded her to come downtown to speak for Elaine. Like the judge—and even Elaine's attorney—Rachel was tired of Elaine's antics, but she went to court to protest the arrangement. "If she needs the support of a Christian community, we can provide that at Riverside Church, Your Honor. The deputy who arrested her, and whose calf she supposedly hurt, is a member of Salvation Bible Church. He's been making money from showing off the calf and claiming that it's speaking Hebrew. And now I'm worried that he'll be trying to get revenge."

The judge listened to Rachel's plea impatiently. "If Ms. Logan can make restitution through community service at Salvation Bible, then we won't have to try to figure out a way for her to pay whatever monetary loss Deputy Schapen sustained. She'll also be spared a prison sentence."

Elaine cried out with rage over the arrangement. "You're a dupe of the Schapen family, Judge. Or, worse, you're part of their cabal. I wish I was a brown recluse spider. Then I'd bite you and poison you for playing up to them."

"You're not making the court wish to change the ruling, Ms. Logan, except to consider a year in prison instead," the judge said, as the public defender uselessly tried hushing his client.

Arnie didn't try to hide his smirk at the decision. He had the deputies take a handcuffed Elaine out to his SUV, where Junior helped transport her to the church. Junior's football coach at Tonganoxie Bible had given him a special pass to spend two days in Lawrence "on Christ's business." Junior would keep Elaine from leaving the church before the Christ-Teen service on Wednesday.

Arnie's smirk faded once he was home and the rabbis arrived to inspect the heifer. Pastor Nabo, Mr. Ruesselmann, and Mr. Greynard showed up as well. Robbie saw how nervous his father was: Arnie shifted uneasily from foot to foot, although he was smart enough not to volunteer information until Reb Meir demanded to know the cause of the evergreen smell and the raw spot on the heifer's skin.

"This is very serious, very serious, indeed, Mr. Schapen," Reb Meir said sternly after Arnie brought out his explanation about Nasya rubbing herself against the slats. "I hope this doesn't cause a permanent marring of her skin."

Robbie held his breath, terrified of what they might ask. They consulted with each other in their own language. Finally, Reb Ephraim and the third Jew, whose name Robbie didn't know, said they would return on Thursday to check the heifer's progress. "She is hanging in the balance, Mr. Schapen. You know that we want to be the ones to proclaim the perfect red heifer as much as you do, but we cannot offer Ha-Shem a sacrifice of an unworthy animal. You worry about your own immortal soul. For us, it's much more serious; the fate of the whole House of Israel depends on the purity of our sacrifice."

With those stern words, the trio headed back to their van. Robbie waited nervously for his father to jump on him for everything that was suddenly looking bleak in the Schapen universe. Instead, Arnie took Pastor Nabo in the house for a private conference. At its end, they summoned Robbie to the front room. Myra, barred from the proceedings, was ostentatiously banging coffee cups around in the dining room.

"I hear you've been seeing a girl who's not a Christian, Robbie," Pastor Nabo said.

"She belongs to the Riverside Church," Robbie said. "I thought that was a Christian church, sir."

"Son, I've done a poor job as your pastor, I can see that." Pastor Nabo shook his head sadly. "I wonder how many of our young people realize that a person can call herself a Christian but still be traveling on a short-cut to hell? Riverside calls itself a church, but they don't preach the inerrant Word of God. They not only admit to blasphemies of the Word, they boast about them. I could show you a file of their so-called pastor Albright's sermons that would make you shudder. I should say, that *ought* to make you shudder. We'll call it ignorance, young Robbie, not willfulness, that has led you into error. Have you given this girl—what is her name, Lara?—a chance to witness true Christian worship?"

Robbie's shoulders twitched with nervousness. "I invited her to come tomorrow night, Pastor, to our Christ-Teen service."

Nabo and Arnie exchanged significant glances, but Robbie was too tense to pay attention.

"That's excellent, young man. You bring her along."

"If she gets her father's permission, sir. I don't know for sure that she'll be with me."

"If she knows enough to ask for parental guidance, then we know she has the humility to follow a Christian path if we show it to her." Pastor clapped Robbie heavily on the shoulder. "Why don't you phone her now and persuade her to join you?"

Robbie laughed, a nervous reflex, because the idea of Lara believing that she needed anyone's permission to do half the stuff she thought up was pretty ludicrous. Still, she did seem to respect Jim Grellier, so maybe Pastor was right.

He hurried to the kitchen to use the phone. Myra hovered behind him, listening so blatantly he almost handed the receiver to her.

Lara was startled to hear from him. Their relationship had been so secretive before that he'd never actually called her. "Where were you today? Are you all right? Did you get my e-mail? Elaine Logan came to our house last night, and my dad is pretty pissed off at me."

"Yeah, she was here, too. She spray-painted Nassie." He spoke quickly, almost in a whisper, trying to keep Myra from hearing him. "I can't talk much right now, but Pastor Nabo is here. He wants to know if you're going to come to our Christ-Teen service tomorrow."

"Why did you talk to him about us?" she cried.

"I didn't, Eddie, he saw, and—I'll explain it all when I see you tomorrow, it's too long to do right now. Can you come?"

"I guess," she said, remembering her earlier plan, to sneak off without telling Jim. Now that she was actually faced with the prospect, it didn't sound so attractive. "But I'm warning you, Robbie, if your pastor tries to convert me or something I'm leaving."

Next day at school, Robbie and Lara figured it didn't matter who saw them together, so they huddled in a corner of the cafeteria at lunch. His arms tight around her, Robbie explained what Elaine had done and how he'd had to stay home on Tuesday to finish cleaning the heifer. All around them, students were roaring with laughter, comparing costumes, talking about what parties they would attend, all except for Amber Ruesselmann, who looked at Lara with a kind of sick misery. Robbie and Lara didn't notice her or the rest of the clamor-filled room.

"All this commotion with Elaine, plus me scrubbing Nassie for hours, it's got Nassie all upset and she won't even eat," Robbie said. "My dad is looking like death, worrying that we'll lose our specialness. He's made so many people mad at him in the valley that he's afraid folks like your father will laugh at him."

"My dad doesn't do that kind of thing." Lara bristled.

"No, of course not. But Dad and Nanny do, so they imagine everyone else acts the same."

The bell rang for fourth period. The two went to their separate classes, and only met again in the Salvation Bible Church assembly room that evening.

Fifty-One

A CHRISTIAN SERVICE

From Pastor Nabo's Sermon

The choice is clear between the rule of Satan and the rule of God. The Bible tells us to choose life. God himself said, "I have set before you today life and Good and death and Evil." And He said—the inerrant Word of the Living God said—"Therefore, choose life."

We have chosen Good. As Christ's people, sanctified in the Blood of the Lamb, the Blood of Salvation, we have chosen Good. But we live in the midst of Evil, and it is hard sometimes to cleave to the Good. Sometimes the two are so closely twined together that we can't easily tell them apart. And we say, "Evil, be thou my Good," and hope that that will make it so. It is one of Satan's oldest, cleverest tricks, to dress himself up in attractive clothes and make us think he's an Angel of Light.

We were given a miracle, a chance to make history, in Kansas. The nation and the world laugh at us. "What is the matter with Kansas?" liberals ask. We have a chance to say, "Nothing's the matter with Kansas, generation of vipers. Everything's right with Kansas. What's the matter is, you have turned your backs on the truth of the risen Lord."

Our miracle hangs in the balance now because the boy who helped bring her into our lives has let Satan trick him, has let Satan dress up in fine clothes and look like Good to him.

Pastor Nabo's voice clanged like a fire-engine bell. Lara could hardly bear it. Instead of the dance that Robbie had promised—him on guitar, Chris Greynard on drums, with canned music on an iPod for later in the evening so Robbie could dance with Lara—she was in the middle of a nightmare.

The church complex anchored one end of a giant mall near Clinton Lake. Lara had driven past it many times but never been inside. Some impulse made her park on the street when she got there instead of in the mall. If she wanted to flee, she could jump into her truck and go.

She saw Arnie's truck in front of the church but couldn't see Robbie. She was already a little nervous about coming into town for the dance without telling her father. Legally, she shouldn't even be driving alone at night until she turned sixteen.

Pastor Nabo was standing in front of the entrance to the Assembly Building, where the church held events ranging from revival meetings to basketball tournaments for the Northeast Kansas Christian League. He was smiling toothily at people coming up to the church, assuring them they were in the right place for Christ-Teen Night.

When Lara crossed the street and stood looking uncertainly for Robbie, the pastor walked over to her. "You're the little Grellier girl, are you?"

Lara was rattled. "I'm not a little girl. I'm Lara Grellier. Is Robbie here?"

The pastor smiled at her sadly. "No, you're not a little girl. You are a very misguided young lady. Let's go inside and work on that, shall we? Brother Ruesselman? Brother Greynard?"

Amber Ruesselmann's and Chris Greynard's fathers sprang forward from the shadows and put their arms around her. Lara shouted in protest. She tried to break free, but they dragged her inside, pushed her through the throng of spectators and into the center of the assembly room, where they thrust her onto a chair. Once she was seated, other men set up a triangle of velvet ropes around her to separate her from the spectators. Robbie was in one corner of the triangle, about fifteen feet from her, and Elaine Logan was in the other corner, with Junior Schapen and two other husky men standing over her in the third corner.

Spotlights were trained on Lara, on Robbie, and on Elaine. Lara took her cell phone from her jeans jacket to call Jim. He'd be at the wellness center on Kentucky Street, starting the group therapy session with Susan. Lara hoped he had his phone turned on. Before she could press the SPEED DIAL number, Mr. Ruesselmann snatched her phone away and put it in his pocket.

"You'll get it back at the end of the service."

"But what about the dance?" Lara cried.

"We're doing things a little different this year, Lara," Mr. Greynard said. "You'll be fine. This ceremony will be a big help to you."

Lara felt shocked, disoriented, helpless. When Mr. Greynard leaned over to fasten a lapel mike to her jacket, she shrank away with a gasp that was suddenly amplified throughout the room.

A dozen or so men were inside the triangle with her, Robbie, and Elaine. Lara recognized Arnie but didn't know the others, besides Mr. Greynard and Amber's father. Myra Schapen stood near the front of the crowd, pressing against the velvet ropes, her face glistening with anticipation.

Elaine was belligerent. She hadn't had a drink for two days. She'd been placed in a cell with a bunk that she couldn't climb into, so she'd spent the night on the floor, and now she'd been brought to the church by a group of gloating hooligans. She didn't hide her opinion of them, as they frog-marched her into the assembly room and pushed her onto a chair—far too small for her buttocks—but Junior and his cohorts only laughed and wrenched her arms farther behind her. She shut up, eyeing them malevolently, biding her time.

Finally, the crowd finished filing into the room. The overhead lights were dimmed, the spotlights were switched from the three seated in the triangle to Pastor Nabo.

"We thank you, Lord Jesus, for the gift of healing, for the gift of tongues, for the gift of casting out demons. Satan is in our midst now. Do we want him here?"

His voice was horribly amplified by his lapel mike. Lara put her hands over her ears but couldn't drown the sound.

"No!" roared the crowd.

"I said, do we want him here?" the pastor repeated, louder. And, once again, the crowd roared back, even more loudly.

"I said, DO WE WANT HIM HERE?"

"NO," the audience screamed, people beside themselves with excitement, joy, frenzy.

"Shall we call him out?"

All around Lara came cries of "Yes, yes!" "Do it!" "Do it in Jesus' name, hallelujah!" "Praise Jesus!"

Lara couldn't make out individual faces, or voices amid the roar. All she could see was part of Pastor Nabo's face, where the spotlight hit it, and the shadows of Robbie and Elaine in their corners. The yelling was so loud that it filled Lara's whole body. The chair she was sitting on seemed to rock, as if she were aboard an old sailing ship in the middle of an Atlantic storm.

"Guide us. Guide us to the source of the possession, to the home Satan has built in this living, breathing body. Guide us there, take us there, Holy Spirit, before this soul is snatched away forever to the lakes of fire, the storms of brimstone, that await all of Satan's friends."

Pastor Nabo went down on his knees. "Help me, Jesus. Come to me, Jesus. Send your Spirit down on me."

The elders formed a circle around him and placed their hands in the air over his head. "Come, come, Jesus. We call on your Spirit, even as you have told us to do. Send us the Holy Spirit, the Spirit of Deliverance, the Spirit of Healing. Bring it into the body and spirit of Brother Nabo!"

"Bring it, send it, give it." The cries came from the audience.

"Guide me, Spirit. Help me, all you angels and archangels. Bring me to Satan's source!" Pastor Nabo got to his feet. The elders parted so that he could move around inside the triangular barricade.

With his eyes shut, he held his right hand in the air: "This arm is my lightning rod!" he thundered. "Come down, my lightning rod, O Blessed Spirit, fill me, electrify me!"

He held out his left arm straight in front of him as he walked around the velvet triangle, facing outward to the crowd. "My divining rod, bring me to the source of Satan! Is he there? Is he anywhere in this room? Help me, help me, Christians. Help me, my sisters, my brothers! If you feel the devil near you, send him forward. Jesus, I feel Ashmed close at hand. Bring me to him, bring me to him, Jesus!"

The crowd pressed closer to the velvet triangle. People moaned and took up the chant: "Lead him, help us, save us." Pastor Nabo turned around and began walking toward Lara. A second spotlight was directed at Lara. When the pastor touched her head with his outstretched hand, she screamed and twisted away.

"Ashmed! Ashmed! Are you in this girl? Speak to me!"

Lara stuffed her fingers in her ears. She was crying. She didn't want this horrible man to see her so upset. Her fear, and her anger at her fear, made her cry harder.

"Ashmed! Ashmed! I feel you in her, demon of lust, demon of horrible carnality, demon who gets between the legs of girls and ties them to lust, who makes the juices run down their legs, so that they entice good Christian boys out of the path of virtue, speak to me!"

"Shut up!" Lara screamed. "You dirty old man, shut up! Shut up!" The mike Mr. Greynard had attached to her jacket collar carried her voice across the assembly room.

"Now you've revealed yourself, Ashmed! Now you've made yourself clear. I command you in the name of the living God, leave this girl, leave her, leave her! She's despoiling a good Christian boy, but it isn't young Lara who's doing it, Ashmed, it's you. Lara, call on Jesus, call on His saving grace now, and the demon will leave you!"

"This is a terrible show. I've seen better by old men with the d.t.'s down by the river," Elaine Logan called. Her mike carried her words around the room.

"Ashmed, is that your controller speaking? Is that the demon Beelzebub speaking?"

"It's me, Elaine Logan, talking, you bag of farts. So shut up and end this dreary performance."

Pastor Nabo left Lara, who was crying and shaking, and walked over to Elaine. Mr. Ruesselmann took Nabo's place over Lara, leaning down so that his face was inches from hers, urging her to accept Jesus. The pastor, his eyes still shut, held his left hand over Elaine's head. "Beelzebub,

Beelzebub! Pay attention to me now, for I am working in the service of Christ Jesus!"

"Amen, praise Jesus," Amber Ruesselmann screamed from the front of the crowd. "I accept Jesus as my living God."

The second spotlight finally left Lara for Elaine. In its light, Lara could see the faces of the people nearest her. They looked greedy, as though, at a word from the pastor, they would surge past the ropes and devour Lara. Myra Schapen was gloating, rejoicing in the humiliation of the Grellier family.

Lara wanted to leave, to race home to the safety of her father's farm, but when she tried to slide out of her chair Mr. Ruesselmann grabbed her and forced her to remain seated. She darted a look at Robbie. Under the harsh white spotlight, he looked sick himself. Anger built in Lara against him. How could he have brought her to this disgusting place? How could he belong to a church that treated people like this?

Most of all, she was upset with herself. How could she have done this, come to this awful service, without talking to her father? She hadn't even left a note for him, she'd been so sure she'd be home before him. No one could help her. She couldn't bring herself to pray, because it seemed as though Pastor Nabo had taken over Jesus. *Chip, Chip,* she begged in her head. *Do something—anything!*

"Jesus' power and glory fill my heart," Pastor Nabo exulted. "His power sends me here to cast you forth from this woman. Beelzebub, Demon Alcohol, Demon Gluttony, in the Holy Name of Jesus I cast you out! Leave this woman and leave this place!"

"Fuck you, and the horse you rode in on, too!" Elaine yelled, her amplified voice booming from the rafters. "I'd rather do a year in the can than listen to your hypocritical ranting."

"Yes, Beelzebub, wrestle with me!" Nabo called, his eyes still shut. "I defy you, Beelzebub, I defy you in Jesus' name. Confess the foul acts you've committed on this woman's body and through this woman's body! Confess! You brought her low; you plied her with alcohol. And then you defaced God's holy heifer. You, Beelzebub, confess it to me now! You tampered with the Lord's anointed, but God's power is greater than yours! The sheriff arrested this woman, but he didn't realize that she was the blind instrument of your will. Come to Jesus, Elaine. Cast out Beelzebub and the sin of drunkenness. Jesus forgives you, for you know not what you did. It was the devil working through you."

"The fuck, you say." Elaine got to her feet. "I knew just what I was doing. Myra Schapen is a murderess. She set the bunkhouse on fire. I watched her sneak up to the bunkhouse in the dark. I saw her light her fuse and laugh when the wood caught fire. She killed my beautiful baby, she made him die. I heard his screams, I saw his beautiful black hair on fire. Now I'd like to hear her screams."

Before the pastor and the elders realized what she was doing, Elaine lumbered over to the barrier. She pushed through the velvet rope, dragging it and the metal stand it was attached to with her as she marched up to Myra Schapen.

"You've done more evil in your life than any other person in this room, Myra Schapen. More than me, for damn sure, let alone Farmer Jones's little girl, even if she did screw around in the hayloft. You're old, Myra, the fires of hell must be licking away at your dried-up old bush. I'm tired of you getting a free ride while I pay for your sins. You go suck on Pastor Fish Breath's dick there. Let him breathe on you. Maybe you'll have an orgasm."

Elaine twisted Myra's nose so hard that the older woman yelped. The crowd was briefly stunned. They moved aside as Elaine muscled through them to the exit. It was only when she opened the assembly-room door that Junior Schapen gave a loud bellow.

"Stop her! She can't leave. The judge gave my daddy custody over her. Stop her!"

Junior's outcry electrified the spectators. People turned away from the pastor and began a stampede for the doors. So many were trying to get to the exit at the same time that for a moment they were wedged in the doors, unable to move.

Junior tried bulling his way through the crowd, but they were packed too tightly for him to do anything except bruise the people right in front of him. When the crowd suddenly moved forward, the surge from behind knocked him over.

Pastor Nabo tried to shout the crowd into quiet. "We need to stay calm. We need to stay here with Jesus' healing power raining down on us. Return to your places. Let Brother Schapen and his son catch up with this tormented woman, so we can remove the stain of Satan from her!"

The emotion in the room had been running too high. The mob needed an outlet. They ignored him, pressing forward to the exits, yelling, screaming, calling out for their children, calling out for Jesus.

Lara crouched by her chair, hoping it might protect her if the crowd trampled through what was left of the velvet triangle. They parted around the ropes, like stampeding cattle around a tree.

The room was still about half full when a new cry passed from mouth to screaming mouth: Elaine had stolen an SUV. Someone—Sister Ruesselmann, no, Brother Schapen, Brother Clifton, maybe Pastor himself—had left their keys in the ignition. Elaine had driven off.

At that, Arnie and Mr. Ruesselmann both ran after the mob. In another moment, Pastor Nabo followed them. Junior and the other casualties got to their feet and started limping toward the exit. The doors swung shut behind the stragglers. Robbie and Lara were left alone, staring at each other under the spotlights.

Fifty-Two

SACRIFICIAL CALF

LARA STOOD ON wobbly legs and tore the mike from her jacket. "I don't like your church very much, Robbie. I'm going home."

"I'm sorry, Lara." Robbie couldn't speak above a whisper. "That was so horrible, I didn't know—they didn't tell me—I never expected— Oh, Lara, I'm so sorry."

He began to sob, the inexperienced wracking sobs of a boy who hadn't cried for years. A minute earlier, Lara had thought she couldn't stand to be in the same room with him, or any other Schapen, but now she found herself patting his head and telling him it was all right, she knew it wasn't his fault, she didn't hate him.

"But I'm still going home. I'm worn-out, and I want to see my dad. He doesn't even know where I am. And that stupid jerk Miles Ruesselmann stole my cell phone, so I can't even call him." She bit her lips, which were swollen from her own earlier sobbing.

"Can I ride with you, Lulu? My dad made me drive in with him and Nanny. I should've known Dad had something awful planned when he said they'd be coming tonight: they've never wanted to listen to me play before, especially not Nanny. I didn't even have time to get my guitar out of the back of the truck—they had Junior drag me in here as soon as we parked."

The two walked slowly out of assembly room, looking around fearfully in case Arnie or Junior was lurking. They kept about a yard apart, neither willing to touch the other. The pastor's description of sex had been so repulsive that they were each privately disgusted by their previous intimacy.

A few knots of people stood in the hallway, talking in excited under-voices. When Lara and Robbie passed, the groups became pointedly silent, watching the pair, who stared stonily ahead, marching on robot legs to the front door.

Cars were still backed up, trying to leave the parking lot. Robbie and Lara had to skirt their way around the cars, trucks, and SUVs to cross Lone Pine Drive. A woman lowered her window and yelled "Harlot! Thief!" at Lara.

When they were safely inside her truck, Robbie gave Lara a sidelong look. "Lara, I don't want to go back there, to my dad and Nanny. Could I come home with you? Just for tonight?"

Lara squinched her eyes shut. "I need to be alone, Robbie. I know that sounds mean, because it must be shitty at your place, but not tonight. I just need to see my dad, and be alone."

He took the rejection humbly—he felt too responsible for the treatment she'd endured at Pastor Nabo's and his father's hands. Both teens were exhausted from the evening's emotions, but Robbie had worked all night Monday and much of Tuesday: he was worn to the bone. He made a pillow of his backpack and drifted off to sleep when Lara turned on to Highway 10. Lara switched on her CD player for company. Jennifer Hewitt was singing *"I just can't take it."*

"I can't, either," Lara said aloud in the dark, "and I have way more to take than you do."

She hoped her dad would be home by the time she got there. As she drove along, all she could think about was flinging herself into his arms, crying against his chest, getting comforted. Maybe a miracle would have happened tonight at the therapy session. Maybe her mother would notice Lara's distress, pick her up—big girl that she was now—and rock her in Gram's old rocking chair.

Lara started to say aloud, "Come back to life, Mom," but it sounded too much like Pastor Nabo demanding that the Holy Spirit descend on him, or that Lara come to Jesus and give up her demon. That memory made her feel sick and shaky. Turn it off, she ordered herself, keep this truck on the road. If you fall in a ditch, it'll be big bad Arnie Schapen they'll dispatch to pull you out.

She pictured having to spend the rest of her life dodging Arnie Schapen. She'd be driving to school, or bringing the combine down the road to the Wakarusa River, and Arnie would be there, barring her path, grinning all over his red face. "Come with me, come to Jesus!" he'd be shouting.

Lara wondered if this was how Susan felt when Lara demanded that her mother snap out of it, wake up, pay attention. Did Lara herself seem like some terrible bully like Pastor Nabo? It wasn't right to run away from your children, whether you did it literally, as Robbie's mother had, or withdrew into a shadow world like Susan, leaving your body behind as a pretend person. Even so, Lara squirmed on her seat, seeing herself haranguing Susan as if her mother were a demon-possessed sinner. She turned up the volume on the CD to drown out her thoughts. No more thinking tonight, no more words about demons in this head, ever.

She braked for the exit to the county road. As she turned north, she saw a glow across the bare fields. Gina Haring's bonfire—she'd forgotten all about it in the drama of the evening. The bulk of the Fremantle mansion lay between her and the Wiccan ceremony, so that their bonfire appeared only as a corona around the house. It was all such a—such a *crock*. That was what Chip used to say when he was furious with someone for making up bullshit. A crock. Dancing around a bonfire to commune with pagan spirits or frothing over the demonically possessed, both were crocks. All that was really on Myra's or Pastor Nabo's or Gina's minds was sex, sex, sex.

There was a huge backup in front of her on the county road, unusual at this hour, unusual at any hour, except on weekends when pilgrims poured in to worship the Schapen calf. The SUV in front of her sported bumper stickers announcing SAVED THROUGH THE POWER OF HIS BLOOD and I CAN DO ALL THINGS IN HIS NAME.

Lara's stomach clenched. Had Pastor Nabo brought his flock out here to attack her? Her hands started to slip on the steering wheel, but as she passed the Burton house, with its collection of old cars on blocks, and got closer to the tracks, she saw the vehicles ahead were turning left toward Schapens'. Probably Arnie had invited the Saved Ones to hold a powwow and decide what to do next to rid Kaw Valley of the devil.

The SUV ahead of her braked so abruptly that she almost rammed it.

The truck bounced on its shocks hard enough to wake Robbie. He didn't open his eyes, willing himself to go back to sleep, hoping that if Lara couldn't rouse him he could at least spend the night in her truck.

Lara pulled out to drive around the line of turning cars. She bumped over the train tracks. At the turn-in to the Schapen place, a sheriff's car was blocking the way. One of the deputies, a man Lara didn't recognize, was inspecting driver's licenses before he let people through.

Lara nudged Robbie. "Something's going on. I don't want to have a hassle after all the other hassles I've gone through. Can you tell the guy you're a Schapen and get him to let you in?"

Robbie reluctantly opened his eyes. "Oh. Deputy Hardin. He knows me."

He stumbled out of the truck on his numb legs and walked over to the deputy. Lara rolled down her window and caught a fragment of the conversation over the crackling of radios and the noise of the people in the cars around her.

Deputy Hardin put an arm around Robbie's shoulders. *Break-in,* Lara heard. *Only church elders. Grandmother beside herself.*

Excellent. A break-in, with Myra beside herself. The only good news tonight. Lara waited until she was sure the deputy was letting Robbie on the property. In fact, Hardin blew an imperative whistle and another deputy appeared who put Robbie into a squad car and drove him toward the house.

Lara put her truck in gear. She was turning in to her own yard— finally, shakily, home—when she was startled by the hullabaloo behind her. She looked down the county road just in time to see Arnie's out- size pickup bounce out of the sorghum field and somehow leap across the drainage ditch. The cars backed up on the county road scat- tered, and just in time: the pickup roared across the road, cleared the sec- ond ditch, and headed in to the X-Farm. Behind it—far behind it—Arnie chugged along on his tractor, with Myra next to him and Junior standing behind.

The yard lights at the track crossing showed the back of the pickup clearly. Lara laughed out loud. Someone had stolen the perfect red heifer and was taking her for a joyride.

Fifty-Three

SAMHAIN

WHEN LARA REACHED her own home, her heart sank: her father's truck wasn't in the yard. Her parents weren't back from group therapy. What were they doing, going out for dinner and a movie? Didn't they know their daughter was home alone after the shittiest evening of her life, worse even than the day she learned Chip was dead or the night Susan tried to kill herself?

Her parents were always home by nine at the latest and here it was— She looked at her watch: eight-ten. No. She stared at the dial, watched the electronic seconds tick away. The watch was working. How could that be? She had left her house a little after six. How could a year's worth of unbearable emotion been squeezed into so little time?

She couldn't go into the dark house alone. She put her head in her hands, wanting to howl like a baby until mommy and daddy came home to comfort her, but she found she was too exhausted even to cry. She leaned back in the seat, turned up the volume on her CD player, and nodded off. Five minutes later, she was startled awake by an explosion, followed by pistol shots and screams.

Lara screamed herself. The noise was terrifying, terrible, but when it stopped, her tired brain tried to make sense of it. Had one of the Saved Ones thrown a stick of dynamite or hand grenade at Arnie's pickup with the heifer in the back? Morons. Imbeciles. The sooner they all went home to Jesus, the better off ordinary people like her family would be. They didn't even think about all the pain they brought to the people around them. And what if there were wounded people lying around the X-Farm now?

She climbed from the truck, her legs still shaking from her fright. She needed to bring first aid to the survivors, that's what she'd learned in 4-H, in the disaster-preparedness class she'd done when Chip shipped out to the Gulf.

She forced her tired body into a run. It was like at the end of a basketball game, when you didn't think you could move another foot, and Coach yelled, "Call up your reserves! There's always a little extra your body's holding back."

She'd stowed her first-aid kit next to the fire extinguisher in the kitchen. A flashlight stood there, too. She grabbed them and pelted back to the truck, drove across the train tracks past the lineup of cars, and turned in to the X-Farm. People were running madly through the disked sunflower field. Trucks, Hummers, SUVs were stopped at crazy angles along the ditch, and everyone was screaming.

Lara jumped out of her pickup, kit in one hand, flashlight in the other, and went into the field searching for casualties but not seeing any. As she looked around, bewildered, she spotted Chris Greynard. He was sitting cross-legged on the hood of an abandoned truck.

"What happened?" she demanded.

"Lara Grellier! What are you doing here?" He slid off the truck.

"I live here, don't you remember? I heard the explosion and the gunshots! What happened? Did they get the shooter? Is anyone hurt?"

Chris laughed. "Elaine Logan blew out the engine on Arnie's truck. That's what you heard—pistons and pins shooting out the sides of the engine and whacking the hood. Can you believe Robbie's dad, Mr. Law-and-Order-of-Douglas-County Schapen, left his keys in the ignition when he parked at the church tonight?"

"So Elaine took it? Serves him right, bullying busybody!"

"Yeah, maybe," Chris said. "Anyway, old Arnie put out an APB for his truck. I heard the deputies at the crossroads about splitting their pants laughing at Mr. Schapen for leaving his keys in the ignition. Someone spotted Elaine doing eighty on K-10, so everyone from church came roaring out here. Only Elaine had like a twenty-minute head start before we knew where she was going, so she had time to steal the calf."

"But how did she get in the pen? How could she get Nassie on the truck?" Lara demanded.

"My dad drove Mr. Schapen to the pen. He says, as far as they can tell, Elaine rammed Nassie's enclosure hard enough to bust down the door and part of one side, then backed up to the pen and forced the heifer onto the truck bed: the platform was just about the same height as the bed. I don't know what she thought she'd do with Nassie, take her to the witches' bonfire and roast her or something. Anyway, once Elaine got the calf in the truck she took off. Somehow, she managed to clear the drainage ditches, but she ran into a hole in your field here and the truck went into dirt up to the axel. She gunned the engine so hard she blew it apart."

Chris started to laugh again. "You should'a heard Myra Schapen. I never knew anybody could swear like that without using any bad words."

"Where's Nassie?" Lara asked. "Is she still in the truck?"

"Nah. Elaine scared the shit out of the heifer: Nassie freaked when the engine blew. She jumped over the backboard and took off. For all I know, she jumped over the moon. Arnie and my dad tore off after her; so did Myra. She got Junior to drag poor old Robbie along, too."

Lara looked around the X-Farm at all the vehicles. It was as if she had sown sunflowers and reaped a car wreck. "Why are you just sitting here laughing your head off? Why aren't you joining the rest of the Saved Ones in destroying the heretics in the valley?"

Chris shifted uncomfortably from foot to foot. "I've had enough heretic saving for one night. I'm waiting for Robbie, see if he wants to crash with me. If you see him, tell him I'm waiting in my old man's car over by the crossroads."

"Yeah, okay."

Chris turned back toward the road, but Lara hiked through her field, looking at the abandoned cars and trucks. A number sported IN CASE OF RAPTURE, THIS CAR WILL BE UNMANNED bumper stickers.

"The wise men followed a star to the manger, you followed a calf away from the manger!" she shouted at the night sky. "Hypocrites!"

In the distance, she could see the Saved Ones heading onto the Fremantle land, going toward the bonfire. Lara walked through the heavy, dry clods to her own truck, then bumped down the dirt track to the county road. At the train tracks, she stopped to stare at her house: it was still completely dark; her parents weren't home yet. She turned east, toward the Fremantle place.

She parked in the big circular drive under the arms of a giant cottonwood, planted as a seedling by Una Fremantle in 1857. She jumped down from the cab. The Fremantle house was dark, too, so she used her flashlight to find her way around to the back of the house. She gasped in fright at a shape moving toward her. Taking a step back, she held up her flashlight.

Elaine Logan looked up. The turquoise pantsuit she'd been wearing when she was arrested was black with mud. Her face was smeared with dirt as well. At the sight of Lara, her mouth twisted into a bitter leer.

"Oh, it's you, Goody-Two-Shoes Farmer's Daughter. You got us all into that scene at church tonight. I hope you're proud of yourself."

Lara couldn't speak.

"Your pious little boyfriend is off lassoing his calf. It can't be that much of a miracle. It came with me, and that didn't bring the wrath of Jehovah onto my head, did it?"

Lara edged away.

Elaine laughed derisively. "Everyone out here thinks they're better than me. They're not. They just do their dirty deeds in the dark, where no one can see. Ask Farmer Jones. He'll tell you I'm right, even if you are his darling little girl."

Lara hadn't realized how much venom could be packed into the word *darling*. She stood frozen until Elaine's laughter abruptly stopped.

"I'm tired and no one cares, no one wants to help a poor little lost girl." Elaine reverted to her whiny-child voice, which unnerved Lara even more than her invective.

"I can't help you. You're on your own!" Lara cried, turning to run.

At the edge of the orchard, she looked back. Elaine was unlocking the kitchen door—she'd somehow found a key to the house. Probably she stole one while Gina wasn't looking.

Lara trudged into the apple orchard and followed the shouts and cries coming from the bonfire. When she reached the clearing where the Wiccans had their fire, she pulled herself up on the low branch of one of the trees.

Gina and her friends, a number of them naked despite the chilly night, were arguing with the Salvation Bible people. Everyone was shouting so loudly that Lara couldn't make out what anyone was saying, beyond the occasional "bigots" on one side and "harlots," or "whores" on the other. She saw Pastor Nabo and the Ruesselmann family, including Amber, but didn't recognize any of the other Saved Ones.

As she watched, Arnie Schapen approached, leading the perfect red heifer by a rope. Junior was with him and Robbie was following after, head sunk in his chest. Far behind them came Myra, her head upright, her jaw moving, although whatever words she was snapping out were drowned by the uproar around her.

Poor Nassie. The calf was covered with mud and was trembling, from her perfect umber crown to her ruby tail. Lara longed to take the calf away, wash her, rub her down, get her away from this assembly of maniacs.

To her horror, she saw Arnie pull out his gun. She jumped from her perch into the high grass, where she lay flat, her hands over her ears. She was afraid he was going to shoot Nassie, or even Gina, but he fired into the air. People screamed, ran, and Arnie fired again. This time, the crowd subsided into an uneasy, muttering silence.

"You witches!" Arnie bellowed. "I could shoot every last one of you and not blink an eye, for harming my calf."

Gina stepped forward. "We have done nothing to your calf, Mr. Schapen. Don't bring her here all muddied and lathered and pretend we hurt her."

"You've been giving houseroom to Elaine Logan. She stole this calf and tried to bring her to your bonfire. Don't you pretend to me, you filthy dyke. Don't tell me she wasn't acting on your orders."

"Very well. I won't tell you that, although I still know nothing about what Ms. Logan did tonight. The last I heard, she was in your custody, so anything she did must have been under your direct command. If I were you, I'd stop trying to spread blame around and spread a blanket over your unfortunate animal."

"You brought Satan into this valley!" Myra shrieked. "We were living in peace until you showed up with your hellfire and your devil worship."

"Ms. Schapen, you are definitely unwell," Gina said. "Go home, take an aspirin, and don't talk to me unless you can speak rationally."

Gina spoke with a cool contempt that awed Lara. She tried to memorize the words, the tone, the way Gina curled her mouth in distaste, as if Myra were a piece of rotten fruit she'd bitten into by mistake.

The other Wiccans laughed. Pastor Nabo thundered threats of damnation, Arnie bellowed hysterically, but the Wiccans turned their backs. Someone started drumming, another began playing the flute, and in a minute the Wiccans were dancing around their fire again.

Mrs. Ruesselmann screamed in fury. She darted around, collecting jeans and shirts and jackets and tossing them in the bonfire. "You wanted to flaunt yourselves before Satan, you keep on doing it. This is what it will be like in hell, the fires burning you but not keeping you warm! You witches destroyed our calf, but we are protected by the Lord of Hosts, His power is greater than your demons. In His Name, we will destroy you. We will wipe you from the face of the earth. Begone, Satan, begone!"

The Wiccans saw what she was doing and made a mad scramble for their clothes.

A movement at the corner of Lara's eye made her turn her head in time to see Eddie Burton get to his feet behind her. His face glistened in the firelight, and he began cackling in excitement as the naked women ran after Mrs. Ruesselmann, trying to grab their clothes from her. He was rubbing himself through his jeans.

Lara felt a wave of nausea rise up. She bent over and vomited. What was left of her supper came up, but even when her stomach was empty she couldn't stop retching. She kept heaving and heaving, even though her chest and throat ached from it. Finally, she grabbed an apple from the ground near her and forced herself to bite into its sour, mealy flesh, to suck on it until her spasms subsided.

She put the apple down and started into the orchard, away from the fire. Eddie looked around and spotted her.

"Junior! Junior! Here she is. Here's the girl I seen with Robbie, she's right here. Lala Grellier!"

For a moment, Lara was too frightened to move. Eddie yelped again for Junior, on the far side of the fire from him. Somehow, Junior heard him above all the other clangor from Wiccans and Christians. Lara saw his shadow, a distorted, distended monster, moving around the fire toward Eddie, toward her, before his actual body came into view. She tried to run on legs turned to rubber from fatigue and fear. "Call up your reserves, call up your reserves," she cried to herself, but she had a stitch in her side, way worse than any she'd ever gotten in a game, and couldn't make herself move any faster than a lumbering trot.

She could hear Junior and Eddie crashing through the trees behind her, even thought she heard Robbie calling out for Junior to stop. She managed to keep moving and reached the kitchen door while they were still in the orchard.

Elaine had locked the door behind her. Lara rattled the knob, banged on the panels, screamed to Elaine to open the door. There was no response. Elaine had gone to sleep, or passed out, or maybe was watching her with that horrible leer on her face: *Get out of this one if you can, darling little girl.*

Lara staggered around to the front of the house and found the pillar she'd shinnied up before. Her knees were shaking. *Stop that!* she ordered her body. *Pull yourself up.*

Chip, in basic training, had written that in an e-mail home:

You can't believe how much your body can do even when you think you've reached your limit. A hundred push-ups in the sun today before the obstacle course. My shoulders were wobbly before I started running, but Sarge reminded us we'll have to keep going in the desert sun, get used to it now.

Get used to it now, Lara admonished herself, and managed to pull herself onto the porch outside the bathroom window. She pushed the window open and slipped inside. She could hear Junior and Eddie banging on the doors and windows below. In another minute, Junior would start breaking the glass. Panic swept through her. She hobbled down the grand staircase, through the dining room and into the kitchen, and heaved open the great flour bins where Una Fremantle had hidden the Free Staters from Quantrill's mob. She crouched down into the bin just as the first piece of glass splintered.

Fifty-Four

BURN, BABY, BURN

AT THE BONFIRE, Robbie had sat on the ground next to the perfect red heifer. He was so tired he didn't know if he would ever get to his feet again. His last act before collapsing was to take off his jacket and rub down Nassie with it.

"You get that jacket filthy and you're paying to clean it yourself, young man, out of that money your father gave you. You ruin it, don't expect us to buy you a new one," Nanny clacked at him.

He stared at her, too dumbfounded to respond. The horrible scene in the church, the mad hunt across the Ropeses' fields for the calf, and the calf herself, sides lathered in sweat, covered with mud, her red skin torn in a dozen places from tangling with barbed wire, all seemed to mean nothing to his grandmother. Her circle of hate was so tightly wrapped around her that she couldn't see anything outside it.

Finally, he sank to the ground. Robbie wrapped his arms around the calf's flank; she was so exhausted, she was lying down. It wasn't her fault everyone around her had gone insane. She was just a helpless calf who'd never been allowed to live in the sunshine.

As they walked the heifer to the fire, Dad had said he was going to put her down. Dad said there was no way to keep the Jews from finding out that Elaine had touched her. "All my hopes went up through that damned bitch's hole, her and Jim Grellier's brat of a daughter," he'd said to Nanny. "I bet Grellier set his girl on Robbie just to make a fool of me."

Robbie would stay here all night, until all the witches and all the

Christians had left; then he'd take Nassie into the Fremantles' barn. He'd get Chip's sleeping bag down from the loft and spend the night next to the poor calf. Leaning against her side, he drifted into sleep.

Eddie's cry to Junior didn't rouse him, but his brother's bellowed response did. Robbie groaned—he didn't want to watch Junior do one more horrible thing, but if his brother was going to shoot Nasya Robbie would have to try to protect her. He sat up. To his relief, he saw Junior moving away from him and the calf. He was about to lie down again when he caught sight of Lara through the apple trees. Junior and Eddie were heading after her.

Robbie struggled to his feet. His legs were thick and heavy, as if they were logs from the bonfire. No one, none of the witches, not Nanny or his father, seemed to notice him. Only Amber Ruesselmann saw him plod dully along in Junior's wake. She cried out to him to come back to Jesus, come back to her—to leave Lara Grellier to Satan, with the other witches.

The words felt like something physical: wet saplings flaying his skin. He didn't ever want to hear Amber's voice again, or Pastor Nabo's. Or his father's or Nanny's, and certainly not Junior's, but he was doomed to live with them forever. Robbie didn't turn around, didn't see Amber run to her mother and gesture at him and the nightmarish parade he was following.

Junior was moving much faster than Robbie could at this point. Robbie could hear him, yelling insults as if he were on the football field, but he lost sight of his brother in the trees. By the time he reached the incinerator in the back garden, where the Fremantles used to burn papers and other trash, he couldn't see Junior or Lara. He hoped Lara had managed to get away from them; Junior and Eddie were so wound up with rage and desire, they might tear her apart. Lara the deer in the path of coyotes. That thought made him force his legs into a tottering run, but he could only move like Nanny, like an old person with swollen ankles.

He made it to the front of the house in time to see Junior swing a branch and splinter the etched glass in the double doors. Junior stuck an arm through the shards, trying to open the lock. The door was barricaded, and he couldn't budge it.

Eddie was cackling with excitement. "Do you see her, Junior? Do you see her?"

Junior didn't answer, just moved to his left, to the windows that opened into the formal front parlor. He used his branch again. When he'd splintered the glass in one window, he stepped back and kicked it in all around the frame, then shoved his heavy body through. Once he was inside, he put out a hand to pull Eddie through after him.

Robbie shambled behind them, up the stairs to the veranda. He swung one leaden leg over the windowsill and felt the glass slice into his pant leg. He managed to drag himself into the parlor. He could hear Junior and Eddie knocking over furniture and breaking china, but he couldn't tell where they were.

Robbie knocked his shin against the old piano, reeled away from it only to bang into the marble mantle over the fireplace, and finally found a light switch. It turned on a single bulb in an old chandelier, but it gave off enough light for him to find the door leading to the front hall.

Above him, he heard Eddie cry, "She ain't here, Junior. I don't see the Grellier witch anywhere. But the big one, she's in here. She's asleep in here."

His brother's heavy footsteps pounded down the hall over Robbie's head. "Whoa, we caught ourselves the biggest witch of them all, the one Pastor says is totally under Beelzebub's control. Come on, cunt, wakey, wakey. Time to face the court."

Junior grunted as he pounded on Elaine; Robbie could picture him trying to move her. "Ah, hell, Eddie, bitch is passed out cold on the floor. Here's a quart of vodka, she must'a drained the whole bottle. We'll have to smoke her out."

"Smoke her out?" Eddie's voice went up a half register in excitement. "How we gonna do that?"

"Set the place on fire. That'll give her a foretaste of hell, should bring the old cow to her feet fast enough. I just need to find me some matches—there's enough papers in here to burn down a town, if we can get them going."

Junior's feet thundered along the floorboards again. Robbie heard him pounding down a far flight of stairs. There were three other doors into the front hall besides the one Robbie had used. He saw a sliver of light under the far door to his left. He pushed it open. He was in a room with a long table and a dozen chairs. Beyond it, he saw his brother in the kitchen.

"Candles, matches, everything we need. Okay, boy."

"No, Junior, don't!" Robbie managed to shout.

Junior turned around. "Hey, shrimp, about time you showed up. You decide you're on the side of the angels after all? Come and get a candle. Help Eddie and me smoke out the Wicked Witch of the West."

Robbie hobbled into the kitchen and knocked the candles out of his brother's hand. "You—shit for brains! This is arson. This is a house, it's where the Fremantles used to live. How could you do this? You can go to jail for this! Where's Lara? Have you hurt her?"

Junior hit him so hard that Robbie fell over. "Whose side are you on, brat boy? Ours or those devil worshippers who ruined our calf? You going to be in heaven when the Lord comes in glory or stuck in the mud with the mud people?"

"Jesus hates people who kill other people," Robbie shouted, getting up on his hands and knees.

Junior kicked him in the testicles with the toe of his boot. Robbie collapsed, screaming in pain. Through his fog of agony, he heard Eddie Burton cry out, "Jesus loves Junior, He gave us the calf, she made a miracle for us, she gave us her blessing! She didn't bless you, shrimp twerp, she sent you a witch, a Grellier girl witch."

"That's right, boy, that's right. Jesus loves us, but He can't stand loser crybabies, that's for sure." Junior scooped up the candles. Putting an arm around Eddie, he led him up the back stairs.

Robbie rolled over onto his side. The pain was so immense that everything else faded behind it. *Find Lara, stop Junior, save Nassie*—those were little pinpricks of thought that he couldn't hold on to. When he heard Lara's voice near him, calling his name in an urgent whisper, he thought at first he was dead and in heaven with her.

"Robbie! I'm in the flour bin, but I can't open it from the inside."

He finally pushed himself to his hands and knees and followed her voice to the bin. Clutching his sore scrotum with one hand, he pulled on the handle and the bin swung forward. Lara emerged, covered in spiderwebs and the white remains of a hundred years of flour.

"Oh, Robbie, you poor thing, I could hear him. He really hurt you, didn't he? I'm so sorry." She put her ghostly arms around him and smoothed his dirty hair.

They clutched each other, not speaking, until Lara said, "I heard him and Eddie, but I couldn't make out what they were saying. Where did they go? Is it safe to leave?"

"He went upstairs with Eddie," Robbie said. "They found Elaine. She was passed out, I guess, and— Lara, Junior said he was going to set fire to the room. That's when he hit me, when I tried to stop him. We've got to call Sheriff Drysdale."

"Maybe we should drive back to my place," Lara said, unable to imagine how she and Robbie could stop Junior. "My truck's out front. My dad should be home by now, he'll know what to do."

She helped Robbie to his feet. The worst of the pain had passed. He hobbled with her to the side door. She opened the bolts, and they went out onto the small porch.

"Oh, no," Lara whispered.

The crowd from around the bonfire was pouring through the orchard. The Ruesselmanns, Pastor Nabo, and a dozen others were already standing between Lara and Robbie and her truck. They backed into the kitchen again before anyone spotted them. They heard a loud shout from the people nearest the front of the house, and the whole group swarmed away from the kitchen toward the front. Lara and Robbie slipped out the door again, hoping to cross the yard and get to her truck before the mob turned back toward the kitchen.

Lara had her keys out and was climbing into the truck when she saw flames leap up in the house's corner window. Junior appeared at another window, waving a burning candle.

He kicked out the glass and yelled to the people below, "We're smoking out the biggest witch. We'll see if the little one follows after her."

The crowd cheered, as if Junior had sacked an opposing quarterback. He did a victory dance and disappeared from view.

Lara pushed her keys into Robbie's hand. "Elaine, they'll kill her. And Abigail's diaries. My mom will never forgive me, she'll go away forever— I have to rescue them."

Before Robbie could make sense of what she was saying, let alone realize what she was doing, Lara had run back across the yard and up the stairs to the kitchen door.

Fifty-Five

THE AWAKENING

JIM AND SUSAN saw the glow of the fire as they drove up the county road but thought it was just the Samhain bonfire. When they came to the long line of abandoned vehicles, they were puzzled but not especially alarmed. Jim figured it was some nighttime vigil involving Arnie's calf, which he was frankly sick of. At the turnoff to Arnie's, they saw the squad car with its flashing lights.

"Arnie is pulling out all the stops," Jim said.

Behind him, a truck was honking and flashing its brights in his rearview mirror. He stuck out an arm to wave it around, figuring it was some kid in a hurry. The driver pulled up next to him.

"Jim." It was Peter Ropes. "That bonfire over at Fremantles' is way out of control. They managed to set the house on fire. I called the Eudora Fire Department, but I'm heading over to see if I can help."

"The Fremantle house?" Susan spoke with the first real emotion Jim had heard from her in months. "Oh, no! Jim—we need to go over there!"

"We'll join you in a minute," Jim called to Peter. "Let me just check on Lara—she's been home alone all night. Although she may be over at the fire," he added to Susan.

He called the house on his cell phone, and then called Lara's phone. When she didn't answer either number, he turned around and followed Peter down the road to Fremantles'.

At the entrance to the drive, they almost collided with Lara's truck, which was heading for the road at high speed. Jim slammed on his breaks and honked, and his daughter came to a halt.

He jumped down and ran to her window. And found himself looking at Robbie Schapen.

"Mr. Grellier!"

"Where's Lara?" Jim demanded.

"She went back to the house. She sent me to find you. How did you know—"

"What's going on here?" Jim saw the fire playing along the upper story and licking the eaves under the roof. He couldn't understand the throng of people, milling around, even cheering when they blocked a woman with a bucket from getting close to the house.

"It's Junior, he went in there with Eddie. Elaine stole Nassie, and Junior wants to burn her to death and—"

"But Lara, where is she?"

"We were leaving, we were going to find you." Robbie was breaking down. "Then she saw the fire. She said Mrs. Grellier would never forgive her if the diaries were destroyed."

Susan had climbed out of the truck and joined them. "Abigail's diaries? She went back in there for Abigail's diaries?"

"I didn't hear the name, I didn't know what she was talking about, I didn't know what to do. I can't fight Junior, so I was coming to get you. But Junior, he's in there with Eddie, they're setting fire to everything and—"

Jim ran back to his truck, but Susan sprinted across the lawn. By the time he reached the giant cottonwood, Jim couldn't see his wife. The front doors of the house were burning now, and Junior, Eddie at his side, appeared at the kitchen door, waving a burning chair in the air. The crowd cheered again as he set the door on fire.

Jim charged up the steps, but Junior blocked his way. "Now you eat Schapen dirt, Jim Grellier."

"The witches are in there, the big fat one, and little skinny Lala. They'll smoke to death and burn in hell forever," Eddie screeched.

Peter Ropes ran to help Jim; Clem and Turk Burton suddenly appeared as well. The crowd saw a battle was under way. They didn't know the issues, but they surged up to take on anyone who was trying to fight Junior.

Jim backed away for a moment, looking for his wife. A surge from the mob thrust him back into the fight. He didn't know until later that Junior threw Susan out of the kitchen when she had run up a minute earlier. She didn't try to fight him but ran around to the back of the house to the cellar doors. The bolts were loose; she hefted one door up and slid down the coal chute. The floor was muddy, and the smell of mold was thick. Little furry creatures were squeaking around her, moving away from the burning front of the house.

This was the cellar where Una Fremantle had hidden her children when Quantrill's raiders came through. Susan's fingers felt on the left for the joists to the small rooms that used to hold coal and root vegetables in the winter. Six more paces to the kitchen stairs. They rose steeply along the north wall. Fifteen of them and then the kitchen door. She pushed against it, but it didn't open. She shoved, but it was nailed shut. Oh, yes, Jim and Blitz—they'd done it one night when Gina had been frightened by a prowler. Who was probably Lara, sneaking into the house, hiding Abigail's diaries.

Susan made her way back down the stairs and went into the front half of the basement. It was warm in here from the fire overhead, but there was no help for it. She'd have to go up this way.

Her fingers, as sensitive as a counterfeiter's, felt along the walls, finding the furnace room. The Fremantles had put this system in fifty years ago. It was antiquated now, the air vents too big to be fuel-efficient, but now that was a good thing. Susan felt for the metal tentacles, reaching up an arm and finding the one that went straight overhead into the back parlor. She ran her fingers along it for the join that Mr. Fremantle had soldered when the tube split; the metal would be weak there. She pushed against it and felt it give a little.

Above her, she could hear pounding feet and animal-like cries— Junior fighting someone. She slammed her shoulder into the weld. This time, it gave, and she kicked away the bottom half of the tube, which was connected to the boiler.

The top half dangled above her. She reached inside, found a metal ridge, and pulled herself up inside the tube. It was a tight fit. Good thing she had lost all that weight or she'd never have made it. Bad thing she'd lain around and let her muscles go; she was struggling and trembling as she inched up the tube. She kept putting her hand up, checking for the grate. The air above her was hot but not unbearable. *Thank you, Jesus, for small mercies. I'm grateful for them.*

When she found the grate, she leaned against the tube so it would take the weight of her hips. She needed to put all the muscle she had left into pushing up, pushing against the cast-iron grate, pushing against the cherrywood table that stood over it. Just when she thought her back would tear in half, metal and table gave, toppled over. *I'm grate-ful,* she thought again, and laughed, a little hysterically, at the pun.

She heard the wooden table crack as it landed. Una brought that table with her from Boston. The Marquis de Lafayette had taken tea at it, or so Una always bragged to Abigail. Now it was broken, but it would burn soon, anyway.

Susan hoisted her skinny body through the opening, tripped on the grate, and cut her ankle. She felt the blood wet around her foot, but the foot wasn't broken, she could put full weight on it.

"Lara! Lara, it's Mom. Where are you?"

She strained to listen, trying to hear her daughter above the crackling of the fire and the noise of the crowd. She called again and again but heard nothing.

The whole front of the house was on fire now. She couldn't use the front staircase, and flames were lapping the north side. The back parlor was full of smoke, but the blaze gave her some light, too. She took a moment to take off her jacket, pull her sweatshirt off to wrap around her face, and put the jacket back on to protect her skin from the embers falling into the room from the outer walls.

Stay down for smoke. Move slower but safer on your knees. The instruction she had given Etienne and Lara when they were little. In the country, no fire truck will come in time to save you. Children have to be able to save themselves. But that was impossible, children can't save themselves. And their mothers were pretty useless protection, too.

Not today, though. She would save Lara today. Her daughter was alive; Susan was certain of that. She was in the house and alive. If her remaining little chick had died, she, Susan, would have known, would have felt all that was left of her heart die in that instant, so she knew Lara was in here waiting for her.

Susan crawled from the back parlor to Judge Fremantle's study and through there to the tiny bathroom the Fremantles installed in the 1920s. She ran water in the rusty shower, stood under it to soak herself thoroughly, then went up the back stairs.

The smoke was thicker here, so thick she started to choke. The fire had grabbed the front of the house, devoured the bathroom there, and run along the long wood floor. Flames were dancing around the doorway to the master bedroom, licking along the polished walnut base of the drinking fountain.

"Lara! Lulu!" she called over and over.

She crawled past the room Gina had used as her study. Through the haze of smoke, she saw Elaine Logan's bulk. Elaine was sitting on the floor, kissing her hands.

"Elaine!" Susan cried. "Elaine, where's my daughter?"

"Dante," Elaine crooned. "I found my baby's picture. Gina stole him from me, but he's come back to me, he's come back to his lily maid, Elaine the lovable, Elaine the fair. He never loved anyone but me, did you, my darling?"

"Elaine!" Susan screamed. "Get up! Where's Lara?"

Elaine didn't look at her, just kept kissing the snapshot in her fingers. Susan went far enough into the room to see that her daughter wasn't hidden behind Elaine's bulk. Choking from the smoke, weeping with despair, she crawled back into the hall and called again to her daughter.

Over the crackling of the fire, over the sirens of the arriving fire brigade, she finally heard Lara answer. Susan found her daughter huddled underneath the faded prom dress in the closet of the far back bedroom, clutching Abigail's tin trunk. Susan pressed Lara against her breast so hard that their hearts beat through each other's chests.

"Mom? Mom? Oh, Mom, I thought— I'm sorry, Mom, I'm sorry.

I put Abigail's trunk in here, and now I can't get out. I'm sorry, I'm sorry— I tried to rescue Elaine but I couldn't move her, and then I got trapped in here and now I'll kill you, too."

"Oh, Lulu, these papers, they weren't worth the price of your life. No one is going to die in here. Not you, not me, not Elaine, if we can get the fire brigade. We're getting out. We're going home, you hear?"

The smoke and heat in the hall were too intense now for them to risk returning to the stairs. Light was filtering into the room from the flames along the roof and the strobes of the fire trucks on the far side of the house. Susan tore the gray prom dress into strips and knotted them together. She tied one end around the legs of the bed and opened the window. She could hear the shouts from the front of the house and the kitchen, but the window opened away from all the action. No one was underneath.

She tied the makeshift rope around Lara's chest and lowered her daughter, Susan's unused muscles trembling with the effort. "Undo the knot, Lulu," she shouted when Lara was on the ground. "Undo the knot and find your daddy."

Part Five

CODA

Fifty-Six

HISTORY LESSON

From the *Douglas County Herald,* November 3
HELL NIGHT IN KANSAS

Nasya the Miracle Calf Injured;
Historic Mansion Destroyed in Blaze

The calf which has drawn pilgrims from as far away as Israel went on a pilgrimage herself Wednesday night that ended her prospects as the harbinger of the Second Coming and led to disastrous consequences for the Lawrence woman who abducted her. Reb Meir, of the Bet HaMikdash yeshiva in Kansas City, says the calf's injuries were too extensive for her to be considered a perfect red heifer, even if her hide retains its lustrous color into her third year.

Arnie Schapen, who was raising the calf, wants to put her down, but area residents, including Animals R Kin, are protesting and have taken the cow into their custody.

More serious are the injuries to local resident Elaine Logan. She is in critical condition at Lawrence Memorial Hospital for burns and smoke inhalation she incurred when a Halloween bonfire at the old Fremantle farm east of town burned out of control. The fire, set by Gina Haring, who is a Wiccan, or so-called "white witch," spread to the Fremantle home, which was almost completely destroyed.

"That's such a crock," Lara cried, reading the paper at breakfast Saturday morning. "Gina's fire was a million miles from the house, which the stupid paper would know if they could get outside of Lawrence and actually look at the land. Anyway, Junior set that fire, him and Eddie!"

"*He* and Eddie," Susan corrected.

"Hank Drysdale told me the district attorney is trying to work out how to charge Junior," Jim put in. "Junior's persuaded Eddie to take the blame, and of course that isn't right."

"But what about Gina and her friends? They saw Junior setting the fire, and so did Robbie and me."

"Let's not go overboard until we see what the DA decides, okay, Lulu? I'm not crazy about the idea of you getting up in court to testify against Junior unless there's no other choice. Arnie feels enough ill will toward us without you adding to his grievances. Besides, Junior is an aggressive guy, with the muscle to back it up. You and he are going to be neighbors for a long time, unless one or the other of you gives up on the land."

Jim had a black eye and a cracked rib from fighting Junior Wednesday night. By the time he and Peter Ropes, with help from Turk and Clem Burton, had battled Junior away from the door, it was burning so fiercely that Jim couldn't get in the kitchen. He still felt a kind of shame for not helping Susan rescue Lara. By the time Lara found him, after Susan lowered her to the grass Wednesday night, he was working feverishly with the fire brigade, who were trying to get enough of the blaze under control to get into the house. When he saw his daughter, he abandoned the fire brigade and got to the far side of the house just in time to catch his wife as she slipped down her makeshift rope.

He and Susan spent the remainder of Wednesday at the hospital, the two of them brooding over Lara, not sleeping, not quite believing the doctors, who said she'd made it through the inferno without major injury. When they brought her home, on Thursday, she spent the day in his and Susan's bed. Her mother wouldn't leave her side, and Jim had to fight back a panicky fear that this was the prelude to another, larger collapse for his wife, worse this time because she'd take their daughter with her.

On Friday, though, Lara was ready to get up again. She was still subdued, picking at her food. She still clung to her mother, as if afraid, like Jim, that with the crisis past, Susan would start to retreat from her again.

Late in the afternoon, Lara finally decided to tell her parents the whole story of her Halloween. "It was so horrible, Dad, all of it. But the worst was, all that stuff at the church. It was, oh, it was disgusting. You never heard anything like it. Pastor Nabo went on and on in this totally gross way about sex and women being agents of the devil! He was touching me, he was saying *I* had the devil in me, that *I* had ruined Robbie's life. I should never have gone, I should have told you about it, I'm sorry, I'm sorry."

Both parents rushed to comfort her. Jim secretly thought it was very nearly worth all the traumas of Halloween night if rescuing Lara had brought Susan back to this world. He stepped back and let his wife have the major share of reassuring their child.

He remembered Lara's comment a month or so ago about the prince coming to kiss Susan and wake her up. Maybe he'd made a mistake, all these weeks since Chip's death, in trying to console his wife. Instead of trying to comfort her, should he have tried to make her feel needed or even heroic?

Lara returned to the paper and started reading it aloud to her parents:

> Elaine Logan is a well-known local figure often seen panhandling near popular student watering holes in downtown Lawrence. Logan used to be an honors English student at the University of Kansas. She dropped out in 1970 to join the Free State Commune, which the Fremantle family allowed to live rent-free in an unused bunkhouse. When the bunkhouse burned down thirty-six years ago, Logan's boyfriend, Dante Spirota, died in the fire. Logan suffered a miscarriage as a result of the shock. Logan accused Schapen's 87-year-old mother Myra of causing the bunkhouse fire, which led to escalating hostility between Logan and the Schapen family.

"That's true." Lara looked up from the paper. "At the—the thing they were doing to me, Arnie and Pastor Nabo and them—Elaine said she saw

Myra set the fire. She says Myra lit a fuse right up against the bunkhouse and waited for it to go up in flames."

"Lit a fuse? That could mean anything, you know that, Lara. Anyway, if Elaine watched her set the fire, why didn't she say something at the time?"

"Maybe she did and no one listened to her then any more than they do today," Lara suggested.

"Maybe she was high," Susan said. "They used a lot of drugs out there. She could have thought she was saying something but couldn't get the words out."

"Maybe she was high and imagined the whole thing," Jim said. "No, Lulu, don't get wound up about this. If Myra set the bunkhouse on fire, we'll never prove it. It's Elaine Logan's word against hers, assuming Elaine even survives."

> Last Monday, Logan broke into the special calf's private pen and spray-painted it. According to witnesses, the Schapen family retaliated against Logan's attack on their calf by holding an exorcism on Logan and some area teens at the Salvation Through the Blood of Jesus Full Bible Church. Pastor Nabo stresses that his church considers this a "service of deliverance," not a Catholic exorcism rite.
>
> Witnesses say the attempted exorcism so enraged Logan that she ran away from the church, stole Arnold Schapen's Ford truck, and used it to break down the walls of the perfect red heifer's special enclosure.
>
> Arnold Schapen had served as a deputy sheriff in Douglas County for the past six years. Sheriff Drysdale has informed the *Herald* that Schapen has turned in his deputy's badge and will no longer be working for the county. Schapen's son, Arnold Jr., is a widely acclaimed local football hero now in his first year at Tonganoxie Bible College.

"It doesn't say how Elaine is," Lara said. "Is she—will she—"

"We don't know, baby," Jim answered. "She was in pretty bad shape by the time the fire brigade could get to her. Rachel Carmody has organized a fund to take care of her hospital bills if Medicaid doesn't cover them all."

"And what's Gina going to do?" Lara asked. "Is she going back to New York?"

"I think Gina is living with Autumn Minsky right now," Jim said, his color heightened. "That's what Curly says, and he usually knows, doesn't he? What about Robbie, Lulu? Is he still at Greynards'?"

Lara nodded, her own face flushed. She and Robbie—what would she say to him when they met at school on Monday? They could never go back to the barn. Their private idyll had been made so public, so ugly, she didn't think she could ever let a boy get close enough to her again to touch her.

"It will pass, Lulu, darling, it will pass," Susan said. "You're too lovable not to find love again."

"I'm leaving for New York now," Gina told Jim a few weeks later. "I suppose you'll be glad to see the last of me."

She had sat in her battered Escort, watching the Grellier house from the side of the barren cornfield until she saw Jim go into the barn. She crossed the field, in her impractical red suede boots, lugging a heavy box, and confronted him as he started to sharpen a coulter blade.

He put the blade down. "What will you do?"

"My old job. I worked for a PR company that supports nonprofits. It's where I met my husband, my ex. He heads a foundation that we did work for. Someone quit, so they can use another hand on the telephone. I came out here hoping to make big changes in my life, but I feel as though I'm going back to where I started."

"Maybe you are," Jim said, "but that doesn't mean you can't go in a different direction. It's like the harvest, you know, life is, I mean. You start in the same place every year—seeds, fertilizer, soil—but every year is different." He paused, sheepish at his pompous words. "What about your book, the story you wanted to write about Elaine and her dead lover?"

"I may still do that. *Hatred in the Heartland,* I'll call it, or something like that. How the hatreds of the seventies still obsess people and make them do unbelievable acts of violence. There's poor old Elaine, back at New Haven Manor, where she's going to be on oxygen for the rest of her life because of Junior Schapen. And what happens to him? Nothing at all. He's still at Tonganoxie, playing football, while Arnie and Myra try to blame Eddie Burton for burning down Uncle John's house."

"I wouldn't say nothing at all happened to Junior," Jim said. "Clem Burton took a potshot at him and got him in the ass at last Saturday's game."

"He did? Really?" Gina laughed, exposing the crooked lower tooth that still seemed endearing to Jim. "What will happen to Clem?"

"I don't know. My older brother is handling his defense. Junior wasn't badly hurt, so they may work out some kind of lawyer's agreement." He didn't add that the injury had been a boon to Junior's career: Curly had brought home the news that the Cowboys and the Eagles were both recruiting him, now that they'd seen him on national television.

Gina stopped laughing and said, with an abrupt change of mood, "People think New York or other big cities are violent places, but New York doesn't have anything like the concentrated venom I've seen up close here in Kansas."

"Do you think so?" Jim said. "Maybe it's because I know all these people that I see it differently. You say you want to connect this time to the seventies, but you're ignoring thirty-five years in between where we all got along well enough."

"Arnie and Myra are obsessed with how liberals took over Douglas County in 1970," Gina argued. "They kept saying I represented the same threat to law and order as the hippies."

"You do like to stir people up." Jim tried to make it sound like a joke, but his voice had an edge.

Gina shut her eyes as if trying not to see something painful. "I guess I've done a lot of damage, too. If I hadn't come down here, Elaine would still be cruising the bars, and Etienne would still be alive."

Jim leaned against the milling machine. "Don't imagine yourself bigger or more important in the world than you are, Gina. Maybe Chip would be alive, but you know my wife, you know she needs a big cause to wrap her heart around—she might have found the anti-war people without you. If she had, Chip might have reacted the same way.

"Elaine—I don't know. Maybe you did injure her. Indirectly, so to speak, by stirring her up with all your Wiccan nonsense and getting her out here, remembering Dante and the Schapens and the bunkhouse fire. But you weren't responsible for the Schapens and their grandiose ideas about their calf and the Temple in Jerusalem and Jesus. Arnie and Myra won't learn anything from this except to blame their neighbors more than ever for their troubles, but maybe you can take something away with you. Something along the lines that even a woman like Elaine Logan is human, not a machine you switch on and off when you feel like it."

She bit her lip. "Or you? Is that what you're trying to imply?"

"Maybe. But I made my own choices, too." Jim spoke with difficulty. "I let loneliness and grief and fear take over my head. Also, I liked your coffee."

She laughed but said seriously, "You're a good person, Jim Grellier. I'm not used to meeting good people. Not that I hang around with bad ones, but there's a difference between being ordinary and being actively good."

He was embarrassed by her speech and turned away, saying quickly, "What's in the box?"

"Those are your great-great-grandmother's diaries. Lara had hidden them in the house, you know. The tin trunk they were in was in one of the few rooms to survive the fire. I brought some of the Venetian fireplace tiles, too. I thought Susan would want them, but then I thought I should check with you first."

"Take them up to the house. Susan's in the kitchen. She and Lara, they're cleaning out the cupboards."

He felt her lips brush his cheeks—soft, full lips, like a butterfly—and then she was gone. He found the push broom and began shoving metal shavings across the floor as if it were essential for saving the farm.

Fifty-Seven

TIDYING UP

From: dgrellier@douggrellier.com
Date: November 17
To: grellier4farms@chiefsworld.net

Jimbo—

When I fled Kansas for Chicago, I didn't expect the valley to catch up with me here! I've talked to Mimi about letting young Schapen stay with us. I agree, he sounds very different from Arnie and Myra, but I don't know how well a Full Bible fundamentalist will cope with our secular world. I haven't been in a church for thirty years, except for Gram's and Chip's funerals, and even though Mimi is Jewish she's not like those red heifer loonies. Also, Nate's only eight, and Mimi doesn't want him getting weird ideas from Robbie. Still, she's willing for him to come for a trial visit to see how it goes. I can understand why it would be a disaster to have him live with you. Aside from Lara, it would be hard for Robbie to have his father and Myra across the road.

Did you know Clem Burton called me? You know he shot Junior Schapen at the football game last week, right? You do hear some local news, don't you, O see no evil? He says it was because the DA was going to put Eddie in a group home in exchange for Eddie pleading guilty to setting the fire at Fremantles'.

Clem was furious that Junior got off the hook by framing Eddie when Eddie was just infatuated and willing to do whatever his hero wanted. I'll be coming down next week for the initial arraignment, so I'll take a look at Robbie then and maybe bring him home for a few weeks.

Cheers,
Doug

From: dgrellier@douggrellier.com
Date: December 11
To: grellier4farms@chiefsworld.net

Jimbo,

Yes, Clem has retained me to defend him on assault and attempted murder charges, so I guess I'll be spending a fair amount of time back in Kansas. Any chance you could put up my associate when she comes down to take depositions next month?

Having Robbie Schapen here is working out pretty well so far. We've persuaded University High to let him take their entrance exams to see where he places. I think it helped him coming to someone who knows the land and the people, even though Chicago is quite a big jump for a country boy. He's taking guitar lessons at the Old Town School of Folk Music. His music seems to keep him grounded. He misses his cows, but he doesn't miss the four-thirty rise and shine, that's for sure.

Mimi being Jewish is another hurdle for him, although after everything he went through last fall he's kind of shying away from religion these days. Mimi was afraid he might want to convert her or Nate, but that never comes up.

I've hired a detective to try to track down his mother. If we find her, and her life is in the right place, that might be the best solution for him in the long run. But, for the time being, he's welcome with us.

Right now he's playing "Noah Built Himself an Ark" on his guitar for Nate—seems nonsectarian enough. He also writes reams of C & W love songs to Lulu. I'm starting to get gripes from Mimi about why don't I ever write love songs for her!

Doug

http://www.schapenfarm.com/newsandnotes.html

Pride goeth before destruction and a haughty spirit before a fall. The inerrant Word of God teaches us that, but some of our neighbors have a long way to go before they learn it. They thought they could bring us low. They thought they could break our spirit when they stole our miracle calf. They thought they could destroy us when they shot the apple of our eye, our beloved Junior.

Well, we just got word that our milk is considered blessed by the Lord for its extra rich creaminess, and that we are the supplier of choice for Christian Cream and Ice Cream. The miracle heifer may not have fulfilled her destiny in bringing us the Lord of Hosts in glory, but she guided the Schapen family to a better place.

And Junior's injury brought him the national attention his play has always deserved. The Dallas Cowboys and the Philadelphia Eagles are both scouting him. His coach says his recovery is astounding. He should be back to his full strength by summer.

Pride, pride the sin by which the angels fell. When will our neighbors finally find themselves cured of this heinous sin? They are trying to lead our younger boy, Robbie, out of the path of righteousness, but the Lord loveth whom He chasteneth.

From: dgrellier@douggrellier.com
Date: January 23
To: grellier4farms@chiefsworld.net

Dear Jimbo,

Yep, I got Clem released on an I bond. I don't know if that's good or bad as far as Ardis is concerned, having him home again. Although Clem is mighty peeved at the news about Junior, it will help our defense in the long run.

Robbie did get into U High, although they're making him go back to ninth grade to catch up on his math and science. Still no word on his mother.

I guess it's true that only the good die young. I saw the story in the *Douglas County Herald*, about Nabo holding an Advent Revival at Salvation Bible and bringing in five thousand people over the seven days of the meeting! And then Arnie gets to capitalize on his heifer and Clem shooting Junior by becoming the martyr of the Christian farm movement. His milk is commanding a premium, I read in the *Wall Street Journal*. Oy veh, as we say up here in the big bad city.

Love to Susan and Lara. I know Robbie wants to see Lara, but I think you're right to let that particular fire cool down. I'm glad Susan's better. Lulu wrote Robbie that's she's taken up tile making, trying to replicate the Venetian tiles from the old Fremantle house. Sounds promising.

Peace,
Doug

Fifty-Eight

SPRING

THE WINTER WHEAT had broken dormancy and was starting to grow. All week, a pale green had shimmered under the brown tufts, barely visible, like a shy girl at a school dance: don't look at me, I'm here. This morning, though, the whole field was suddenly alive.

The sky was still dark, barely paler than the land beneath it, but Jim could smell the greenness of the plants, a fresh tang like lime rising from the land. When he bent to feel the stalks, they were supple and soft as bird down between his fingers.

He heard footsteps whickering through the grass, and then Susan knelt beside him. Like him, she bent to feel soil and roots.

"Mmm. It smells like spring."

They squatted for a time without speaking. All the poetry about spring that Lara was studying for her English class—*April is the cruelest month . . . Blossom by blossom the spring begins . . . Now that April with his showers sweet*—and Lara's own earnest, clumsy lines that celebrated the coming blue skies, pink roses, nestlings, why did no one write a poem about the winter wheat coming to life?

Susan seemed to read his thoughts. "At group therapy, they say to be grateful for small things, but I'm grateful for this big thing—spring again, the wheat again. Perhaps this is the only vision I'm allowed, seeing the wheat come to life. I have to keep reminding myself that it isn't small just because it isn't the Mother of God in chains."

He squeezed her hand.

She took a deep breath. "Jim, I'm sorry about the farm. Thank you for protecting the X-Farm for Lara, but you had to sell the river section, and you had to sell it to Arnie. I'm sorry for—for letting you down, for being the reason you had to do it."

He put his finger over her lips. "Listen."

The bobolinks were calling to each other, their long line of song drowning out the meadowlarks. The bobolinks had come back from South America a week ago, as they had each spring for twenty thousand years, and were working in earnest on their nests. They sailed around Jim and Susan in the dark, paying no more attention to the humans than to the silos across the field. In the east, a faint stain of pink heralded the rising sun.